LEGACY
of the
LIGHT

By
Todd A. Gipstein

Cover and all photographs by Todd A. Gipstein

www.Gipstein.com

First published by Dog Ear Publishing
4010 W. 86th Street, Ste H
Indianapolis, IN 46268
www.dogearpublishing.net

dog ear
PUBLISHING

ISBN: 978-145750-357-3

This book is printed on acid-free paper.

This book is a work of fiction. Places, events, and situations in this book are purely fictional and any resemblance to actual persons, living or dead, is coincidental.

Printed in the United States of America

Dedicated to Ed, Fuzz and Rick, my foundation, and to Marcia, my light.

Prologue

Millions of years ago, in a steaming prehistoric jungle, a tiny spider makes its way down the trunk of an enormous tree. He stops to explore something on the bark. Behind him, a bead of thick golden resin trickles down, moving very slowly because it is so viscous and sticky. Its path is random, constantly altered by the rough texture of the bark.

The spider continues to probe and nudge what he's found. He dallies too long: the resin catches up to him. It touches the spider's rear leg. He turns to see what is there. In the time it has taken him to react, the resin has oozed a bit further. It clings to his leg and is touching a second. The spider pulls away, but the liquid is far too sticky, too thick. It holds him in a grip that he can't escape. The resin continues down, pooling around the spider like a miniature ocean wave. He struggles desperately, but in a few moments the resin has engulfed the spider's body completely.

Inside his sticky prison, the spider cannot move, cannot breath. He dies, not the victim of a predator, but of staying too long in one place, oblivious to the approaching danger. The bead continues down the tree, carrying the dead spider along in a golden tomb. The resin oozes into a patch of sun. The heat dries it a bit, slowing its descent even more. It finally stops. In a few hours, the bead has hardened into a tiny glowing sphere that is impervious to rain and heat and ice and time. The spider is perfectly preserved. It will not rot. It will forever be as it is now, a tiny speck entombed in a jewel-like bead of amber.

Over time, the jungle will die. The amber itself will be entombed in the ground. There it will rest, hidden in the darkness for millions of years. Eventually humans will find the bit of amber. It will be prized for its beauty and the evocative power of the ancient life it holds within. They will fashion the amber into a piece of jewelry—a ring. Like so many things, it will journey far, touch many lives. Its exact drift through history is not documented and cannot be known.

People will be fascinated by the amber and the tiny prehistoric spider, whose fatal moment of inattention is captured, as if in a photograph. And like an old photograph, the bead of amber has captured a moment in time and preserved it forever. It is haunting and mysterious. It invites us to shine the light of our imaginations into it. In the glow of that light, the spider lives again and its story is given new meaning.

PART 1

1907

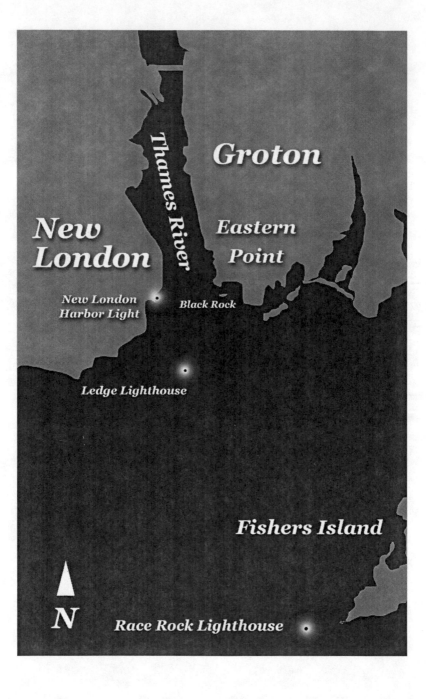

1

"**A**nother goddamned storm!"

Race Rock lighthouse stood alone in the storm, its own little island, surrounded by an angry sea that was willfully trying to destroy it. Or so it seemed to the keeper of the light, locked inside, assaulted by the roar of the waves and the rattle of rain against the windowpanes.

"Another goddamned storm!"

Nathaniel Bowen cursed the weather again, and poured himself another whiskey. It was a late afternoon in February, 1907. The sky was beginning to darken. He should light the light soon. The whiskey was only to ward off the chill, or so he told himself. The chill he was really feeling could not be so easily warmed. It came from within—a deep, cold sadness that swept through his heart like the winter wind.

He poured the whiskey into a small glass and stared into it, as if it held the secret to his happiness. Though he knew it didn't, it dulled the pain, and that was enough. He was not much of a drinker, but he gulped the glass down in one swallow. Earlier, the first few drinks had burned as he'd sipped them. Now the liquor was just a pleasant warmth as he tossed back the shots. He sighed. He was feeling a little better.

The icy wind blew a spray of seawater against the windowpane. The drops hit the glass like buckshot. Nathaniel slowly turned to look at the window. It was encrusted with ice. The howling wind rattled the casement and whistled through a tiny crack. Something to be fixed. There was always something to fix on the lighthouse. Besides lighting the light, his main job was to fix the lighthouse. To maintain the building and its mechanical systems. To try to slow the relentless deterioration of the man-made presence in the middle of the sea. The light-house was besieged by a harsh and unforgiving nature. Wind, rain, ice, waves and salt spray all took a heavy toll on metal, wood and stone. So he fixed things.

This cold, stormy winter afternoon, repairing the window was a distant abstraction to him. He noted it somewhere in the back of his mind, his thinking dulled by the whiskey. He raised the glass and toasted the window and the raging sea beyond it.

"To fixin' what's broken," he said.

The nearest land—the nearest human—was a mile away. He had lived for several years with this isolation, yet for some reason it had gotten to him today. Made him take a drink. Why? He had to think. Nothing was coming quickly to him. He sorted through the day. He remembered. It was the boy. His son. Caleb. He twirled the glass and watched the liquor ride up on the edge like a wave striking shore. He shook his head. His son. When had he last seen him? How long had it been? He mulled it over. Two years? Three? Caleb would be a teenager now. He would have changed. His son would be a stranger to him. Thoughts of his missing son had made Nathaniel sad this stormy winter day. The sadness had made him seek solace in a bottle. Something he had never done before.

The waves crashed outside, roaring like an angry mob attacking his castle. Race Rock *was* like a castle. The keeper was its king; the surrounding sea his kingdom. The enemy was the wind and sea.

A gust rattled the window. Nathaniel was tired of the storms. The winter of 1906 and 1907 had been a rough one. The wind, the cold, the icy dampness of his world were relent-less and depressing. Now this sadness. Colder than the winter. Bleaker than the sky. More numbing than all the wet wind that swirled around him. He could contend with the winter weather. He could seal the drafts, turn up the furnace, bundle himself in more sweaters. But this inner storm: there was no way to pro-tect himself from it. He knew the liquor was a flimsy refuge even as he sought its temporary shelter.

Why today? Why had the sadness washed into his soul like a piece of driftwood today? Driftwood: now he remembered. It was the piece of driftwood. He had found it in a drawer this morning. It lay on the table now, ghostly white in the encroaching gloom.

Nathaniel picked up the small piece of wood. It had naturally weathered to look like a bird, with a pointed end like a beak and a flared end like tail feathers. Two little pieces on the sides looked like wings. He'd carved in some eyes, daubed a little yellow paint on the beak and had a passable sculpture of a seagull. He had given it to Caleb on his seventh birthday. His son had loved it. Nathaniel twirled it in his hands, examining it from different angles. A piece of driftwood. A gift. A memory. He put it down with a heavy sigh.

It was a little thing, but it reminded him of how much he missed his son. How much he missed doing things for and with Caleb. It had triggered his sadness. Usually, he was good at keeping his loneliness suppressed. But sometimes it popped up, like a Jack-in-the-box. Nathaniel would suffer a while then push it down into the deep dark box of his heart and secure the latch. He never knew what might trigger it. Today it was the little driftwood bird.

Without even realizing it, he had been brooding all afternoon, and as the sullen skies had turned darker, so had his mood. It soured into melancholy, then deepened to regret and anger as he remembered that awful day when his wife had left with his son. The day his world had started to crumble.

Nathaniel poured himself another drink. The glass of whiskey caught the candlelight and glowed. He gazed into the amber liquid, seeing in it the images of a summer morning two years earlier.

2

The day began as countless others had. Nathaniel dressed in his crisp Lighthouse Board uniform. It was heavy for summer wear, but he didn't mind. The Board required the uniform, and Nathaniel found it gave him a sense of pride to wear it. He checked the buttons were polished and gleaming, that everything was neat and tidy. He was a man of an era that valued formality and obedience, that prized a deep sense of duty. His little island home was surrounded by the ocean, and the ocean was a place of chaos. In the face of nature's uncertainty, he sought and found predictability in the daily routine of a lighthouse keeper.

As he did every day, he picked up a small daguerreotype picture. It was a portrait of him and his wife, Carla. He looked at it and quietly whispered "Love, luck and longevity." It was a kind of morning prayer for him, a way to start the day on a hopeful note. His gaze lingered for a moment on the photograph, on their smiles, on an instant of happiness preserved forever. He smiled.

Nathaniel went down to the kitchen and found his wife and son there. Two satchels were on the floor beside them. Caleb looked scared. Carla looked agitated.

"Are you going somewhere?" he asked, surprised to see them with the two suitcases at the ready.

Carla sighed. Looked down. Her small fists clenched. She looked up at him and held his gaze for a moment.

"I ... we're leaving," she blurted out. "We're leaving."

Caleb fidgeted and looked away, unable to meet his father's eyes. Nathaniel was stunned. Leaving?

"What? Why?"

Carla's face was anguished, her green eyes moist. Her words tumbled out with a desperate urgency.

"Nathaniel, I've tried to talk to you about it. You know I have. And I've tried to make this work. But it's like being in a prison out here. This is no place to raise a child. Caleb has no friends. He has no place to play. He can't be a child."

Nathaniel was not completely surprised by what she said. They *had* talked about this before. It seemed to come up every so often. They had never resolved the matter. Their conversations about it always seemed to end with a "we'll see." He began the defense he always used when Carla complained about their son's life on Race Rock.

"He's learning about all sorts of things, Carla. He helps me here. We fish. We get ashore…"

She shook her head. She didn't want to hear this again. He didn't understand. He never had. Maybe never could. She cut him off.

"That's not a childhood, Nathaniel. Learning to grease gears and fill tanks, to polish brass and mend ropes. That's man's work. That's *your* work. This is *your* world. Our son is ten and he's never done the things a boy his age should do. He's never ridden a bicycle or flown a kite. He's never been to a circus or played baseball. He's never even been to school for God's sake!"

Caleb stood there watching his parents. Though they kept glancing over at him, it seemed as if they were talking about someone else.

"He may not do those things, Carla, but he gets to do things a lot of boys don't. And as far as schooling, well, we read to him," said Nathaniel. "We have a wonderful library courtesy of the Lighthouse Board. Better than the school's I bet. You help him write. I teach him mathematics. He learns. He'll learn what he needs to know." Nathaniel sounded small and desperate.

Carla glared at Nathaniel, anger building in her. "You teach him what you think he needs to know. To be a lighthouse keeper. But maybe that's not what he wants to be. Did you ever

5

think of that? Maybe he wants to do something else with his life. If we stay here he'll have no choice, will he? He won't know any other life. He'll be trapped."

"I would be proud if my son were a lighthouse keeper."

"But what about Caleb, Nathaniel—would *he* be happy? Or would he just follow in your footsteps because that's the only path he knows? Why do fathers always think their sons have to carry on their lives? Finish their unfinished business? Why can't they be something different? *Somebody* different?"

"I could leave him worse legacies," said Nathaniel.

"Or better," Carla shot back.

Silence. Nathaniel had never really thought this through. They'd had the child and just started rearing him. The years had passed. He looked at his son. How he'd grown! Caleb looked like his mother, though he had Nathaniel's deep brown eyes.

A thought bubbled up in Nathaniel's mind, unexpected. Unbidden. Unremembered for a long time. It was a hot, dry afternoon. He was maybe eight or ten. About Caleb's age. He remembered standing in a field and watching a train approach from a great distance, roar by, then slowly shrink until it vanished. He remembered that as the train had passed, he had longed to get on it. To go wherever it was going. To get away. But he didn't. He couldn't. He was left behind, fixed to the spot.

His life was spent being fixed to a spot. Then. Now. That was the very definition of a lighthouse, after all. A fixed point, a precise coordinate on a chart. It marked a place that was dangerous and best kept away from. Was that what Race Rock was saying to Carla? He looked at his son. He looked at his wife. Was this about Caleb, or was this really about her? Was she so unhappy? Did she really hate their life?

Nathaniel could think the questions, but could not voice them. He was not good at confrontation. He merely croaked out a beseeching "Carla...."

Carla had enough determination for the two of them. "I'm taking him ashore. We'll stay with my cousin in New London a few days. Then we're taking the train to Virginia, to my mother's." Carla had her course charted.

Nathaniel could not leave Race Rock. His commission was to be the lighthouse keeper. It's all he had done for years. Mariners depended on him. He was dedicated to the light.

"You can see Caleb. You can visit us in Virginia. Or maybe we'll come visit here. I don't know." Carla was on the verge of tears. But she had made up her mind. She would not be deterred. He wondered how long she had been planning this, how long she had bottled up her emotions. He wondered why Carla hadn't asked him to leave with them. Had she come to hate him? It hurt him to realize he didn't know. Really didn't know how his wife felt. She was leaving and taking his son with her. He would be alone. With a stunning suddenness, his life was changing.

Carla picked up one of the satchels. "You have your work to do. I'll take the dinghy and row us to Fishers Island. We'll take the ferry to New London later. You can have Chester bring you the dinghy tomorrow when he makes his supply run."

Caleb looked at his father.

"Caleb," said Nathaniel, "do you want to leave here?" It was all Nathaniel could do. In desperation, he would try to let his young son make the decision. The boy looked at his mother. At his father. He looked down at the floor.

"Caleb?" Nathaniel repeated.

"I guess," was the boy's quiet reply.

So there it was. There was silence in the small kitchen.

"And you, Carla. Will you miss me?"

Carla dropped the bag and put her hands over her eyes. She began to cry. Her crying was loud in the small room. Caleb fidgeted, frightened by the emotions swirling about him. He was too young to understand any of it. Through her sobs, Carla finally spoke.

"Yes, I will miss you Nathaniel. You're a good man. You've been a good husband. But you don't have room for him—for us—in your life. This lighthouse, this godforsaken rock: this is your life. But it's not for me anymore. And not for Caleb. We can't live out here. It's so isolated, Nathaniel. It's a prison. Caleb needs to get away. Needs to be a boy. And I ... I ... just ... can't..." She could go on no more.

Carla's sobs filled the kitchen. Caleb looked down at the floor, distressed at his mother's crying. At what she was saying. Nathaniel said nothing. He'd been stunned into silence, and he was never good at expressing his emotions anyway. It was a burden of his time that men remained stoic. They believed they showed great strength in their reserve, even when it cost them dearly.

Pulling herself together, Carla wiped away her tears. She approached Nathaniel and rose up to give him a quick kiss. "We will see you again soon," she said. She urged Caleb forward and he gave his father a quick hug. Knowing that if she did not act quickly and decisively she would not act at all, Carla picked up their two suitcases and nudged Caleb toward the door of the kitchen. Nathaniel stood still. He should go with them, row them the mile to shore. But the suddenness of it, Carla's words, and his helplessness had paralyzed him. He was fixed in place, as he had been that day when the train passed him by.

Carla threw back the bolt on the front door. She opened it and for a moment bright daylight flooded the room. She ushered Caleb through it and followed. They seemed to dissolve into the light. Then the door swung shut behind them and Nathaniel was left alone in the lighthouse.

Carla and Caleb crossed the short porch on top of the cylindrical caisson that was the foundation of the lighthouse. They climbed down the iron ladder, somehow getting the suitcases to the stone pier at the bottom. They moved to the small rowboat that lay moored there. As if watching himself in a dream, Nathaniel crossed over to the window and looked out. It was a heavy, humid, foggy July day. Fishers Island, a mile to the East, was just a dark shape. Everything was wrapped in a gentle blue gauze of fog. He realized he had been holding his breath.

He looked down and saw Carla and Caleb in the tiny boat. She pulled the oars smoothly and strongly, accustomed to rowing the mile to the island. The water was dead calm. Caleb sat with his back to Race Rock, a small hunched figure in the stern of the boat. Nathaniel picked up a telescope from a table and walked outside to the porch railing. He sighted the scope on the rowboat in the fog and looked into the eyepiece. His wife's anguished face was clear. It was dreamlike, as looking through a scope always is. He was up close to them, but there was no sound. It didn't seem real. None of it seemed real.

As Carla and Caleb rowed away, they seemed to slowly dissolve into the fog. They were becoming phantoms, as insubstantial as dreams. Soon they would be only memories. Just as the fog obscured them from view, his son turned on the little bench at the rear of the boat and looked back at Race Rock, back to his father, the lighthouse keeper. Nathaniel watched through the telescope as his son said something. It was easy to read his lips. Nathaniel smiled—the only time he would smile on that painful, grim morning and for many mornings thereafter.

Then they were gone. Swallowed by the fog.

Nathaniel was alone.

He stared at where they had been, trying to will them back. In a daze, he went inside. He wandered over to a mirror and straightened his uniform coat. Brushed a bit of dirt off his shoulder. The brass buttons gleamed brightly, as they should on a well-kept uniform. He found a stray thread hanging from a button, wrapped it around his finger and gave it a hard yank. It snapped off. He watched as it drifted to the floor.

He should turn on the foghorn. He'd have to light the boiler to get the steam up to power it.

He lit a lantern and descended into the gloomy basement. He crouched by the foghorn's boiler, pumped some fuel and lit it. It would take a few minutes for it to build the steam. He waited, replaying the scene in the kitchen in his mind. Maybe Carla would change her mind in an hour or two. Or in a day or two. Maybe she would come back with Caleb. They could sit down and talk this through. They'd figure out what to do.

The steam valve hissed. Nathaniel threw a small lever that directed it into the pipes for the horn, a third class Daboll trumpet. It bleated for three seconds. Then a three second pause. Then another cry. Another three second pause. A final three second sounding before a forty-five second pause. A secondary pipe stole away a little of the steam to run the mechanism that timed the horn's sounding. Above him and outside he heard the horn.

Nathaniel went back to the main floor. He opened a small closet and removed a few rags and a bottle of cleaner. He opened the fire doors and started a slow climb to the lantern room, sixty-eight steps up and around the metal spiral staircase that wound its way up the tower. His footsteps echoed off the heavy masonry walls. The foghorn sounded its cry, echoing his own sad mood. Up and around he climbed, up and around, a spiral that seemed to go nowhere but gradually brought him to his destination.

He reached the top of the stairway and opened the metal door that led to the lantern room. He went in. Falling to his knees before the glittering glass Fresnel lens, he took a rag, poured some cleaning fluid on it, and carefully wiped one of the glass prisms that made up the complex array of concentric circles. He touched it with great care and respect. Though it was already spotless, he nonetheless cleaned it, as he did every day.

Nathaniel looked out the lantern room to the surrounding sky, thick and dull with fog. He was sixty-eight feet above the water and couldn't see it through the fog. The featureless sky was a blank canvas onto which he could project his thoughts.

Those thoughts were memories. Memories of life with Carla and Caleb. Little moments. Happy moments. Sad moments. Images from a life that was suddenly without a tomorrow. It scared him.

Damn Carla. Why did she have to go? Why couldn't she sit down and talk about this reasonably? What had she told the boy? When would he see them again?

For a moment, just a moment, he did not want to be on Race Rock. He wanted to be ... where? He didn't know. With his son, certainly. Perhaps walking in the woods or at a parade. Maybe Carla was right.

Nathaniel turned his gaze to his reflection in the lens. He could see the sadness in his eyes. He stared a long while, thinking about what Carla had said, conjuring up images of Caleb and trying to fix them in his mind.

He thought of things he wished he'd said but hadn't. Too

late now. There was an ache in him that was like a hard knot in his chest, as if all his emotions had solidified and come to rest there. Alone at the top of the lighthouse, he felt adrift, alone in the middle of nowhere, a disembodied spirit suspended in the air.

Nathaniel Bowen sat there for a long while. Thoughts drifted by like clouds. Carla had made a choice. *He* had made a choice. Could he change anything? He had been here too long to go anyplace else. He was trapped in a web of his own making.

He looked down at the rag in his hand. He remembered his chores. He leaned towards the light and began polishing another sparkling glass prism. Nathaniel took comfort in his daily routine, in the repetitive chores that gave his life meaning.

* * *

Nathaniel's memories lost their focus, and the images in his mind's eye blurred and evaporated. He found himself staring into an amber glass of whiskey, lit by a candle, on a cold February afternoon. He had been so lost in memories the storm had faded away. He was surprised to find himself where he was, as groggy as a man wakened from a sleep heavy with dark dreams.

A clap of thunder boomed. He turned his head slowly and looked out the rain-streaked window. The drops were backlit by another flash of lightning. They looked like tears. He picked up the little wooden seagull again, turning it over in his hand. Carla had left, taking Caleb with her. He had never seen them again. His dedication to the light had proved costly. Nathaniel was overwhelmed by a profound melancholy.

He shook his head and poured another drink.

3

While Nathaniel was struggling with his memories, the steamship *City of Lawrence* was struggling to make its way across Long Island Sound. The storm had worsened since the light at Montauk Point had disappeared into the night an hour ago. Captain Smith was holding his boat on a course of 348 degrees NNW, but the heavy currents were pushing him east. The wind was howling, the sleet unrelenting, the seas high—maybe fifteen to twenty feet—the ragged waves layered on top of large swells. The slow, heavy steamer—234 feet long, powered by steam-driven side-wheels—was plowing through the waves, and her decks were often awash. Ice had begun to form on those decks, but it was far too rough to send men out to try to chip it off. It was not a good situation. The ship's roll in the heavy seas was sickening.

He had no time to tend to the passengers. Many were sick. All of them were frightened. He'd sent what crew he could spare to comfort them. There was little any of them could do but ride out the storm. He could feel the boat getting sluggish in its response to the helm. The ice was adding weight and the weight was bogging them down. The storm clouds obscured the moon and stars. They were steaming through a deep and impenetrable darkness. On the bridge, Smith and two officers peered into that darkness searching for the light at Race Rock. He prayed it would show itself so they could steer by it. But they were only halfway across the Sound. Race Rock was still at least six miles away. As he had figured, in this severe weather, they would be lucky to spot it a mile or two before they were upon it. Smith lit up another cigarette. Its tip was an orange glow in the bridge, traveling an arc back and forth from his mouth to the ashtray by the wheel. He smoked it nervously, stubbed it out, lit another. He was earning his keep tonight.

* * *

On Race Rock, Nathaniel Bowen awoke with a start. A very large wave had slammed into the lighthouse with an echoing boom. He must have dozed off. On the table in front of him were the empty whiskey bottle, a shot glass, and the little piece of white driftwood carved into a seagull.

He had not bothered to light a lantern. He had not lit the light yet, either. The room was dark. He wasn't sure what time it was. He was confused. He pulled out his pocket watch and flicked open the cover. 6:30! He really should go light the light. The storm raged even worse than before. He must have dozed off. He felt cotton-headed. He stood up and felt dizzy. He stumbled towards the door to the spiral staircase and opened it. The shadowy, cold, dank stairwell was like a cave. The thought of winding his way up three flights to the lantern room was not appealing, especially in the dark. It smelled of fuel and that made his stomach churn. He needed to lie down for a minute to let the nausea pass. He shouldn't have drunk so much. He seldom drank more than a single beer, and had no tolerance for hard liquor. He needed to lie down. For just a few minutes.

He shuffled back into the room. It was lit by a flash of lightning. Everything was etched clear, as if illuminated by a photographer's flash powder. The afterimage lingered—strange, blue shapes that drifted like ghosts.

He needed to find a lantern. He needed to light the light. The room seemed to tilt. No, he needed to lie down. He headed across the room, bumping into furniture on the way. He collapsed onto a couch. He'd rest for just a few minutes. Then he'd get back to work.

He was asleep again almost as soon as he stretched out on the cushions. Waves crashed against the rocks below. Salt spray rattled against the windows. The keeper of the light slept.

The *City of Lawrence* pushed on, slowly making its way towards Race Rock, a dark presence in the dark night.

4

Keeping the light lit. That was the main job of the keeper of the light. That and turning on the foghorn. Yet a keeper did countless other chores devoted to mainte- nance. He tried to mend what nature had injured. A light keeper was constantly caulking holes in window frames, shin- gles and doors. He was always scouring away rust, burnishing metal, painting and polishing, greasing and calibrating. A keeper repaired or replaced ropes. He oiled pulleys and hinges and gears. He tightened screws or replaced rusted ones. He bought and stored provisions. A keeper needed to fix balky motors, tune compressors, scrub stairs, sand wood, patch leaks and paint walls. All the while, he needed to keep an eye out for trouble on the water.

The light itself was a mechanism of exquisite precision and worrying vulnerability. Race Rock had a fourth order fresnel lens, a complex and beautiful array of beveled prisms that took a small flame, magnified it, and focused it into a beam that could be seen, on a clear night, for fourteen miles. It was an ingenious and effective mechanism. Its vulnerability lay in the fragility of the glass. Over the course of a night, it absorbed the heat from the flame. If cold water touched the hot glass, the sudden cooling could cause it to crack or even explode.

Inside the array of prism lenses, the wick for the flame was fueled by reservoirs of kerosene. The reservoirs needed to be filled every day, and the wick carefully trimmed of residue. Keepers spent so much time and care tending to these wicks that they were sometimes called "wickies."

The lens rested on a pan of mercury which provided a vir- tually frictionless rotation, so long as the pan and the lens were kept level and adjusted. The light was rotated by a series of gears, driven by weights threaded through the center post of the spiral stairway. Much like a grandfather clock, the slow descent of the weights turned the light. Every four hours, the keeper had to crank the weights back up. From the sea, the light appeared to blink as the beam spun in or out of view, giving Race Rock its unique and identifying red flashing pattern.

A keeper tended his light as if it were a living thing. He knew exactly how to balance it, clean it, adjust its gears. Every day, a keeper tended the wick, carried cans of fuel from the basement storage tank to the lantern room, filled the reservoirs, polished the glass, raised the weights and checked the rotational gears. Every night, he lit the light and unlatched the weights. A keeper might never know the names or faces of the people sailing by through fog or storms or night, but he knew they depended on him to keep the light lit. His lighthouse was a beacon of safety. Its beam warned of dangers and provided a known point to navigate by.

Every day, a keeper entered notes of the weather, unusual events, and his daily chores in the official lighthouse logbook—the "Journal of the Lighthouse Station" as they were known. There was a journal for every year, kept in a leather-bound book. At the start of the new year, the old journal was taken by the Lighthouse Board to be stored in the National Archives in Washington, D.C. A new book was started.

Though keepers were busy, it was still a job that offered them plenty of time to pursue their own interests. The Board provided a rotating library of books, and keepers read a great deal. Some were avid fishermen. With assistant keepers or family, they passed time playing cards, making music, working on puzzles, painting, building model ships, carving driftwood, writing poetry—a multitude of activities to help relieve the tedium and isolation.

There was plenty of time to think. The repetitive chores did not require a great deal of intellectual engagement. They required dedication and competence. They required a sense of duty.

For all the work, all the responsibility, all the regime of duty, keepers were still men inside their crisp uniforms. Men whose hearts held dreams—and demons.

One morning, about six months after Carla and Caleb had left, Nathaniel lowered his skiff into the water. He was a strong rower. He set out in his small boat often, for the exercise, to fish, or just to circle his little island and see it from a different perspective. If he ventured toward the western tip of Fishers Island, he would pass the treacherous rocks off Race Point, on a line with Race Rock. In his small boat, he could skim among them—ominous black rocks encrusted with barnacles and trailing strands of seaweed like hair. They lurked just a few feet below the surface—deadly to all but the smallest of boats.

This day, he made his way slowly out toward the open waters of Long Island Sound. The seas were calm. The water was glassy, with light rolling swells that barely disturbed the surface. Race Rock was mirrored perfectly in the calm waters, undistorted, an inverted reflection of the real thing. Nathaniel gazed at it until a gull landed and sent a gentle ripple across the sea. The image of the lighthouse silently shattered into a chaotic abstraction, like a pristine memory that had become jumbled by confusion and doubt.

When he was about a mile from Race Rock, Nathaniel let the boat drift to a stop. It was morning, and quiet, and the sun was still low in the sky above Eastern Point in Groton. He could see waves gently breaking on Black Rock, just offshore. He watched a cormorant fly across the water, a sleek black shape skimming just inches above the surface, mirrored by its own reflection. Its wing tips never quite touched the water. Of all the birds that lived in the area, the cormorant was his favorite. Pitch black, shiny and sleek, their flight was gentle, effortless, beautiful. They fished by swimming along then disappearing below the surface. After a half minute or so they popped back up, usually quite a distance away. He watched as the bird arced around him and landed on Black Rock. A group of cormorants stood there, wings outstretched to dry, looking like Count Dracula spreading his cape. It was a pose that inspired some to call them "sea bats." They looked as though they were standing around having a meeting—perhaps planning their day of fishing.

From his pocket Nathaniel pulled out the small daguerreotype photograph of him and Carla, taken at the studio of William Jennings in Norwich shortly after they were married. Its gray metal surface glinted in the morning sunlight.

"Love, luck and longevity." The words he had uttered looking at the photograph every day seemed to mock him now. He looked at the picture where he and his wife looked back at him. He touched Carla's face with his fingers, as if the cold metal might feel like her soft, warm skin. The photograph triggered so many memories. He could recall her laughter, her humming as she cooked or sewed. He remembered her sitting at her small vanity, combing her long hair, turning and smiling as she caught him looking at her. He remembered their walks around the porch of the lighthouse, miles and miles of walks taken in sixty-pace circles. So many miles, so many memories!

He had loved her. She had loved him. What had happened? He hadn't noticed their drift apart. But drift they did, until one morning they were too far apart to reach out to one another. Carla was caught in a current that pulled her further away, and she took Caleb with her.

The keeper sat there in his gently bobbing boat, holding the photograph, lost in a frozen instant from his past.

He remembered the day the photograph had been taken. They had dressed up and taken the small rowboat to Fishers Island and then the ferry to New London. From there, it had been a carriage ride of several hours to Norwich to the studio of the photographer.

The picture's long exposure required they remain motionless for almost a minute. Smiles were too hard to keep, so they stared at the camera with a stoic determination. Though they were happy, they did not look it. Nathaniel looked at himself. At Carla. The photograph captured their likeness, but it did not capture their essence. Missing was Carla's vitality and grace, his own determination and strength. In and odd way, the photograph seemed to be of some other couple—strangers who just looked like them.

Nathaniel realized that he and Carla had become strangers. His memories seemed a betrayal now. As if the happy, shared life was a lie. Perhaps the photograph had captured their essence after all.

As if the metal photograph were too hot to hold, too painful, Nathaniel dropped it into the water. The stiff plate floated on the surface for a second, then drifted down, fluttering like a leaf. The metal picture caught the morning light and glowed as it sank. He watched as his face and Carla's grew dimmer. The water distorted their image as it sank into the cold green depths of the sea. It was a lazy descent; gentle, like a sigh dying in the wind. A final glowing glint and the picture vanished into the obscuring depths. Nathaniel continued to stare, as if he could still see the photograph. But he was only seeing the memory. So much of his life now seemed to be reliving memories.

He could not have explained, if asked, why he had thrown the picture away. It was an unconscious ritual, a symbolic separation from Carla, from their life together. The photograph was the talisman that enabled him to let go of her. Yet though the photograph was gone, the memories lingered on. If anything, more fragments of their life together bubbled into his consciousness, a jumble of impressions, like the turning of a kaleidoscope.

Nathaniel sighed and sat back in his boat. He pulled out his Lighthouse Board pocket-watch and checked the time. Nine o'clock. He should get back. Get going on his daily routine. He wondered how long the picture would lie on the sandy ocean floor before it rusted away. The corrosive salt water would claim it eventually. He wondered if his mind would likewise erode the memories. Did he even want that?

Nathaniel set his oars and headed back to his lighthouse, his ritual enacted, though not with the sense of finality he had hoped for. He had rid himself of the picture, but not the pain. Their past was fixed like the instant in the photograph. It could be distorted by memory, but not rewritten.

Beneath the waves, sixty feet down, the small metal photo-graph of the keeper and his wife lay on the sandy bottom. Their moment of happiness was beyond the reach of light, obscured by the sea's dark waters, lost forever.

5

The storm raged. The rumbling thunder joined the howling winds and hiss of waves crashing into the rocks and caisson. Lightning lit up the interior of the light-house. On the couch, Nathaniel Bowen, keeper of Race Rock, slept, oblivious to the maelstrom that raged outside. His dreams were troubled, poisoned by the liquor and his own melancholy.

Captain Smith, on the *City of Lawrence*, was living his own nightmare. One all too real. He peered into the dark, violent seas with a mad intensity, willing vision where there was none. The rest of the crew on the bridge looked, too. No one spoke a word. He gripped the wheel so hard his hands were white. They betrayed his fear.

The *City of Lawrence* crept across the Sound, assaulted by the storm, its crew searching for a light that was not lit.

6

When Carla left with Caleb, Nathaniel's world, already defined by the small island that was his kingdom, shrank. It was very hard at first. Whatever problems they may have had, they were still a family. There was love. The sudden silence they left behind was deafening. Gone were the shouts from room to room, the hugs and kisses given while passing on the spiral stairs. He missed Carla's gentle laugh, the sounds she made cooking, the whisper-like rustle of her skirt. He missed the way she read stories to Caleb, how she used different voices for different characters. He missed her humming songs while she worked.

Nathaniel missed Caleb, too. He missed explaining things to his son. He missed Caleb's endless questions about the workings of the light or the weather or the seas. He missed how intently the boy watched him when he made his daily entries into the lighthouse journal. He missed catching a glimpse of Caleb out on the porch that encircled the top of the stone foundation, waving his arms and giving commands to imaginary pirates. Caleb and Carla had both seemed happy in their lives at Race Rock. Without them, the place felt so different, the loneliness heavy and palpable. Nathaniel was a man grieving. Not for the dead, but for the living.

For the first few days, he had wandered around in stunned disbelief. He kept expecting to hear the creak and splash of oars, to look out a window and see them rowing back. He busied himself with chores, hoping that by losing himself in them he would forget the pain. But it was always there, riding along on top of his thoughts like an angry bird floating on the waves.

As the passing days stretched into weeks and then months, he came to accept they were gone. Slowly, reluctantly, he started to let them go. Time, as it always does, dulled the pain. His solitude became part of the daily routine on his joyless rock. Eventually, the voices of his wife and child were replaced by those that droned on in his head, an internal monologue that became his only companion.

Regulations required Bowen to report his changed circumstances immediately to the Lighthouse Board. They would send an assistant keeper out to share the chores and to keep him sane. It was generally believed, if not explicitly stated, that it was not healthy for a man to be alone on a lighthouse. There had been cases where the isolation had caused keepers to go mad. A few had jumped into the sea. One kept a crew of men at bay for several days, convinced they were an invading army. Some loners were able to cope, but most men could not, at least not for long. Human beings were not meant to live alone.

Solitude and isolation are a sort of madness. However well tolerated, however efficiently a man might adapt to them, he lacked the perspective and balance another person provided. A man alone was his own world, his own lever and fulcrum. He had no way to know if that world had tilted off balance.

Yet Nathaniel did not report Carla and Caleb's leaving. In part, he could not admit to himself that it was permanent. Whether it was or not, he wanted to be alone. He *needed* to be alone. He needed quiet reflection to come to grips with what had happened. Healthy or not, he embraced the solitude that was his. He worked hard, kept the light lit, and found satisfaction and meaning in doing so.

Nathaniel tended to the light and kept house for himself. He read. He continued his walks around the lighthouse's porch. It took nearly fifty laps to walk a mile. Sometimes he walked lost in thought; sometimes he simply watched the birds. There were so many and so varied: large, angular white herons, flocks of geese in their tight vees, gulls wheeling and chasing each other across the sky, graceful cormorants skimming silently inches above the surface like black arrows. Sometimes a bird would land on the railing and study him curiously. Nathaniel would stop his walk and talk to the bird.

7

The morning of December 1, 1905, Nathaniel was walking around the base of the lighthouse, stopping every so often to check the rocks below for flotsam. It was something he did every few days. Flotsam was nature's roll of the dice. He never knew what might wash up. Mostly it was driftwood—gnarled, knurled, grotesque sculptures cast onto the rocks. He wondered where the wood had started its journey. What tree in what forest had fallen and made its way to the sea? What about the pieces clearly shaped by human hands? What were they? A pier? An oar? A boat? How long had they journeyed, pushed by tides and winds and fate, to finally wash up on his tiny island? Bleached by the sun, the wood was ghostly white, like the bones of a skeleton. He had collected a few of the more bizarre and intriguing shapes, and carved them into toys for his son. The seagull was one of them.

He piled most of the wood in the boiler room deep inside the cistern of Race Rock. There it would dry, then he could burn it in the lighthouse's various fireplaces or wood stove.

Other things washed up too: shoes, tires, fishing nets, bits of rope, bottles (though none with messages), fishing floats, pieces of ceramic, odd bits of metal, sea glass, bricks—polished round and smooth by the water—the bones of fish and birds. It was hard to know how some of these things had become afloat. Were they cast off? Lost by accident? The result of a shipwreck? Once, a section of white piano keys drifted up, like a lost set of dentures. Another time, a gilded kerosene lamp. He found a perfectly good rocking chair. A letter addressed to a Mr. Harrison T. Kat. The ink had run into an unreadable mess, except for the words "vaudeville band." Nathaniel found a cocoanut from God knows where. He found a bible, which he dried out and consulted when he went to church on the mainland. A top hat. A life-preserver from the *Fantadia*, which had sunk months earlier off the coast of Maryland. One afternoon, he found an injured cat on the rocks. How it had gotten there he had no idea. He named it Neptune, nursed it back to health, and gave it to the daughter of a friend in New London.

It fascinated Nathaniel what washed up, and he speculated endlessly about where it may have come from and how it had found its way to him. Hunched over an atlas, he tried to figure the route a bottle or a cocoanut might have taken as it rode the ocean currents, drifting thousands of miles in an aimless wander across the globe. Had the flotsam visited other shores only to be pulled back out to sea by the next tide? Who had last touched it? Where? When? It was all a mystery.

These stray objects, like many antiques, were tantalizing. They hinted at lives; they evoked vague impressions of places and times. Yet they did not reveal their true origins. The imagination could make up whatever story it wanted about a piece of driftwood or a washed up top hat or anything else. The truth could never be known. Flotsam had a kind of anonymous immortality.

Nathaniel could not help but sometimes attach a bit of mystical significance to what arrived on his island. Sometimes he thought that it was not random at all, but ordained by a higher power. Like the time a chest of dolls washed up just a week before Christmas. He donated them to St. James church in New London, and they made many children happy. Perhaps the junk that drifted up was like tea leaves that held portents and meaning if you knew how to read them.

On this gray December day, as he scanned the boulders below, it started to snow. Nathaniel delighted in watching the millions of flakes drift down and disappear into the sea. He could hear them as they hit the water, hissing softly like gentle sighs. The scene was rendered in shades of gray, and the white snowflakes were distinct against the dusky sky. The lighthouse took on a fairy-tale look as the snow gathered and frosted the stone building, dock and rocks. A few gulls circled silently overhead. It was dreamlike, beautiful, a day of crystalline beauty. He felt that his lighthouse was encased in a little snow-globe. Someone had shaken it and now the snow swirled and descended in a slow, mesmerizing drift. It was magical.

As his eyes swept across the rocks, he noticed a bright glint of metal. Shading his eyes, he peered harder. There was something down there. Probably junk, but worth a closer look. Curious, he descended the ladder to the flat stone pier. He paused and looked out at the surrounding fringe of massive boulders that formed the island that supported the lighthouse. It was always risky stepping onto the rocks, even when it was calm. When the tides were low, the rocks showed off beards of brown, slimy seaweed. The stuff was very slick. In the winter, on rocks made even more slippery by snow and ice, it would be easy to twist an ankle or fall and break a leg. Easy to slip and fall into an ice cold sea. No one would rescue him. Another reason being alone at a lighthouse was not a good idea.

He was ever mindful of the terrible fate of Shane Fitzgerald, keeper of a light that, like Race Rock, stood alone in the middle of the sea. It, too, rested on a base of huge boulders. Fitzgerald, alone at the light, had gone out on the rocks for some reason. One of the huge boulders, prodded by wind and waves, had become unstable. When Shane stepped on it, it rolled over, pitching him down onto the rocks at water's edge. Then the huge rock had continued to roll over and trapped Shane in a crevice. There was no one to see his fall. No one to cry out to for help. It had been Shane's poor judgment to go out on the rocks at low tide. A few hours later, when the tides rose, the crevice slowly filled with water. No one could hear his frantic cries. Shane Fitzgerald drowned, alone and helpless in the rocks at the base of his own lighthouse. No, it was never wise to go out on the rocks, especially at low tide. Yet for Nathaniel, low tide was when much of what washed up on Race Rock was visible and accessible. So he risked it.

Cautiously, Nathaniel stepped onto the boulders. He scanned the jagged shapes. Twenty feet away, he could see a small wooden box inlaid with metal. Bending over, holding on, keeping his center of gravity low, he made his way to where the box lay wedged in a crevice. Bundled in his coat, Nathaniel was a dark figure crawling across the icy rocks. He slipped once and cursed. If he broke a leg, he would never make it back and up the ladder. He pushed on, driven by curiosity.

Finally he reached the crevice where the box was wedged. It was about seven inches square. He was intrigued. Where had *this* come from? Nathaniel pried it loose. He sat on a rock and studied the box. It was made of wood and every side had inlays of brass in a checkerboard pattern. There were no clasps or hinges, and Nathaniel assumed that somewhere the box pulled apart. This was not like so much of the junk that washed up; this was a little work of art, and it seemed intact. The lid— wherever it was—was tightly sealed. No water dripped out. He doubted any had even gotten in.

When he tipped the box, something moved inside.

The box held a secret.

It looked like it had been traveling around on the seas for quite a while. The wood was a little chipped, the brass squares scratched. His imagination crafted a dozen scenarios. It had come from a shipwreck. A spurned lover had tossed it into the water in anger. A shipment had been stolen and then lost again. Perhaps it had come all the way from Europe or Asia. Perhaps it had been afloat for decades or longer, bobbing along, swept by currents and winds, stranded for a time on this beach or that until a storm freed it.

He thought of the ancient myth of Pandora's box. All the ills of the world had been put in a box, a box Pandora was forbidden to open.

But she had.

The ills escaped to haunt mankind forever. Maybe this was Pandora's box. Maybe it had been adrift for centuries—since the dawn of history? Who knew? It was a box of mystery, and he hoped that something inside held a clue to its origins. Like Pandora, he would open it. It would be impossible not to. Whatever the consequences, he would be responsible, as Pandora had been. It was the price of satisfying curiosity.

Whatever was inside shifted again as he turned it. He could feel it. Nathaniel shoved the box into one of the deep pockets of his big coat and carefully made his way back across the boulders. They were even slicker from the snow now, and it took him ten minutes to clamber his way back to the base of the ladder. He slipped a few times but managed to make it back. He climbed the slick metal rungs of the ladder and stood on the porch. Anxious as he was to open the box, he had to admire the scene.

The thick flakes fluttered down more heavily now, and the snow obscured both Fishers Island and New London. The snowfall was as gentle as a caress. Race Rock was alone, the whole world, a planet adrift in a universe of cold white stars. He felt exhilarated in his solitude, a wonderful connection to the vast nature that surrounded him.

After a few minutes, getting chilled and drawn by curiosity, Nathaniel opened the heavy wood door, which swung silently on its massive hinges. Like everything on Race Rock, it was built solidly to withstand the rigors of the weather.

He stepped inside, closed the door, slid the big iron deadbolt in place, and hung up his wet coat on a peg by the door. He took the box from the pocket and put it on a table. The fire in the wood stove had dwindled during his excursion, so he added a few logs. He went to the kitchen and started a pot of water boiling to make some coffee. He rubbed his hands to warm them, then sat down at the table where the box rested, mute and tantalizing.

The box. What was in it? Should he open it? Of course, he should! How could he not? It had come to him from the sea, given to him by the waters like a gift. It was his now. He owned whatever was inside it. He picked it up and turned it in his hands, examining it closely again. It was exquisite. The craftsmanship was superb. The brass inlays were all the same and precisely set on the wooden sides. Though it seemed solid, without any lid or hinges, he finally detected a very fine line below the second row of squares on one side. There *was* some sort of lid.

He grasped the box and pulled at the edge, hoping to slide the top off. It didn't move. Either the fit was very tight or the wood had swelled from immersion in water and stuck. Perhaps both. There had to be a way to open it. Maybe a hidden lock mechanism. He'd once seen a Chinese puzzle box of inlaid woods that required some of its inlays to be slid in a particular sequence to trip the lock mechanism. If this box, with all its inlaid squares of brass, were such a box, it could take him a long time to discover the right sequence.

As it happened, it would take Nathaniel only a few minutes to solve the riddle of the washed-up box. As he was turning it in his hand, one of the brass squares moved under his finger. Like a button, it depressed into the wood. Keeping it pressed in, he pushed on others. After trying sixteen, the seventeenth square depressed into the box and there was an audible click. When he released them, the two squares stayed in.

He applied a steady, hard pull and the lid begrudgingly opened a little. He wiggled the lid and pulled again. It gave another fraction of an inch. He could feel it getting a little easier. Steady. Steady.

The lid finally came off. The box was open. Nathaniel sat back. Exhaled. He lifted the lamp. Inside the box, there was a leather pouch. He pulled it out. It was dry. It looked like a very old bag. The neck was fastened with a drawstring. It was heavy, and it felt like there were a number of things inside. He put the lamp down. His hands were trembling slightly as he started to untie the drawstring. He finally got the knot undone. He opened the mouth of the bag, and something shiny caught the light. Nathaniel reached inside and felt around. His fingers touched cold stones. He pulled one out.

It was about the size of an almond. It glittered a deep blue in the lantern-light, and though Nathaniel was not too experienced in gems, he believed he was holding a sapphire. A huge one. The beautiful stone was cut with many facets. He gazed into the jewel, whose deep cobalt blue color reminded him of a twilight sky. It was a lovely color. His favorite. He turned the sapphire in his fingers. The gem's facets refracted the lantern light onto the walls in streaks of blue that looked like a thousand streaking comets.

He carefully placed the gem on the table. He sat back and looked at the sapphire and the pouch. He took a sip from his coffee. Finding something as beautiful and refined as this stone stunned him. Where had this come from? Whose was it?

He reached in and withdrew another gem. It, too, was very big. Green. The deepest and most seductive green he had ever seen. This jewel also sparkled with a focused perfection. Nathaniel let out a slow whistle. Again his mind bubbled with images of camel caravans and sumptuous palaces, of noblemen and kings, of dowries and pirates and shipwrecks. Nathaniel picked up the green stone. Somehow, the purity of its color seemed to define the very notion of "green." He held it to his eye and looked through the broadest facet. There was no distortion to the room he saw through it, just a tinting of color. It was like looking at his world from the depths of the sea.

He put the emerald on the table alongside the sapphire. He reached in and pulled out a clear faceted stone that seemed afire in his hand. Its icy clarity left no doubt: it was a diamond. It was huge—the size of a large raisin. It was cut in a complex pattern of facets, with a broad face and sides that tapered to a point. It glittered in his hand like a bundle of sparks, though it was cold and hard to the touch. He put it down, hands trembling.

Nathaniel realized he hadn't been breathing. He sat back in his chair and stared at the three gems that shone on the rough wooden table. The leather bag still had treasures within. He knew he was already looking at more wealth than he could ever hope to amass in a lifetime of being a lighthouse keeper.

He took a gulp of coffee. Then another. He was tempted to take a shot of the whiskey he kept in case a cold, wet sailor needed to be revived. But he had little taste for liquor. It just put him to sleep.

Sleep.

He hoped, he prayed this was not a dream. It seemed dreamlike. Unbelievable. Perhaps he had gone mad after all and he was hallucinating. Nathaniel went to the sink and splashed some water on his face. He was awake. This was real.

He had retrieved much from the rocks of his little island over the years. Most of it worthless junk. He could never have imagined finding a real treasure. His eyes returned to the gleaming gems on the table.

Nathaniel sat down and reached into the leather bag. He withdrew an ornately carved gold ring. The miniature, detailed sculpture on it depicted a cross section of a nautilus shell. It was an intricate working. He could see each of the shell's spiral chambers. The gold was a buttery yellow color, and it, too, captured the dim lantern light and beamed it around the room. He put the ring on the table next to the sapphire, emerald and diamond.

He reached into the pouch and pulled out another ring with a diamond. A large, square one. The next jewel was a ruby. Its deep red was like a fall sunset sky or the last embers of a winter fire. He held it at arm's length in front of the lantern. The stone caught the light and sent a red beam glowing across the room. He was holding a miniature lighthouse.

Nathaniel Bowen continued to empty the pouch. The gems were so beautiful, so perfect, so mesmerizing, that he had to admire and savor each one. There was another gold ring, an intricate carving of Medusa, head full of writhing snakes. The artistry was amazing; he could see each miniature snake's eyes and fangs. A few more gemstones followed— star sapphire, topaz, amethyst. The pouch was yielding up a spectrum of jewels. Nathaniel scarcely noticed the room or the sounds from outside. He was somewhere else, transported to a world of pure luminous colors captured in cold hard stones. Again the questions surfaced. Whose were they? Where were they from? How old? He knew he would never know.

The final thing he pulled from the bag was another ring. It had an oval of translucent material, about an inch long, that was a rich tobacco color. There was something inside it. He brought it to his eye and peered in. There was a tiny spider embedded there. Nathaniel knew what this was. It was amber. He had read about it in "Streeter and Hale's Encyclopedia of Fossils, Gems and Minerals," one of the books circulated by the Lighthouse Board.

Of all the gems he had pulled out of the bag, the amber ring with the tiny spider inside was somehow the most intriguing. Not the most valuable, but certainly the most evocative. He held it close to his eye and turned it in the light. The spider was a silhouette, its little legs visible. It wasn't a fossil; it was the real spider, trapped in resin and preserved for millions of years. He was holding a bit of the past in his hand, and he marveled that sometimes that past did not decay or fade away. It endured, unchanged, beyond the reach of time.

Nathaniel imagined a hot primeval jungle. A huge tree. A tiny spider becoming trapped in a golden bead of resin. As if in a photograph, that moment was captured for eternity in the bit of amber he held at his fingertips.

The leather pouch was empty. Nathaniel had twenty remarkable jewels and rings laid out on the table. He gazed at the treasure for a few moments. His mind's eye played the scenes again. Pirates. Shipwrecks. Exotic bazaars. Traders and murderers, noblemen and thieves. He shook his head in disbelief.

Nathaniel Bowen stood, put his overcoat back on and walked over to the fire door, opened it and headed up the spiral stairs. He stopped on the second floor to retrieve a well-used Meerschaum pipe, carved into the head of a turbaned Arab, and a pouch of tobacco. He went back to the stairway and continued up. Though it was not time to light the light, he opened the hatch to the lantern room. He squeezed in beside the light. Its Fresnel lens was the largest gem of them all and, until tonight, the most valuable thing on Race Rock. He crawled out the small door that led from the lantern room to the outside catwalk. He needed the fresh winter air to clear his head. He needed to think for a bit.

Snow still drifted down, and he watched as it disappeared into the dark green waters, nearly seventy feet below. The waves surged against the boulders, sending a frigid spray into the air. It rained back down onto the rocks with a hiss. He watched as the water washed off the rocks back into the sea, leaving them glistening. A frosting of ice glowed on the highest boulders and upon the rest of Race Rock.

Nathaniel filled his pipe, turned away from the wind and lit it. The wind swirled the blue smoke around him like a veil. He thought about the treasure. The gems were worth a fortune.

He knew that. When he sold them he would be a wealthy man. He'd never coveted wealth, anticipated it, dreamed of it. He didn't know what it meant to have money and the freedom it could bring. He liked to work. His thoughts turned to his family. It was too bad Carla had disappeared. Maybe his new-found fortune would bring her back to him. They could live anywhere, do almost anything now.

As he watched a puff of his smoke drift into the night sky, he realized, sadly, that there was no "they" anymore. Just himself. Alone. He couldn't even use the money to help Caleb. He had vanished with his mother, moved to who knows where. He hadn't heard from them in over a year. It would be a wonderful legacy to leave the boy. But how? Caleb was gone from his life, and he had no way to bring him back. Too bad the little box hadn't washed up a few years earlier. Life might be very different.

He was happy being a lighthouse keeper. This was his life. It had been his life since his teens. Someday, he would travel to the faraway lands he had read about in the travelogues. Someday. It did not seem time to do that yet. He was still young. He could travel later. When he was ready, maybe in a few years. He would remain the keeper of Race Rock and plan. Read about places. Think it all through. When he knew what he wanted to do, when he was tired of his life on Race Rock, he would see the world in style. Distant lands, exotic cultures, the wonders of nature—he would see them all. There was no rush. The gems and rings were safe as they were. Small and durable. Though he had a bank account, he didn't have a safety deposit box. There was no need for one. He decided he would hide his treasure on Race Rock and only take it when he left for good. Nathaniel thought about the lighthouse. There were hundreds of places he could put the box. After considering the possibilities a few minutes, he had a sudden inspiration. He smiled. He had thought of the perfect place to hide the treasure.

Snowflakes drifted slowly to the sea. A gull wheeled by and gave a plaintive cry. A ferry worked its way toward New London. The muffled hush of the snowy evening embraced him. He let his mind roam. He looked out over Fishers Island Sound, to Eastern Point in Groton. He turned and admired the slender white lighthouse at the mouth of the Thames River. Here and there, lights twinkled on the shore. He listened to the waves on the rocks. This was his world. His kingdom. The kingdom of the light. Now he had his crown jewels.

Nathaniel Bowen was a man who had some regrets about his life, yet a man who had found peace. His future had changed today, and though he could only see to the horizon twenty miles away, his thoughts carried beyond it to a world that was suddenly wide open to him.

The snow swirled, caught by a freshening breeze that blew across Long Island Sound. The scene was one of perfect beauty from his vantage point in the middle of it. He felt alive and happy—more so than he had for a long, long time.

Night had crept in.

It was time to light the light.

8

The days and weeks and months passed. Nathaniel worked as hard as ever. For his own memory, he had noted the discovery of the little box of gems in a simple, sparse entry into his log of the day.

"December 1, 1905. Snowy. 28 degrees. Winds from SSW at about 10 knots. Visibility 4-5 miles. Seas 1-2 feet. Oiled lamp bearing. Caulked window. Found wood box, a real treasure. Checked kerosene levels. Need 100 feet of rope."

The only change brought on by his discovery of the box of gems was in his reading. He read more travel commentaries and had started a list of places he wanted to see. He circled them on a world map he kept in his study.

The winter faded away; spring was warm and rainy. Migrating birds stopped at Race Rock to rest, as did Monarch butterflies. Monarchs fascinated him. The colorful butterflies migrated back and forth from Canada to Mexico. They lived only a few weeks, so it took generations to complete the journey. In the spring, they started the long trek to where their ancestors were born in Canada. They inherited their flight paths and bearing to their destination. It was a history that repeated endlessly. Nathaniel enjoyed the few weeks every year when his lighthouse was dotted with the butterflies' fluttering orange wings.

The days grew longer. Summer settled in.

One hot morning in July, 1906, Race Rock was wrapped in a dense blanket of fog. Visibility was only a hundred feet. The sea feathered off into an infinity of luminous gold as the unseen sun lit the thick air. Sounds drifted by. An occasional fishing boat materialized from the fog like an actor parting a curtain on stage, motored by, then disappeared again. Standing at the top of his light, Nathaniel was alone in the fog in a way that was both calming and eerie. The world was hushed and heavy with a sense of anticipation. It was impossible to tell what loomed out there, just beyond the periphery of his vision.

Though he loved the fog, Nathaniel was also leery of it. More ships were wrecked in the fog than in heavy storms. Fog was deceptive and disorienting. Sounds echoed and often seemed to come from an entirely different direction than where they really were. Some sounds were muffled, others amplified in the heavy air. A dog barking on Fishers Island might sound like it was at the base of the lighthouse. Race Rock's foghorn ricocheted off distant shores and rolled back.

There were no horizons, often no distinction between sky and water. Just a surrounding blankness sprinkled with half-glimpsed phantoms. Poets and painters love the fog, but mariners dread it. Sailing in the fog is nerve wracking. The imagination fills in the emptiness with things that never appear. The featureless world of fog can lull a mariner into a daze. There is nothing to focus on, no sense of progress. Fog cuts a helmsman's reaction time down to almost nothing. If something does suddenly appear ahead, shockingly close, there is no time to steer out of harm's way. Fog is expectation often becoming the unexpected.

Nathaniel stood on Race Rock and listened. There were ships out there. The blasts of their foghorns cut through the heavy air. They were carrying on a conversation of sorts as one sounded its horn and another answered. Their trumpeting always sounded like great beasts to him. It was eerie to hear the grind and hum of their motors but not see them. They were ghost ships, passing by Race Rock, their exact size and location unknowable. Race Rock's horn added its voice to the chorus. Between the sounding of the horns, the sea was cloaked in a heavy silence, a silence that was almost tangible. The waves lapped gently at the rocks around the lighthouse. The keeper listened in these silences for subtle, faint sounds. If he closed his eyes and listened intently, he could start to make out the threads of the gauzy tapestry around him. It took concentration and a conscious filtering out of the obvious noises, like boat motors and lapping waves. As the near sounds fell away, he could hear a distant train, a barking dog, children laughing as they played. In a fog this heavy, he could even hear the beat of a bird's wings. A foggy day was a waking dream, a world of suggestion and ambiguity.

As he listened, Nathaniel heard the sound of rowing. The unmistakable creak of wood in metal oarlocks and the rhythmic splash of the oars in the water. He opened his eyes and peered into the fog. He saw nothing. The sound continued, slowly getting closer. He though he saw a shape in the mist, but it might just have been his imagination desperately trying to conjure up something—anything—in the infinite blankness that surrounded him.

Creak. Splash. Creak. Splash. The sound grew louder. Then he saw it: a darkening of the golden air. It was a faint silhouette: a woman in a rowboat. She was as transparent as a piece of gauze at first, but slowly gathered form as she approached. Creak. Splash. Creak. Splash.

Was it Carla returning? For a moment, he was excited and hopeful. Then he saw her a little more clearly and realized the woman was not his wife.

Though it was not common, unexpected visitors sometimes followed life's drift to Race Rock. Someone whose boat had sprung a leak; a fisherman in need of assistance; sightseers drawn to the castle-like house perched on the rocks in the middle of the sea. Once, a writer working on a book stopped by to research life on a lighthouse. Another time, a couple eloping sought refuge on Race Rock as they tried to elude the bride's father. A spiritualist made a visit hoping to contact ghosts from nearby shipwrecks. He believed the seagulls talked to him, though he could not divulge what they had to say. The great magician Howard Thurston, vacationing in New London a few days and unable to conjure up biting fish, spent an afternoon charming Nathaniel with his tricks. Nathaniel welcomed them all, happy for a little company, though just as happy when they left and he could return to his solitude and work.

He gazed at the woman rowing toward him.

When she had left Fishers Island, Race Rock was invisible in the fog. She had put a compass on the bench and headed in the light's general direction. She could hear its horn, but that was all. Every few strokes, she'd looked over her shoulder toward where the light should be. From time to time, the drift of the fog would reveal a dark blob out on the water. Just a shape, an impression. She rowed on.

As she drew closer, the details of Race Rock began to crystallize: the boulders of the riprap, the heavy stones of the drum base, the house itself with its windows, tower, roof and chimneys.

Nathaniel opened the hatch to the lantern room and crawled in. He opened the heavy metal door, stepped onto the spiral staircase and wound his way down and around, past the heavy metal fire doors that sealed off each floor. Sixty-eight steps brought him to the first floor. He opened the massive wooden door and stepped out onto the porch that encircled the house. He walked around a few paces to where he had last seen the woman approaching.

She was much closer. Just fifty feet or so from the notch in the rocks that led to the stone dock. She rowed with smooth, assured strokes. She had her back to him as she rowed, but peered over her shoulder to adjust her course as she neared the large boulders. She saw Bowen standing there, looking very official in his uniform. She stopped rowing and let the boat drift towards the lighthouse as she called up to him.

"Hello there!"

"Hello!" Nathaniel yelled back.

"Can I dock my boat?"

"Yes!" he yelled back.

Nathaniel saw that the woman was perhaps in her late thirties. She had a narrow face, fine features and long brown hair. She was quite attractive. She was slim, dressed in a blue shirt and khaki pants. She wore a wide-brimmed hat, and a green scarf around her neck.

He welcomed visitors. He had realized, after his wife and son left, how much he missed contact with other people. Though somewhat of a natural loner, he still enjoyed company. Nathaniel could be friendly and talkative, unlike many keepers, who were quiet, even surly hermits. Visitors were a break from his routine, and he truly enjoyed most anyone who ventured to his rock. Attractive women didn't show up on his island every day. During the past year, the sea had been kind to him. First the box with its treasures, and now this lovely visitor.

She started to row again, slowly guiding her small boat between the massive rocks surrounding the dock. It was a flat stone platform at the end of a short protective channel. The dock was about ten feet wide by twenty long. A metal ladder rose from its center to the top of the caisson that supported the lighthouse, a height of thirty feet. Nathaniel climbed down the ladder and took the line she threw. He tied it with two half-hitches to one of the heavy iron cleats set into the dock. He wrapped the rope around his hands and gave it two hard tugs to make sure it was tight. Satisfied the little boat was secure, he held out his hand. The woman stowed her oars, gathered up a knapsack, and accepted his hand as she stepped onto Race Rock.

"I'm Nathaniel Bowen," he said, "keeper of the light."

"Pleased to meet you Nathaniel. I'm Madeleine Covington. Friends call me Mad for short." She laughed. "Well, no they don't. They just think I'm mad. They call me Maddy."

"Pleased to meet you, Maddy," said Nathaniel as they stood on the dock. The seas were calm and made little noise as they lapped against the stones at water's edge. The foghorn sounded and echoed in the fog. There was a moment of silence. Maddy studied the man. She was surprised at his attire, at the neat suit, shining brass buttons, tie and hat. It looked very formal and not very comfortable. He was a handsome man, with deep brown eyes. His hair was also brown, and he kept his mustache neatly trimmed. He was a little under six feet, thin and angular, like a seabird—maybe a heron.

"What brings you to Race Rock?" asked Nathaniel.

Maddy smiled. "I'm a painter. I've always wanted to come out here and paint. I was on Fishers Island visiting a friend. So today, with this mysterious fog, I decided I wouldn't put it off any longer. An impulse. So I rented this boat and here I am. I'd like to roost here today and paint. If it's all right with you, of course. I won't get in your way."

"It's fine," said Nathaniel, smiling. "You row well."

"Thanks. I grew up on the water."

"Where was that?" asked Nathaniel.

"Newport," Maddy said. She picked up her bag and took a step towards the ladder. "Mind if we go up?"

"No. Fine," said Nathaniel. "Here, let me carry that."

Maddy gave him her bag of painting supplies and started to climb the ladder towards the lighthouse. He caught a faint whiff of perfume in the heavy air and smiled. It had been a long time since he'd been in the presence of a woman. The sweet smell of hyacinth drifted behind her like a caress. Maddy ascended easily and Nathaniel followed. It brought them to the circular porch with its white iron railing.

"Whew," she said, as she paused to catch her breath. She craned her neck back to take in the granite house. "This place is bigger than it looks. And higher."

"They built it to last," Nathaniel said. "It's a fortress."

"And you're the king?" Maddy said with a laugh.

"Yes, the king and the keeper," he said, sweeping his arm around to the sea. "And this is my kingdom." He pointed to the light. "That's the queen."

Maddy followed his point to the light tower and looked at it a moment. "How come it's not lit?"

"It doesn't help much in the fog during the day. It just gets swallowed up. You couldn't see it a quarter of a mile away in this stuff. I'll light it when it gets dark, as always."

As if on cue, the foghorn sounded, very loud.

Maddy jumped and bumped into Nathaniel. She clutched him for a second then backed away.

"Jesus!" she spat.

"The foghorn, on the other hand, is quite effective in the fog." He smiled at her. He was so used to the horn that it didn't startle him. But for someone who'd never been so close to one it was like having a train whistle blow a few feet away.

"It's going to do that again, isn't it?" she asked.

"Yes, in about forty-five seconds," Nathaniel said.

"Then let's get away from it." She said and turned towards the door of the lighthouse. Then stopped. "CAN you get away from it out here?"

"Pretty well. The walls and windows are thick, and most of the sound goes out away from the house. You can hear it inside, but it's not bad."

They arrived at the front door. Like the rest of Race Rock, the door was heavy, thick, and built to last. To its right was a small metal dedication plaque. It read:

Race Rock Lighthouse
Built by
Captain Thomas Albertson Scott & Francis Hopkinson Smith

May this light forever aid mariners as they sail these waters.
May God protect all those who serve here.

October 26, 1878

"A nice sentiment," said Maddy.

"It's mine," said Nathaniel. "The original plaque wore out. The salt and the wind had all but erased it. When I got here you could barely read it. That didn't seem right. So I replaced it and added the last few lines."

He turned the large brass handle on the door. He pulled it open towards them slowly. Its great weight fought him. They stepped inside just as the foghorn sounded again.

It was a strange feeling for Nathaniel to have a woman in the lighthouse again. He had left some of Carla's and Caleb's things around. If an inspector came, he wanted it to look like they still lived here so he wouldn't be assigned an assistant. Chester, who came out once or twice a week with supplies, suspected what was up, but discreetly said nothing. Over time, the connection to Carla and Caleb had weakened. When he saw her hat on a peg by the door he did not stop and think about her as he once had. Time had eroded away the intense emotions of loss.

As Maddy looked around, Nathaniel was caught between feeling he was doing something wrong having this woman inside and being delighted to have her company. It was an ambivalence common to someone who has ended a relationship and found himself with a new person in a familiar place. Though Carla was long gone, Race Rock was still the home they had shared and where they had forged their memories. Her presence haunted the place still.

Maddy Covington was lithe and graceful. Her mane of chestnut hair flowed wildly down her shoulders and back. She had green eyes the color of shallow water, and they sparkled like water, too. She was trim, with a nice figure. Prettier, he thought, than Carla.

"Mind if I smoke?" she asked.

"No, not at all."

Maddy took out a pack of cigarettes, tapped one out. She fished in her pocket and came out with a gleaming gold lighter. She noticed Nathaniel noticing it.

"One thing my father taught me was to always carry a little gold with me. If I run out of money, I can always trade something made of gold for what I need. Or hock it for cash." She lit the cigarette.

"Good advice," Nathaniel said.

"If nothing else," she said, "my father knew about money."

Maddy continued her examination of the small living area: a heavy desk, a few chairs, a fireplace and a bookcase. She browsed the bookcase and was surprised to find an eclectic assortment of fiction, poetry, history, science and travelogues. "The Alchemy of the Arts." "The Marriage of Loti." "World Travels and Adventures." "The Poetry of Samuel Taylor Coleridge." "Greek Mythology." "Lhasa and Its Mysteries: With a Record of the Expedition of 1903-1904" "Atlas of the South Pacific."

"The Lighthouse Board provides those," Nathaniel explained. "They have a library of books that circulates among the lighthouses. Keepers tend to read a lot. One of the few amusements to be found out here."

"Do you read anything in particular?" she asked, running her fingers along the spines of the books on the shelf.

"These days, I like travel books and atlases."

Maddy looked around. There were a few pictures on the walls. Some seascapes with square-rigged ships and a little oil painting of a field with horses and a farmhouse. Nathaniel noticed her looking at it.

"A change of pace," he said. "We see water all the time. The original keeper left that and it's never been replaced. Sometimes, out here, you get a craving for solid land, for a view that isn't always in motion. For flowers, a tree—something that would change with the seasons."

"Can you decorate as you please?" asked Maddy.

"Pretty much. It's our home, after all, so the Board likes us to feel comfortable. Every keeper or family usually adds a few touches, though some things seem to stay on a lighthouse forever. Especially one at sea like this one. It's hard to bring furniture out here, so that changes the least. When keepers change, stuff gets taken off or stored here. There are some boxes in the attic of old pictures, I think."

"Can you have a family?"

Nathaniel lost his smile for a moment, then he answered her.

"Yes. A lot of these lighthouses are kept by keepers who have families."

"Isn't it kind of an isolated place?"

Nathaniel frowned. Maddy realized she'd touched a nerve and regretted the question. He turned away and looked out the window towards Fishers Island, just a long low streak in the fog. She wasn't sure he would answer.

"It depends," he said at last, still looking out the window. "I had a family here once. A wife and a son." He lapsed into silence. The foghorn sounded. Silence. It sounded again.

"They left when he was ten," he continued quietly. "My wife thought it was isolated. She didn't think it was a good place to raise our son. I suppose she was right."

"When was that?" asked Maddy, wishing she had not gotten him on an obviously painful topic, but curious nonetheless.

"A few years ago," said the keeper.

"Do you see ...?" She let the question trail off.

"No, I don't see them. I haven't since they left. About a year ago, a fellow arrived with the supply boat. He had papers for me to sign. Divorce papers. Carla—my wife—had met someone. He would be a good father for Caleb—my son. It was all spelled out in the papers. I signed."

"Couldn't you write Caleb?"

"No. The address was temporary. They were going to move soon. To where I don't know. I've lost track of him."

"I'm sorry," said Maddy. The lightness and energy of their meeting had dissipated. There was an awkward silence. She tried to think of something to say, but could not. It was not a death he mourned. It was a living loss that is sometimes harder to endure. She knew.

After a moment, Nathaniel turned towards her.

"Maddy," he said, and the sadness was gone from his voice. "I don't brood over what happened. Some families love being together out on these rocks, some don't. Like I said, it depends."

She nodded and decided not to pursue the subject any longer. In that brief exchange, Nathaniel Bowen had revealed something of himself to her. His hurt had made him more than just a man in a uniform. More than just a keeper dedicated to his work.

Maddy figured Nathaniel to be in his late thirties, maybe early forties. It was hard to tell. His face was tanned and a bit weathered. His eyes were touched with a trace of sadness. He looked fit and muscular. He was an attractive man. A man with an aura of quiet intensity.

"Can I see the rest of the lighthouse?" she asked at last, hoping to shift his attention away from his memories.

"I'd be happy to show it to you," he said.

The two strangers began their tour of Race Rock.

9

"Maddy, do you know that the blue pigment in your paint comes from copper?"

They were sitting on one of the boulders by the water. Its broad flat top was a good perch. Nathaniel had brought some blankets to sit on. The fog had lifted, and the day was brightening up. The water was very calm. The foghorn was off, so they heard only the gentle lapping of the waves, a few gulls, a bell buoy, and her boat as it thumped against the dock.

Maddy had set up a small portable easel. She had a pad of watercolor paper attached to it. Her paints were spread at her feet. A lit cigarette was on a rock, its ash an inch long. He'd provided her with a mug of water to use for her brushes. She held a palette in her hand and was painting the scene looking back at the lighthouse. She painted with quick strokes, sketching rather than being fussy. She'd finish the ones she liked best later. Nathaniel had done a few chores and then joined her.

"Really?" she said, looking at her brush, tipped in blue.

"Yes. And that green shade is probably made with arsenic."

Maddy looked up from her sketch. "How do you happen to know that?"

"I told you I read a lot. I have the time. I read all sorts of things. I recently read a book that had a chapter about the chemistry of the arts, and I happen to remember where some of the color pigments come from. So in case that green *is* from arsenic, you shouldn't lick your brush."

Maddy shook her head. She picked up the cigarette, flicked off the ash and took a deep drag. She smiled. "Well, Mr. Keeper, I'm impressed!"

He returned her smile. She went back to her picture. Nathaniel went back to idly carving a piece of driftwood he'd pried out of the rocks.

Maddy envied Nathaniel all his reading. She used to love to read. To lose herself in a good story that took her far away to different places and times. But she'd gotten distracted by more tactile and sensual pursuits. A few memories flitted across her mind. If you could only sketch life with as much freedom and control as a painting. She sighed. She put down her brush and looked around. Race Rock loomed in front of her like a small mountain. Behind her, Fishers Island was a green band of land. Beyond it, floating on the horizon, was Long Island and Montauk Point, maybe twenty miles away. To her right were New London and Groton. A few buoys dotted the waters. Men fishing in small boats drifted with the currents, trolling for striped bass and blues. A few were anchored, bottom-fishing for flounder. Sailboats glided by. It seemed that the lighthouse was the center of its own universe, as if everything revolved around it.

"Do you like it here?" she asked.

Nathaniel stopped carving. Looked around. Then met Maddy's eyes.

"I do. There's a satisfaction to doing this job. Knowing how many people at sea depend on this light. I don't know how many of them I may have helped during bad storms. Except for a few of the guys on the ferries and tugs, I don't know who they are. I light the light and they steer by it and make it home safely."

Nathaniel broke off his gaze with Maddy and looked out at the sea, the land, the boats, the birds. He watched a white heron take off from the water in great strokes of its huge white wings. "There's a beauty to this place, Maddy. I'm no painter, and no poet, so I can't describe it very well. But it's beautiful out here. It's always changing. The sea has its moods, like a person. I've seen them all. It can be frightening, sometimes, but even when there's a big storm, when the waves are high and the lightning is flashing, it's beautiful. I get to see raw nature out here. I see the soul of the sea."

"I thought you said you weren't a poet," Maddy said with a laugh.

Nathaniel looked a little pleased and a little embarrassed by her compliment. He went back to his carving.

"I'll bet it's beautiful in the snow," she said.

"Like a dream," he said. He was enjoying sharing Race Rock with Maddy. With someone who appreciated it. At first, Carla had appreciated its beauty, too. Then she came to resent the place. More practical matters concerned her.

"It's never the same. Ever," he said. "The sky is always changing. The water, too. It can be glassy calm, and an hour later rough and full of whitecaps. The sky can be full of clouds, or a blue so deep you get lost in it, or so red from a sunset it looks like it's on fire."

"There you go again," said Maddy with another little laugh.

Nathaniel liked her laugh. He liked her. Their eyes met again and then drifted apart. She smoked her cigarette and stared at the water, quiet for a moment.

"Don't you get lonely? Don't you ever wish you had someone to talk to?" She asked. "Or do you just talk to yourself all the time. Like I do?"

Now it was Nathaniel's turn to laugh. He *did* talk to himself a lot, now that she mentioned it.

"I guess I get lonely sometimes. The Board doesn't like keepers to be alone. I'm supposed to have an assistant keeper. I was supposed to report my wife and son leaving. I intended to. But I thought I'd wait and see. Make sure they weren't coming back. I guess I thought they might. A few months passed. Then a few more. I just never got around to it. I made excuses when the supply boat came out or the superintendent made a surprise visit. I kept some of their stuff around so it would look like they were still here. When they left … I don't know. I just wanted to be alone for a while. Now it's been two years. Time passes quickly."

Their conversation kept circling back to his family. It was like a piece of driftwood that keeps bobbing along the same piece of shore, moving, but going nowhere.

"Do you ever get tired of the same small rooms and the confines of this little island? Do you ever want to get away? Travel?"

"Sometimes," said Nathaniel. "I haven't ever been far from this area. I've heard stories about other places. Read about them, too. I read a lot, as I told you. I'll see the world someday." He smiled. To Maddy, it wasn't a wistful smile. It was different. More of a knowing smile.

"Where?" she asked. "Where would you go if you could just get on one of the ships that passes by and go somewhere— anywhere?"

He mulled it over. He had only recently thought about himself actually being on one of the ships that passed by. He was curious about the world beyond Long Island Sound. The home ports painted on the sterns of the freighters were so exotic. Tangiers. Queenstown. Jakarta. Puerto Limon. Hong Kong. Venezia. Papeete. Christchurch. He knew where some of the places were. Had no idea where others might be.

"Let me show you something," Nathaniel said, and got up and went into the lighthouse. He returned a few minutes later with a book, "The Marriage of Loti" by Pierre Loti. It was a tale of a man who ventured to Tahiti and the romance and adventure he found there. It was set in 1872—the year they started to build Race Rock. The cover of the book showed lovely Polynesian women wearing flower necklaces. Nathaniel sat back down and thumbed through the pages until he found what he wanted.

"I haven't looked at this in a while, but I remember this picture." He showed it to Maddy. It was an illustration of several native women walking along a white beach with palm trees and puffy clouds. There was an old sailing ship in the harbor, and exotic trees and flowers filled the foreground. "I think I'd like to go there first. It's a long way away from here. In the South Pacific."

She studied the picture.

"It would be so warm," he said. "Always sunny. The people who live there are friendly. Gentle. Beautiful. It looks like paradise."

"It does look like a beautiful place, Nathaniel." She took the book from him and thumbed through it, skimming the pages. She read a passage, then another. After a few minutes skimming and reading, Maddy looked up at Nathaniel and smiled. She read aloud:

"Oh! The delightful hours, Oh! The soft and warm summer hours we spent there, each day, near the Fataoua River. The air was all charged with the tropical scents dominated by the fragrance of oranges heated in the branches by the midday sun."

Nathaniel smiled too. The words painted such a beautiful scene. He could almost feel the warm air, smell the oranges. Warm breezes. Sunny skies. Fragrant fruit. Beautiful women. Paradise.

"Maybe you'll get there someday," said Maddy, looking up from the book at him. "You can always dream."

"Oh I'll get there, Maddy," he said. He smiled that knowing smile again. He took the book back and closed it. Contemplated it a moment. "It's a big world. I'll see it when I'm ready."

They both looked at the book in silence. Nathaniel looked up at Maddy who looked up at him. She gazed into his deep brown eyes. She felt she could sink into them, like the sea. The waves were a gentle hiss against the rocks; her boat bumped the dock, as regular as a clock ticking. A gull glided overhead, spiraled around the lighthouse and out to sea. The moment seemed to last an eternity. Nathaniel broke off the gaze. He stood.

"I'll let you work on your pictures," he said, and climbed down off the boulder and headed towards the lighthouse. Maddy watched him. She found this lighthouse keeper—this lonely, solitary man—fascinating. There had just been a connection between them. He'd backed off. She felt his uncertainty. She knew her own. It had been a long time since he'd been with a woman. It had been a long time since she'd been with a man. They were both tentative. Scared as school-kids.

She watched as he quickly climbed the ladder. He went inside then returned holding a telescope. He walked to the railing, raised the scope and focused it. She wondered where his mind was. Was he really seeing a beach in New London, or had his imagination carried his vision to one in Tahiti? Maddy watched him a while. She tore off the page she was working on so she had a fresh sheet of paper. Then she began to sketch a new picture.

10

"It's good," said Nathaniel.

He was looking at the watercolor Maddy had done. It showed Race Rock's big drum base of granite blocks rising above a small island of large, angular stones. There was a bit of the lower floor of the house—a few windows and the edge of the door. Nathaniel was standing at the railing peering through his telescope.

Maddy nodded, acknowledging his compliment.

"May I?" he asked, stretching out his hand towards her. She handed him the pad. He studied the watercolor. He was amazed how, when he looked closely at it, what had seemed like his face fragmented into a few quick brushstrokes. They only formed his likeness with some perspective. Likewise the stones of the caisson and the window of the lighthouse. It was a trick of the mind that made them seem more substantial than they were. It was magical. He held it at arm's length and studied the composition. Maddy stood and stretched.

"Why did you paint it that way?" asked Nathaniel after a moment. "It's only a piece of the scene."

"True," Maddy said. "But sometimes, a fragment can represent the whole. The whole scene can be interesting, but I'm after something else. I try to find the essence of a thing. I don't paint something; I paint the *idea* of something," she said. "An interpretation. I think that's what art is supposed to do. It offers a version."

Nathaniel nodded and then cocked his head. "Tell me, Maddy: how do you decide what details to use? Where do you look for this essence?"

"Ah, well ... that's the hard part. You have to learn to look at things differently." Maddy paused and tried to plan what she wanted to say. "I've been here a few hours. I've observed the lighthouse. Now I could paint the whole thing, and that would be fine. I did, in fact. See?" She picked up the loose sheets of paper and showed Nathaniel a few of her sketches. A couple depicted all of Race Rock.

"As I keep working, I start to try different things. I work the scene. My ideas evolve. When I am looking at something, I'm trying to figure out its true nature. So I break it down into some of its basic elements. What is this place, really? Well, it's a fortress, like you said, Nathaniel. A kind of castle. A big, solid, monumental presence erected by men in the middle of the sea. It has structure, where nature is more chaotic. So I chose the base—the drum—with its rectangular stones. They capture the essence of this building. They are big, rugged, carved, immovable."

"So far, I follow you," said Nathaniel, looking at the lighthouse—*his* lighthouse—a little differently.

"Good!" said Maddy. "Then there is you. You are the heart and soul of this place. The human who lives here. I was struck when you were standing up there how small you seemed beside those big rocks and the stones. I saw how small a man is out here. Then you took out your telescope and started to scan the scene. And *that* really captured the essence of what you do. You keep a watch for ships in peril. So those are the elements I chose for my composition: the sea, the rough rocks, the monumental base, and the small human, vigilant and alert. To me, those things capture what Race Rock is all about." Maddy smiled. She seldom articulated what she did, and she felt a sense of pride in doing so.

"Interesting," said Nathaniel. "But no light. Isn't the essence of a lighthouse? Its light?"

"Yes," Maddy said. "That's true. But that's a different picture. I'll get to that. There isn't only one picture that captures the essence. The heart of something can be expressed in different ways," she said.

"Yes," said Nathaniel. He paused, looked up at the light-house. "The heart of something can be expressed in different ways." He looked at her again with his piercing brown eyes. In the fleeting emotions that seemed to play across them, she sensed so much. She met his gaze. Again the charge flowed between them.

Maddy had the sudden impulse to lean forward and kiss him. Maddy, being Maddy, tended to give in to her impulses. She held his eyes, craned her neck forward, and gave him a quick, but firm, kiss on his lips. Her heart beat heavily as she did. She was scared, scared that he would be offended or recoil from her advance.

He did not.

Nathaniel did not recoil. Nor did he prolong the kiss. Nor grab her to him in an embrace of passion. He accepted her kiss. She wasn't quite sure how to interpret it. Easier to find the heart of this building than the man who tended it.

When she pulled away, their eyes met for a moment. Nathaniel smiled at her. She had broken the ice, and she felt the waters warming. Just a bit.

He handed her back her paintings and she busied herself fussing with them. When she glanced up, he was staring at her. Those brown eyes! "Oh. Maddy," she laughed to herself nervously, "Maddy, Maddy, Maddy..."

After a few moments, when her pictures had been arranged and rearranged and her heart had slowed and she had regained her composure, she looked at Nathaniel.

"Now it's your turn, Nathaniel," she said. "I've told you a little about what I do. What about you? How did you come to be out here on this rock?"

Nathaniel sat back and watched a bird fly off towards Montauk Point. He followed it until it vanished inside the images in his memory.

"I was in my late teens," he began, "when Thomas Scott and Frederick Smith began building Race Rock. It was the talk of New London, where my father had a small fishing boat. He fished for blues and bass, mostly, but took whatever he could get from the sea and sold it to the local markets. I helped out. I spent a lot of time on the water. A lot of time out here by the Race, where the blues and bass run best.

"The Race?" asked Maddy.

"This area is called the 'Race' because it has colliding currents. The waters coming from the Thames River, across Fishers Island Sound and from Long Island Sound meet here. Look—even on a calm day you can see the turbulent water running quickly over there. That's the race. Fish love the strong current. Race Rock, where we are, used to be three nasty spurs of rock. Very close together, just below water level. Ships were always plowing into them. Race Rock claimed many ships and many lives over the years.

"Finally, the maritime folks around here decided they had to do something. They tried putting markers on the rocks, but the winter ice and summer storms carried them away. This is a violent place. As treacherous as it gets along the coast. They realized they had to build a lighthouse. They decided to build it right on top of the rocks. It was an enormous challenge. No one had tried to build a man-made island like this. And it was incredibly expensive. I heard it cost something like a quarter of a million dollars to build Race Rock. Incredible! Then again, you're trying to build an island in the middle of the sea. It was windy, rough, stormy. They piled tons and tons of these huge stones around the rocks. You can't imagine how hard it was, Maddy, to haul all that rock out here and pile it up. All the while being hammered by the sea. Like the sea was fighting us. Like it didn't want our island here.

"After the stones were in, they had to build this big circular base out of cut granite. To do it all, Smith and Scott needed workers. Lots of strong young men to haul the rocks and set the stones. So I signed on. I helped build this lighthouse. The base took four years; the whole thing almost seven. It was brutal, dangerous work. I only worked for about a year out here, but I feel I did my part. I even have this to show for it."

Nathaniel extended his left hand to Maddy and splayed his fingers. She noticed what she hadn't before. The tip of his little finger veered off at an odd angle.

"Caught it between two hunks of granite. Broke it. It hurt like hell. When it healed, it healed crooked: Race Rock's reminder to me of my time building it."

Maddy took a puff of her cigarette.

"Some thanks," she said.

Nathaniel shrugged. "We all got a little roughed up out here. Lots of scars. Anyway," he went on, "the sea was in my blood. I wanted to stay in the area and work on the water. I fished with my father for years. We fished the Race a lot, and he was proud I'd worked on this lighthouse.

"Then, in 1882, I heard about an opening for an assistant keeper at Montauk Point. The timing was good. My father was ready to retire and let someone else catch the fish. I applied, got the job, and spent ten years out there, learning the job of being a keeper. In '92, the keeper at Race Rock got sick and had to leave. I had met Carla, and we had plans to get married. She thought it would be romantic to live out here. When the Lighthouse Board heard there was a young family eager to live on Race Rock, they offered me the job as keeper. A family saved them the expense of an assistant keeper. It all happened quickly. Before I knew it, I was the keeper of the lighthouse I'd helped build. We moved out here and a year later Caleb was born. I didn't plan much of it. It just happened."

"Well, life's like that," Maddy said. "Sometimes you control it. Sometimes it controls you. Like the sea, right?"

Nathaniel shook his head. "No. You never control the sea, Maddy. You might sail across it, fish the waters, take advantage of what it offers. But control it? Never. One thing you learn when you spend a lot of time on the sea is that you're always at its mercy. And it has no mercy."

She looked out at the calm day. At the placid waters. The soothing, gentle sky, with just a trace of fog hanging low in the distance, like the remnants of a dream. It was hard to imagine danger lurking. Nathaniel saw her gaze.

"Don't let it fool you, Maddy. I've seen days like this that turned stormy in a few minutes. Before you know it, there are fifteen-foot waves crashing in. The sea is moody. It can get angry real quick."

"Like a person," muttered Maddy.

"Sort of. But you can reason with a person. The sea doesn't listen. Doesn't care. It doesn't need a reason to kill you."

"I guess I didn't pay the sea much attention when I was in Newport," she said.

They both looked out at the surrounding waters. Maddy thought that Nathaniel might not think of himself as a poet, but he had a poet's sensibilities. An artist's. He could see the essence of things.

Nathaniel peeked at Maddy from the corner of his eye. He liked her. He didn't want her to leave. She had drifted out of the fog into his life, and he didn't want her to drift away just yet. He always liked company. And this charming, slightly wild woman was good company. And very attractive. And she had kissed him.

They spent a pleasant afternoon together. The sun fought its way through the fog for hours. About six, it finally showed as a luminous spot in the western sky, above a grove of trees near town. It would be light for a few more hours.

Slowly, Maddy started packing up her paints, flicking a brush, capping a jar of paint. She seemed ready to leave.

"Maddy," said Nathaniel, "do you like fish?"

She looked up at him. Some of her hair dipped over her left eye, and he found the way she looked out at him through it very provocative.

"Yes I do. You grow up in Newport, you learn to love fish."

"Well, yesterday I caught a couple of big stripers just off the rocks here. There's an old recipe that's been passed down through the Lighthouse Board..."

"You catch your own food?"

"Yes," said Nathaniel. "Some of it, anyway. There are rules, of course, about fishing. The Lighthouse Board is very clear on what we can do. According to regulations, we can catch enough for our own use. No more. I guess they're afraid we'd sell it and turn the lighthouse into a fish market."

Maddy laughed. "This Lighthouse Board sounds like a school principal. It makes you wear a uniform. It gives you books to read. It gives you rules for fishing."

"Recipes, too," said Nathaniel. "Actually, they do pretty well at keeping us happy. They have a lot of lights and keepers to keep track of."

"All right. I'm sold," Maddy said. Nathaniel was a charming mix of seriousness and humor. "I'm hungry. We'll see what your official fish tastes like." She continued packing up her paints, flicking the brushes dry and spraying a spectrum of paint on the rock. She packed up her gear and tidied the pages of watercolors.

"Do you have any potatoes?" she asked.

"Yes. Just had some delivered yesterday."

"Cheese?"

"Vermont cheddar."

"Wine?

"No wine. Water, whiskey and coffee."

"No wine but whiskey?!"

"I don't drink it. It's here in case I rescue someone and they need reviving," said Nathaniel.

"Well, I might need some rescuing," said Maddy with a laugh.

Nathaniel smiled. "I might need some reviving."

So the two strangers went up into the lighthouse and cooked themselves a very tasty dinner. There is something curiously intimate about preparing a meal with someone, especially in close quarters. There's the ballet of handing food around, the sensuous textures of vegetables, the colors and aromas. The kitchen was small, and by the time they were done, in the summer heat, it was hot and they were sweating. Nathaniel had shed his heavy uniform and cooked in shirtsleeves. Maddy found the whiskey and after much cajoling managed to get Nathaniel to join her and take a drink. He was a little giddy after a few sips.

They talked and ate and studied each other as they shared the meal. Sometimes, two people meet and they seem like old friends. An alchemy of comfort and trust happens almost immediately. So it was with Nathaniel and Maddy. The two loners connected the moment she had stepped into his world.

They both knew it would be fleeting. All the more reason to make it burn bright while they could, like a lightning bolt.

It was dusk when they finished cleaning up.

"I need to light the light," said Nathaniel. "Why don't you grab a few lanterns and wait for me out on the porch."

While Nathaniel was up lighting the wicks of the light, Maddy went out to the porch and lit two small lanterns. She went inside for a refill of whiskey. She found a small bathroom and combed her hair. She rummaged in her bag, found some lipstick, and put it on. As she did, she looked at her face in the mirror, trying to see herself as Nathaniel might. So hard to do. So hard to penetrate one's own mask—so familiar, so slowly changing with experience and age. Unhappy with how her hair looked, she shook her head. Her hair flew about, coming to rest on her shoulders and across her forehead. It looked a little wild. "Better," she thought.

Maddy topped off her drink. She noticed he hadn't finished his so she left it behind in the kitchen. She went out and waited for Nathaniel. A wisp of a breeze stirred the sultry summer air. The light came on high above her. She could see its beam, a streak of bright red pushing out against the night.

After a few minutes, Nathaniel came out. They sat side by side with their feet dangling over the edge of the stone porch, arms hooked over the railing. It had cleared enough that there was a ruddy glow where the sun had set. A few stars twinkled.

Nathaniel scraped at a piece of chipped paint on the rail. Maddy puffed a cigarette and watched the smoke drift slowly away, a blue curl against the sky.

"Who are you, Maddy? Tell me something about yourself. Prove to me you're real," said Nathaniel after a few minutes.

Maddy liked the way he'd put it. He had a way with words. She looked at him. The lantern shone in his soft brown eyes. She looked back to the sea, her gaze soon lost in the abstract reflections languidly swirling on the water.

She sighed, and Nathaniel wasn't certain she would tell him anything. Maybe he'd been wrong to ask. She flicked her cigarette and it arced over the railing, its tip glowing like a comet. It hit the water with a soft hiss. She took a sip of whiskey. Dusk blanketed the calm scene. It was a moment of perfect tranquility. Suspended, still, like one of her watercolors.

"I was born into a rich family," Maddy began. "The Covingtons. Maybe you've heard of them. My father was Paul Wyatt Covington the Third. Two would have been sufficient. He inherited a bundle of money and made a lot more in shipping and railroads. We lived in New York and had a summer home in Newport. One of the lesser mansions, I'm afraid. We had money, but not quite of the Vanderbilt class. Still, we held our own. I went to good schools, traveled a bit. Summers were just one big party, rotating from mansion to mansion.

"I was a bit of a wild child. I just never quite fit in to the lifestyle. I lived up to my nickname. I had my own ideas. That was hard for my father to accept in a girl. Girls weren't supposed to be independent, have willpower, their own ideas. He'd rather have had a son, of course. A tidy way to pass on the family business and fortune. Instead, he got two daughters. It always hurt me to know my father was disappointed at the moment of my birth. But Paul Wyatt Convington the Third was determined. He wouldn't let the setback of two daughters deter him. He waited patiently, and when I reached my late teens, he looked around at the sons of his business associates and found Teddy, or Theodore as he preferred to be called. Father picked Theodore for me.

"He found someone for you to love?" asked Nathaniel.

"Not to love, just to marry. Love wasn't important." said Maddy. "That's how it was done. Poor Teddy. He was nice enough. Good pedigree, of course. Ivy league schooling, a year in Paris. He spoke French to me all the time. He though it was romantic. He thought I understood him. I didn't. I just smiled and said 'Oui, merci, non and merde,' the only French words I knew. I don't think he liked 'merde' too much. Not very refined. Whenever he became amorous, I told him 'non!' I explained I was saving myself for marriage. It frustrated poor Teddy, but he understood the rules."

Maddy paused. Lit up another cigarette. Her eyes focused on the glowing water, as if she could see the events of her life there.

"But I wasn't saving myself. I was rolling in the hay—literally—with Jason."

Maddy smiled. She took another sip of the whiskey. It had loosened her tongue. She was a little surprised at herself, at her willingness to tell this stranger such intimate details. Then again, those same details had pretty much become public knowledge anyway.

"Jason worked in the stables. On my nineteenth birthday, I lost my virginity to him. Can you believe it? Not very original. Well, maybe I shouldn't say 'lost.' 'Gave' was more like it. We became lovers. I have to admit, it was deliciously risqué to carry on with him while mother and father thought I was happy with Teddy—Theodore. It was a rich girl's dilemma, Nathaniel. I loved a boy who was poor, but masculine and passionate. I could barely tolerate the boy who was rich, weak and scared of me. I knew Teddy would end up like most of the men I knew. Always boys. Always playing at sports of one sort or another. Always cheating on their wives who cheated on them. God, what a life! It was all as brittle as the teacups we used.

"But I was weak. I went along with the arrangement. You don't say no to Paul Wyatt Covington the Third. Teddy had been chosen for me and I for him. Our parents had dreams of children and grandchildren running around, growing up, building the business for generations. Teddy and I were really just a corporate merger, a way to build wealth and power. The closer the wedding got, the more scared I got of the life that loomed ahead. I was looking at a prison term, Nathaniel. You told me earlier you got lonely out here sometimes. You should try one of those Newport dinners, surrounded by two dozen people you loathe. I hated how lonely I could be in a crowd. So I took solace with Jason."

She stopped her narrative, lay back and looked up at the stars overhead. Orion's belt twinkled. It was the only constellation she knew.

"Something happened?" asked Nathaniel, sensing in the tone of her voice that her story was about to get darker.

"Oh yes, something happened. The night before the wedding, after the partying was over, Teddy's father decided to come out to the stable to look for something. A polo mallet, I think. He found his future daughter-in-law and the stable boy together. We both thought it was the last time. I won't go into the details. Poor man. I thought he might drop dead on the spot. He was furious. It exploded into a very ugly affair. It was in all the newspapers.

"Teddy was humiliated. His family was humiliated. Jason was fired, of course, banished from the perfect lawns of Newport forever. The Covington honor was stained. Our stock tumbled for a spell. Mother was so devastated she was bedridden for weeks. Newport was rocked as if by a huge storm. Of course, some people were delighted. We had enemies. Polite ones, but enemies nonetheless. You don't get to be as wealthy and powerful as Paul Wyatt Covington the Third without making some enemies. There was even an editorial in the paper that said my indiscretion was a symptom of the moral bankruptcy of the entire Covington empire. Yes, I really screwed up."

She had a slight smile but shook her head. Nathaniel imagined what happened had both pleased and distressed her.

"Then what happened?" he asked.

"Father gave me twenty thousand dollars, kissed me on the cheek, wished me luck, and suggested that I never darken his doorway again. I was disowned. Cast adrift. I think he thought he was just firing an employee, not losing a daughter. Or just recalculating an asset as a loss. I was hurt, but I got over it. I didn't mind that much. We weren't a close family, and I really did hate the lifestyle. There was no way I could stay in Newport. No way I could even live in New York, where we had a townhouse on Park Avenue. You may think New York is a big city, Nathaniel, but the circle I moved in was viciously small.

"I should have run off with Jason, but they had sent him off somewhere and I couldn't find out where. When the well-to-do close ranks, you can't break through. I gave up. I left and traveled around Europe for a while. I dabbled at painting and discovered I had a flair for it. When I got back, I settled on Block Island. It's been home. Now I'm ready to move on. I want to go across the country. Get away from the water. See the Southwest. New Mexico. Arizona. Maybe head north to Alaska someday. I don't know. I'm like a seabird, Nathaniel. I fly and I land somewhere and then I take off again. I guess I'm just a restless spirit."

"You've really never seen your family again?"

"No. I've followed their exploits in the papers. Father's in the midst of helping bankroll some huge new ships in England for the White Star Line. They're building three. The Olympic, the Gigantic and another one. The Titanic, I think. Biggest ships ever. He's sure to make a fortune on them."

"What about your mother? Your sister?"

"My mother wrote me, and my sister visited a few times. But they drifted away, too. I was interested in traveling and exploring and painting. They were interested in forgetting about my exploits, repairing the damage to the family name, planning their parties, and finding a suitable mate for my sister Eleanor. Which they did."

"It's hard to forget a child," Nathaniel said. "They're a part of you, good or bad."

Maddy shrugged. Her quiet betrayed a hurt she could not conceal.

"It's all history now," she said. "Ten years ago. Life moves on. You have to live for the present. You have to keep moving forward."

Nathaniel listened. An image of the amber ring drifted into his mind; the spider, trapped inside it for eternity.

"Time is a ship that never anchors," Nathaniel said.

"Pardon?" Maddy asked.

"'Time is a ship that never anchors.' It's painted on the side of the keeper's house at the New London Harbor Light."

"Really? Hmmm. That fits me," said Maddy. "I'm a ship that doesn't want to be anchored. That's why the prospect of a secure and predictable life with Theodore was so hard to accept. I'd have felt trapped. Dead."

"I guess I'm the opposite," said Nathaniel. "I'm anchored to this rock."

"You don't mind?"

"No. Because I can weigh anchor anytime I want. I can go anywhere I want."

"They must pay you well," Maddy laughed. Nathaniel smiled too, that odd smile she'd seen already, but he didn't say anything.

Maddy thought about her past and how she somehow felt divorced from it, as if it had happened to someone else, or she'd read it in a book. It was *her* past. *Her* memories. Yet time distorts things, separates us from them. It's good when it is pain or grief, but a bit unsettling when so much of one's own history seems both familiar and strange at the same time. The reality becomes a dream, and like a dream, it drifts to the edge of memory and becomes less certain.

They sat in the warm night and listened to the lap of water against the rocks below, a few distant boat horns, and the sound of a train rumbling through New London. Nathaniel had always liked the train whistle. Like the boat and lighthouse horns, it sounded as if it were a living thing—a great beast, howling in the distance.

Like castaways on an island, Nathaniel and Maddy had revealed much about themselves. Perhaps the remoteness of Race Rock encouraged them to confide in each other. They shared a deeper isolation, too. They were both adrift from their families, something that caused them lingering hurt, whether they admitted it or not.

Maddy thought about how she had shared her story with Nathaniel. With a man she'd only met today. She felt comfortable with him. It hadn't taken her long to sense the strands that were woven into his character: his strong attachment to the past. His sense of dedication. The pain that, like most men, he was reluctant to share. He was an intriguing mix of a man bound by duty and routine and a man who dreamed, who had a poetic perspective on life.

She looked over at him. He was a silhouette against the evening sky. She slid closer and rested her head on his shoulder. He didn't flinch. He didn't say anything. Was he perhaps breathing just a little but faster? She couldn't tell.

Maddy wondered about Nathaniel. About his ambitions. It seemed to her he was content to be where he was. For him, the horizon was a place in the distance that would never get any closer. It would always be where it was, fixed, a defining line between sea and sky. Then she thought about herself. She was always moving, always looking to the horizon and then crossing it, only to find a new one in the distance. She wandered forever, never settling down, never really reaching her elusive destination. How different they were. She searched endlessly, he never moved. He was an island, she a bird. Yet in her movement and in his repose, they were both alone, away from other people. She looked over at him and smiled. They were so different and so much alike, loners who knew the joys and anguish of their solitude.

Maddy rested against Nathaniel and looked at the lights around them, some on shore, a few in the water, the stars overhead. The beam of the lighthouse reached out, spinning slowly around, bright against the night sky. From the sea, the beam appeared as a simple blinking dot of color. But here, at the base of the lighthouse, it looked like the spoke of a great wheel spinning overhead whose hub was the very top of Race Rock. The moon had risen and sent its own trail wiggling across the calm waters. Maddy thought it might be the most beautiful scene she had ever seen.

Everything seemed to move in slow motion. Or maybe it was just that this moment was one of rare perfection, a moment to savor. Maddy took it all in. Then she felt an impulse and, as usual, gave in to it.

She shifted around so that she was facing Nathaniel and looked into his face. She smiled and slowly leaned forward and kissed him. He returned the kiss more than he had before. They hugged, their foreheads touching. Neither spoke. She kissed him again. Their breath mingled, hot in the humid air. She kissed him again, more urgently, but he did not follow. She could sense a tenseness, an unease. She backed off a bit.

The moment had passed.

She didn't know why.

Nathaniel shifted and turned back to the railing, and Maddy had to do the same. Their conversation drifted, slowed, stopped. No mention of the kisses. Maddy tried to coax Nathaniel back to her, but he seemed either shy or uninterested. Which? The age-old question when people meet. How to interpret reticence.

For Nathaniel, it was a mix of emotions that swirled through him and measured his spontaneity. She was the first woman who'd been out here since Carla left. It felt strange to have her here. Yet, at the same time, it felt wonderful to have her here. He was attracted to her and obviously she to him. Maybe Maddy was to be a new chapter for him?

Decorum demanded he honor his uniform and do nothing unprofessional. Then again, he was in shirtsleeves, his uniform thrown over a chair, and who the hell was the Lighthouse Board to tell him not to return the kiss of a lovely woman? He smiled. He knew it wasn't the uniform or any regulations that stopped him. The truth was, he was scared. He'd once been a married man. In what seemed another life. Now he was tentative and self-conscious again. For some men, women were easy to engage. For him, they were not. Maybe he thought too much. Or he was too polite. Perhaps they picked up on his lack of confidence and that only made it worse. He wasn't sure. He caught himself: there he was again, thinking too much! He had the feeling that once the mood passed, it might not ever come back. Perhaps it had already passed. As they sat in a charged silence looking at the evening, and as they started to talk again, he knew it was so. The moment was gone. He had let it slip away.

Nathaniel had asked Maddy to stay and stay she had. As the night wore on, as they grew tired, the awkward subject of where she would sleep was inevitable. Nathaniel seized the initiative.

"I have some of my wife's gowns and robes," he said. "You are welcome to use them. And my son's room is empty, of course. The bed is made."

Maddy smiled, a bit in disappointment.

"Thank you," she said. "Nathaniel?" she started.

"Yes?"

"I..." She stopped. Her smile changed. Had he been able to see her eyes, Nathaniel would have seen them narrow and sparkle a bit. "Nothing. Let's go in."

They went inside and cleaned up the kitchen. As they did, Nathaniel glanced over at Maddy, but could not read her mood. Their talk was light. Inconsequential. They walked up the spiral staircase to the second floor, where Nathaniel opened a closet and showed her some clothes of Carla's. Maddy was a little taller than Carla, but found a robe she liked.

"Good night," she said and again kissed Nathaniel full on the lips. It was a quick kiss. She did not try to make it more.

"Good night," said Nathaniel quietly. He watched as she turned and walked down the short hall to Caleb's room. Her perfume lingered in the air behind her. He stood there a few moments, thinking about Maddy. He considered walking down the hall and opening her door and taking her in his arms.

Instead he turned and went to his room. He slowly undressed. He hung his uniform in the closet, straightening the seams of his pants as he hung them. He carefully put his shoes near the closet, side-by-side. He put his pocket watch on the table by his bed. He stripped down to his shorts.

He should act. He should be like one of the men in some of the books he read, sweeping a woman off her feet. But somehow, he could not. Perhaps it had just been too long. Or maybe not long enough.

He crawled into bed and listened to the caress of the sea on the rocks below, letting his mind wander. His thoughts always took him back to this afternoon, to his conversations with Maddy, to her paintings, to her hair backlit by the sun or the soft caress of her breath on his neck as she'd rested her head on his shoulder. And her kisses—it had been so long. He was so lonely.

He should go to her. He should take her in his arms and make love to her. But here? At Race Rock? Where he and Carla had shared their intimacies? Why not? Carla was gone. She had left him to his loneliness. She had no claim on his heart anymore. He mulled over his options.

The door to Nathaniel's room opened. A silhouetted figure entered. Nathaniel looked up to see Maddy standing by his bed. She still had the robe on, but with a quick gesture shed it. Her naked body was lit by the faint light coming in from the moon.

She glowed like a ghost. She was beautiful.

"Mad..." Nathaniel started, but she reached out and put a finger to his lips. She pulled the covers off the lighthouse keeper and in a quick graceful motion lay atop him. Her body was light and warm. She smelled of hyacinth. Her mane of hair flowed down and over his shoulders as she nestled into him. She raised her head and he could see her eyes sparkling. She leaned forward and kissed him, parting his lips with her tongue. Her kiss was insistent and deep and he responded to her, wrapping his arms around her, his hands sliding down her sleek flanks. He moaned as she ground into him, urging on his arousal.

She pulled down his shorts. Then she was astride him and he slid deep inside her. She moved slowly and gracefully and it was a delirium of pleasure for them both. Her hair swayed as she moved. His hands swept along her back, now slick with sweat, and up to her breasts and hard nipples.

She had not spoken. She panted and moaned as they made love, and he marveled at this sensuous, mad woman who had rowed out of the fog and swept over his island and his life like a sudden summer squall.

She made love with a kind of desperate urgency, as if this might be her last time. He suspected she lived her life this way—seizing what she wanted and consuming it fully.

His musings gave way to pleasure and he abandoned himself to that wonderful place beyond thought.

* * *

After they made love, she lay nestled against him, her head on his chest. Her hair cascaded across him, and Nathaniel idly played with it. Maddy gazed across him to the window. She could see the moon sparkling on the water, its iridescent beam shimmering like diamonds. It cast a shadow of the window-panes on the wall.

She raised herself up on her elbows and peered out at him from under her tresses.

"I've bared my soul to you," said Maddy.

"And a lot more than that," he interrupted. They laughed for a moment.

"I don't tell my story to just anyone." She looked at him, eyes bright with a trace of mischief. "I've told you some secrets. Now it's your turn, Nathaniel," she said. "Tell me a secret."

And so he did.

11

In the morning, she was gone. Gone from his bed. Gone from the lighthouse. Gone from his island altogether.

There was no trace of Maddy except a watercolor she'd left for him, propped up on a table in the living room on the first floor. It was the one of him standing in his uniform at the porch railing, looking through his telescope. She'd signed it with an "MC" in the lower right corner. If it weren't for the watercolor, he might have imagined that Maddy was not real, that she was just a delusion created by the heart of a lonely man.

He picked up one of the glasses from dinner. An impression of her lips, rendered in her red lipstick, was on the rim. No, she was real.

Nathaniel looked at the watercolor. He sat down and looked at it very closely, marveling again at how just a few quick, simple brushstrokes created his body. How a few more defined the edge of the lighthouse. How just the lightest wash of color suggested the sky and sea. It was magical. He liked the watercolor. Not so much because it was of him, but it seemed to capture the essence of being a keeper of the light. Maddy had done was she'd set out to do.

He liked it, too, because it reminded him of her. It was a souvenir of the wonderful afternoon and night he had spent with Maddy. Her visit had been an infusion of energy and color to his drab, solitary daily life. Her brief, passionate visit had rekindled in him a humanity too long suppressed by his service to the light.

He felt the picture deserved a permanent place of honor in his home. He recalled that in the attic there were some old boxes of pictures. Maybe he could find a frame that would fit Maddy's painting.

He opened the metal fire doors and stepped onto the spiral stairway and wound his way up to the attic. Its pitched roof made him hunch over a bit as he looked around, trying to remember where he had seen the box. It was about like any attic. It held bits and pieces of past lives. Boxes of things that should have been discarded but never were. Attics are like beaches. Sometimes things drift into them and there they stay. Nobody ever looked at the stuff. No one cared about it. What was here had accumulated over the years, discarded by successive keepers. The attic was an archive of life at Race Rock, but it was a place of forgotten memories. Whether it held secrets he did not know. Some of the boxes were his. Some held Carla and Caleb's clothes. Others contained books or letters or old pictures. There was a pile of newspapers. He picked one up. It was from 1888. The paper was yellow, stiff, and brittle, and little pieces broke off and fluttered to the floor as he held it. He scanned the headlines. Ancient history. What had seemed so important, so urgent on the 14th of May, 1888 had faded away with time.

Nathaniel bent lower and finally had to get on his hands and knees and crawl as the sloped roof got lower and lower. He made his way to a pile of boxes in a far corner, half hidden in the shadows. The boxes rested between a tracery of spider webs. He wondered how the spiders had gotten out to Race Rock, and what they hoped to catch here in the middle of nowhere. It seemed impossible they could sustain themselves, but they did. He brushed a few webs away and saw the edges of some pictures in one old box. He took one out. It was a faded portrait of a lighthouse keeper, in uniform, and his wife. They stared at the camera and across the years. He wondered if they were the first keeper and his wife.

Another picture was a painting, not very good, of a sailboat. Another painting, only half done, was of a vase of colorful flowers. There were others, mostly crude, done by keepers or their families. None compared to the assured artistry of Maddy. Finally he found a sketch of the New London waterfront whose frame looked to be about the same size as Maddy's watercolor.

He opened the back and removed the picture. He scrambled back out of the dark corner, flicked a spider off his arm, and made his way out of the attic, clanging the metal doors shut behind him. He went down the stairs to the living room. With a rag he cleaned off the dusty glass. He'd been right: the frame was a good fit for the watercolor.

He put the paper into the frame, put the back on. He walked over to the mantle and took down the picture of the barn. In its place, he hung Maddy Covington's portrait of Race Rock. He stood back and smiled. It would always remind him of her. Of the time they'd shared. A good memory.

As Nathaniel looked at the watercolor, scenes from her story played across his mind. He imagined the parties in Newport. The mansions. The suffocating mores. He tried to imagine the hapless Theodore and the passionate Jason. He conjured up the painful scene of a father saying goodbye to his child. Then his thoughts turned to their day together. It came back in a flood of impressions.

Nathaniel opened his logbook and made a brief entry in it, noting that he was visited by the "painter MC." As he wrote, he wondered if he would ever see Maddy Covington again. He suspected not. She was like one of the Monarch butterflies that rested at his lighthouse for a few moments on their long migration. They were beautiful visitors who came in on the breeze and left by it, guided by instincts they could not resist and he could not know.

So it was with Maddy. She'd said as much.

"Time is a ship that never anchors," me muttered to himself. "And so are some people."

* * *

Whatever happened on any given day or night at Race Rock, whatever variation there might be from the daily routine, a keeper could never drift far from the demands of the job: to maintain the lighthouse and light the light. Like Prometheus, chained to a rock by an angry Zeus for giving mankind fire, the lighthouse keeper is chained to his rock. Bound to it by duty. Lighting the light might seem a simple, small thing. But to those at sea, it means everything.

Until you've been at sea on a moonless night, near a rocky shore, pushed by a steady wind over the inky waters, and sailed a course for hours by following a distant blinking light, you cannot know how powerful that light is. For sailors, a lighthouse is a beacon of hope and safety. It guides them through the darkness.

12

"Captain, maybe we should turn west, just a bit?" Alexander was wide-eyed and beginning to crack under the strain of the storm. His fear was getting the best of him. Smith could see that. He was not far behind. This was one of the worst storms he'd ever been in. The *City of Lawrence* was far too heavy with ice. The seas had become increasingly wild and erratic. It was almost impossible to know how to steer across them. And still no Race Rock. No light to tell them where they were and to help them get to where they were going.

"I mean, sir...." Smith couldn't hear him over the howling wind and pelting sleet.

"What, Mr. Alexander?" Smith yelled. Alexander cupped his hands around his mouth, leaned towards Smith and yelled.

"I said maybe we could assume we've reached Race Rock and start to arc around to the mouth of the Thames!"

The boat pitched hard to port. Alexander flailed out and grabbed a pipe. Smith used the wheel to keep himself upright. He held it in a death grip.

"I don't know," yelled Smith, "I think we should...."

He never finished his sentence. The boat hit something. It twisted to the right and the bow seemed to rise straight up. Smith, Alexander and the rest of the men on the bridge were thrown backwards. The ship kept going hard to the right. There was a loud deep rumble beneath them. A grinding, growling boom. It lasted two, three seconds. Their momentum was directed upwards and the boat climbed skyward, into the night. Then it slammed down. The ship shuttered. Chunks of ice flew off the deck like cannonballs. Windows cracked on the bridge. The metal hull deflected and bent. The *City of Lawrence* ground forward and into a wave that washed over the bow.

The collision left the men on the bridge stunned.

Alexander was moaning. He had put his hand out to stop is fall and broken his wrist. Captain Smith had sideswiped a valve handle on his way down and had a nasty cut above his eye. Blood trickled down his cheek. Olson lay in a heap in the corner, unconscious.

Lightning flashed. The men saw their world in an instant of backlit silhouettes.

"We hit something!" yelled the First Officer, King. "Jesus, we hit something hard!"

Smith was dazed. He sat up in the pitching room, trying to get his bearings.

Alexander was holding his arm. His hand dangled limply. The lights were flickering. The boat felt strange, as if it was going in different directions at the same time. They could hear metal grinding and squealing as they were tossed by the seas. The *City of Lawrence* was still under power. Still moving forward. But everything was at angle. Something was terribly wrong.

The men in the bridge were far from the engine room. Down there, the violence of the collision was worse. Water was gushing in. The engineers had had no warning. The collision was sudden and devastating. For a second, Chief Engineer Olmstead saw a wet black rock ripping through the metal hull. Then the rock was gone and seawater rushed in the gash the rock had made.

Chief Engineer Speltz was knee deep in ice-cold water. He spun around to the intercom pipe and bellowed into it.

"We've hit a rock. We're taking on water!"

It was a barely audible, garbled message on the bridge. Alexander, nearest to the pipe, heard it.

"Engine room taking on water!" Alexander yelled at the Captain. Smith was still stunned by his impact with the pipe. He was shocked by the suddenness of the ship's collision. It had happened so quickly. Now he had to act quickly.

Alexander was trying to stand up in the rolling ship. The lights flickered out. The crippled steamer kept moving forward, slowly, out of control.

There was a lightning flash and Alexander saw a shape to his left, silhouetted by the sky. The shape was unmistakable: Race Rock Lighthouse. Its light was out. In that instant, Alexander knew what happened, He leaned over Captain Smith. "We hit Race Point, sir."

Smith struggled to his feet. In the next flash of lightning, Smith saw what Alexander had seen. The sky lightened for an instant, and he saw the silhouette of Race Rock against it, quickly sliding away and into the distance. He knew they had steamed between Race Rock Lighthouse and Race Point, the rocky tip of Fishers Island. It was a treacherous channel. Take it too close to the island and you sailed over jagged rocks. Without Race Rock's light to warn them, they had done just that. They had scraped over the ledge and the rocks. Torn out part of the bottom of their ship.

Smith shook his head, partly to clear it, partly in disbelief. "Do we have steering?" he shouted at Williams, who had jumped to the wheel, trying to control the ship.

"No, sir. We must have lost the rudder or it's jammed. I can't get the helm to respond."

They steamed on. Fishers Island and Race Rock were behind them now. They were heading towards Eastern Point in Groton. There were bad rocks there, too. Black Rock was a known ship-killer. If they could steer, they might be able to head to the soft sandy beaches of New London or Waterford. Smith grabbed the wheel from Williams and tried for himself. No luck. The *City of Lawrence* was heading on its own course, driven by the waves and the wind, not the hand of man.

Smith had always felt competent at sea. In control. A captain to be trusted. A captain who had sailed many years and had great confidence in himself. All that changed in an instant when he realized he was now commanding a stricken ship. He was about to become one of those captains who lost his ship. Just another able seaman who had foundered on the treacherous, merciless rocky shores of New England.

The bridge door burst open. It was Speltz. He was soaked and wild.

"Sir! The engine room is flooding. I saw a rock. I think the rudder's gone. The collision ripped off a big chunk back there. We're spilling debris out. We lost some crew. The C deck gave way. I saw some passengers go in. We may go down!"

Smith blinked. He had no idea what to do. They were in a nightmare. Kill the engines and lose all headway? They'd be turned by the wind and knocked over by the waves. Abandon ship? In this weather? In this frigid cold? Out of the question. Stay aboard and ride a sinking ship to their doom? There was no good choice. Alexander and Speltz looked at him. The burden of command was upon him, and he alone could tell them what to do. For a moment, his courage left him. He wished he were someplace else. His thoughts seemed frozen.

"There was no light," said Alexander. "No Race Rock."

Another lightning bolt lit up the western sky. No Race Rock. It was behind them. They were still four miles from Eastern Point. Smith did not believe his shattered ship could survive that long. The winds howled and made concentrating hard. His head throbbed. The waves tossed them violently. Sleet and spray hammered the metal. He could hear the ship groaning as its sections and decks buckled with the strain. The *City of Lawrence* was a ship at the mercy of the sea.

"God help that keeper," muttered Smith.

* * *

The keeper slept. He did not see the ship tear itself on the rocks. He didn't see it tossed by the violent seas, coming apart from its collision with Race Point. He did not see it steam on towards Groton, its lights flickering as the ship began to die. He could not hear the screams of the frightened passengers as they scrambled about or were swept into the icy seas. The pain and fear and death and destruction all played out to an empty sea on a cold and unforgiving night. The wind covered the sounds of the dying ship, as if the storm were committing a crime and concealing the evidence.

The *City of Lawrence*, headed through the black cold night. The crew was powerless to control it. All but a few men had abandoned the wrecked and flooding engine room. The mortally wounded steamer crossed the four miles of Fishers Island Sound ponderously, zigzagging like a drunken man. It wobbled side to side in the heavy seas, almost capsizing. It was low in the sea and getting lower as water filled its hull and more ice built up on its decks. It was helpless, and this night the sea would show it no mercy.

With a sudden jolt and wrenching twist, the *City of Lawrence* hit Black Rock, just a hundred yards off Eastern Point. It might as well have been a thousand miles.

The ship steamed head-on into the low rock. Its bow bounced skyward. The midsection caught and the ship stopped dead. The bow broke off and crashed forward into the water. The hull canted severely to port, dumping wreckage and people into the churning waters. The boilers hissed, and when the icy water hit they exploded into clouds of steam. The few engineers still in the engine room never had a chance.

The voyage of the *City of Lawrence* was over. Its lights were out, its engines were dead, its boilers gone. The waves smashed against its metal hull, tearing away chunks of loose steel like hungry animals at a carcass. The sleet continued adding to the ice that coated every surface of the wrecked ship.

The passengers and crew who were thrown into the sea succumbed quickly to the icy waters. Their cries of pain as the frigid water claimed them were lost in the howling winds. The sea swirled into the ship and flooded rooms and cargo holds. The heat and life were sucked away by the cold.

Stunned survivors clambered about the wreckage in desperation, looking for a safe perch away from the raging storm. Though they were close to shore, it was too cold and the storm too severe to attempt to leave the ship. By the flashes of lightning they could see what happened to those poor souls in the water.

There were no people at the few summer homes that dotted Eastern Point to see the wreck and attempt a rescue. For those who had survived the two collisions, the night would be long and cold. Some would die of injuries or exposure before dawn. Some would live.

Just minutes after hitting Black Rock, the *City of Lawrence* was a frozen, lifeless corpse. The seawater that sprayed it turned to white ice. It was barely dead and already it was a ghost ship. The waves crashed against the torn metal with a hollow, leaden sound, like giant bells, tolling the tale of death.

13

Nathaniel awoke. His head hurt, his mouth was dry. He was still dressed in his uniform. When he sat up on the couch, the room spun. He put his head in his hands and groaned. Bright daylight streamed in the windows. He pulled out his Lighthouse Board pocket watch and checked the time. Eleven in the morning!

He stood up, teetered, steadied himself on a chair. Dear God, he had slept a long time! The damned whiskey. He never should have started drinking. He never drank; had no tolerance for it. The empty bottle and glass stood on the table as a reminder of his weakness the night before.

The night before.

He tried to remember the night before. Then his eyes widened at the thought: he didn't remember lighting the light!

He stumbled through the metal fire doors and wound his way up the spiral staircase. He was hoping that he had lit the light, that he would find it still burning, and that he just didn't remember.

In spite of his grogginess, he bolted up and around, up and around. He reached the top of the stairs and threw open the door to the lantern room.

The light was not lit.

It was cold, full of fuel, waiting for him to do his duty.

Nathaniel Bowen stood staring at it. He had not lit the light! For the first time in his dozen years at Race Rock, he had not lit the light. During a bad storm, at that.

The bright, sunny day hurt his eyes as he looked out of the tower. He had always marveled at how often the day after a storm was so clear, as if the winds had scrubbed the sky clean.

Storms were like a madman's rage. They were savage, violent, destructive. When they passed, they left behind an extraordinary calm. A quiet that was all the more gentle for the sound and fury that had preceded it.

Nathaniel looked down on the rocks that surrounded the lighthouse. There were dark shapes, maybe eight or so, scattered about. What were they? Seals? He had seen a few seals on the rocks over the years. Yet never so many.

He had to take a look. He left the lantern room and walked quickly down the spiral staircase to the main floor. He crossed the living room and opened the heavy wooden door out to the porch.

Even though he was much closer to the rocks, he still could not figure out what the shapes were. If they were seals, they were sleeping, motionless. Something was not right. A feeling of dread crept over him.

He turned around and climbed down the metal ladder onto the landing platform, then out onto the rocks. He knew no caution this day. He made his way across the huge boulders until he reached one of the forms.

It was a man. Dead.

Nathaniel recoiled and gasped. In that instant, he knew how terribly he had failed.

He crouched over the figure. It was a man in a crewman's wool coat. Nathaniel turned him over. His eyes were closed. He looked uninjured. His skin was a pale blue. It looked like he had frozen to death.

Not far away was another body. Also a crewman.

The third body was a man dressed in a suit. A gold pocket watch chain stretched across his waist. He was older. He, too, was pale blue, but the odd angle of his neck spoke of a more violent end.

Nathaniel crawled along the edge of his island. The next body brought home the full horror of what had happened. It was a beautiful young girl, no more than twelve or so. Her lifeless eyes were open, her lips slightly parted, as if she was whispering a secret. Her long red hair spread out across the rock beneath her. She was so peaceful. So young. Her arm was in the water. It bobbed gently, like she was waving.

Nathaniel sat back, stunned. He looked around and saw more bodies cast upon the rocks. There was some wood, too, and other objects. What had happened? Even as he asked himself the question he knew the terrible answer: a shipwreck. He had not lit the light. He prayed that it had not caused the wreck, but the grim evidence around him told another story. Tears began to fill his eyes.

It was then that he noticed the small launch heading his way. It seemed to be coming from New London. He could make out four or five figures standing.

He should go to the dock to help them land, but he could not take his eyes off the dead girl. He stared at the girl's bobbing arm. It transfixed him. It was so frail, so light on the water. He looked at her lifeless body with profound sadness and thought: her hair will never blow in the wind; that bobbing hand will never write a love letter; those eyes will never see another sunset. She was dead, and he may have killed her.

Nathaniel was dazed, staring at the dead girl, his mind full of grim thoughts, his heart broken.

"Keeper Bowen? Keeper Bowen?"

He heard a voice. Repeating his name. Distant, like someone trying to wake him from a sleep. He hoped they *would* wake him from this nightmare.

"Keeper Bowen? Keeper Bowen?"

He looked up. There were four men standing there, all in Lighthouse Board uniforms.

He blinked. "Yes, I am Bowen," he said.

"Keeper Bowen, you need to come with us," the man closest to him said.

"What happened?" asked Nathaniel.

"You need to come with us, please," the man repeated. "Now!" he added.

Nathaniel stood up shakily to face the four men.

"Keeper Bowen, I am Senior Regional Commander Kane. This is the assistant keeper of New London light, Mr.

McGuire. This is seaman Bullard. And this is Mr. Adams of the New London office."

"Was there a shipwreck?" asked Nathaniel.

"Yes there was," Bullard said. "Last night."

"Oh, God."

"Sir, please come with us to the boat."

"Now? I need to go inside and…."

"Yes, sir, now," Kane cut him off.

"But the light…."

"Mr. McGuire will be manning the light for now. And Mr. Adams will stay here to assist and to investigate," Kane said.

"Investigate?" asked Nathaniel, bewildered.

"Yes, sir. He will determine what went wrong here at Race Rock last night. Check the equipment. See if it is operating correctly," said Kane.

"Determine if it was mechanical or human failure," added McGuire. He stared at Bowen with a cold, angry glare.

"Come with us to the boat," said Bullard, a muscular man with a thick neck, blotchy face and piercing gray eyes. He took Nathaniel by the arm, making it clear he was ready to escort him.

"I would like to pick up a few personal effects," said Nathaniel. He was suddenly afraid.

"Not possible right now," Kane said. "Maybe later."

Bullard nudged Nathaniel forward, and they turned away from the carnage on the rocks. They clambered their way over the boulders and around to the dock area. As they did, Nathaniel noticed pieces of wood and steel and other objects washed up. More dead bodies. He could not look at them.

When they got to the dock, Kane ordered McGuire and Adams into the lighthouse. "Do your jobs, gentlemen," he said as he dismissed them. He jumped into the small boat and motioned Nathaniel to join him.

"After you," said Bullard. Nathaniel stepped into the craft as Bullard untied them from the pier and jumped in himself.

Bullard started the engine and put the boat in reverse. They gently slid away from the dock, through the flanking piles of rocks. Nathaniel could see a leg dangling over one. Bullard spun the boat towards New London.

"Did the ship sink?" Nathaniel asked Kane.

"No, sir, it did not. It ran aground on Black Rock, off Eastern Point."

"Casualties?" Nathaniel whispered.

"What you see here and more. We aren't sure yet. We're still reviewing the ship's manifest and counting survivors."

Bullard turned to Nathaniel. "Seems your light was out. They hit the end of the Island. Race Point. It ripped their ship up pretty bad. Amazing they made it all the way to Groton." There was a sneer of anger in his tone that chilled Nathaniel.

They were four miles from Groton. It was hard to see that far, but looking towards Eastern Point, Nathaniel thought he could see a dark shape silhouetted against the shore.

"The Board will investigate carefully, Keeper Bowen. We will find out what happened," said Kane.

"I know what happened," muttered Bullard.

"Enough, Bullard!" Kane said. Nathaniel's face was anguished. He looked up at Kane.

"I..." Nathaniel began.

"Don't talk now. Save it for the investigation. That's when you can tell your story," Kane said.

Nathaniel nodded and moved to the bench at the back of the small boat. They made their way across the choppy seas to New London. The keeper turned and watched Race Rock—his light, his duty, his life—fade into the distance.

14

Nathaniel stayed at the house of a friend in New London. The one whose daughter he had given his rescued cat Neptune to. The Lighthouse Board planned an inquiry hearing in a few days. Word had spread quickly around Groton and New London, and Bowen dared not even go out in public, afraid of the anger he knew would be directed at him. He stayed in a small room at the back of his friend's home and brooded. He came out for meals, shared with the family in awkward silence. Nathaniel was grateful someone would take him in, and appreciated that the family did not rush to judge him. True friends. They did not ask about the night of the storm, and Nathaniel did not bring it up in their measured conversation. Still, it was there, an unspoken drama that threatened to break through their studious avoidance of it. He noticed a copy of The Day newspaper on a table. "*Death toll in Lawrence sinking rises to twenty-nine.*" He could not bear to read it. Alone in his room, he spent his hours reliving the night of the storm. He thought about his past and his future. Only Neptune seemed to want to be with him, perhaps remembering the kindness Nathaniel had shown nursing him back to health when he had washed up on Race Rock.

"Well, at least I saved you," Nathaniel told him.

On the day of the hearing, Bowen made his way across New London to the Custom House on Bank Street. It was a small granite building perched on the river bank. It had seen its share of history. In 1839 the slave ship Amistad had been moored behind it and the start of the fight to exonerate and free those slaves had begun within its walls.

The hearing was held in a large room on the second floor. Tall windows overlooked the Thames River. There was a table where the three commissioners sat, another for Bowen, angled sideways to them, a chair that served as the witness stand, and some chairs and benches for a gallery.

Nathaniel entered. A few people were milling about. He recognized Kane and Adams, two of the men who had picked him up. Bullard was there. Kane motioned to Nathaniel to take a seat. A few more people filed in and sat. A stenographer entered with her legal pad. Then Captain Smith walked in. His forehead was bandaged and he had a slight limp. Following him, Alexander entered, his arm in a sling. A few other officers and crew from the *City of Lawrence* came in and took their seats. They saw Bowen for the first time and looked him over, trying to take the measure of the man who had failed them. A few whispered to each other. Nathaniel looked back at them. His expression was stoic, masking the heartbreak and guilt he felt.

Kane cleared his throat and brought the meeting to order. He spoke slowly for the record.

"This is the investigative hearing of the United States Lighthouse Board, Commander Kane presiding. Location is the Custom House in New London, Connecticut. The date: February 10th, 1907. Present are Assistant Superintendent Burdick and District Commissioner Cole, as well as other officers and personnel of the Board. We are here to accept testimony regarding the failure of the Race Rock lighthouse on February 7th, three days ago. For the record, there was a very severe storm that night. Further, the steamer *City of Lawrence*, having hit the rocks at Race Point, causing severe damage to the ship, ran aground on Black Rock around midnight. There were twenty-nine casualties. Several passengers and crew remain hospitalized. No further fatalities are anticipated. The bodies of those lost have already washed ashore, as usually happens in this area. This inquiry seeks to determine if there was a causal relationship between the failure of the light and that wreck. We hope to discover why the light was not lit. The keeper of Race Rock that night, Nathaniel Bowen, is present." Kane paused and looked around. "I believe that covers the formalities."

As Kane was speaking, Nathaniel looked around the room. It was charged with energy. The appraising looks had hardened to cold stares. The Captain met his eyes with an angry glare. "You wrecked my ship!" was what that glare said.

Kane continued: "The board would like to call as its first witness Captain Smith, commander of the *City of Lawrence*."

Smith stood up and limped his way to the small chair directly in front of the committee. He was at a forty-five degree angle to Nathaniel. Again he glared at the lighthouse keeper as he took his seat.

"State your name, please."

"Captain Leo Smith, master of the steamship *City of Lawrence*."

"Captain Smith," said Kane," would you please tell us what happened three nights ago?"

"Yes, sir. I will. The *City of Lawrence* left Wilmington, Delaware in the morning, bound for New London. We carried 96 passengers, a crew of 12, and a cargo of lumber, rum, and textiles. The storm blew in early in the afternoon. By the time we were at Montauk Point, the storm was fierce. I would estimate the waves were 15 to 20 feet. The sleet was heavy. It was bitter cold. I'm sure you know how bad the storm was."

"Yes, we do. It was a particularly nasty winter storm. Continue," said Kane.

"We rounded Montauk Point. The light there was lit, as we expected. We then headed 348 degrees NNW. That should have taken us near Race Rock. Of course we were expecting to pick up the light itself to adjust our course and then head in to New London."

"And what happened," asked Burdick. "Did you see the light?"

"No sir, we did not. We looked and looked but could not find it. We never saw a single flash on our crossing from Montauk. The light was dark."

"You're sure of that?" asked Kane.

"Yes, sir, I am. Neither I nor any of my crew saw the light. Christ, you can see that light from fourteen miles away! Even in a storm, we should have been able to see it a few miles out. No,

Race Rock lighthouse was not lit three nights ago." As he said this, Smith turned and again glared at Bowen.

"So you never saw Race Rock?" asked Kane.

"Not exactly, sir. We saw it silhouetted by the lightning in the western sky after we had hit the rocks off the tip of Fishers Island at Race Point. By then it was too late. Our ship was mortally wounded by the collision. That's when I got hurt. We saw the building for an instant. But not the light."

"And you never saw the lighthouse lit by earlier lightning?" asked Burdick.

"No, sir. We did not. It was too stormy, and the lighthouse is too dark an object. Only when we had almost passed it and were east of it looking west could we see it. As I said, just its shape lit by the lightning in the sky behind it. And then for only an instant."

"Continue."

"We were east of Race Rock. The currents had pushed us that way. Those are treacherous waters. That's why there's a lighthouse there. We hit the rocks. Hard and head on. No warning. The collision tore off our rudder. We lost steering. It ripped a huge hole in the engine room, and we started taking on water. We lost some of the crew right then, and I believe some passengers shortly afterwards when the lower deck collapsed down into the engine room and into the water. There was enough of one engine working that it was turning the propeller keeping us moving forward. We could do nothing to help ourselves. I would never have thought we'd have stayed intact long enough to cross Fishers Island Sound to Eastern Point, but we did. Only to smash into Black Rock."

"Did you consider abandoning ship, sir? Trying to get to Fishers Island?"

"No. Fishers was behind us quickly. We had no steering. It was freezing cold and the seas were rough. We had a lot of ice on deck. I doubt we could have launched any lifeboats, or kept them upright even if we had. Not in those seas. Staying on the bigger ship was our only chance. At the time, I'll admit, I didn't think we had any chance in either case. Like I said, we had no steering. It was almost five miles to Groton. We were in God's hands. I was saying my prayers. It was a terrible trip across the Sound. We lost some more crew and passengers. Thank God, the ship held together long enough to run aground on Black Rock. We didn't sink. So it was the correct choice. We didn't lose everybody." He paused a moment, looked over at Nathaniel, then back at Kane.

"The lighthouse keeper at Race Rock let us down!" Smith said, no longer trying to contain his anger. "He didn't light the light or he let it go out. I don't know. But he didn't do his job. Our ship hit the rocks and people died. That I do know."

Nathaniel looked down at the table. The captain was right. He had failed. Failed miserably. He was responsible for the death of twenty-nine people.

"Do you have anything to add?" asked Kane.

"No, I've told you what happened. I did what I could to save my ship and the lives of my crew and passengers. I hope God will forgive the lighthouse keeper." He paused. "I know I won't."

There was a moment of silence. Captain Smith was shaking with fury.

"Thank you, Captain. You may step down," said Kane.

Captain Smith composed himself, nodded, stood up, and turned to Bowen.

"This is on your conscience!" he said. Then he limped back to his seat. There were hushed whispers in the room. Smith's account had been compelling and damning.

"We call First Mate Alexander," said Kane.

Alexander's testimony matched that of Captain Smith. He reinforced their desperate search for Race Rock and the horrific collision that doomed their ship. When he was finished, he too turned and spoke directly to Bowen.

"You are safe on your lighthouse, sir. We at sea are not. We are at the mercy of the seas, and they have little mercy. We depended on your help. You let us down. You are a disgrace to your uniform."

They were not saying anything Bowen did not already know or feel. If he could have willed himself to die right then and there, he would have.

"We call Mr. Adams of the Lighthouse Board," said Kane.

Nathaniel recalled Adams was one of the two men Kane had left in charge of Race Rock two days ago. The one who would investigate.

"Mr. Adams, would you please state your name, position and your duties for the Lighthouse Board?" asked Burdick.

"Yes sir," replied Adams. "My name is Edwin Alan Adams. I am an engineering and facility analyst for the United States Lighthouse Board, Southern New England Region, District 6. I inspect lighthouses and make sure that their lights and other mechanical systems are in proper working order. If not, I am authorized to order such repairs as may be necessary to remedy any problems."

"And did you, Mr. Adams, at the request of this office inspect the Race Rock lighthouse?" asked Burdick.

"Yes, sir. I did."

"Would you please tell us what you found?" asked Burdick.

"Yes, sir. I inspected and tested the light. Everything was in working order. The wicks were trimmed, the oil reservoirs full, and the siphoning tubes clear. The rotation mechanism was greased and functioning smoothly. The fresnel lens was spotless. The gears, pulleys and chains were all in good working order. Indeed, I would have to say that the light was kept in impeccable condition by Keeper Bowen."

"I see," said Burdick.

"Mr. Adams, did you investigate the rest of the lighthouse?" asked Kane.

"Yes, sir. I did a thorough inspection. I wanted to make sure everything was operating correctly and all supplies properly stored. I even tested the fire doors and light room hatch to be sure the keeper had access," said Adams.

"And you found everything satisfactory?" asked Kane.

"Yes. Everything was in order. Like the light itself, impeccable." Here Adams hesitated. He shot a quick glance at Nathaniel. He seemed uncomfortable.

"Is there something else, Mr. Adams?" asked Kane.

"Well, yes, sir." Again Adams looked at Nathaniel.

"Go on," urged Kane.

"Well, in the course of my investigation, I found a bottle of whiskey—an empty bottle of whiskey—and a single shot glass on the living room table. The glass was still wet." Adams had revealed the damning evidence. All eyes swung to Bowen. Kane seemed stunned. There was a tense silence in the small room.

"Well, Mr. Adams, I am sorry to hear that. Very sorry indeed," said Kane. "Anything else?"

"Not much, sir. A little piece of driftwood carved like a seagull. Some pictures and other personal effects as you would expect. Nothing out of the ordinary."

"Mr. Adams," Burdick asked, "in your opinion, is there any reason why the light at Race Rock should not or could not have been lit the night of the storm?"

Adams paused a moment before he answered, glancing over at Nathaniel. "No mechanical reason," said Adams. The way he phrased it made the implication of human failure quite clear.

"I see," said Burdick. "Mr. Kane, do you have any further questions for this witness?"

"None."

"Then you are excused, Mr. Adams. Thank you," said Burdick. The presiding officers made some notes and whispered to each other a moment. There was a low mumbling of voices in the room as the officers of the ship and others reacted to Adams' testimony.

"Quiet, please," said Kane. "We call Mr. Bullard."

Bullard stood and swaggered to the seat. He was an imposing, if somewhat brutish figure, with his crew cut and muscular body. He projected an air of self-assurance.

"State your name and position for the record, please."

"I am Dirk Bullard, seaman and junior officer of the Lighthouse Board, New London district."

"Thank you, Mr. Bullard. Please tell us your observations at Race Rock."

"Well, we arrived at Race Rock late morning the day after the storm. We'd heard the light was not lit and went to investigate. It was a grisly scene. I observed several dead individuals on the rocks. We found Keeper Bowen hunched over one. He seemed dazed. We took him to the skiff. I smelled alcohol on his breath. The light was not lit. Keeper Bowen, like I said, seemed dazed. Maybe hung-over. We put him in the boat and took him back to New London. I think it's clear what happened: he got drunk, let the light go out or never lit it, and caused the wreck of the *City of Lawrence.*"

"Mr. Bullard, the board would appreciate it if you would let us draw the conclusions. We only need testimony of what you saw and did. Not what you think happened."

"Well, with all due respect, sir, it don't take a genius to figure out what happened out there."

"Thank you, Mr. Bullard. Since there are no geniuses on the board, I trust we will be able to figure out what happened. You are excused," said Kane, obviously annoyed at the man's bullying tone.

"That's it?" he asked.

"That's enough," Kane shot back.

Bullard shook his head and stood up and swaggered back to his seat at the rear of the small room. The three inspectors huddled and whispered for a moment. Kane spoke next.

"We would like to call Keeper Bowen."

The room went silent, though it was energized with expectation. Nathaniel Bowen stood up and made his way to the chair before the judges. He sat and faced them.

"For the record, your name and position, sir," said Burdick.

"Nathaniel Bowen. Keeper of the Light at Race Rock."

At the back of the room, Bullard snorted in scorn. Kane glared at him then turned his attention back to Bowen.

"Keeper Bowen, we have not heard your side of the story. Would you care to tell us what happened that night?" asked Kane.

Nathaniel wondered what he could possibly say. There was no excuse, no defense for what he had done. Or not done.

"No," said Nathaniel.

"No?" asked Kane, surprised.

"I am afraid there is nothing I can say, sir. There is no excuse for my failure. I did not do my job. The light was not lit. A ship was wrecked and people died. I have no defense. I won't insult the magnitude of the loss by saying I am sorry. No, sir. I failed in my duty. Why I did so is something I will take to my grave with me. I can ask only hope for God's mercy and forgiveness." Nathaniel spoke these words slowly, sadly. Then he sat back and looked at the three men. It was essentially a guilty plea.

They returned his gaze, a little surprised he had no defense. No explanation. The men of the Lighthouse Board knew Bowen. They knew the demands of his job. They knew the code of dedication and responsibility that motivated keepers. They wanted him to say something in his own defense, to offer up some reasonable explanation that would lighten the weight of his failure. But Nathaniel would not. He sat silently, staring at them, a man who had accepted his failure and whatever fate it would bring.

"Very well, Keeper Bowen. Very well," said Kane with a sigh. "We will take a short recess. The officers of the board stood and walked out of the room.

The Captain, Alexander, Adams and Bullard all remained seated. They spoke quietly among themselves. Nathaniel picked up a few words, none of them flattering. After a few minutes the Lighthouse Board officers returned to the room and took their seats at the table. Kane looked at Bowen. He was perhaps hoping that Nathaniel had changed his mind and was ready to say something that would illuminate what had happened. He waited a few seconds to give the man a chance—a last chance—to speak. Nathaniel said nothing. He returned Kane's gaze with a look of such sadness that it made Kane hesitant to speak.

Looking down at his notes, he began: "This inquiry is ready to render its recommendation to the Superintendent of the Lighthouse Board. We will draft the official language later today, but the essence of our decision is as follows. We shall recommend that Keeper Bowen's duties as a lighthouse keeper be terminated. He is to be immediately suspended as keeper of Race Rock Lighthouse. We will further recommend that he shall never be allowed to be a keeper of a lighthouse—any lighthouse, anywhere—again. Mr. Bowen, you have betrayed the sacred trust given to all lighthouse keepers. You did not light your light. Given the loss of life, we will turn this matter over to local authorities for further civil or criminal action. We therefore order you to surrender yourself to the police chief of the City of New London tomorrow at nine o'clock in the morning at the courthouse. He will take you into custody and proceed with legal action against you. We know you will not oppose these sanctions and orders. You will not attempt to flee. Do you understand?"

"I do," said Nathaniel quietly.

"Is here anything you wish to say at this time?" asked Kane.

Nathaniel thought for a moment. "May I return to Race Rock this afternoon to collect my belongings?" he asked.

"Well, sir, I think that would be all right with...." Kane began, but he was interrupted by Captain Smith, who stood to speak.

"I object to that!" shouted Smith, his face flushed with anger. "He should *never* return to Race Rock! The men, women and children—my crew—none of them ever had the chance for a final visit home to set their affairs in order. Neither should the man who killed them! Have the supply boat pick up whatever belongs to him. The light is no longer his. Keep him away from it!"

Seeing the depth of the Captain's emotions, the three men whispered among themselves. Smith was clearly, desperately venting his rage. It would make little difference if Nathaniel went out to collect his belongings. But in deference to the captain, they agreed to his demands.

"Very well," said Kane. "We shall do just that, Captain Smith. Mr. Bowen, a crew will collect your personal effects from Race Rock and bring them here to New London. You have no need to return to Race Rock. Ever."

Nathaniel nodded and bowed his head, looking at the table. There was only one thing he really wanted to retrieve from Race Rock. Now he could not. Nothing was working out for him. He exhaled and seemed to shrink.

"Mr. Bowen, I suggest you make good use of the remainder of this day," said Kane. Then he stood and looked at Captain Smith and the rest of his crew, commanding their attention with his fierce stare. He spoke with deliberate forcefulness: "We advise no one in this room to take the law into his own hands. Due process will be done in this case. The Lighthouse Board will no doubt accept our recommendation. Mr. Bowen will no longer be a keeper of the light. As for any justice to be meted out in connection with the loss of the *City of Lawrence* and the death of her passengers and crew, that will be for others to decide in a court of law. I hope I make myself clear. This hearing is adjourned."

Captain Smith stood and faced Nathaniel. "God have mercy on your soul," he said. He leveled a withering glare at Nathaniel and limped out of the room.

Nobody else wanted to talk to him. The room emptied.

Nathaniel sat and watched a drip of water slowly make its way down one of the frosted windows. It glowed in the morning sun. Its path was not straight. Encountering the smallest obstacle on the window—a bump in the glass or a bit of dirt—the drip veered away on an unpredictable path, seeking its own destination and destiny. Nathaniel knew his life, too, had veered off from the path it had been on. He had the blood of twenty-nine people on his hands, his conscience. He had lost his wife, his son, and the respect of the very men he had labored so hard to serve. He felt empty. He knew that if he had had an assistant keeper, the man would have lit the light. No ship would have foundered. No lives would have been lost. But Nathaniel had embraced solitude. It was like a magnetic aberration that affects the accuracy of a compass, deflecting it so that the course it points to is askew. He had followed his solitude and it had led him to disaster.

He had the rest of the day and night to himself. He had already decided what he must do. In this, he realized, he could not fail.

15

Nathaniel left the Custom House and walked to the New London Savings Bank, where he had deposited his money over the years. It wasn't much. He withdrew it all.

He backtracked to lower State Street, to a jewelry store. He had them engrave the back of his Lighthouse Board pocket watch. It took them about an hour, during which time he browsed the jewelry cases. With more than a little regret, he noted that none of the gems on display came close to matching those he'd left behind on Race Rock. He wondered if the treasure would ever wash up into someone else's life.

The clerk returned with his watch. Nathaniel inspected the engraving. They'd done a good job. He paid and left.

He made his way up to the top of the street, past the Public Library and Courthouse to Broad Street. About a mile up the road he went into another establishment, a stone carver. He spent a while there, making arrangements, being sure they got what he wanted exactly right. They were a bit surprised and uncomfortable with his request, but he spun a good story and offered them enough recompense to overcome their doubts. Nathaniel paid in cash and left. He walked slowly down Broad Street, his collar turned up against the winter wind.

The late afternoon sun cast long shadows across the streets as Nathaniel made his way to Pequot Avenue that ran along the bank of the Thames River. A gangly man in a rumpled black suit cut across the street and fell into step beside Nathaniel.

"I'm Don Sutherland, a reporter for The Day," he said.

"Go away," said Nathaniel. "I don't want company. I want to be alone."

"Come on," the man continued, unfazed by Nathaniel's brush off. "I have a story to file. I was at the trial..."

"Hearing," said Nathaniel. "It was a hearing."

"Right. A hearing. Let me fix my notes." He scribbled in a small notebook as they walked. "Anyway, I was there and you didn't say anything in your own defense. Here's a chance. Anything you want to say for the newspaper?"

Nathaniel looked at the man.

"No."

"Nothing?"

"No."

Nathaniel walked a little quicker.

"Come on! I'm gonna write the story anyway. Go on the record. If not a defense, maybe a thought or a quote. Something."

Figuring that if he said something to Sutherland the man would leave him alone, Nathaniel stopped and faced him. He thought for a moment.

"You can write that I will pay my debt."

Nathaniel started to walk again, quickly, as the reporter wrote in his notebook. He was relieved when the man did not follow him. Nathaniel didn't really care what he wrote. It wouldn't matter.

It was a cold day, and there were only a few people out. That suited Nathaniel fine. He was in no mood to talk, and he did not want to endure any more accusing stares and angry looks.

He walked slowly, thinking, reflecting. He thought about Carla and Caleb, about life at Race Rock, about the few friends he had ashore, about that painter who visited him. He smiled. "Maddy." What a day they had spent together. What a night! He wondered where she was now. Had she gone west like she said?

The wind had picked up from the south and he was walking into it. He pulled his heavy wool coat tighter around him.

The setting sun lit up the windows of the houses that dotted the Groton shoreline. The orange glow reflected in the windows made the houses look like they were burning.

Nathaniel Bowen thought about how his life had changed. He was stunned by his change of fortune. It had all happened so very quickly. With no warning. Events spread over years had connected to result in an awful outcome.

First, Carla had left with Caleb. That had taken him by surprise. In retrospect, he wished he had listened to Carla more. Wished he had looked ahead at the life facing Caleb. He wished he had gotten to know his son better, that he had not been so blindly dedicated to the light.

Then, after they had been gone for several years and he thought he was over their loss, he'd found the little carved seagull. With it he'd also found an ocean of sadness and regret in himself. He'd unleashed a storm and it had overwhelmed him. In a moment of weakness, in a moment of stupidity, he had turned to drink, something he never did. He'd paid dearly for the little comfort it had given him.

After thousands of days of doing his job perfectly, he had failed. Just once, but at just the wrong time. Why couldn't he have let the light go out on a calm, clear night? Why had it happened on a stormy night with almost no visibility. On a night when, of all nights, the light of Race Rock was crucial to those at sea? Though he wanted to with all his heart and soul, he could not change what had happened. He laughed a bitter laugh. Fate was cruel. He shook his head. It didn't matter.

Nathaniel Bowen lived in a time when duty both molded and measured a man. Now he was branded as a man who had not fulfilled his duty. The supervisor was right. He *had* betrayed a sacred trust, and in doing so he had damned himself. His shame was overwhelming. It was too much to bear.

Nathaniel walked on, bending into the wind, head down, his thoughts tumbled as if blown by the wind.

So abrupt had been the end of his days at Race Rock that he hadn't even had a chance to take the treasure he'd found. That extraordinary box of gems. Then he thought: even if he had, what would he have done with it? It would have been a perfect legacy to leave his son. But he couldn't find Caleb. He hadn't heard from Carla in years. He had no idea where they were. Caleb would probably never find the few clues he'd left.

Perhaps he could have helped one of the charities dedicated to the families of lost sailors. Somebody could have benefited from all that wealth. Who could he tell? Who could he trust? He would have told the friend he was staying with, but he had shipped out last night. There was no time to figure it out. The box of jewels was hidden on Race Rock and would most likely stay hidden. A final punishment.

He walked, alone with his bitter thoughts. It was dusk. He arrived at the tall white octagonal tower of the New London Harbor Light. It was an old light, one of the very first in America. It was built in 1761, then rebuilt in 1801. It was a brownstone and brick tower, eighty-nine feet high, with octagonal sides. He knew the keeper, Samuel Hawkins. Nathaniel stood at the base of the light and looked up at it. The light was lit, alternating three seconds on and three off. Life would have been so much easier on a light on shore like this one. It wasn't isolated. It wasn't assaulted on all sides by the sea. It was just another building on the bank of the river. You could almost have a normal life being the keeper here. But Race Rock had lured him to its rocky isolation. It had given his life meaning. So many days, so many nights, until one night betrayed him forever.

Nathaniel kept walking.

A little beyond the light he came to the long beach that was part of the Guthrie Estate. A stone wall bordered the beach along Pequot Avenue. He walked alongside the seawall, peering over it into the gloom below. He spotted what he wanted.

Nestled against the wall was a small rowboat, turned over. He could see two oars beneath it. Perfect.

He jumped over the wall. He flipped the little boat over and slid the two wood oars into the oarlocks. He dragged the boat down the beach to the edge of the surf.

He walked back up the beach and took the last of his money and laid it on the sand where the boat had been. He covered it with a rock. Payment.

He returned to the boat and pushed it into the water. The waves were small and the little boat slid into the surf and bobbed there. Nathaniel took a few steps in the shallow water and hopped in over the stern.

He sat down on the middle bench, pushed the oars out and began to row. His stroke was slow and steady as he aimed across the river and south, out toward the mouth of the Thames, toward Eastern Point.

There wasn't much current. He only had to correct a little for its push north up the river. The sky was clear and deep—the infinite, inky black that comes with winter. Stars appeared and the moon was rising over Groton. His breath condensed into white puffs as he rowed. He heard the wind, and he heard the splash of his oars in the water. The oarlocks creaked. It was a rhythm as old as mariners. Creak. Splash. Creak. Splash. Again it reminded him of a hot summer's day when Maddy had rowed out of the fog. She was something, that Maddy. He wished she'd stayed for more than a night. He wished she'd stayed forever.

Nathaniel rowed on across the black waters.

The Thames was about a mile across where he rowed, and it only took Nathaniel half an hour to approach the far shore. He had avoided looking at his destination, but now he was close. He could hear it. Finally, he turned and looked.

The ruined hulk of the *City of Lawrence* was right in front of his little wooden boat. His course had been true. The remains of the ship were huge, a looming silhouette blotting out the stars of the night sky. The waves swirled against its hull, into the ragged holes in its side and the sheared off stern. It was tilted to port, hard on the rocks where it had finally foundered, a few hundred feet from shore. The bow was broken off, and rested half-submerged in the water. Only the smokestack rose high above the water, as if in defiance. The ship's giant side-wheels were bent and broken, pieces dangling. The ship was an abandoned wreck. Already the sea was working at claiming what was left of her. It creaked and groaned as the waters pushed against it. It was an eerie sound, metal against rock, water against wood, deep and hollow.

He had caused this. His negligence, his weakness, his inattention to the light. The remains of the *City of Lawrence* would be an ugly reminder of his failure for months as it slowly rusted and fell apart. It was a sad legacy.

Nathaniel let his boat drift near the wreck.

It was so close to shore, so close! Had the seas been calm and the weather warm, maybe more could have survived. Some could have swum to safety. But in the winter storm, they had no chance in the frigid waters. He just hoped they had died peacefully. He'd heard that dying of exposure to cold was not so terrible. Drowning was horrible, but dying of exposure was a gentler, calmer death. The body shut down. The mind drifted away. It was like falling asleep.

He hoped so.

He took out his Lighthouse Board pocket watch, unhooked it from his jacket. It had been his faithful companion since the first day he'd served as a keeper. He'd measured out his days by it. His life. It was a beautiful timepiece. Nathaniel looked at the time: 6:52. He turned it over in his hands. The new engraving caught the moonlight. He could just read it: "JLS 12~1~05." Well, it wasn't much, but it was something. He carefully placed the watch onto the bench. The crystal face glimmered a bit in the starlight. "Time is a ship that never anchors," he murmured as he looked at it.

It was cold. The wind was light, but out here in the open, it was biting. A sharp chill cut into him. His hands were numb. He made his way to the bench that ran across the back of the small boat. He sat down, looked over the side at the black water, as deep and infinite as the night sky above. Then he swiveled his legs around so that they hung off the back. In a single move, pushing up with his arms, he levered himself up and off the boat into the frigid sea. The boat barely rocked as the keeper went overboard.

The initial shock as Nathaniel was submerged in the icy water was knife-sharp. It knocked the wind out of him.

He surfaced. The boat was already a few feet away.

There was no desperate flailing. No fear. No attempt to swim back to the boat. Bowen's destination was elsewhere. His boots were heavy. His wool coat grew heavier as it soaked up the seawater. He started shivering, then shaking. His teeth chattered. His body heat was no match for the icy waters around him. He laid back and looked up at the stars. He could see the big dipper. The North Star. Orion's belt. They were like old friends.

Slowly, Nathaniel turned his head to the left and saw the looming silhouette of the *City of Lawrence*.

"Forgive me," he said.

As his body sank, his head pivoted upright. He looked south and saw Race Rock, its light blinking in the distance. It was lit again. McGuire was doing his job.

A few minutes ticked by. His body cooled. The shock of the cold was gone. Then the shivering was gone. Nathaniel started to feel a warm glow, and weariness came over him. He no longer moved his legs or his arms. He barely felt them. They seemed far away. It all seemed far away, as if he was watching himself in a dream. The moon laid down a stripe of shimmering sparkles on the ebony sea. The stars twinkled overhead, and Race Rock blinked before him. New London light answered with its beacon. It was a beautiful scene. The little rowboat bobbed gently, Nathaniel's pocket watch glinting in the moonlight like a tiny lighthouse.

His head bobbed above the waves, but just barely. He was really quite warm now. And so very tired. He could hardly keep his eyes open. His body was adrift somewhere. He didn't feel it. A peacefulness washed over him. Stray images drifted across his mind. Bits and pieces of his life. Big moments, little moments, all sorts of moments—like a file cabinet tipped over, its papers a jumbled pile. He thought about what he'd said to the reporter. He'd paraphrased a line from Shakespeare's *The Tempest*: "He that dies pays all debts."

Nathaniel's head dipped beneath the water. Surfaced. Dipped again. He felt it a little against his closed eyelids. A gentle wet surge. That was all.

Nathaniel Bowen sank beneath the waves at last, his face tinted green by the waters of the Thames. It dimmed as he sank, like an ember gently dying. As he slowly faded away, Nathaniel dreamt of a long beach with white sand and swaying palm trees. He could almost feel the sun, so bright and hot, shining down on him. He could smell the tropical scents.

Especially the fragrance of oranges, heated in the branches by the mid-day sun.

He was in paradise.

The keeper of the light drifted down, down into the embrace of the sea's cold darkness.

PART II

September 21, 1938

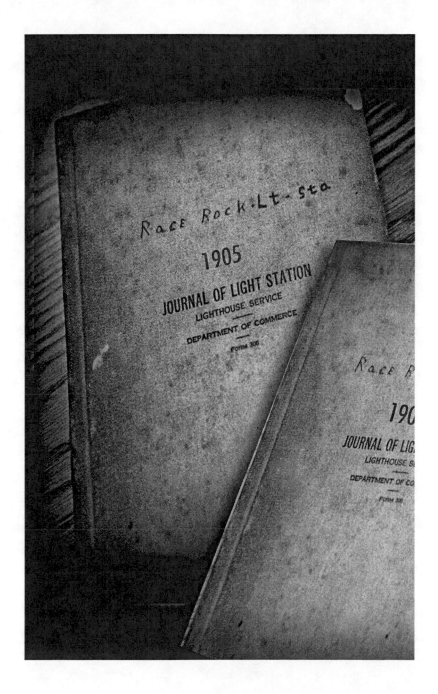

1

Light flooded into the dawn sky over Eastern Point in Groton on the morning of September 21, 1938. The seas were calm. The gentle swells caught the first light of day and glowed like burning mercury. Seagulls bobbed on the water or kept silent watch from the tops of buoys and rocks. Fishing boats chugged out to sea, spreading rippling wakes across the glassy waters. A distant train rumbled through New London. It was a sunny morning after a rainy week. New England had been a steam bath in August, and the heavy rains of the past four days had rivers and streams threatening to overflow their banks. The ground was saturated. This morning was like a gift—a beautiful, tranquil start to the day.

Caleb Bowen was on the catwalk outside the lantern room of Race Rock Lighthouse admiring the dawn. He was dressed in his Lighthouse Service coat and cap. His uniform was impeccable, made even more formal by the tie and white shirt he wore. The Service insisted that its keepers and their lighthouses be spotless and crisp, and conducted surprise inspections to ensure compliance. A dingy home, a dirty light, an unkempt keeper could result in dismissal.

He liked to get an early start, intermingling a chore or two with mugs of hot coffee. After taking a sip from a battered tin mug, Caleb sat the steaming cup on the narrow metal walkway. He looked down through the mesh grate at the rocks below. They were big and angular. They were the riprap that formed the man-made island Race Rock was built upon. He turned his attention to his daily chores, and began scraping some rust off the metal strips that held the windows in place. He noted any tiny holes that might need caulking. The hinges on the panel of the octagonal room that opened to the catwalk squeaked a bit—more rust to deal with. He glanced up at the lightning rod. A three-foot iron spike that topped the metal cupola, it had begun to wobble in heavy winds. He'd been putting it off, but eventually he'd have to fix it before it fell off and killed somebody. It was hard to get to. He'd need help.

He stopped and looked at the sunrise. He couldn't put his finger on it, but there was something a little odd about the morning stillness. It was as if the sea was holding its breath, waiting to exhale. His years at sea had fine-tuned his senses, and like anyone who lived or worked on the water, he had an intuitive feel for its moods.

Caleb Bowen was the keeper of Race Rock light, as his father before him had been. He had grown up at the lighthouse until his mother took him away. She thought he would never return, but she was wrong. Light-keeping, the sea, and Race Rock were in his blood. Even at ten, he had somehow known it. As they rowed away that foggy morning, he had turned to the light and silently said to his father "I'll be back."

He had been upset and confused that morning. He had told his father he wanted to go, just as Carla had asked him to. It had been a lie. He liked living on Race Rock. As soon as he had said he wanted to leave, he regretted it. The look in his father's eyes at that moment had haunted him for years. Still haunted him. Too young to know better, he had unwittingly broken the man's heart. He had never had the chance to set it right. Never even spoken to him again.

His mother had taken him south to Virginia. Within a year, she had met a wealthy insurance agent. He found a lawyer who worked up the divorce papers, and another lawyer had delivered them to Nathaniel on Race Rock. His father signed.

Carla and the insurance man had married, then moved west to Colorado, far, far away from the sea. His stepfather was a decent man who loved Carla and tried very hard to be a good father. Caleb liked him. But he didn't love him. His love would never drift from Nathaniel, his real father. He thought he would see him again. At first, he believed he and Carla would visit Race Rock often. Or so he hoped. Then she met Frank, and Nathaniel, Race Rock and New England drifted away like an abandoned boat. For Caleb, his memories of his father and Race Rock were a jumble of impressions, some vivid, some vague. With time, like a dream, some faded. Others he clung to and treasured.

Caleb settled into life in the West. He made friends, went to school, played sports, studied history. Whenever he went to the little pond in the woods to swim in its tepid, muddy waters, he closed his eyes and tried to imagine the white beaches of New London and Groton. He tried to remember the smells of low tide, the sounds of gulls, the foghorns of the lighthouses. He could almost conjure them up. Yet when he opened his eyes, he was in the little pond, its glassy waters untroubled by any waves or tides. It was not the sea, and it was the sea he longed for.

Caleb worked for Frank in the insurance business for almost ten years. He hated it. He was engaged once but it didn't work out. One day he was in a bookstore and happened upon a book called the "Lighthouses of New England." There was a picture of Race Rock on the cover. He stared at it for a full five minutes.

The next day, he packed his bags, said goodbye to his mother, and left.

He drifted back toward New England, working odd jobs to get by, determined to keep on his course, like a Monarch butterfly unerringly returning to its ancestral home. He would return to Race Rock. He did not know if his father was still the keeper of the light. He had never tried to find out, never tried to track him down and telephone him. Caleb wasn't sure why. He was busy with school and friends and his life. The years passed. The memory of the man in the uniform tending the light was something that surfaced from time to time. It was a cherished memory, one he held onto like a secret. A few times, he had thought about writing or calling, but life has a way of intruding on things, of getting in the way of life.

As he headed east, the images from his days at Race Rock came back as they never had before. It was as if the place was calling to him, trying to beguile him with memories, pulling him along a path of memory to his destination.

Finally he arrived in New London. When he inquired about Nathaniel, he was shocked to learn what had happened on that stormy night in 1907. He was devastated to learn his father had committed suicide. He went to the office of The New London Day newspaper and found the reports of the storm. The newspaper was old and faded, but the story was clear. It was all there: the storm, the wreck of the *City of Lawrence*, the Lighthouse Board hearing, his father being blamed, and, a few days later, his body washing ashore. He found a passage where a reporter said that Nathaniel Bowen promised to pay his debt. He had—with his life. In just a few days' papers, the drama ran its course, then disappeared. A new keeper took over and the world forgot about Race Rock.

It was a wrenching ordeal for Caleb to read the reports, to imagine the harrowing story unfolding, to picture his despairing father. He left the newspaper office and went to the Old Dutch Tavern for a beer, saddened and shaken. He had hoped to return to Race Rock and find his father still there, still the lighthouse keeper, still impeccably dressed in his smart uniform. Instead, he had found a gloomy history of failure and death.

A few days later, Caleb went to the Colonel Ledyard cemetery in Groton. It was a small place near the bank of the Thames River. At a far corner he found his father's tombstone. Through teary eyes he read the inscription:

Nathaniel Bowen
1864 ~ 1907
My legacy is in my dedication to the light.

It was a final, defiant statement from the disgraced lighthouse keeper. He would not let the one night he failed totally outweigh the thousands he had done his job with such devotion. He had arranged for the tombstone on that last day when he was censured by the Lighthouse Board and took his own life.

Whatever the record in the brittle, forgotten newspapers might say, he had fashioned his own in enduring stone.

Caleb stared at the grave and wondered about his father. Had he ever really known the man? His memories of him were fragmented glimpses of a life they had shared years ago. They came back to him—a series of impressions like photographs in a scrapbook.

He remembered walking up the spiral stairs to the lantern room, the echo of their footsteps on the metal stairs, the view from the small, glass-enclosed summit. He remembered the slow turn of the light, and the complex glittering array of glass that made up the fourth-order fresnel lens. He remembered seeing his face perfectly reflected in the pan of mercury the light rested on. He remembered the smell of the oil they burned in the light. He remembered watching his father make daily entries into the Journal of the Light Station books. He remembered clambering over the huge rocks with his father, looking for driftwood and other curiosities that had washed up. He remembered eating dinners around the small table in the dining room. He remembered the smell of his father's pipe. He recalled the day his father had given him a little carved seagull. He remembered Nathaniel teaching him how to shut out sounds, to isolate a distant horn or a single bird's cry.

There were a few fragments of conversations, too, and little moments of life that floated up like bits of flotsam: the muffled sound of his father and mother talking downstairs after he'd gone to bed. The way a curl of hair always dipped over Carla's right eye and how she brushed it back as she spoke. A gull gliding by a window. The sound of the waves hitting the base of the lighthouse. Caleb wondered: did the memories add up to a portrait of his father and the life they'd shared? Not really. They were just stray pieces of a puzzle. Fragments that did not connect into a coherent picture.

Caleb was taken away before they had spent much time together, and now there was no chance of being together again.

Who was this man buried beneath his feet? What had driven him to drink that night—something he never did? What price had he paid for his dedication to the light?

It was a hard time for Caleb. He was full of remorse. He believed he should have been at Race Rock that night in 1907. Even though he was just a kid back then, he could have helped his father. He was sure of it. The light never would have gone out; no ship would have been wrecked; nobody would have died. His father would still be alive.

As he stood there by the grave, his regret turned to resolve. He vowed to return to Race Rock as its keeper. To serve with the same pride and faithfulness his father had. He would give the Bowen name the luster and respect it deserved. That would be *his* legacy. A gift to his father.

The next day, he went to the Lighthouse Service office in New London. It was in the Custom House building where his father's trial had taken place. Caleb stood on the stairs and tried to imagine his father in the same spot arriving to face his judgment. He shook his head. New London was full of ghosts for him, as if the past had waited for his return.

He found the office of Commander St. Clair, the officer in charge. When Caleb gave his name, he got no reaction. Years had passed since that stormy night. New people were in charge. Commander St. Clair asked him why he wanted to be a lighthouse keeper. Caleb answered: "To help mariners."

St. Clair smiled. "It's not that simple," he said. "Keeping the light lit is the easy part. Living out there in the middle of nowhere—that's hard. You ever lived in isolation like that?"

"A bit," replied Caleb.

St. Clair went on: "Listen: Race Rock has a keeper, a fine one, Mr. Hesky. And he has an assistant keeper who would be in line to take over from him. That probably won't happen for another five or six years."

"I see," said Caleb, his tone betraying his disappointment.

Catching his tone, St. Clair looked at him thoughtfully a moment. He seemed to be weighing something in his mind.

"Let me look," St. Clair said. "Let's see what's going on in this area." He went over to a bookcase in his tiny office and retrieved a journal. He looked through it, thumbing back and forth through the pages.

"Ah, here," he said. "The senior keeper in Saybrook at the Outer Light is set to retire next spring. The assistant keeper, Mr. Rowbotham will take over then. That would create an opening for a new assistant keeper. That's how you learn the job. I don't see anyone penciled in for that position yet. If you like, I will put your name in. No promises. It's a tough spot. A metal can of a light at the end of a half-mile breakwater. It's dangerous to get to. It's cold, damp. Tight quarters."

"I don't mind," said Caleb. "If it will get me into the Service, I'll work there."

St. Clair nodded. Again he looked at Caleb, studying him a moment.

"Okay. I'll put you down. Until the position opens up, you should try to find some work around here to learn the area. The waters, weather, shipping patterns, marinas, and so on. Get to know some of the fishermen and other keepers."

"I already know a lot about the area," said Caleb.

"Yes, I imagine you do," said St. Clair. He paused, caught Caleb's gaze and held it. "I know who you are," he said. "You're Nathaniel Bowen's son, aren't you?"

"Yes, sir. I am."

The two men looked at each other intently. Inwardly, Caleb cringed. The disgrace of his father would come back to haunt him. His dream could end here. A few seconds passed that seemed an eternity.

Finally St. Clair spoke.

"Caleb, what your father did—or didn't do, to be more accurate—that night was sinful. He failed at his job. People died. Ultimately, so did he. I was a young crew member on a tugboat back then. I heard all about it. It was big news in the area. I was one who felt there had to be more to the whole story than ever came out. There never was a trial, of course. Just the Board's hearing. I can't forgive what he did. But I also can't forget all the years he served us well. I sailed into new London hundreds of times in the worst weather New England could serve up. Race Rock was always lit, and I was grateful for that. It's too bad your father never told his side of the story. Who knows what really happened out there? But that was a long time ago. I'll give you a fair shake. How *you* conduct yourself as a keeper, if you make it that far, will determine how you are judged."

"Thank you," said Caleb. "That's all I can ask."

He realized he had been very lucky to meet a fair, open-minded man in a rigid, judgmental bureaucracy. He was also bitterly disappointed. He hadn't imagined it would be so hard to get back to Race Rock. The Lighthouse Board of his father's day had evolved into the Lighthouse Service, and with that change had come new rules and procedures. He'd have to bide his time and hope that someday there would be an opening at Race Rock. It was a setback, but not a dead end.

Caleb stood, thanked St. Clair again and left. On his way out, he wandered into a large open room on the second floor. He knew from the newspaper accounts that it was the room where his father's hearing had taken place. He tried to imagine the scene. He wished his father had said more at the inquiry. Explained what had happened. But he hadn't. He took that story to the grave with him. Dedication to the light may have been his legacy, but so too was silence. A silence filled with unanswered questions.

Caleb had only to wait a few months before he started work for the Lighthouse Service. Good to his word, St. Clair offered him the assistant keeper's post at Saybrook when it became available. It was a remote place at the end of a rocky breakwater, but it was not as isolated Race Rock. Though much of it was familiar, Caleb learned the job of a keeper and learned it well. What he had seen his father do he now did himself. The technology had changed, but it was still a demanding and often numbingly repetitive routine.

Caleb worked hard at the job. He was more driven than most keepers, who tended to be quiet men of placid disposition. From time to time, his travels took him by Race Rock, but he never once went there. He had his reasons. He wanted his return to Race Rock to be to work on the lighthouse, his old home. He didn't want to visit and have the wrenching pain of leaving again. If he ever got back to Race Rock, he would never leave it before he was ready to. Race Rock lighthouse was a part of Caleb, an almost mystical part of his makeup. It was a piece of his past and the focus of his future. He would have to be careful it did not consume him, as things we love can do if we love them too much.

Quite suddenly, in the winter of 1931, the head keeper at Race Rock became ill. He had contracted a virulent case of tuberculosis. He went ashore, never to return, and the assistant keeper, Fletcher, took charge.

A week before Christmas, Caleb Bowen was about to fill the light at Saybrook when the phone rang. It was Commander St. Clair.

"Caleb, there is a position open for the assistant keeper at Race Rock. While we have Hawkins penciled in for that, well, you know, we could shuffle things around. I don't think Hawkins has his heart set on Race Rock. In fact, I think he'd prefer a land-based light to that God-forsaken rock. Are you still interested?"

He was, and on December 28, Caleb Bowen was officially assigned as the Assistant Keeper of Race Rock Lighthouse. He spent the New Year's holiday a happy man. At last, he would return to his childhood home. He was scheduled to go out on January 3.

On January 2nd, he received a telephone call asking that he report to the office of the district superintendent of the Lighthouse Service, a Mr. Bullard. Caleb had no idea who he was or what was up. He figured just some paperwork or formalities. Maybe a briefing about what was expected of him.

Bullard's office was in an old warehouse building on Bank Street in New London. He found the office, and a secretary told him Bullard would see him soon. After nearly forty minutes, she said, "Superintendent Bullard will see you now."

Bullard was a large man in his sixties. He had a crew cut, thick neck, a ruddy complexion and a broken nose. He looked like he'd seen too many beers or brawls—or both. The man raised his head from some paperwork, grunted, nodded toward a seat. Bowen sat down. Bullard did not look up from his work, so Bowen took the moment to study the man. He was stuffed into his uniform and looked stiff in it. The buttons gleamed against the dark wool fabric. The collar of his white shirt was tight, and his neck bulged out around it. His hands were big, his fingers thick. Everything about Bullard was coarse. He was a large man and gave off an air of military bearing, of no-nonsense command. Maybe even arrogance.

At last, Bullard squared up his papers and clasped his hands in front of him. He sat bolt upright and looked at Caleb with a piercing glare.

"I have heard that you are to be assigned to Race Rock," said Bullard, with no introductions, no small talk. He was all business.

"That's correct."

"Well, I don't think that's going to happen," Bullard said, his gray eyes fixing on Bowen.

Caleb was stunned. "What do you mean? Why not?"

"Why not? Because we had a Bowen at Race Rock and he let the light go out on a stormy night and twenty-nine people died. That's why not." Bullard paused. He stared at Caleb, pinning him in place like a butterfly.

"I never did care for your father. He screwed up. Gave all keepers a bad name. Disgraced the Service. Far as I'm concerned, we don't need another Bowen. Ever. Especially at Race Rock."

The past had caught up with Caleb, just as he had feared. He was speechless.

"If I could, I'd bar you from being on *any* lighthouse. But you've already served and St. Clair seems to want you around. He can have his way, but so can I. You can be a damned keeper. But not on Race Rock."

"Why? Do you think I'd let something happen again? Do you think just because I'm Nathaniel's son I'd let a light go out? My father served for many years and served well. He was dedicated to that light. One night does not define his career."

"It does in my book," said Bullard. "I was one of the men who took him off Race Rock the morning after. I saw the dead bodies washed up. I smelled the alcohol on his breath. It was a sickening situation. As far as I'm concerned, he got off easy. I wish he'd spent years in jail. He'd have had plenty of time to think about what he'd done."

"So you intend to make me pay."

Bullard shrugged, his face set in a stern look. He was enjoying this moment. He had harbored his hatred for Nathaniel for years. He never could have dreamed he'd ever have a chance at revenge, even if it was twisted and misplaced. Bullard picked up a notebook and leafed through it. "Let's see, I think I could reassign you to a support job in, say, Maine."

"You can't..."

"Oh but I can. St. Clair doesn't have the final say on who goes where. I do. I can assign you anyplace I goddamn please!"

Bullard sat back. He looked at Caleb, saw his stricken look. He looked through the journal again. The faintest trace of a smile played across his thin lips.

"No, I have a better idea. I think I'll stick you on Southwest Ledge Light, at the mouth of the Thames River. You can see Race Rock from there. It's just four miles or so away. You'll see Race Rock every damned day, Caleb. But that's all you'll do. You won't serve out there. So close, Caleb. But so far. Southwest Ledge Light. Take it or leave it."

Caleb could barely control his anger. He wanted to jump across the desk and pummel Bullard senseless. He was a bastard, a sick and vindictive jerk. He saw in his eyes what is always in a bully's eyes: weakness masked by aggression.

Bullard went on, enjoying Caleb's torment.

"I'll take your silence as having no objections. You serve on Ledge Light, do your damned job, and keep out of my way. When I come for inspection, you better have that fuckin' place shined and polished and oiled and painted like new or I'll dismiss your ass out of there faster than you can blink. Understood?"

Caleb nodded in a daze. He could not believe it. This man had harbored a grudge for a generation. He would punish a Bowen. Even an innocent Bowen.

"Get out of here," said Bullard. He returned to his papers, head down. The meeting was over.

Caleb stood. His fists were clenched. It took all his will not to attack the man. He walked out of Bullard's office and out to Bank Street in a state of shock. Like St. Clair, Bullard was one of the few people left over from his father's days, and now he had the power to thwart Caleb's plans.

He went to the Custom House and found St. Clair there. He told him what had happened.

"Oh, Jesus," said St. Clair. "I'd forgotten Bullard was around back then. He's a vindictive asshole. We all think so. You put a guy like him in a uniform and he suddenly thinks he's an emperor or something. Really, he's a first-class pain in the ass. But there's good news for you, Caleb. He'll be retiring in six months—a year, at most. Then I'll be in charge. I'll get you to Race Rock and there's nothing that asshole will be able to do about it. You'll just have to wait it out. God, that son-of-a-bitch is a pain!"

"I could kill him," said Caleb.

"You'd be doing us all a favor. Bullard wields regulations like weapons. He beats us all down with them. If he was ever in battle, one of his own men would shoot him in the back and everybody would cheer. Then again, he's the sort of guy who would probably run away from any real danger. He's a desk warrior."

St. Clair shook his head. He looked up at Caleb with a gentle smile. "If you really want to get to Race Rock, Caleb, just hang in there. Think of Bullard as a headwind you have to sail against. He'll blow himself out eventually."

St. Clair had offered Caleb a bit of solace and hope. It calmed him down a bit.

"Maybe he'll drown," he muttered at last.

"Maybe he will," said St. Clair. "Nobody'd throw him a life-preserver."

Caleb found his elusive goal slipping a little further away. At least he had hope. And an ally.

He would bide his time. He had no choice.

2

Southwest Ledge Light was a square red brick building built in 1909. It bridged the gap between Race Rock and New London Harbor light, marking the entrance to the Thames River. It was a unique building. Square, red, with white trim and a mansard roof, it looked like a French chateau, not a lighthouse. It was built that way because two wealthy men of the area, Morton Plant and Edwin Harkness, didn't want to look at an ugly metal can from their mansions in Groton and Waterford. They wanted something more refined, more genteel, more old world. They had enormous clout in the area, and they got their way. Thomas Scott, who had triumphed in building the foundation for Race Rock, rose to the challenge again with Southwest Ledge Light, also built out at sea on a ledge. It seemed to float on the water as if a grand old building had drifted over from France.

For Caleb, serving on Southwest Ledge Light was a kind of torture, just as Bullard had planned. He could see Race Rock. He was only about four miles from it, four miles that seemed an infinity at times. He could hear its horn, see its light. Determination tempered his anguish. He would outlast Bullard.

Caleb polished and painted and kept Ledge Light like new. In spite of his threats and bluster, Bullard never paid him a visit. As St. Clair had promised, Bullard retired on his 65th birthday. There was no party.

St. Clair called him the minute Bullard was officially out of the service. "Okay, Caleb. The jerk is gone. Pack your bags and head out to Race Rock before something else happens."

"Thanks," said Caleb, truly appreciative.

"And Caleb?"

"Yes, sir?"

"For God's sake: don't let the light go out!"

It was a good-humored remark, but Caleb winced when he heard it. Though it had happened decades earlier, his father's failure was a blot on the record of the Lighthouse Service. Time may have faded its memory, but it had not erased it altogether.

On July 10, 1932, twenty-seven years after he had left, Caleb Bowen returned to Race Rock. He had kept the promise made to his father on that hot foggy day. "I'll be back." Now he was.

The emotions swirled through him like wind as the small Lighthouse Service boat from New London approached the lighthouse. His heart beat hard. He was nervous. He had anticipated this day for years. The familiar boulders loomed large as they approached the landing area and passed into the light's shadow. The boat slowed and nudged gently into the cement dock. Caleb looked up at the stone block base and granite lighthouse above. The building was silhouetted against the glare of the sun. For a moment, Caleb just took it all in. Then he stepped onto the dock and into a new chapter in his story.

He ascended the ladder and was greeted by Keeper Hastings, a big man with a moon face, a full beard and an easy smile. He wore wire-rimmed glasses. His uniform was clean, but a little tight. He extended a big paw of a hand to Caleb.

"Welcome aboard," said Hastings.

"It's good to be here," said Caleb. "I've waited a long time."

"So you *wanted* to serve out here?" asked Hastings.

"Yes," said Caleb.

"Well, suit yourself. It's a little hard at first, but you get used to it. To the isolation."

"Won't be a problem," said Caleb, who was looking around, trying to match what he saw with his memories.

"I'll give you a tour," said Hasting, who then turned his attention back to the boat driver.

"Hey, Sheldon!" he yelled.

"What?" the driver yelled back.

"You bring me any beer?"

"It's not allowed. And you don't drink!"

"How about women?"

"It's not allowed. You'll have to catch your own. Maybe you can hook a mermaid."

"Screw you!" yelled Hastings.

"No way!" yelled back Sheldon, who promptly put the small boat in reverse and headed away from the lighthouse.

The two men began their tour. As he walked through Race Rock, Caleb felt an odd mix of familiarity and strangeness. He was trying to reconcile memory with the reality of the place. He had vivid memories of the lighthouse, but much had changed in the intervening years. The walls had been painted many times; most of the furniture had been changed. It was hard for him to tell if some of the pictures on the walls or objects in the rooms might have belonged to his family. He didn't recognize much from his childhood. Perhaps the rocking chair or the desk? The lamp in one of the bedrooms? He went to what had been his bedroom. It was a small room, and looked out toward New London. It was still a bedroom, but that was where the similarity ended. He had never had a calendar with a pinup girl like that! He hadn't expected to find anything of his there and that was the case. A generation of keepers, their families and assistants had lived there and made it their own.

Still, the architecture of the place remained the same, as did the views through the windows in the rooms and along the spiral staircase to the lantern room.

Race Rock was smaller than he'd remembered, but that was a trick often played on people when they return to a place of their childhood. To a three-foot kid, a doorway is enormous. To a six-footer, it's a tighter fit.

Certain rooms and certain views did evoke strong memories, and Caleb let them flood over him as he walked about. The sound of his father trudging up the metal stairway ... his mother humming to herself as she folded laundry in their bedroom ... walks he took around the caisson with his father, endlessly circling the lighthouse as they talked .... watching through one of the arched windows in the stairway as a sailboat disappeared into the fog … clambering over the rocks to fish or collect driftwood … watching his father polish the glass fresnel lens as if it were a rare and priceless jewel.

We all have our personal archives. In the scrapbooks and drawers and shelves of our memories, the events of our lives—big and small—are kept. Sometimes we retrieve them voluntarily. Sometimes we stumble upon them. Reliving memories becomes a new experience added to the archive. Our lives become a palimpsest of experience and memory, a collection of recollections.

It didn't take long to tour the lighthouse, and when they were done, Caleb and Hastings sat in the kitchen and discussed the everyday work of running Race Rock. As they talked, Caleb realized Hastings had no idea he had once lived at Race Rock. He saw no reason to bring it up.

They drank coffee and talked about themselves, like college roommates getting acquainted. "I snore like a bear," said Hastings. "And for that I apologize in advance. If it bothers you, you can turn on the foghorn. That'll drown it out." The big man laughed. "Other than that, I don't have too many annoying habits. I hope."

He continued: "I like to read. I build model boats. I like to play cards. I seldom cheat. I don't drink, but I do chase women. Not that it's easy out here. I go to dances in town. I try not to step on too many toes. If I don't come back, I got lucky." He laughed and Caleb joined him.

"Other than that, Caleb, I don't know what to tell you about myself right now. Oh, I like to cook, as you can see." They laughed at that, too, and Caleb knew that he and Hastings would get along just fine.

"Your turn," the big man said.

Caleb thought for a moment.

"Well," he began, "I don't know if I snore, since I'm usually asleep." He got a laugh with that. Then with a smile, he continued.

"I like to read. I don't build boats. I like to play cards. I sometimes cheat. I don't drink, but I do chase women. I'll go to dances in town. If I don't come back, I got lucky."

Hastings laughed as Caleb parroted his profile back at him. Then he turned serious.

"Well, Caleb, I guess it will take a little time before I know who you really are."

Caleb shrugged. "You'll have plenty of time," he said.

"Yes," said Hastings, "plenty of time. If there is one thing we have out here, it is time. No shortage of that. Time and rust."

Keeper Hastings and Assistant Keeper Bowen settled in to their lives on Race Rock, two men isolated on a tiny island at sea, one working there because it was his duty, the other because it was his destiny.

True to his word, Hastings had few annoying habits and was an excellent cook. He was an easy-going and hardworking man, and the two fell into an easy friendship. Hastings, for all his size, was quite agile. He had the hands of a surgeon, and Caleb marveled as he watched him build his model ships. He strung the lines and glued the tiny pieces in place with great delicacy and precision.

And he did snore like a bear.

Caleb served as assistant to Hastings for a year. At a Fourth of July picnic in New London, enjoying a day of shore leave, Hastings met a woman, got lucky, and decided he'd had enough of the rock's solitary location. He asked for a transfer to a land-based station. It took the bureaucratic wheels a while to turn, but finally, on Christmas Eve 1933, Caleb received the best present of his life: he was officially named head lighthouse keeper of Race Rock.

By the morning of September 21, 1938, Caleb had served as the head keeper at Race Rock for five years. He was in his early forties, his face creased and ruddy, aged prematurely by exposure to sun and wind. His brown hair had only a few wisps of gray here and there.

Caleb was a man of fierce determination and purpose. He enjoyed being keeper of the light, and he served with a pride born of the need to redeem his family name.

Many things from his father's day had not changed much. The light mechanism had been refined, but much of its characteristics and operation were the same. It still ran on kerosene. It still floated on a pan of mercury and spun slowly, driven by weights and gears that needed winding every four hours. The light and the fresnel lens still needed daily attention and maintenance. As he worked, Caleb often thought of the hours, days, and years his father had spent laboring at Race Rock. Polishing the lens. Scraping rust. Painting. Oiling. The daily routine connected them. It was timeless.

Yet some things had changed since Caleb had left Race Rock. New ships plied the waters of Fishers Island Sound. There were sleek submarines, built at Electric Boat, a mile up the Thames and berthed at the sub base a few miles beyond. They came and went on their practice patrols. Airplanes flew overhead on their way north to Boston or south the New York. The loud hum of their propellers could be heard a long time before they appeared overhead and a long time after they disappeared over the horizon. There was even a small airport in Groton, opened in 1929. More homes dotted the shores.

It was a different world from 1907. A busier, faster, more complex world. Yet the rhythms of the sea, of the tides and weather, of daily life on the light were the same. At Race Rock, time seemed to sail in a circle, moving forward yet not really going anywhere.

Sometimes, Caleb wondered if his life was following the same course. He had started here, drifted far away, then returned. The days had become months that had became years. Five years. It had become a blur of maintenance, of the slow passage of the seasons, of weathering storms and living his quiet life. Assistant keepers came and went. Some had become friends, others stayed strangers with whom he shared his home and his work.

Though he would never admit it, the stretch of years and the isolation of his life had begun to take their toll on him. No matter how dedicated they may be, no matter how much they loved their lights, keepers sometimes resented them, too. They resented the metal and stone and wood and glass that consumed their days and eroded away their years.

On the morning of September 21, 1938, Caleb worked his way around the catwalk that circled the lantern room, lost in thought as he scraped away the rust on the metal mullions between the windowpanes. From time to time he would stop and look out to sea, like a cat catching a scent. He could not shake the feeling that there was something just a little off about the day. He studied the sky, the waves, the wind, but he couldn't point to any one thing that seemed amiss. Maybe it was just the pressure changing. He made a mental note to check the barometer and returned to his work.

A gull flew by the top of Race Rock, screeching at the keeper of the light, then banked and headed to sea.

3

As Caleb Bowen was working at the top of Race Rock, Jennifer Hays was slowly getting dressed in her small home on Fishers Island. About a mile off the western point of the island, Race Rock Lighthouse punctuated the sea like the dot of an exclamation point. Jennifer was lost in thought, her mind a swirl of memories and plans, hopes and fears. She lived in the home where she'd grown up, a modest cottage she'd inherited when her parents died. Her mother first of tuberculosis, her father several years later of cancer and grief. She had cared for them both, a wrenching ordeal as she watched them sicken and fade away.

Fishers Island was small, about four miles off the coast of Groton, home to wealthy people who valued their privacy. Her parents had worked on the island, her father at the marina in West Harbor, her mother as a cook at the country club. Jennifer had few friends on the island. Most young people eventually moved away to the mainland where there were more opportunities for work, for love, for life. She had stayed because it was home, but increasingly it felt like a prison.

Jennifer took the morning ferry to New London, where she worked at "Mariner's Widows," a small, underfunded charity that helped the families of men lost at sea. With so much maritime activity in the area, it was a sad fact of life that men often set out to sea never to return. Fishing boats were lost in storms. Freighters sank or succumbed to horrific fires. Men fell from ships and drowned. Some ships disappeared in the fog. Others were lost on distant oceans.

Living on a small island, working at a small charity, Jennifer didn't meet many men. Sure, there were sailors aplenty around

New London, but they were a rough lot and she was wary of them. Their love was about as deep as a reflection on the water and just as fleeting.

The years had passed. Jennifer found herself in her early thirties living a life that was satisfying but lacking. She knew she wanted a man and a family. But where to find that man and how to change her life she did not know. Like so many people, she lived the life she had—always dreaming, always hoping, thinking that next week, next month, next year she would find what she wanted and her "real life" would finally begin. Time, however, is indifferent to such desires. It is a ship that never anchors. It moves and carries us with it, and "pretty soon," can easily become "too late."

Jennifer knew in her heart that there was more to life than her work, to coming home, cooking dinner, then turning on the radio and listening to big band jazz while she read romance novels. The music and the stories took her far away from Fishers Island, to glitzy nightclubs in New York and to far away places where heroic men and beautiful women found adventure and enduring love. She knew that somewhere there was a different life waiting for her, but it was obscured as if by a heavy fog. She did not know how to navigate to it.

Yet fate has its way. Life has its surprises. Like something long adrift that finally washes up onto a beach, the opportunity for change sometimes finds its way to us. We need only see it and seize it.

The morning opportunity came to Jennifer was a clear, crisp, mid-November day. Caleb Bowen had taken his motorboat to the island to fetch some provisions. The supply ship came to Race Rock once a week to restock his staples, but he went ashore every few days to get fresh meat, vegetables, milk and fruit. As he walked from the harbor to the store, Jennifer had been walking down the street coming toward him, holding a bag, her long raven hair peeking out from a floppy hat. She was petite and pretty and smiled at him when their eyes met. He was drawn to her.

Though he had had a few relationships, Caleb was awkward around women. He had no idea how to engage Jennifer, a stranger on the street.

The wind took care of that.

Just as they neared each other, a gust blew her hat off and toward Caleb. He took a few quick steps and retrieved it, then jogged across the street to her.

"Here you go, Miss," he said, smiling at her.

She returned his smile with a dazzling one of her own.

"Thank you," she said.

She was struck by how handsome he looked in his uniform with its shiny brass buttons. There was a moment of silence.

"Well," he said, "I am heading to the store." He couldn't think of anything clever to say to break the ice, and as soon as he said it, he thought how stupid it sounded.

"I just came from there," she said. She looked down at her bag. "Oh, darn. I forgot the corn." She smiled at him. "I guess I'll have to go back."

"It looks like we're headed in the same direction," said Caleb, and they fell in step beside each other.

"You're the lighthouse keeper, aren't you?" she asked.

"Yes. I've been on Race Rock five years. My name is Caleb Bowen."

"Pleased to meet you, Caleb. My name is Jennifer Hays."

They walked to the store, making small talk. Inside, they roamed around together as he picked up some groceries. He picked up a tomato and started to put it in his basket.

"No, not that one," said Jennifer. "It's not so good. This one is better." She handed him a plumper, redder tomato. They shared the often revealing act of shopping for food. Foods reflect one's tastes which reflect one's personality. Jennifer noted he picked basic foods. Nothing exotic. Nothing adventuresome. Was he the same? A straightforward man comfortable with the ordinary?

That was their first meeting. A few days later, Caleb was again ashore and again ran into Jennifer. Later, he would learn that their second meeting was not accidental. She had a view of

Race Rock from her home, and when she saw him leave, she planned another "chance" encounter.

She was interested in him.

From time to time, Caleb would leave Race Rock in the hands of his assistant keeper, Franklin Shaw, and spend an evening with Jennifer. They'd go to a movie at the Garde Theater, in New London, or to a dance at the Lighthouse Inn, a beautiful place that had evolved from the old Guthrie Estate. They'd take the late ferry back to Fishers Island. After a quick kiss, she would head home and he to Race Rock. The ride back at night in his small boat was sometimes an adventure, but worth it to be with her.

She would sometimes visit him during the day on weekends. Though he hoped she might stay a night and make love to him, she would not. Not unless they were married. He understood and accepted her wishes, though he did not stop dreaming about being intimate with her. He would watch her row the mile back to Fishers Island at dusk, a small lantern bobbing at the stern of her boat. She would signal that she was safely home by flashing a light in her bedroom window.

Over time, their love blossomed. Jennifer brought new life to Caleb's small world, and he brought hope to hers. One beautiful June day in 1937, they were strolling along Pequot Avenue. They stopped and sat on the sea wall. The tall white New London Harbor Light was to their left. Ledge Light was out at the mouth of the harbor. In the distance, a small smudge on the horizon, was Race Rock. It was a beautiful panorama. It was a beautiful day. Jennifer was a beautiful woman.

Caleb turned to her and kissed her, lingering more than usual. He reached in his pocket and pulled out a little velvet bag. He opened it, fished inside and pulled out a small diamond ring. He took her left hand and slowly slipped it on her ring finger. It was a good fit. She noticed his hands were shaking.

"Marry me?" he asked. She was surprised, but happy.

"I'd loved to," she replied.

"I wish it were bigger, Jennifer. Something that better reflected how much I love you. But it's the best I could do."

"I love it," she said, wiggling her fingers and watching as the diamond caught the sunlight. It was like a tiny lighthouse on her finger.

"And I love you, Caleb."

They were engaged, and they made plans to marry the following spring.

But life on Race Rock intruded.

In the early spring, Assistant Keeper Shaw was severely hurt in a boating accident. The Lighthouse Service had no replacement ready. The depression had forced cutbacks. Assistant keepers were reassigned to other lights or let go. Caleb was told to make do alone. He asked if Jennifer could join him living there. They were, after all, engaged. But the strict and rather prudish Lighthouse Service said no. Not until they were married.

Jennifer suggested they get married immediately. She could help out at the light. Caleb did not agree. He said he needed some time to get used to doing his work alone. He needed to figure out how to manage all the chores. He would determine what she could do, and it would take time for the Service to approve the plan. It wouldn't take too long. They would get married soon and then they could live together.

Jennifer was disappointed, but did not push. She wondered if he was having second thoughts about marrying her. More likely, she thought, Caleb just needed to make changes in his deliberate, methodical way. Marriage would be a big change for him. She wanted him to be ready. She could wait a few months.

So they postponed their spring wedding and had to settle for being a mile apart. The two shared what time they could, frustrated by being so close and yet so far from one-another. Even when she hadn't been out to visit him, Jennifer would signal Caleb goodnight by blinking the light in her bedroom on and off. It was her own little lighthouse, intended for only one soul at sea.

Time sailed on. Spring turned to summer, summer to fall. The months slipped by, and still they had no wedding date. Caleb was busier than ever at Race Rock, and couldn't seem to focus on the wedding. Whenever she asked, he would say, "soon," and smile and kiss her. He meant it. But soon always became later. She grew angry at Race Rock for consuming his time, and became jealous of the attention he paid the cold stone of his lighthouse.

Now it was September 21, a date that had loomed like a dark cloud for months. Jennifer had decided she had to force Caleb to make a decision, and she had vowed that come hell or high water, she would do it on September 21. It was the autumnal equinox, a date that signaled change, and it was change she wanted. Today would be their moment of truth. It made her nervous. She dressed with a sense of foreboding and dread, thinking of what she wanted to say over and over. She was distracted and tense, her stomach in knots.

She looked at the diamond ring on her finger—the engagement ring Caleb had given her almost a year before. It wasn't big; it was all he could afford on his keeper's salary. She wondered if engagement really meant commitment?

It was time to find out.

Either she and Caleb would set a date for a wedding or she would break off their engagement. She could not drift along like this forever. There was more: she wanted him to leave Race Rock. Once they were married, she did not want to live out there, away from other people, leading a life of isolation. She had grown up on a small island and knew how stifling it could be. How limiting. She had fallen in love with a man who lived on an even smaller island. She could not imagine life on Race Rock. No amount of love could make it bigger. It had taken Caleb's mother, Carla, years to come to the same realization. Jennifer would not repeat that history.

Jennifer knew that asking Caleb to leave would be difficult. Maybe impossible. Race Rock was his life. She knew how wrenching it had been to leave when he was a boy. She knew how long he had worked to get back. Asking him to leave it again would be like asking him to cut out his heart.

His heart.

Hadn't she captured his heart? Did he love her enough to turn his back on his past? If she really loved him, could she ask him to do so? She had debated it in her mind a thousand times, and a thousand times more. On ferry rides, at slow times at work, as she walked to the store, or cooked dinner, or lay in bed listening to the foghorns. For months she had agonized. Finally, she had decided that she *would* ask him. If they were to be happy together and have a life of their own—truly their own—he would have to cast off the anchor of his past. He would have to leave Race Rock.

She thought of the first time she had met him, their lives brought together by a gust of wind. She thought of their early, tentative days getting to know one another. Of their blossoming love and all they had shared. Their love was strong. She wondered if it was strong enough.

Caleb's fierce dedication to Race Rock was born of a need to find some sort of redemption for the Bowen name. She knew all about Nathaniel and what had happened on that stormy night thirty-one years ago. She knew how much it had molded Caleb's personality. She wondered if the side of him that she so loved—his compassion, his wit, his easy manner and generosity—might have developed to balance a more unhappy side. If she took him away from Race Rock and his mission of love, how much would he change? Would the good in him blossom or wither away? It was hard to know. People were complex. They wore their personalities like shells, sometimes trying to protect hidden vulnerabilities within.

Yet she knew that without a push, Caleb might drift along in his life at Race Rock for years. He was not a man of action, not a man to go out and make things happen. Few lighthouse keepers were. They tended to be men who reacted to life: to the weather, to mariners in trouble, to whatever came their way and required them to act. A friend told her that you cannot live somebody else's life for them. Was that what she was trying to do? She shook her head. No. They were engaged; they had a shared life now. She was only trying to move it along to their future.

She sat down on her bed and took a deep breath.

"Caleb," she whispered, "I love you so much. You are my light. Your love guides me, and after my years of being alone and lonely, you have given my life direction and purpose."

She stopped. That was the easy part. Her heart talking.

"I want to be with you. For all our lives. Come what may. And I know you feel the same Caleb; you've asked me to be your wife. But, Caleb, have you thought beyond that to our future? Our lives together?"

No, she thought. I have to talk about the wedding first. She shook her head. Damn! She had figured this out weeks ago. Why couldn't she remember what she wanted to say—how she wanted to say it? Her heart beat fast. She felt a little sick to her stomach. She stood up, walked around, took a deep breath and began again.

"Caleb," she whispered, "I love you so much…."

Jennifer Hays paced in her small room, rehearsing her speech, a woman carrying the terrible burden of a love that was drifting, a love she hoped to guide back on course even as she feared it would run aground and sink.

"You are my light," she continued.

4

As Caleb worked at his morning chores and Jennifer rehearsed her words, Eliot McPherson stood in the dining room at the Lighthouse Inn in New London. He had come up from Washington, D.C. the previous night. Before that had been a long train trip from his home in New Mexico. His first stop had been Washington so that he could visit the National Archives. In its vast storage rooms one could find the minutiae of history—the everyday life at libraries and schools, military bases and post offices, congress and state legislatures, police stations and hospitals, endless government agencies and public facilities.

And lighthouses.

Eliot arrived in Washington early on the morning of September 20. After breakfast at Union Station, he walked down Constitution Avenue to the imposing building of the Archives. Most people came to see the Declaration of Independence and the Constitution. Eliot was after something else. He passed the graceful statues of women seated in flowing gowns that flanked the stairway to the huge old building. Carved into the heavy granite base of one was the phrase "What's Past is Prologue." It was a line borrowed from Shakespeare's *The Tempest*, and it was the motivating spirit behind the archives. Eliot hoped it was true.

He wanted to look at some of the journals from Race Rock. There were logbooks going back to the very first day of the light's operation. All neatly stored in boxes on shelves in rooms at the National Archives.

He walked up the broad front steps and entered what some called the "nation's memory." He went to the front desk and

asked how he should request something. He was directed to
another desk. There he filled out a card: "Journal of Lighthouse
Station of Race Rock Lighthouse, N.Y. for the years 1904, 05,
06 and 07." He handed the card to the woman behind the desk.
She looked at it and pointed to a corridor. "Please go down
there and enter room six. It's the seventh door on the right. We
will pull these journals and bring them to you. It will probably
take us about 30 minutes to find them, if you care to browse
around or go look at the famous documents."

There were already lines to see the Declaration of Independence and Constitution, so Eliot wandered around various
displays. Most featured dry material about preservation tech-
niques, how items were acquired and catalogued, and histories
of the Archives' various departments. He stopped at one labeled
"The Full Landscape of History." What captured his interest
was the description of the "spirit" of an archive. It read:

*What's past is prologue. Our actions and our decisions of today are
based on events of the past. How we deal with our world, our fellow
humans, cultures, lifestyles, and the ebb and flow of history are all
based on what has previously happened. An archive is a repository of
the past—in all its glory, all its tragedy, all its mundaneness. Here
you will find not only records of the great events of history, but also the
minor ones. The small, seemingly insignificant moments that occur
each and every day.*

*History is like a beach. The big events—wars, pioneering voyages
of discovery, revolutions, elections, assassinations, natural disasters—
are like large rocks on the beach. We notice them for their prominence.
The beach the rocks rest on is made of billions upon billions of separate
grains of sand. Likewise, history is made up of the billions and billions
of small decisions and actions of everyday people. It is a landscape of big
events and small ones.*

*An archive is the only place where one can find the full landscape
of history, from its most dramatic features to its smallest and most
humble. They are here for all to see, to study, to interpret and understand. It is we the living who give history meaning and context. It is
upon our past that we build our future. What's past is prologue.*

Eliot found it to be an eloquent and thought-provoking description. One that certainly fit his own life. It was in his mind as he made his way to Room 6, seventh door on the right.

Room 6 was not much more than a cubicle. It had a small table with a lamp, a chair and a wastebasket. No window. On the table, neatly squared with its edges, were two sharp pencils, a pencil sharpener, and a pad of lined paper.

He sat down and waited, still thinking about the metaphor of a beach and history. He wondered what he would find in Race Rock's past.

After a few minutes, the door opened and a white-haired man in glasses rolled in a cart. It was really just a bookcase on wheels. On the top shelf rested four old leather-bound journals.

"I'm Charles Roby, Archivist in the Marine Division of the Domestic Services Sector of the American History Department. I have your materials. You are the patron who requested the Journal of the Light Station Race Rock from 1904 through 1907?"

"Yes. That's me."

Charles Roby continued: "Please be careful of them. Do not mark the pages in any way. Make sure none gets folded or damaged. If you sharpen your pencil, do so away from the documents. Lead dust will soil the paper. Touch the pages only at the edges, as the oils from your fingers can cause stains. Please sign this receipt for the books and this one confirming your responsibility for them until you turn them back over to me. Print your name in block letters where indicated, and please initial here, here and there. Do you have any questions? Is there anything you need?"

Eliot said he understood, and would be very careful of the books. He signed and initialed the forms. He thanked Mr. Roby, who left and quietly closed the door. Eliot smiled. Washington!

The ledgers were about 8 by 13 inches, bound in leather. They smelled musty. The journals of the light station were like old men: ragged at the edges, age spots on their browned covers, somewhat forgotten, but full of stories to tell.

Keepers were required to write daily entries, in ink, noting weather, repairs, supply deliveries, shore leave, visitors, and so on. The books were to be available for review by inspectors on their visits. Yearly, they would be collected and sent to the National Archives, where the journals would be stored in drawers and all but forgotten.

He picked up the first one. On the front cover was printed:

"Race Rock - Lt - Sta.
Journal of Light Station
Lighthouse Service
Department of Commerce
Form 306

Inside, on the first page was written:

"Race Rock Light Station
New York
Year 1904
Nathaniel Bowen, Keeper
United States Lighthouse Board Appointee."

Eliot thumbed through the book to get a feel for it. Written in careful longhand were entries for every day. They were usually short and quite matter-of-fact.

A typical entry read: *"Thursday, April 28: Sunny. Winds from the SSW at 10 knots. Variable. Seas 1-2 feet. Polished lens. Trimmed wicks. Filled fuel reservoirs. Refilled tanks from cistern reservoir. Caulked window above desk. Scraped rust from third-floor stairway railing. Replaced dock rope."*

Each page had maybe ten such entries. Eliot flipped through the journal, and gazed at page after page of meticulously recorded notes, marking the passage of time—and the lifetime of the keeper. Mostly, it was a numbing repetition of weather conditions and daily chores, a procession of weeks and months.

"Saturday, May 14: Stormy. Heavy Rain. Winds from the NE at 30 knots. Waves 4-5 feet. Repaired pulley for davit."

"Friday, June 3: Polished brass window latches. Oiled light gears. Repaired broken mooring ring. Received supplies of oil and water."

"Monday, October 3: Cleaned soot from lantern chimney and fresnel lens. With help of metal worker William Todd, reset loose lightning rod"

"Saturday, December 24: Chipped ice from mooring cleats. Brought coal to first floor. Temporary patch of cracked window glass. New London Harbor Light horn sounds weak—report to Board."

The rhythm of the light was the rhythm of the sea. The tides rose and fell. Storms came and went. The seasons slowly changed the face of the sky and water. Visitors stopped by, and supplies arrived regularly. Occasionally something out of the ordinary warranted mention in the log:

"Aided injured lobsterman."

"Found top hat."

"Rescued near-drowned cat. Scratched me."

"Visited by minister."

The events were written down plainly, without flair or interpretation. If the keepers of the light ever waxed poetic, those lines were written in another journal. The official log-book was, like so many in the archives, a minute—and perhaps meaningless—account of daily life. The grains of sand might create a beach, but that beach might just be a numbing blankness.

Eliot wondered if a keeper ever looked back at the entries, which marked the passage of his life. Each entry was like the tick of a clock, measuring another day spent—and lost—forever. The entries reminded him of the lines scratched on a prison wall marking off the days. The lighthouse seemed, to him, like a prison. A remote place where nameless men served long sentences. The routine seemed relentless and boring. Fuel the light. Scan the horizon. Oil anything that moved. Repair minor damage. Dry things off from the dampness. Polish. Polish. Polish. How did a keeper avoid going crazy? Would he know it if he did? Then again, Eliot thought, does any madman know he's crazy?

Eliot wondered about the keepers' lives. He imagined it must have been very difficult to live in such confined quarters.

A keeper with a wife could not stroll, hand in hand, across a field. They could circle the big drum base, maybe sixty steps around. If they had a child, there was no yard to play in. No friends. The vast expanse of water that surrounded them was more often than not a threat. The weather could be very rough. In the winter, when the building iced up, they would have to stay inside. How did they endure the isolation? The confinement?

Eliot supposed they went ashore from time to time. From Fishers Island they could take a ferry to New London. And from there a train to Boston or New York. How odd a huge, congested, noisy city would have seemed to a keeper of the light! Instead of looking out to the horizon, their view would be stopped short by the city's walls. He wondered if, in the city, they felt a different sort of isolation and confinement?

To browse through the journals was saddening. Nathaniel Bowen seemed a forgotten man living out a forgotten life. He served with dedication, but what he did was taken for granted. Eliot thought of all the books in the archives, of all the forgotten people doing their jobs. Each a grain of sand lost among a billion others.

Some pages were stained by water. A few included a rough sketch of a repair job or an idea for some small improvement to the workings of the light. Most were just a few lines of entry for the day. Eliot was not sure that Nathaniel Bowen had written down what he sought. The only way to find out was to read through the logbooks, the record of his daily existence. Eliot didn't know exact dates, so he'd have to review every day and hope he found what he was after.

Eliot started reading carefully, entry by entry, page by page. Nothing in the first book. He moved on to 1905. It took him an hour to find the first entry he sought. The second took longer, almost an hour and a half. It was in the 1906 Journal of the Light Station. He very carefully wrote them down verbatim, using one of the Archive's pencils, in a little notebook he carried.

Eliot smiled. He closed the old journal. He tried to imagine it on a desk at the lighthouse, the keeper hunched over it, filling in the entries. The notes gave little feel for the man who wrote them. There was nothing personal in the pages, no suggestion of emotion or character. For them he would have to search elsewhere.

He rang a small buzzer and in a few minutes Charles Roby appeared again. Eliot showed him the journals, carefully piled on the small desk. Roby thumbed through all three of them, nodded and methodically wrote up a final receipt for the books. "Journals of the Lighthouse Station Race Rock, Years 1904–1907, returned in the condition of delivery."

He asked Eliot to sign and initial the receipt, a carbon triplicate. He ripped off the top paper and gave it to Eliot. He retained the other two. No doubt they would go into files somewhere in the Archive. Files about files about files. A maze of interlocking references, an infinity of grains of sand.

"Has anyone ever requisitioned these journals before?" Eliot asked Mr. Roby.

"Nope. According to the records, you're the first. What did you think of them?"

"To be honest," said Eliot, "I found them kind of sad. The daily chores. Endlessly repetitive. Fixing things. Polishing things. Lighting the light. It seems like a numbing kind of life."

"Perhaps," said Roby. "But some jobs require that kind of repetitive precision, you know. Some people like having structure to their work. They take comfort in the familiarity of the routine. Instead of trying to always master new things, it lets them concentrate on perfecting what they know."

"I suppose," said Eliot, "but it seems boring. Never much change except the seasons."

"Change is our least efficient behavior," said Charles Roby. "It can cause problems. Routine helps things run smoothly." He carefully inspected the two pencils, sharpened one a bit, and placed them both back on the desk, perfectly aligned with its edge. He placed the books on the rolling cart.

"Anything else you need?" he asked Eliot.

"No. Thank you for your help, Mr. Roby."

"You're quite welcome, sir," said the archivist. "If we can ever be of further assistance, please don't hesitate to visit the Archives again. I hope you found what you were after."

"I did, Mr. Roby. I did. Thank you."

Eliot went to the request desk and thanked the woman for her help and left the vast old Archives building. The Washington day was sunny and cool. He decided to walk to Union Station, where he could catch the 2pm train north. He would be in New London by mid-evening.

He whistled as he walked along Constitution Avenue. The old dead files of the archives had yielded up their secrets.

5

The train ride from Washington to New London had been relaxing. Eliot watched the countryside glide by as the train made its way up the East coast. Baltimore, Philadelphia, Wilmington, Trenton, Newark, and New York all passed by. Businessmen in suits chatted away and smoked cigars, filling the car with a blue haze of smoke. He ignored them, preferring to gaze out the window, watch the scenery, and think.

As the train began to hug the shore, he caught frequent glimpses of the ocean. He had only seen it a few times before, always at a distance. Eliot had grown up in Kentucky, Texas, even central Alaska for a time. He lived in New Mexico now. Most were places far from the sea, and he was excited to be seeing it at last.

He had called ahead and arranged to stay at the Lighthouse Inn. He'd also rented a small motorboat. He had done enough boating on small lakes to feel confident on the water. He knew the ocean would be more challenging, but he was determined to get out to Race Rock.

The train left New York and made its way along the coast of Connecticut. As they passed through Stamford, Bridgeport, and New Haven, Eliot saw fishing boats, sea gulls and the occasional lighthouse drift by the large picture window of the train. The water stretched to the horizon. It was beautiful country, so very different from what he'd known. At Old Saybrook, he left the train long enough to stretch his legs and smell the salty air. He was excited. His long journey across the country to Washington and through the journals of Race Rock was behind him. Tomorrow he would at last see the lighthouse first hand.

He arrived at Union Station in New London at eight o'clock and took a taxi to the Lighthouse Inn. It was a grand old place, once the private Guthrie mansion. It was decorated with panels of dark wood, floral wallpaper, and plush carpets. The furniture was Victorian—heavy and comfortable. Beautiful chandeliers and sconces provided the light, and a dramatic winding staircase curled to the second floor. The main dining rooms, lounge and bar were inviting, warmed by crackling fires.

The dining room had a beautiful view of the Thames River and Long Island Sound. He dined there watching the changing mood of the sky and water as night fell. After dinner, he walked down to the street to Pequot Avenue. He hopped over the stone seawall and walked along the beach. He thought about that passage he'd read at the Archives. The landscape of history. A beach. Grains of sand. He picked up a handful. It was fine and white, like silk to the touch. He let it trickle through his fingers and watched it float away in the light breeze. Eliot savored the smells, the sound of the surf, the lights of passing boats reflected in the calm sea.

He could see the area's three lighthouses blinking. Closest was New London Harbor Light, at the end of the beach. It was a tall white octagonal tower. Out at the mouth of the harbor, where the Thames River met Fishers Island Sound, was the square red Southwest Ledge Lighthouse. Way out, was the tiny light of Race Rock. It seemed a long way away, blinking on the horizon like a fallen star. While most sailors used it to steer by on their way through the Sound, for him, it was the end of a long journey. His destination.

"Tomorrow," Eliot thought. "Tomorrow I'll finally go out there."

He retuned to his room and fell asleep to the sound of the surf.

* * *

The next morning, September 21, he was up early and back in the dining room for breakfast. While he waited for coffee, he sauntered over to a telescope by the window. He swung it around and trained it on the distant speck that seemed to float on the sea. Race Rock. Eliot brought the image into focus. What had been a dark spot on the horizon now resolved into the distinctive shape of the lighthouse: its small island of rocks, the massive circular stone base, the sturdy granite house and the tower that rose along one side. The day was clear, and he could even see a figure moving around the catwalk at the top. That would be Caleb Bowen, the lighthouse keeper.

The red sky was giving way to pink tinged with blue as the sun rose higher over Eastern Point in Groton. He could see Black Rock just offshore, a low, jagged shape. The full moon was still large and bright in the sky.

Eliot had to get to Burr's Dock, a few miles down Pequot Avenue toward town, by late morning to pick up the small boat he'd rented. He hoped to squeeze in a quick trip to the local paper, the New London Day, to search its archives. There were still bits of history to be researched and verified, pieces of the puzzle to be filled in.

The waiter brought coffee and muffins to his table. He ate a bit then returned to the telescope and studied the lighthouse some more. It was strange to look at it through the telescope. It brought the lighthouse up close, but in silence, as if the sound had been switched off in a movie. Visually, he was out there four miles, looking at the keeper as a seagull flying by might. But he was hearing the clatter of dishes, the cooks and waitresses talking about the baseball pennant race. It was an odd dissonance, a merging of two worlds.

Eliot took out his small notebook. Thumbed through a few pages and read the notes scribbled there. He looked back through the telescope. He was looking forward to his visit to Race Rock.

He went to the bar to pay for his breakfast. As the cashier tallied his bill, Eliot glanced at the rows of pictures that lined the wood walls of the room. They were a capsule history of New London, the Inn, and the surrounding seas. His eyes settled on one of Race Rock. It was a sepia photograph, slightly tilted. Probably taken from a small boat.

"Ever been out there?" he asked the cashier, pointing to the photograph.

"Not on it. Nope. But I've fished out there. Great spot for blues and bass, right along the riptide. You a fisherman?"

"Of a sort. I'm a journalist."

"You going out to the lighthouse?"

"Yes, I am. I'm working on a story about it. I hope to spend the day learning how it works and some of its history. I want to talk with the keeper about his job." Eliot paused a moment, smiled, and continued. "I guess I'm fishing in a way—for information."

"Well, good luck. Looks like you picked a nice day."

"Yes, sunny and calm."

"Hope you find what you're after."

"Thanks. Me too." Eliot gathered his change, left a tip, and headed out of the restaurant.

* * *

Out on Race Rock, Caleb Bowen slowly made his way around the narrow metal catwalk. He spotted a tiny hole in one of the lead mullions. Something to be patched. A whiff of a breeze stirred the calm morning waters.

Jennifer Hays left her home and made the short walk to the nearby pier where her rowboat was docked. Her mood was a mix of dread and hope. She curled a lock of hair nervously in her fingers as she went through her words to Caleb yet again. Seagulls wheeled overhead, seemingly agitated.

Eliot McPherson rode a cab along Pequot Avenue to the offices of The Day in downtown New London. He jotted some thoughts in his notebook.

The sun crept higher into the sky. The morning of September 21 unfolded calmly as summer turned to fall. As with any change of season, the day brought with it a sense of expectation.

6

On the morning of September 21, something else was heading toward Race Rock.

A storm.

The first signs of it had been noted weeks earlier, on September 4. A French weather observer at the Bilma Oasis in the Sahara Desert noted a wind shift. The man, Phillipe Le Tendre, of the French Foreign Weather Information Gathering Service, sat in a tent. It was large enough to accommodate a few cots, a table, some chairs and piles of testing gear. Le Tendre was not too thrilled with his current assignment in the middle of nowhere watching flags flap and measuring temperature and barometric fluctuations. It was a kind of punishment, one he'd earned by being just a bit too wild for the folks in Provence.

Le Tendre sat in the shade of the tent reading a magazine. He heard the wind and looked out at the desert sands. It was afternoon and blindingly bright. On top of a tall pole, a red flag flapped in the breeze. It had been pointing east for most of the day, then suddenly swung west. It stayed there as the wind picked up a bit. "Merde," he mumbled as he noted the wind shift in his logbook. It was a book full of numbers and directions and notations that only a few could read and probably no one ever would. Someday it would wind up in an archive. The 180-degree wind shift created a small vortex that carved a gentle swirl in the pattern of the sands, like a comma. A tiny spin. It kicked up a small cloud of sand that quickly settled as the breeze moved on. Le Tendre watched it pass and returned to his reading.

The whiff of wind drifted west slowly, ebbing and flowing, never quite dying out. It traveled for miles, a gentle swirling breeze that fed off the radiant heat of the desert. As this mild disturbance moved west off Africa and over the ocean around September 10, it gathered more energy, fueled by the temperature gradient where warm water met cool air. It grew larger and started to rotate. Alone at sea, it tracked west. Its spin tightened and it picked up speed. Across the vast expanse of the ocean, it grew and gathered form: a tight elliptical core, long tendrils flaring out. The spin grew tighter; the winds grew faster; an eye formed in its center. By the time it reached the Cape Verde Islands, the breeze had evolved into a tropical storm. It was like an angry person, muttering to itself, getting more and more agitated with time.

The storm continued to move west across the Atlantic, picking up speed as it did. By September 16, when the Brazilian freighter *Alegrete* sailed through the storm, it had winds of 75 miles per hour. By September 19, it was just east of the Bahamas, and ships at sea were estimating its winds at a frightening 160 miles per hour. The gentle breeze of the African desert had turned into a ferocious beast in the southern waters off America. It was dangerous, and it was quickly heading toward the coast.

As the storm neared Florida, forecasters at the Washington, D.C., Weather Bureau office assumed it would follow the same path other storms had for decades. They believed its track would take it back out to sea. Just its fringes would brush the coast.

At 9 in the morning on Wednesday, September 21, the storm was reported off the coast of Cape Hatteras, North Carolina. Passing near the Cape, the Cunard liner *Carinthia* reported a barometric pressure of 27.85 millibars. This storm was not heading out to sea, but was moving straight north, following the track of the devastating storms of 1635 and 1815. A few weathermen noted this trend and began to worry. If a storm this big followed the course of those two storms, the results would be catastrophic. Their worry lagged behind the reality of the storm. It shot up the eastern seaboard like a bullet, and their cry of alarm would be left behind, too faint, too late.

Rain had been falling in the northeastern United States intermittently for days before September 21, fueled by a trough of low pressure in the atmosphere. The hurricane moved rapidly in this warm, moist pathway. A large high pressure system over the Maritimes of Canada blocked the storm from moving out to sea as it headed north. The earth was already saturated from the days of rainfall, with streams and rivers full to their banks across New England. The tide was astronomically high at the autumnal equinox, when both the sun and the moon's gravity tug at the sea. The stage was set for an attack by all aspects of the storm: wind, rain, and storm surge.

The storm barreled up the coast. It crossed the Outer Banks, then Maryland. It raced toward New Jersey and Long Island, inexorably heading to New London. If it stayed on that trajectory, Race Rock would be directly in its path.

Ashore, barometers in New England, which had started the day at 30 millibars of pressure, began to dip. The needle inched from "fair" to "change." At the weather station in Groton, the officer on watch—Michael Shivers—noticed it. He looked up from the morning newspaper and listened. Flags flapped in a freshening breeze, their snapping sounds a percussive accompaniment to the windchime-like music of halyards striking masts on moored sailboats. The wind was strong enough to dislodge leaves from trees—the first of the fall season. A stiffening breeze was nothing unusual in New England. No warnings had been issued.

People went about their daily lives, oblivious to the danger bearing down on them.

7

Eliot spent a few hours looking through the archives at the offices of The Day. After reading brittle old newspapers, he'd had enough of the dusty past. He was eager to get out into the air and the sun, out on the sea, out to Race Rock. He made it to Burr's Dock by late morning to pick up the small motorboat he'd rented. A guy named Paul Tremain was working. He held the 15-foot boat's bowline and walked it to the end of the dock where there was a ladder. Eliot paid him and climbed down into the boat. He handed a spare life vest up to him. "Right. Got it!" Tremain said and tossed the bowline down to him.

"Sure you know how to handle this?" Tremain asked.

"Yes, positive."

"Maybe you oughta wear that," Tremain said, pointing to another life-vest on the boat's bench.

"Maybe when I get out a ways," said Eliot, absently.

"Have a safe trip. Watch out for the currents. Careful of the tides," Tremain continued.

"Don't hit anything," muttered Eliot.

"Don't hit any rocks," Tremain called down.

Eliot gunned the engine and the boat jumped away from the dock. He pulled the tiller and the boat swung toward the mouth of the Thames River a few miles to the south. He could see Race Rock, a tiny blob on the horizon.

The wind had built to a steady 20 knots. Enough to ruffle the waters and slap the face. Eliot gripped the motor throttle and tiller and tried to figure out how to ride the chop. This was nothing like puttering around on the lake back in Kentucky. He'd left Burr's Dock full of confidence. Thirty minutes later, as he neared the New London Southwest Ledge Lighthouse, he was getting anxious. Though Long Island Sound wasn't technically the Atlantic Ocean, it connected to it and behaved like it. The dark, green, foaming and hissing waters around him were unnerving. The spray was cold.

Eliot caught himself imagining sharp-toothed fish and nasty crabs down below in the murky water, just waiting for him to screw up. Were there sharks up here?

The boat pitched and yawed and bucked and rolled as he made his way toward Race Rock. It still seemed a long way away. He was going very slowly. He thought that would help, but it didn't seem to. A few times he caught a wave sideways and thought he'd capsize. He'd drown in the sea. The thought started to rattle him. He clenched the tiller and tried to steer and willed the lighthouse to get closer. His free hand dipped into his pocket and fingered a cool metal case. It lingered a moment, then withdrew.

As he passed Southwest Ledge Light, with its massive concrete base and mansard roof, he almost turned toward it. The red brick building, three stories high, perched on its thirty-foot base, looked solid and inviting. He wanted to give up, head over there and seek refuge. Get the lighthouse keeper to take him back to shore. He didn't belong out here. He should have hired a bigger boat, or better, a bigger boat with a captain to get him to Race Rock in one piece!

But he didn't turn. He wouldn't let his fear deflect his course. He just had to do this once. Get out there and get back. He wasn't out in a storm, after all. It was just a little wind. He rocked the tiller and kept his boat pointed toward the shape ahead.

By noon he had cleared Ledge Light and was into Long Island Sound. New London dropped back behind him. Eastern Point curved off to his left, a spit of land dotted with impressive summer cottages. More like mansions. They were huge Victorian buildings of cedar and stone. They had broad porches and big green lawns that stretched to water's edge. They were the homes of the wealthy who flocked to New London and Groton for summer fun. The stately Griswold Hotel stretched along

Eastern Point, a broad white edifice. A few yachts bobbed in the waters off its pier.

It was an area full of boats and tradition. June brought hordes to see the Harvard-Yale rowing regatta, the oldest college event in America. Some summers, impressive yachts came to the area as the wealthy descended to watch the America's Cup, held in Newport, Rhode Island, just a day's sail up the coast.

New London had once been a great whaling port, second only to New Bedford in the hundreds of ships it sent to sea. Though it still boasted a large and active fishing fleet, New London had evolved over the years into a recreation and transportation hub, where trains and ferries moved people to Boston and New York and Long Island. Except for the downtown district, most of the New London coast was dotted with homes perched near the water. Especially where the river widened into the Sound. There, the wooden cottages were packed tight, like a flock of ducks trying to stay as close to the water as possible.

Groton, on the east bank of the Thames, became an industrial power. The Electric Boat shipyard built submarines, and its cranes and sheds spread along much of the Groton bank. Next to it, where the coast widened at the mouth of the Thames River, Atlantic Coast Fisheries filled the shore with buildings and docks.

Halfway between New York and Boston, the Groton-New London area was a less pretentious alternative to the mannered and stifling social scene of Newport. The area was a vibrant mix of sprawling mansions and trim summer cottages, industry and transportation, rowdy bars catering to sailors and fine restaurants welcoming the wealthy.

Eliot took it all in despite his growing anxiety. Another day, he might have enjoyed his visit as a tourist. But this late September morning, he was on a mission. He pushed his little powerboat on, into Long Island Sound, where the waves grew steeper and the wind blew stronger. Race Rock still seemed an ocean away.

Eliot knew why Race Rock had gotten its name. He knew that around the lighthouse, three currents collided to create treacherous waters. As he looked ahead across the Sound, he could see up ahead, in front of the lighthouse, the whitecaps were more frequent, the waves more violent.

"Watch the currents. Mind the tides. Don't hit any rocks. Shit!" he cursed to himself.

He slowed his boat as he hit the open waters at the tip of Eastern Point with its grand old beach house. He spotted the small Coast Guard weather shack down the road from it. Just off the point, Black Rock looked like the back of a whale breaking through the waves. A few cormorants sat on the rock, holding their wings up and out, drying them. The birds slowly turned their heads to watch the little boat go by.

Gripping the tiller, jaw set in grim determination, Eliot continued on toward Race Rock.

8

B y early afternoon, the storm was beginning to pummel New Jersey. It was hugging the eastern seaboard as it raced northward at sixty miles an hour. It showed no signs of veering off to sea. No signs of weakening. If anything, its spiral had grown tighter, its winds more fierce. It pushed ahead of it a storm surge that added to the already high waters of the equinox high tide.

The Groton Regional Weather Station was located at the corner of Shore Avenue and Beach Pond Road near the Eastern Point Beach. "Station" was a name that was official sounding but inaccurate. It was a small building, not much more than a wooden shack. The instruments themselves were outside collecting data on wind speed and direction, rainfall, barometric pressure, temperature and humidity. It was manned by Coast Guard junior personnel, who pulled eight-hour shifts.

The shack had a single window that looked south toward Long Island. One could see both Race Rock and the Ledge Light from it. Other than that, it had a folding chair, table, hot plate, a few shelves of reference books, some cans of coffee and a file cabinet. There was no phone, just a radio link to the main Coast Guard base in New London. Tacked above the radio was a small hand-lettered sign "If it's broke, fix it." The men were expected to keep the gear operational. It was a cramped place, hot in the summer and cold in the winter. There was no bathroom. The men had to use a bucket or take a stroll down to the beach.

It was usually a boring assignment. The man on watch would note the hourly readings in a small notebook. Some guys slept half their watch and made up whatever readings they missed. They could listen to the radio, read newspapers, books, or dirty magazines. Sometimes they flirted with the girls who came down to the beach. The shack was so cramped it was hard to sneak a girl in for a little fun, though it had been tried. One time, in the middle of fooling around, a girl managed to lean on the radio transmit button. The couple's sounds of passion was broadcast back to base headquarters. After listening in amusement for a while, the commander of the watch put an end to the tryst by blowing a very loud air horn into the microphone of the open channel. Both the girl and the cadet were scared half to death. She left quickly. The cadet was reprimanded and disciplined by being assigned another thirty days at the weather shack. It was the worst punishment the commander could think up.

On this day, Seaman Michael Shivers was on duty, taking the 8am to 4pm shift. He was well into his second pot of coffee by early afternoon. He frowned as he noted the barometer had dropped to 29. The winds were steadily increasing with some strong gusts. The seas were more choppy, dotted with whitecaps. High tide would come later in the day. He knew it would be a very high one. The radio squawked.

"Shivers?" It was the commander of the watch.

"Yessir?"

"Shivers, looks like you will have to stay there until 8 or so tonight. Jenson's delayed in Newport and I have nobody else to relieve you."

Shivers thought to himself, "Fuck! Shit! Trapped in this little hellhole an extra four hours! Goddamn!"

He said: "That will be fine, sir."

The radio clicked off without an acknowledgement. In the military, after all, it was an order, not a request.

"I'll relieve myself, sir," mumbled Shivers. "I'll relieve myself on your fuckin' desk!"

On the hour, he wrote the data in his logbook and returned to reading the sports section of The Day. He'd already read the comics. The Red Sox had won again. This year, he felt in his bones, the Sox would finally win the World Series.

The barometer ticked down to 28.8, but he was too absorbed in the box scores to notice.

At about the same time, the steamer *Catskill* left New London for the three-hour trip to Montauk Point on Long Island. There were 65 passengers and 10 automobiles aboard. Captain Charles Freedman had made the trip hundreds of times. The ferries from New London to Montauk Point, Block Island, Fishers Island and Orient Point were like buses. One always seemed to be passing by. They kept to a rigid schedule. Head out, make the transit, spend an hour or so at dock unloading and reloading people, cars and supplies, then head back. Over and over, all day, every day. The ferries went in winter storms and summer fog. It was an area with good lighthouses to help with navigation, and the skippers relied on them.

Freedman wasn't bothered by the wind or chop. His boat was broad and heavy and rode the seas well. He knew the area so well he didn't need charts. He knew every rock and buoy, every current and riptide, the shallow spots and the ledges. He knew how the wind came off the land and where to watch out for boaters who had no idea what they were doing and strayed into the shipping channels. The *Catskill* rounded Southwest Ledge Light and headed SSE toward Montauk Point. He noted a small motorboat on its way to Race Rock. He thought it crazy to be out in this ragged sea in such a small boat. He shrugged and lit a cigarette.

9

The oars slapped the water in a steady rhythm. The wind was brisk and the seas were choppy, but nothing Jennifer couldn't handle. She had a motor, but she preferred to row. She liked the exercise, and this morning, it helped her burn off some of her nervous energy. She rowed with her back to Race Rock, judging her course by her house on Fishers Island. If she kept it centered on her stern, she would hold a straight line to the lighthouse. Nonetheless, as rowers do, she turned around every so often to look at Race Rock. It got unnerving to head for too long at something you could not see. Which, in a way, was why she was heading to the lighthouse today. For too long, she and Caleb had headed toward something blindly. Yes, they would be married. But when? The currents of life seemed to slow their progress, to push them away from their goal. She needed to do something.

"Caleb, I love you so much. You are my light. Your love guides me..." She didn't even realize that she had been whispering her words as she rowed.

"After my years of being alone and lonely, you have given my life direction and purpose..."

A few gulls swooped in circles around her, calling in their throaty squawks. Their paths were jerky, full of quick turns and changes of direction. They seemed agitated.

Her favorite bird, a black cormorant, flew by. She smiled as the bird streaked just inches above the water, wings close but never touching. Its reflection was like a shadow beneath it. She watched until it disappeared in the distance. She had once heard that birds were the spirits of dead people, free now to swoop and glide and watch mortals go about their lives. She liked that thought and wondered who the cormorant might be. She hoped that someday she would be a spirit riding the wind. The sun, though up, was losing its battle against some gathering clouds, and the color began to drain away. The scene was turning gray.

She was nearer to Race Rock. Even without turning, she could tell by the growl of the waves breaking against the huge boulders at its base. She turned and saw Caleb standing on the catwalk, facing in her direction, watching her approach. She pulled in an oar for a minute and waved to him. He waved back and headed into the lantern room.

She started to row again. She looked back at Fishers Island and over to Eastern Point in Groton with its fringe of offshore rocks. Lost for a moment in reverie, she thought of a night long ago when Caleb's father had triggered a series of sad and fatal events. Her mind played the movie she had crafted over the years. The fierce storm, the collision with Race Point, the ship shattering and going on, spilling parts and lives into the cold black sea. She shook her head and cleared the images and turned toward the lighthouse again. Caleb was walking on the caisson toward the ladder.

Jennifer switched to alternate oars as she threaded the passage in the rocks to the landing area. Right oar, right oar, left, right, left. She crabbed her way in, riding the waves toward the dock. By the time she got there, Caleb had arrived. With finesse she parked the boat gently against the slab of stone and tossed him the bowline. He caught it and snugged it to the cleat. She smiled as she saw him give it his extra safety twist and pull tight checking it. He always did so. He was never careless tying a boat to the lighthouse. She flipped rubber bumpers over the side and crawled across the bench toward Caleb's outstretched hand.

"Permission to come aboard, sir?" she asked with a smile.

"Permission granted," he said. It was their standard greeting, another ritual.

She hopped off the boat just as a wave rolled under it throwing her off balance. She collided with Caleb. He caught her in his arms and wrapped them around her in a hug. He gave her a kiss and they stood here, two small figures amidst the crashing waves at the base of the heavy stone structure. The wind blew, the sea surged. They hugged and enjoyed the moment, though Jennifer's mind was in turmoil over what she wanted to say this fall day.

"It's getting cold," said Caleb. "Let's get inside."

They climbed the ladder to the caisson. Jennifer was agile and seemed to float up the rungs. Caleb turned the heavy knob of the massive wood door and pulled it open. It didn't make a sound. Not a creak or groan. It was well oiled.

They stepped inside and Caleb closed the door. The world of wind and water vanished. They were in the cozy living room.

"I missed you," said Caleb, smiling at Jennifer. "I didn't expect you out here today, but I'm glad you came."

Jennifer smiled back. She looked at him and felt such conflicting feelings. She knew what was about to happen. He didn't. His smile made him seem so vulnerable. So innocent. She had steeled herself to be combative and forceful with him. But now that she was with him, her resolve was not so fierce. She mustered up a smile and walked past him so that he wouldn't catch the anxiety in her eyes. She tried to think of what to say.

"I've missed you too," she said. They hadn't seen one another in over a week. She *did* miss him. No lie there.

"Would you like some coffee?" he asked.

"Yes, I need to warm up from the row. It's getting windier."

"Yes, I noticed. Funny ... at dawn, the day was so still. It was eerie. Unsettling. I can't put my finger on it, but something's in the air."

She thought that maybe he was picking up her mood.

"I think a storm is coming, Caleb. A front's moving in. Fast."

"I think you're right. The barometer's been dropping all morning. You might get trapped out here."

"I'm sure you wouldn't mind that," she said.

"I'm here to aid mariners in need," he said with a wink.

The living room had three doors. One went to the spiral staircase in the tower, one to the kitchen, and the third was the door that led out to the caisson. Caleb walked into the kitchen, went to the coffee pot that steamed away on the stove, and started preparing two cups. As she waited, she looked around at the small living room. It was functional but cozy. A sofa, small table and two chairs. A beat up Oriental rug. A few lamps. A bookshelf full of books. The mantle over the fireplace held a few knickknacks, a candlestick and a clock. Above it was a watercolor of a lighthouse keeper peering through a telescope.

"Anything interesting happen this week?" she asked, wondering if he heard the tremor in her voice. She would have to get to her talk quickly or she'd lose nerve.

"Out here? Not much. The usual," he said.

Caleb walked in and handed her a steaming mug of coffee. She took it, grateful for the momentary diversion. The bubbles from the cream he'd stirred in spun in a tight spiral, like a cloud. She looked down into the black liquid and saw herself reflected in it, her face shimmering and pale. A ghost.

She took a sip. The tick of the clock on the mantle seemed to fill the room. Or maybe it was her heartbeat. She was nervous. Her stomach fluttered. It was now or never.

"Caleb, we need to talk." It was the timeless prelude to all serious conversations about love and relationships.

"Talk?" he asked.

"Yes."

She sat down. She glanced up at him and then down into her steaming mug again, as if the swirling galaxy of bubbles held the secret to the universe. Why was this so difficult? She loved him. He loved her. All she wanted to do was get on with their lives together.

She cleared her throat, looked up at him and held his gaze. She composed herself, took a deep breath and began.

"Caleb," she said, "I love you so much."

10

The motor hummed in a steady drone. When the boat headed down the face of a wave, the prop came out of the water and revved with a nerve-wracking whine. Eliot was out in open waters, a few miles from land, and he was anxious. At least the damned lighthouse was at last close. Race Rock had slowly transformed from a dark shape to a series of parts: the jagged boulders of the riprap, the heavy rectangular blocks of the caisson, the mix of stone, windows and angular roofs that made up the house. It looked like a Bavarian castle incongruously awash, like nothing Eliot had ever seen. It was dreamlike. It looked a lot more imposing than it had through the lens of the telescope. Then it has seemed like a phantom place, afloat on the water. Now it seemed a fortress, a heavy stone building rising out of the sea like a sculpted rock. Solid. Immovable. A defiant challenge to the sea.

He was only a few hundred yards away from Race Rock. There was a clear spine of sharp, pointed waves that defined the edge of the rip tide. He could see how the waters changed around him. The sky had become more threatening, the wind was gusting, and the seas had grown heavier in response. Eliot found himself riding six-foot waves. Some rolled under him while others crashed over the bow of the little boat. He tried taking them at an angle as he worked toward the light. He was beginning to wonder how he would dock at the lighthouse and where. He'd have to circle it and see if there was a dock.

The wind and spray were cold, but Eliot was sweating. Partly from the exertions of steering and trying to keep his balance in the pitching boat, and partly from anxiety. Though he'd never been on the ocean, Eliot thought he had a feel for it from books and movies. The real thing had turned out to be quite a surprise—bigger, more unpredictable and more threatening.

The closer he drew, the more Race Rock loomed, isolated and forbidding. The lighthouse was its own island, its own little world, perched on a pile of rocks in the middle of the water. From afar the rocks looked big, but at a hundred yards they were huge—each the size of a car! The waters around them swirled and boiled. The waves crashed against them and the wind caught the spray. Water threaded through the gaps between the boulders.

"I hope this is worth it," he mumbled to himself as he gripped the tiller and dodged the cold salt spray.

The motor rumbled and Eliot eyed it nervously. If it stopped he'd be in trouble. He'd have no way to steer and he'd be smashed against the rocks. He tightened his grip on the tiller and swung out to orbit Race Rock and look for a place to land his boat. He circled around toward Fishers Island and spotted the slot in the boulders. There was a small boat already there. He swung around and tried to line his boat up with the entry notch. He realized he would get only one chance at this.

The waves and wind and currents made it hard to hold a true course, and he had to saw the tiller wildly to keep the nose of the boat headed into the narrow slot. He managed to do so with only a few bumps along the sides. It was a bit calmer once he was in the narrow channel in the rocks. He nudged the bow against the end of the dock with a thump. He killed the engine and stumbled forward to grab the line at the bow. He realized he needed help to tie the boat up.

He looked up at the dock. It was only twenty feet of flat concrete, covered with bird droppings and glistening wet. In its middle, a metal ladder rose up the side of the stone caisson. The lighthouse rose above that, a forbidding angular shape against the stormy sky.

He was shaking. He wanted to get off this damned little boat and on to solid ground—if that's what Race Rock was.

He had come a long, long way. He was finally at the lighthouse. He hoped he could get what he wanted and head back home and leave the sea far behind. He didn't care if he ever saw it again.

11

Jennifer had spoken but one sentence of her prepared speech. Her serious tone had caught Caleb's attention and sent a sudden chill threw him. He could see that she was troubled. Her face was anguished.

"Is everything all right?" he interrupted.

Jennifer sighed. She tried to remember her speech, so carefully considered and rehearsed over the past few months. But now, looking into his bewildered eyes, she was not sure she could continue. She had taken the leap, and now she wished she could reverse her fall.

"Caleb," she said, "I'm fine. I just want to talk about us." She tried to get back on track. She began again.

" I love you so much…."

They both heard it. A shout from outside. Near.

"Ahoy!"

They looked at each other, frowning. They heard it again.

"Ahoy!"

Who the hell said: "Ahoy?" No mariner used that word anymore. It was something from adventure novels and swash-buckling pirate movies.

"Ahoy! Ahoy!" The cry was repeated with increasing urgency.

"Just a sec," said Caleb as he walked by her and gazed out the window next to the door. "I can't see anyone."

They heard it again. An anguished cry. Caleb opened the front door. The wind gusted in and swirled around the small room. A napkin drifted off a table. Caleb stepped out and Jennifer followed him. They walked the few steps to the edge of the caisson railing and peered over at the dock. A small boat had landed there, and a man was in it, swaying, waving a rope.

"Ahoy! I need help!" he shouted.

Caleb walked to the ladder, turned and lowered his foot to the first rung. He stopped and looked up at Jennifer.

"I have to help this guy. We'll talk in a bit, okay?"

"Sure," she said, knowing that duty called. Duty always called.

Caleb descended the iron ladder quickly and disappeared from her view. She looked over the railing and watched as he crossed over to the edge of the dock. The man tossed him the line and Caleb snugged it onto one of the cleats, careful as always to give it an extra turn and test it. The man stood, unsteady and arms flailing as the boat pitched. He waited for a lull and jumped onto the dock. His foot hit some wet bird droppings and he wheeled wildly and tumbled forward, falling to his knees.

"Shit!" he yelled.

Caleb bent and offered him a hand up.

"Thanks," the man said. "Jesus, what a spot!" he huffed.

"Let's go inside," said Caleb. His standard greeting. Inside the lighthouse was generally a better place to be than outside. The man looked at the wet iron ladder with wide eyes, but said nothing. He followed Caleb up, gripping ladder for all he was worth. He noticed that there was not a spot of rust on the iron rungs. They gleamed in the light.

Jennifer had already gone inside. The door was closed. As Caleb opened it, Eliot noticed the plaque by its side. He read the last line, *"God bless all who serve here,"* and thought that, on the contrary, this seemed a godforsaken place.

He followed Caleb inside. When Caleb closed the heavy door and slid the bolt home, the loud crashing of the waves and the hiss of the wind dimmed. He felt safe inside the heavy stone building. It was a secure shelter from the elements.

"Hello," said the man, offering his hand. "I'm Eliot McPherson."

Caleb nodded. Shook the man's hand. "Caleb Bowen, lighthouse keeper. This is my fiancée, Jennifer Hays."

"Pleased to meet you, Miss Hays." They shook hands.

"Would you like some coffee?" asked Jennifer.

"Yes! I'm half frozen from my trip out here! It was windy out there and I got sprayed a lot."

Jennifer poured a mug and handed it to him. She noticed his hands were shaking. His hair was wild from the wind. The man drank, eyes darting about. He was obviously unnerved by his journey to the Race Rock. Jennifer looked at Caleb who just shrugged his shoulders.

When a few minutes had passed and the man had warmed up, calmed down, and finished most of his coffee, Caleb spoke: "Now, how can we help you?"

"I'm Eliot McPherson," the man said again, as if that explained everything.

"Yes?" said Caleb.

The man frowned. "You know, the reporter. From New Mexico."

Caleb shook his head, confused. "Sorry, do I know you?"

The man frowned again. "No, but I made arrangements to be out here today."

"You did?"

"Yes," said the man. "Through the Lighthouse Service. I've been corresponding with a Commander, uh, oh, what's his name?"

"St. Clair?"

"Yes! St. Clair. I'm a writer for a newspaper in Santa Fe, New Mexico. I'm doing a series about people who work in remote places. My editor wanted a piece about Race Rock. Seems he sailed by here once when he was in the navy and never forgot the place. I can see why. So here I am. Surely St. Clair told you about my visit. He wrote me it was all arranged."

Caleb was perplexed. It wasn't like St. Clair to not mention this to him. But the man did have a lot to deal with as commandant, especially with some of the changes being talked about these days.

"I didn't receive any notification about your coming out here. Not a word."

"Really? Damn! I have been working on this for months. I thought everything was arranged. I've come a long, long way to be here."

Caleb looked at Jennifer. She did not look happy about this stranger's intrusion. He wasn't happy either. The timing couldn't have been worse.

"Could you come back tomorrow?" asked Caleb.

The man's eyes widened. "Come out here again? No, no, I can't do that. God, no! I thought I wouldn't make it in that little boat." His voice rose and quickened as he talked. "It's rough out there. I'm lucky to be here today. I could have died out there. This weather! My God, no! Besides, I have to be on the train. Tomorrow. On my way back to New York. Tomorrow. I only have today. Damn!" He paused. Composed himself a bit. "Listen, I don't need anything from you. I just want to watch your routine and take a close look at the place. Make some notes. Ask some questions then go. Get back to the desert as quick as I can. I'll stay out of your way."

Caleb looked at Jennifer again. She sighed and with a slight shake of her head, turned and went into the kitchen. The wind gusted. Salt spray rattled against the windows.

He looked at McPherson. He was warming his hands with the coffee mug. He looked frightened. It occurred to Caleb how scary the ocean must be to someone who lived in New Mexico, surrounded by a flat and placid sea of sand. Out there, nothing moved. Out here, everything moved.

He looked in the kitchen. Jennifer had her back to them. She was gazing out the window. He knew she had something serious to talk about. Maybe they still could. He could let this guy stay a few hours, let me get what he needed, answer his questions, and send him on his way. He certainly deserved a little time after the trip he'd made all the way from New Mexico. It wasn't his fault—St. Clair probably just misplaced the letter in a pile on his desk. The man looked so upset Caleb didn't have the heart to send him back out right away. If the weather got worse, he could go to Fishers Island, just a mile away. He'd be on land and safe. How he got to New London would be his problem.

"Okay," said Caleb. "You can stay. Look around. Ask your questions. Watch me work. But stay out of the way, and you have to head back before dusk." He didn't know if the man wanted to see him light the light, but he didn't want him around all night or getting himself killed trying to get back to shore in the dark.

"Oh, that's fine with me," said Eliot. "It was bad enough being out on the water in broad daylight."

Caleb started to gather some supplies to continue his chores and while he did, he started to explain life on Race Rock to Eliot. The reporter had taken out a little notebook and a pen and began writing.

"The daily work is not exciting. In spite of the stories, a lighthouse is not that romantic a place to be. It's dangerous out here. This is a rock in the middle of the ocean. That about says it all. This place takes a beating from the waves and the wind. The salt is corrosive. I clean stuff. Oil stuff. Fix things. I light the light at dusk. Switch on the foghorn in the fog. I keep my eye out for trouble. If a fisherman or someone else needs help, I do what I can. In bad weather, I just ride out the storm and keep the light lit."

Eliot nodded and kept scribbling.

"Look, Mr...."

"McPherson," said Eliot, "Eliot McPherson."

"Look, Mr. McPherson. If you want to ask me questions, you'll have to follow me around while I do my work."

"Fair enough."

"And don't get in my way."

"Watch out for the currents," Eliot thought to himself. "Don't hit any rocks. Don't get in the way." He wondered if he exuded incompetence.

Jennifer was still in the kitchen, still looking out the window. It rattled a bit as the wind continued to gust. Caleb would have to fix that, she mused. Caleb glanced over at the anemometer on the wall of the living room. There was a row of small gauges that measured humidity, wind speed and direction, barometric pressure and temperature. The wind was hitting 40 miles an hour in gusts and was steady at 30. He frowned when he noticed the barometric pressure had dropped quickly in the last hour. The weather would be getting worse. Maybe a lot worse. He wished this McPherson guy wasn't here. He wished Jennifer wasn't here. He'd rather have her onshore, safe at home. He knew he couldn't send either of them out if a storm blew in. Whatever was coming their way, they'd have to ride it out together.

Caleb looked at Jennifer. She was silhouetted against the kitchen window, still looking out. What was she going to tell him before this Eliot character arrived? Caleb walked into the kitchen and stood behind her.

"I'm sorry," he said. "I had no idea this guy was coming out here."

"I know," she said. "Maybe you can answer a few questions and then get rid of him?"

"The weather's deteriorating quickly. I don't think I can send him out just to go rescue him."

"Maybe he could just go to Fishers Island?" she suggested.

"We'll see."

She turned. He thought her eyes looked a little teary. She snuggled against him and wrapped her arms around him tight. She seemed to want to hold him forever.

"I love you so much," she whispered.

"I love you," he replied. "Maybe we can still talk. I'll let him poke around the basement and we can head to the attic."

"No, let's wait until he's gone," she said. She didn't want to start talking only to be interrupted again. She needed to air her thoughts and unburden her heart completely. She didn't want to do it in bits and pieces. She wanted Caleb's full attention.

"I'll make myself useful," she said. Though Caleb kept Race Rock very neat and clean, it was a man's neat and clean. She'd spotted some things that needed work.

"I'm sure you will," he said, a smile returning to his face.

Jennifer turned before he could read her expression, but he still sensed she was troubled. Not knowing what was bothering her gnawed at him. Was she going to call the engagement off? Had she met someone else? Was she sick? Dread began to swirl in him like a wind. Caleb turned and went back into the living room. McPherson was studying the watercolor of the keeper that hung above the mantel.

"Mr. McPherson, I'm heading up to the lantern room if you want to follow me."

"Terrific," said McPherson. "I really appreciate this."

The two men stood and looked at one another for a minute, each trying to gauge the other. McPherson looked younger than Caleb. Maybe thirty or so. He was thin, about Caleb's height, with brown hair, still askew from the wind. Like Caleb, he had deep brown eyes. He did not look like a man who did much physical activity, certainly not outside. He was lightly muscled. He was pale, his hands smooth. Caleb thought he looked like what a reporter should look like. He was wearing corduroys and a sweater and a coat a little too thin for a chilly sea passage. Probably fine for a stroll in the desert.

Meanwhile, Eliot assessed the keeper. His uniform made him look crisp. Official. They were about the same height, but Caleb looked stronger. The work at the light and rowing ashore no doubt kept him fit. Caleb's face was weathered and tanned, which made him look older than he was. His hands were rough, with a few scrapes and scars. He looked like what a lighthouse keeper should look like.

Eliot glanced at Jennifer. Petite, dark hair, pretty face, nice figure. He found her quite attractive. She turned away after their eyes met for just a second. She had an intense look that could have been anger or anxiety. He couldn't tell. He wondered what he had interrupted.

Caleb walked over to the double metal doors in the living room that opened onto the metal spiral staircase that ran up the center of the tower to the light. Stenciled on the gray metal was the warning: *"Fire Door. Keep Closed."*

"As you can see," said Caleb, noticing where Eliot was looking, "these are the fire doors. There's a lot of kerosene up at the light. If a fire starts up there, these doors will contain it in the stone tower. The stairway is metal. It might turn into quite an inferno in there, but at least the main house would be protected. These doors are always closed."

Caleb lifted the heavy metal latch. A small cotter pin on a chain dangled from it. If need be, it could be used to secure the latch in place, locking the doors. Reflexively, Caleb examined the connection where the chain was attached to the door. It was a little loose. It looked like the screw that held it in place was rusting. It wiggled when he tugged on the pin's chain. Something to be fixed.

Caleb opened the doors and stepped onto the metal spiral staircase. The light tower ran up the west side of Race Rock, like a chimney on the side of a house. A metal pole ran down the center. The stairs were cantilevered off of it in a dizzying spiral. The stairway was only about eight feet across. A thin metal railing wound around it, spiraling inside the stone walls at the perimeter. An arched window was punched into the heavy masonry wall, and Eliot could see the wall was at least nine inches thick. The lighthouse was a fortress, built to withstand whatever attacks the sea could mount against it.

Caleb turned and closed the fire doors. They clanged loudly in the empty tower. Eliot looked up. The stairway spiraled away into the gloom. The center pole was striped with the rings that attached the stairs. It looked like a spine, with vertebrae and ribs. The tower was damp, claustrophobic. He heard waves crashing outside and felt a vibration in his feet.

Caleb led the way up. Their footsteps echoed in the cold tower. Around and around they climbed. Eliot gripped the thin metal railing that hugged the curved wall. It was cold to the touch.

"So you're from New Mexico?" asked Caleb.

"Yes. It's a little different from here," Eliot said with a laugh.

"I can imagine. Ever been at sea before?"

"Not really. I've seen it from the shore a few times, from New York and once from San Francisco. But it's not the same. Not the same as being on it. Like this."

"So what's your impression of the sea?" Caleb asked.

"Big. Cold. Violent. Deadly. You can keep it."

"Well, it's not for everybody," said Caleb. "You've managed to come out here when a storm seems to be brewing. You're seeing its angry mood. It can also be calm and beautiful, you know. It gets in your blood. You learn to love it and all its moods."

"Like a woman," Eliot offered.

"Yes," said Caleb with a chuckle.

"How long have you been keeper of Race Rock?" Eliot asked.

"Oh, about five years."

As they talked, they spiraled slowly up the stairway.

"Doesn't it get tiresome out here? Doing the same thing day after day?" asked Eliot. He had taken out his notebook. Every few steps he stopped and scribbled a note.

"Yes and no. There is a daily routine that is, well, routine. But it's *where* you are doing the work that makes it special. The sea is amazing. The water is always changing. The sky is always changing. You see more types of boats go by than you can possibly imagine. You see birds of all sorts. Catch fish of every kind."

"But not too many people," said Eliot, scribbling away in his notebook.

"That's true. To a degree. A lot of keepers are married. They have their families. Where there's just a keeper and an assistant, they generally get to be good friends. And having one good friend is better than having lots of not so good friends, right?"

"True," said Eliot.

"We get ashore, too. It's not a prison. We can leave. People visit."

"Like Jennifer," said Eliot. Caleb didn't say anything.

"Is it dangerous?" asked Eliot after a moment.

Caleb stopped and waited until Eliot caught up. The two men were standing shoulder to shoulder on the narrow spiral stairs. They were at the level of a window. Caleb pointed out to the waves.

"You see that water?" he asked. "That water is the edge of four thousand miles of ocean. Those waves have had all those miles to build their momentum. This is where all that power hits the land. The sea crashing into the edge of the continent.

Add in the tides and the winds—those enormous natural forces."

Eliot stared out at the water, his eyes a little wide again. He was beginning to see the lighthouse in a new light. Caleb watched a gull for a moment, noting how it struggled against the wind. Birds were a natural barometer. How they flew, how they acted showed a lot to someone who knew how to read their behavior. The wind had picked up even more. It had started to rain. He saw a distant lightning flash. He checked his watch. 2pm. He didn't like the look of things. A line from Macbeth floated into his thoughts: *By the pricking of my thumbs, something wicked this way comes.*

He turned to Eliot.

"All the danger isn't out there, Eliot. I could trip and tumble down these damned stairs. Sixty-eight of them. I could fall off the catwalk onto the rocks. I could break an ankle out on the rocks and drown. I could be hit by lightning—we're the highest spot around and there's a lot of metal out here. I could get a fever and waste away in my bed."

Eliot was writing furiously.

"I'll make it simple so you don't have to write so much. It's dangerous out here. You can't run. You can't hide. You have to be careful, and you have to deal with whatever comes your way."

They had arrived at the base of the lantern room. The spiral staircase ended at a metal door that opened up and into the lantern room. Caleb shouldered it open.

"You have to lug the kerosene all the way up here?" Eliot asked.

"Yes. I fill the cans from the main tank in the basement, which is deep inside the caisson. A supply ship fills it once a month. It takes about three cans to keep the light burning every night. I always have extras for good measure."

"Isn't that kind of a fire hazard?"

"Sure, if you were careless with it. A burning liquid can be very dangerous. Hard to control. Hard to stop," said Caleb.

"I see. That's why you have the fire doors."

"Right. Like I said, they'd contain a fire."

The octagonal lantern room of Race Rock was a small place, about eight feet across. It was dominated by the gleaming Fresnel lens that sat atop a metal stanchion. The stanchion was the top of the center column of the spiral stairs. It contained the gears for turning the light and weights that hung down its center on long chains that reached to the basement.

One small panel of the Fresnel hinged open to provide access to the fuel reservoir and lamps. Cans of kerosene were clustered on the floor around the stanchion. There was just enough space around the gleaming lens to walk around it. The outer walls of the room were metal to about waist height, then panels of glass. One section of metal was a hatch that opened to the catwalk outside. The catwalk that circled the lantern room was also narrow, just three feet wide, with a metal mesh floor and railing.

The lantern room was capped with a cupola made of copper. At the pinnacle was a three-foot iron lightning rod. It was creaking in the wind. The connection to the roof had rusted and it was beginning to wobble.

Eliot walked around so he was on the other side of the lens. His face was magnified by it, distorted like some strange apparition. He watched as Caleb opened a small door in the beautiful glass lens array. He lifted off a cylinder of red glass that gave the light its color, and checked the reservoir. Seeing it needed fuel, he filled a small pitcher with the last few ounces of kerosene from one of the cans and carefully poured it into the reservoir. He adjusted a small wheel and checked the wick. He re-seated the red glass cylinder and closed the door.

Caleb pushed the lens gently and it began to turn on its nearly frictionless bed of mercury. Eliot reached out to touch it.

"Don't!" shouted Caleb. Eliot stopped, his fingertips just inches from the gleaming glass.

"Never touch one of these lenses with your bare fingers. The oils will stain the glass."

"Oh," said Eliot. "Sorry." He studied the lens, then asked: "So it's fragile?"

"Yes, especially when it's hot. That's why I have to be sure there are no leaks in any of these windows or the roof. If cold water were to hit the hot glass, it would contract, shatter, and explode."

Eliot leaned back away from the huge spinning array of prisms.

Though they were almost seventy-five above the water, the waves crashing on the rocks were loud. The wind howled. Eliot looked out the lantern room windows and saw a growing maelstrom of rain and spray, all lit by lightning. The storm was getting worse quickly.

"When will you light the light?" he asked Caleb.

"Soon. It's going to be dark early with this storm. Maybe in another hour or so. I need to get more fuel up here."

"Can you control how bright it is?" he asked.

"Yes. You can pump it and increase the pressure and the flow of the fuel. Like any light, the more fuel it gets, the brighter it is. But you can go too far. These lights have limits. Get them too hot and they can burn out. In normal operation, these lenses are incredibly efficient. They do all the work of focusing and enhancing the beam. This light can be seen for fourteen miles."

Eliot was amazed. Fourteen miles!

"In a heavy storm, visibility goes way down. You should still see it a few miles away, and that's enough to help any boats unlucky enough to be at sea."

"Once it's lit, does it stay lit?"

"If the light is maintained correctly, if the fuel is good, the pipes clear, the reservoir pumped right, and if the wicks are trimmed and clean, the light will stay lit until it runs out of fuel. It doesn't take much tinkering once it's going. That means working on it almost every day. It's like anything, I guess. The more you work at it and take care of it, the better it is."

"What about the spinning?"

Caleb opened a small door in the stanchion below the light to check the gears and weights. Two long chains hung from the mechanism and disappeared into the shadows inside the stanchion column. Eliot moved around to look inside. Caleb fiddled with the weights as he explained how they worked. "These weights turn the light through a series of gears. Once I crank the weights up here from the basement, the light will spin as they slowly drop down. That takes three hours."

"So you have to stay up all night and baby-sit it?"

Caleb laughed. "No, not at all. I get my sleep. Just three hours at a time. That's not to say that I don't get up and check on it between windings. I do. Habit. I trust it, but I like to be certain."

"Yes. You wouldn't want the light to stop. Or go out."

Caleb looked at Eliot. He wondered just how much Eliot knew about him and his father. With a bit of an edge to his voice Caleb said: "No, I wouldn't want to let the light go out. And I never will."

"It's your job to light it and keep it lit," said Eliot.

"Yes. My job," said Caleb. He watched Eliot write in his notebook. "And your job is to ask a lot of questions."

Eliot looked up. "That's right. I'm a reporter, I ask questions. Try to find out about things. How they work. Why they work." He paused a moment. "Am I asking too many questions?"

The two men looked at each other. Eliot had a bland smile on his face. Perhaps there was nothing more to Eliot's questions than curiosity. Perhaps there was more. Caleb was on guard.

At last, he answered: "No, not too many. But I think I've told you all you need to know about the light."

"You're right. I know enough."

Caleb closed the door to the weights. He turned to Eliot. "Do you want to go out onto the catwalk?"

Eliot looked a little surprised. "Out there?"

Caleb laughed. "Yes, out there. Take a little walk around the lantern room. It's quite a view."

"Is it safe?"

"It's safe if you don't get blown off," said Caleb. He got down on his hands and knees and opened the hatch to the catwalk. A cold wind rushed in, moist from the waves and rain.

"I guess you wouldn't open that with the light lit?" asked Eliot.

"No, that would be a bad idea."

He crawled out and Eliot followed.

It was another world on the catwalk. They were suspended over the edge of the caisson and the rocks. Eliot looked down through the mesh at his feet and saw waves slamming against the base. They hit the stone cylinder and sprayed upwards, where the wind caught the water and blew it sideways. The sound of the waves was frightening—a mix of hissing and thundering booms. The wind was loud, too, a roar that enveloped and shook them. Eliot instinctively reached out and grabbed the thin metal railing. It was not very substantial and only supported every four feet by a thin post to the catwalk. Caleb and Eliot swayed in the wind and were doused by the rain and spray. Talk was impossible.

The storm was something to behold. It had exploded over the region with almost no warning. The wind was a steady forty knots with gusts hitting seventy or eighty. Lightning crackled to the south.

Caleb saw Eliot's white-knuckled grip on the railing. He leaned over and yelled in his ear. "You aren't writing much."

Eliot managed a wan smile.

"Just soaking it all up!" He was trying to be funny, but his voice was strained with fear.

Caleb took a brief walk around the lantern room. He held on to the railing tightly all the way around. A gust could easily blow him off. A dozen paces and he was back where he'd started. Eliot did not join him. He maintained his death-grip on the railing. When he returned, Eliot was already crawling back into the lantern room. Caleb followed, pulling the hatch closed behind him. Though the wind was still a loud roar inside, it was less deafening than on the catwalk.

"This is some storm!" said Eliot. "Do they usually come on so quickly?"

"No. No, they don't. This is ... I've never seen anything quite like this, Eliot. I don't think this was predicted. It's getting worse. Quickly."

Caleb looked out the window at the storm. The waves must have reached twenty feet on top of enormous rolling swells. Those that struck the base of Race Rock surged upwards and created a swirling, wind-blown mist around the lantern room.

It was hard to see Fishers Island or Groton or New London. Race Rock was becoming increasingly isolated. Thunder added its voice to the howl of the wind. Caleb shook his head.

"I don't like this," he said.

Eliot caught some of his fear. It made his that much worse. The lighthouse keeper must see a lot of storms. If he was scared ...

"I guess I'm stuck out here?" Eliot asked, his voice shaky.

"Yes, you are. My job is to save lives, not put them in danger. No way I'd let you try to go back in this. You get to ride out a storm on a lighthouse. Should give you a good story for your editor."

Eliot nodded, but his gaze was fixed on a very large tree being tossed by the waves. The lightning rod creaked and groaned above. Caleb looked up at the ceiling. Eliot looked up, too.

"It's the lightning rod. It's loose. Hard to fix. If it lasts the storm, I'll have to get some help out here. We'll have to climb up there and reset it."

Eliot looked out at the darkening skies. At the lightning. Not a day to lose the lightning rod.

"There's always something to fix, isn't there?" he said to Caleb.

"Yeah. Always something. No surprise. Look at where we are. The wind, the waves, the rain—they attack this place like they hate it."

"Race Rock seems pretty solid," said Eliot. He was fishing for reassurances from the keeper of the light that they were safe.

"I think we're going to find out today," said Caleb.

Eliot blinked. That was not what he wanted to hear.

"You ever hear that conundrum," continued Caleb, shouting to be heard, "about what happens when an irresistible force meets an immovable object?"

Eliot nodded "yes."

"Well, here we are on what would seem to be an immovable object. And out there is—or should I say: 'are'—the irresistible forces.

Eliot nodded again.

"So it should be interesting."

Eliot nodded. Did he say: "interesting?"

"I think it's time to light the light," said Caleb.

He opened the hinged panel of the fresnel lens. Checked the fuel reservoir again, then pumped a small handle with short hard strokes, increasing the fuel pressure. From a small box attached to the light stanchion, Caleb took out a box of matches. He lit one and reached inside the lens. He touched the flame to the wick. It caught immediately. The Fresnel lens blossomed with bright red light. Caleb blew out the match and closed the lens door, then toggled a small lever and the light began to turn, slowly and silently. It was incredibly bright. Eliot had to squint. He was amazed at how much the array of glass prisms magnified the small flame.

"Light's lit," said Caleb. "Now you've seen how it's done."

"God it's bright!" said Eliot, still stunned by how the tiny flame seemed to flare so brightly within the Fresnel lens, like a captured sun.

"It needs to be in a storm like this," said Caleb.

"How far will it be visible tonight?" asked Eliot.

"Hard to tell exactly from here," said Caleb. "You'd have to be out there on a ship to know. Even with all this rain and spray and mist, probably three or four miles. Enough to warn any ships around of danger. Caleb looked at the light, making sure the small flame was okay and the fuel was flowing properly.

"This is what a lighthouse is all about," Caleb said to Eliot, his tone almost reverent. "The big stone foundation, the caisson, the granite building, the stairway, the Fresnel lens, the keeper. Everything. It's all here to take this tiny flame and beam it out to sea as an aid to navigation."

"It's pretty impressive," said Eliot. "I don't think many people realize what's involved. They just take it for granted."

"That they do," said Caleb. "Well, I have to go get more kerosene." With that, he opened the door to the lantern room and headed down the spiral staircase.

Eliot looked out and was surprised how little he could see. The storm swirled around them, rain pelting the glass of the lantern room, angry clouds scudding by, lightning knifing through the gloom. The top of the lighthouse seemed a small and fragile place. He walked around and onto the spiral stairway. The red light swept around, bathing him in its blood-red beam. He closed the hatch to the lantern room and descended into the shadows.

12

A little after 4pm, the steamer *Catskill* left Montauk Point for the return trip to New London. There were 41 passengers and 18 cars aboard. The ship was an hour or so behind schedule. Captain Freedman had debated canceling the return trip due to the high seas. He'd called the ferry company's dispatching office and talked to one of the men on duty there. They'd discussed the storm, the encroaching darkness, and the need to keep on schedule. Freedman sensed a bit of a challenge in the man's voice when he asked if Freedman was "scared of a little rough weather." He wondered if the guy was anywhere near the ocean. In the end, it was Captain Freedman's call, and he decided that, no, he wasn't scared of a little rough weather. It was only two hours at sea. Maybe three in this storm. He knew the waters well. As long as all the lights along the way were lit, he'd have no problems navigating into New London.

He had his crew batten down everything extra securely and told the passengers it would be rocky. If anyone didn't want to go, the company would make arrangements for them to stay the night and return tomorrow. Only five passengers cancelled their passages. The *Catskill* headed out of Montauk Point up Long Island Sound toward New London. It would be a rough trip. The high winds and waves were coming from the south and hitting the ship broadside, rocking it on its side. A half mile out of Montauk, Freedman wondered if he'd made a mistake. He debated turning around. In the end, he decided to keep on going into the darkness, into the storm.

13

The base of Race Rock was a huge cylindrical drum, a caisson, made of blocks of granite. It rose 20 feet from the middle of huge boulders. They'd been set on top of the foundation, which had been poured on top of Race Rock itself. The caisson housed coal bins, fresh water tanks, mechanical systems, and the supply tank of kerosene for the light. It was a dingy place, always damp, and often loud with the rumbling sound of the waves striking outside. On a stormy day like this, those rumbles were like explosions—loud and visceral.

Eliot and Caleb stood in the yellow glow of a single electric bulb. It hung from the ceiling and seemed too dim to light the gloomy basement. The lighthouse was electrified, power brought to it by an underwater cable from Fishers Island. The light itself wouldn't be converted to electricity for another year or so. Caleb had taken six cans from the light down to the caisson. He needed to fill them and bring them back up to the lantern room. He would be ready for the night. He put the first under the spigot on the kerosene tank and began to fill it.

Eliot was looking around. The caisson ceiling was mostly in shadow, but he could see huge iron beams radiating out from the support column. The round room was a jumble of tanks, pipes, rope, chains, boxes of spare parts, some life vests, paddles, paint cans, boxes of rags and brushes, and tins of provisions. It was a place of shadows and cobwebs, smelling of oil, noisy from the incessant pounding of waves. The wind had picked up and so had the seas, and now the waves were hitting Race Rock higher, coming in over the riprap at times and hitting the caisson directly. This, Caleb had explained, was unusual. The seas seldom rose so high. But on this day, there was a significant storm surge superimposed on the highest tide of the year and altogether that probably added 15 to 20 feet to the normal sea level.

None of what Caleb said made Eliot feel any better about being marooned on Race Rock. He cursed his bad luck at picking this day to be here. He kept thinking about that damned tree going by, tossed by the waves like it was a twig. Just how big could waves get, anyway? He flinched with each percussive boom of one hitting the caisson.

He had been poking around in the shadows. He felt an itching on his forearm and looked down and saw a large spider on it. He shrieked and waved his arm trying to dislodge it. He hated spiders! Caleb was startled and looked up.

"Jesus! What's wrong?" he shouted.

"A spider. Damned spider on my arm. Probably bit me!"

"Dangers everywhere," mumbled Caleb, returning to his work.

Eliot came into the light, rubbing his arm.

"Writers!" Caleb thought. "Useless."

"I think I'll go up and look around a little, if that's okay with you," said Eliot. He wanted to get out of the dark, damp, claustrophobic basement. He didn't like the idea of being below sea level.

"Sure," said Caleb, happy to get rid of him for the time being. Eliot was clearly rattled and getting panicky. Just what he needed.

"Just don't break anything," said Caleb.

* * *

While Caleb and Eliot were down in the caisson, Jennifer had been busy. The electricity was still on, but who knew for how long. Knowing what storms could do, she was getting ready for a day or two of self-sufficiency at Race Rock.

She had gone to various closets and gathered all the lanterns and flashlights she could find. She'd taken one of the supply cans of kerosene and filled the lanterns. She checked their wicks and valves. Then she'd distributed them to each floor of Race Rock. They would have light.

The lights taken care of, she found some empty bottles and filled them with fresh water. These, too, she distributed to the various levels. They would have water.

She was in one of the bedrooms, making sure the window was locked, when she heard a strange sound. She frowned, stopped and listened. Even with the storm raging, the wind howling, the thunder booming, she could hear it. She cocked her head, closed her eyes and listened. She knew what the sound was. It was drawers being quickly pulled out then put back in. She almost called out, but did not. Instead, she went out into the hallway. She could see a vague shadow on the floor coming from one of the bedrooms. She tiptoed across the hallway into the shadows, then made her way down the wall until she was across from the bedroom where the noise was coming from.

She craned her neck and looked in. Eliot was standing with his back to the door in front of a small desk. He pulled out one of the drawers. All the way out. He looked inside it, then turned it around and examined the back panel of the drawer. He put the drawer on the desk and reached in to where it had been and felt around. Then he slid the drawer back in. He did this for three more drawers, quickly but thoroughly inspecting each one and its place in the desk. Then he started on the bookshelf. He took out several books and reached in behind where they'd been, poking and taping the wood.

Jennifer leaned back against the wall. Why would a reporter be examining the backs of drawers? Tapping bookshelves?

She stood in the shadows and tried to think as she listened to him roaming about the small room, opening things, looking, looking. What on earth was he looking for? She felt a shiver of fear. Something was wrong. This frightened reporter was not what he seemed. Eliot was after more than a story about Race Rock.

She needed to tell Caleb.

She gingerly walked backwards along the wall. A floorboard creaked loudly. The noise from the bedroom stopped.

He'd heard.

Eliot put the book he was holding back on the shelf. He turned toward the door. What was that? Someone in the hall?

He headed to the doorway and poked his head out. No one was there. He studied the fire door at the end of the hall. Closed. It was probably the wind. He returned to the bedroom and resumed searching.

Jennifer let out her breath and opened the small closet door and stepped back into the hallway. She tiptoed to the fire door. There was no way she could open it quietly.

So she wouldn't.

She stood at the door, opened them with a clang and shouted "Caleb! Are you up here?" Jennifer spun around to make it look as if she'd just come through the doors just as Eliot came out of the bedroom.

"Oh, Eliot! Have you seen Caleb?"

Eliot looked startled. A little wild. He quickly regained his composure.

"No, he's not up here. He'd down in the basement. I've just been looking around, getting the lie of the land. Or sea, I guess?" he chuckled.

Jennifer smiled. Her ruse had worked. She shrugged and said, "I guess I'll head down, then." Quickly, she went back through the fire doors and onto the spiral stairway. She closed the doors behind her and let out a breath.

Eliot stared at the fire doors a moment. Then he returned to the small room and sat at the desk.

Race Rock was much bigger than he'd thought. Much bigger. He hadn't figured on Jennifer or the storm. On the train, it had seemed so simple. It was not turning out that way. No, not at all. The wind's howl grew louder. The spray from the waves was hitting the windows here on the second floor regularly. How high was he above the sea? At least fifty feet. He was trapped on this godforsaken rock. He scratched his arm where the spider had been. Wind. Waves. Lightning. Spiders. Jesus, what a place!

His hand dipped into his pocket and he withdrew a silver case. He turned it in his hand.

It was time.

He opened the small case and took out a glass vial filled with white powder and a metal tube, about three inches long. His hands were shaking. He couldn't calm down, not in this maelstrom! He waited a moment, closed his eyes, tried to gain a measure of composure. His heart beat loudly in his ears. After a half minute he was ready, ready as he could be in this damned chaos. Carefully, very carefully, he unscrewed the cap of the vial and placed the tube in it like a straw. He brought it up to his nose and put the tube in his nostril. He inhaled, hard and quick. The white powder swirled in the vial like a miniature storm then shot up the tube. He closed his eyes and felt the familiar tickle in his nose. He carefully replaced the cap on the vial and returned the vial and tube to the case and the case to his pocket. He'd been holding his breath. He exhaled slowly. Very slowly.

Eliot remained at the desk, his eyes closed. Sparks seemed to dance behind his eyelids. His heart thudded louder, a quick drumming overlaid on the rumble of the waves. He opened his eyes. His pupils were wide and his eyes glassy. In the darkness of the room, he could see with great clarity. Wonderful clarity. The powder always helped him focus his thoughts, calm his confusion. Like the penetrating beam of the lighthouse, it was an illumination that showed him the way. In his mind's eye, vivid and clear, he saw what he must do. What he must do to solve this problem. He scratched his forearm. Stared at the pattern of the wallpaper—so vivid, almost alive, lit by the flashes of lightning. Fragmentary ideas began to connect. His mind was buzzing and at the same time calm, and now his fear was just a throb of energy that fueled his resolve. He began working on a plan.

14

J ennifer ran into Caleb on the spiral stairs. He was lug-
ging up two full cans of kerosene, huffing and puffing.
They clanged against the metal stairs and railing. The waves
crashing against Race Rock echoed loudly in the confined space
of the stairwell, its heavy masonry amplifying their sound.

Caleb looked up and saw Jennifer. "You know, sometimes I
really hate this stairway!"

"Caleb!" shouted Jennifer, "I need to talk to you!" Earlier in
the day, she had said these words with a quiet intensity. Now
she shouted them with desperate urgency. The subject had
changed from their future together to the more immediate
worry of Eliot.

"Can it wait? I have to get more cans from the caisson up to
the lantern room. You know the drill."

Jennifer did. It was one of the less appealing chores of the
daily routine. The cans were awkward and heavy, too heavy for
her to lend a hand with. She flattened herself against the wall as
Caleb squeezed by her. She was near one of the windows and
looked out.

The scene was unbelievable.

The waves were level with the second floor. Their tops
were being sheared off by the wind. Huge plumes of spray shot
out. The wind howled and whistled and moaned and keened, a
mix of voices unlike anything she had ever heard. It must be
gusting over one hundred miles an hour! Lightning crackled,
illuminating seas that were enormous, chaotic, foaming white,
and slamming into Race Rock. She saw pieces of boats and
buildings go by, tossed in the churning waters. She saw whole
trees. A cow, flailing wildly. Cars. Furniture. Jennifer was

stunned. She had never seen a storm anything like this. It was as if the Earth had suddenly stopped and the sea and sky had kept on going, propelled by momentum, tearing onward with unimaginable force.

She pulled herself away from the window, from the nightmare outside. She caught up with Caleb as he carried and dragged the dented cans up and around the metal spiral staircase.

"Caleb!" she shouted. "Caleb, I need to talk to you!" He hadn't heard. He shouted down at her, "Jennifer, you need to gather some lanterns and water!"

"I already have!"

He didn't hear her. He was at the door to the lantern room, wrestling the cans of kerosene up and inside. After a minute, he came down, sweat beading on his forehead, huffing and puffing.

"The lightning rod's gone. I heard it blow off!" Caleb yelled as he came back down the stairway. She waited until they were together and followed him down and around, down and around until they were in the basement.

It was even louder in the caisson. The waves were crashing into it, and even though its walls were two-feet thick, the building seemed to shake. Jennifer tried again to talk to him, but he shook her off.

"Let me get all the cans up there, Jennifer, then we'll talk!" he shouted. He was working with desperate intensity. She looked at him a moment and realized he was scared. Scared that this storm might breach the fortress of Race Rock.

Caleb went back up with two more cans, and Jennifer stood in the unlit stairwell. The lighthouse was being assaulted on all sides. She knew the sea had no soul, no personality, but it was hard not to think of it as angry and violent. It seemed to be willfully trying to destroy Race Rock. That was the attack from outside.

And inside?

Eliot, this stranger who had appeared from nowhere—what was he looking for at Race Rock? She knew it was more than a story about the workings of a lighthouse. Jennifer had a bad feeling about the situation. They were trapped inside Race

Rock. There was nowhere to go. Nowhere to run. While the storm outside was menacing, her gut told her that the real danger might be the man who had come here unexpectedly. Like the sea this day, he had at first seemed calm, but had become agitated and unpredictable.

15

Steaming across Long Island sound, the *Catskill* was barely making headway against the sea. Captain Freedman had taken the helm himself and was turning the wheel wildly as he tried to anticipate the waves. That was impossible. While the prevailing swells and waves were from the south, the seas were so high and so rough that the ferry encountered them coming from almost every angle.

"Are the cars chained down?" he yelled to his first mate, Kellar.

"Yes, sir, secured as we can make them!"

"Good. How are the passengers?"

"As terrified as we can make them!" shouted Kellar.

Freedman smiled and looked over at the man. "How about the crew?"

"At the end of this trip, we're all going to become farmers. In Iowa. As far from the sea as we can get."

Freedman nodded. "Save me a barn," he said.

The boat climbed an enormous wave, reached the crest and hung out over the trough, suspended in space. It was a sickening feeling, a moment of weightlessness that seamen dread.

"Hold on!" yelled Freedman. The *Catskill* slammed down on the backside of the wave and ran down it into the trough. Freedman prayed the bow wouldn't bury itself in the water. If it did, they'd keep going to their death in the cold dark sea. The trough curved to a flat bottom, and the ship rode down and across it. The bow stayed above water. They'd been lucky. This time.

"These waves get any higher, sir, and one of them will flip us over!" yelled Kellar, his eyes wide, his hands gripping a small railing.

"These waves get any higher and we might collide with the goddamned moon!" shouted Freedman. He wrestled the wheel hard to port, again trying to find a safe angle across a mountain of water.

It was hard to see anything through the windows, even with the wipers set to their fastest speed. He hoped he'd be able to spot the lighthouses through the spray. They were his only hope for navigation. Buoys were small and hidden by the waves. The shore was obscured by mist. Only the lighthouses, with their bright beacons, would penetrate the gloom. The next one he needed to pick up was Race Rock.

Freedman's eyes narrowed. He had spotted something in a massive wave up ahead.

It was a school bus. Spinning on the water.

"Well, I'll be goddamned!" he said.

16

Eliot's mind was racing. The powder, his adrenaline, and the energy of the storm all fed his manic fear. The storm was beyond his comprehension. It was as if the sea had exploded. As if it were still exploding—an endless, lingering, massive release of energy. He was heading up the stairway. His fear was not helped at all when he looked out the window and saw the roof of a house floating by, tossed by the waves as it did. Three people—two adults and a child—were sitting on it, desperate, doomed, riding what was left of their home to oblivion.

Shaken, Eliot opened the fire doors at the attic level and stepped inside.

As everywhere, it was noisy in the attic. Two triangular windows at the far end, on either side of a chimney, offered dim light. It was all he needed. His dilated pupils took the barest of illumination and magnified it into a shimmering glow. He could see just fine.

There were boxes, some old furniture, window screens, and plenty of spider webs. The floorboards creaked as he walked in. He looked down at them. He stood there in the gloom, studying the floor. Then he nodded his head and smiled.

Searching around, he found a box in a corner. It was a box of tools. He rummaged around and found some pliers, hammer, screwdrivers and a chisel. Perfect.

He saw a large black spider hanging onto a web, just at the corner of the box. He took the hammer from the front and smashed it down onto the spider, over and over. Damned filthy thing! He wasn't going to let another one bite him.

He paced around the attic. Bumped his head against a sloping beam. Cursed. Eliot listened to the pelting rain and thunder, the crash of waves and howl of the wind. All of it was loud, even through the heavy roof. He wished it would stop. Just for a minute. Just a minute of peace without the storm filling his senses.

This was some hell he'd gotten himself into.

He fingered the silver case in his pocket.

17

The weather shack was shaking. Seaman Shivers made a note in his logbook:

"Shack shaking: winds high."

Seaman Shivers had never imagined winds like this. The newspaper lay at his feet. He looked at the readings on the instruments arrayed before him. Sustained wind speed: 105mph. Gusts topping out at 130mph. He blinked. Was the wind really that strong? His ears told him what his eyes could not believe. The roar of it as it swirled around his shack was unearthly. The barometer was at 28. The humidity was 92%. The temperature was 54.

"This is a big fuckin' storm!" he said. He looked again at the anemometer. A gust pushed the needle to 120, where it held a minute before suddenly dropping to 0. He could still hear the wind's roar. It was a sustained explosion laced with an unearthly howl.

"Shit," he cursed. "The wind vane's fucked up." His eyes swept up to the small sign above the radio. *If it's broke, fix it.*

"Shit!"

He would have to go out there and see what he could do.

He started to get dressed for his excursion, yelling at the storm.

"I don't need this, dammit! I should be somewhere else. I can build stuff. I should be building stuff. I can wire stuff. I should be wiring stuff. How did I get stuck doing weather? Who gives a shit about the weather? It is what it is! What are ya gonna do about it? Fuck this! Who cares what the wind is? It's fucking strong! Who cares how much it rains? It's raining lots! I should be doing something else, damn it! I can hit! I can run!

I should be playing on the fucking Red Sox! Why am I here in a goddamned shack? Fuck the shack!"

Shivers' monologue continued as he put on his heavy rubber boots and foul-weather slicker. He put on his hat, then thought about the wind and took it off. He wouldn't have it on for more than a few seconds, and he didn't want to go chasing a hat. Nothing good could come of that. He didn't have that much hair to get wet anyway.

He opened the door and stepped outside.

Shivers was a short, heavyset man. About 220 pounds. He was muscular. It didn't matter. He stepped outside his shack and was knocked over instantly. Then he was rolled by the wind into the water that had flooded over the low-lying point. He struggled to his feet and was knocked down again. Finally he made it to his knees. "Well, Hell! It's goddamned windy!"

He managed to get to his feet and grabbed the railing that ran along the beach. In defiance to the storm, he turned his anger to purpose and began to make his way down the path toward the Tyler House. It was at the side of that path that the wind vane was fixed to the top of a metal pole attached to the railing. He held onto the railing for his life, pulling himself along it.

"I can drink! I should be someplace fuckin' drinking! I can play the harmonica! I ought to be in the symphony playing my goddamned harmonica! Fuck the weather! Fuck the storm!"

Shivers winced when the wind drove cold salt spray into his exposed face. He was shaking, and not from the cold. The howl of the wind was demonic, and it scared him to his core.

He made it to the anemometer. He knew they would want wind readings of *this* storm, and he had to try to fix the damned wind vane. He could see it was still attached to the top of the pole. The wire had come loose and flailed in the wind. With luck, he could reattach it. Maybe they'd give him a goddamned medal! He could see the commendation now: *"As the world was coming apart around him, brave and resourceful Seaman Shivers, disregarding personal safety and doing his duty, fixed the instrument that was broke."*

He reached up and caught the wire with his hand. He stood on his toes but couldn't get a good angle on the socket. Cursing a blue streak, he gave up and bent down and felt around in the water below him for a rock. He found one and jammed it against the pole. He stood on it but it rolled out from under him and he went down on both knees in the cold water.

"Goddamittofuckinshitofasonofabitch!"

Shivers tried again. This time, the rock held. He reached up and jammed the wire into the socket. It came out so he tried again. It clicked into place.

He hopped off the rock and turned to see a monstrous wave wash over the point and surge toward him. He held on to the pole as the water rushed by, lifting his legs high up in the air.

"Holy Shit!"

It seemed like the whole damned ocean had moved up a hundred feet or so. What used to be beach, what used to be land was now sea bottom. Lightning crackled loudly in the black clouds. Bolts knifed down here and there, and it occurred to him that climbing a metal pole had been a very stupid thing to do.

"If it's broke, fix it. Fuck that!"

Another medal commendation flashed through his mind.

"Seaman Shivers was killed while stupidly climbing a metal pole in a severe thunderstorm. He was trying to fix a wind vane that took readings nobody cared about. He got fucked."

Wet, cold, and scared, Seaman Shivers turned, put his head down, and struggled back to the weather shed, holding onto the metal railing warily, walking sideways, cursing. Several times, he was knocked off his feet by a gust of wind or the roiling waves. Pieces of wood and metal were flying by, and had one hit him it would have taken off his head. "Fuck this!" He had to get inside.

Head down, he sloshed back in water up to his waist. This low point at the end of Shore Avenue flooded in a heavy rain. Today, it was three to four feet submerged, both from the rain and the flooding sea. He looked up to get his bearings and see how far he had to go to get to the weather shed.

He stopped dead in his tracks.

The shack was gone. The foundation remained and a few boards stuck up from it like fingers. That was all.

He formulated his next weather report in his mind:

"Shack gone: winds *VERY* fuckin' high!"

18

"Okay, what do you want to tell me?" asked Caleb.

Jennifer thought to herself: "Well, let's see, Caleb. That I love you. That I came here today to give you an ultimatum. To ask you to agree to a wedding date. To tell you that you have to leave Race Rock. To tell you that I am terrified of this storm and think we may die here today. And, by the way, we have some strange guy here taking drawers out of desks and seeing if there is anything behind them!"

They had gone looking for someplace to talk and headed to the attic. They'd heard the fire door to that level clang shut a few minutes before as they made their way up the stairs. She hoped they could be alone up there and finally, finally talk. Jennifer quietly opened the door and they stepped into the gloom.

"Well?"

She decided now was not the time to speak of love and their future. She had more immediate worries in Eliot's odd behavior.

"Listen, Caleb. There's something strange about this guy!'

"Strange?"

"Yes! I saw Eliot in the study. He didn't know I was watching him. He was pulling drawers out of the desk. Looking behind them. He was searching the desk and the bookcase, too, trying to find something."

Caleb listened, trying to hear her above the din of the storm, trying to absorb what she was saying.

She paused and flicked on a flashlight and shone it into the attic. Her face went pale.

"What?" Caleb caught the sudden look of shock on Jennifer's face.

"Oh my god!" Jennifer put her hands to her lips.

Caleb followed her gaze to the floor. A dozen or so floorboards were pulled up at crazy angles, dark holes showing beneath them.

"What the hell!" Caleb couldn't comprehend what he was seeing.

Jennifer leaned in to Caleb and was speaking into his ear in an agitated rush. "It's him. Eliot. He did this. He's looking for something and he'll tear this place apart until he finds it!"

Caleb stared at the floor.

"It makes no sense," he said. "What on earth does he expect to find here?"

"I have no idea, Caleb. None. But I don't think he's after a story for some newspaper. Maybe he's a raving lunatic. I don't know." She paused, playing the light over the ripped-up boards. "Maybe you should ask him."

Caleb hugged her close, looking over her shoulder at the floor. He tried to imagine some explanation for why a stranger would come all the way out to Race Rock to look for something. What? What did he expect to find? Who was he really?

In the few minutes Caleb and Jennifer were in the attic, the wind had slackened. The howl of it faded, and as it did, they realized how thoroughly it had wrapped them in its deep embrace. The rain eased off, too.

It was the eye of the storm.

It would last twenty, maybe thirty minutes before it passed over and the worst of the storm hit. The sudden quiet was deafening.

"I'm scared, Caleb," whispered Jennifer. "How do we deal with a storm *inside* a lighthouse?"

19

C aleb and Jennifer made their way down to the kitchen. They decided to take advantage of the brief calm and eat something. They put on some coffee, and Jennifer made sandwiches.

"I wonder where he is?" said Jennifer.

"I don't know. Maybe he went outside and got blown away." He paused, thinking of something.

"I'm going to radio St. Clair and see what he says about this Eliot writing him asking permission to visit here."

"Good idea."

Caleb went into the small adjacent room, about as big as a pantry, where the radio and telephone were housed. He stood in front of the shelf, and switched on the radio. It crackled with interference. He adjusted the dial to try to home in on the Service's station. Just static. Not surprising in a storm like this. With all the lightning, the electromagnetic fields would be a mess.

"No dice," he said. "Let's see if I can reach him by phone."

He picked up the headpiece and put it to his ear. Frowned. Started tapping the receiver buttons.

"It's dead. Nothing at all. No dial tone. Strange," he said.

"The lines on shore must be down. They wouldn't stand a chance in this wind," said Jennifer.

Caleb nodded. They moved into the small living room. A puddle of water glistened beneath the big wooden door and extended a few feet into the room. Solid as it was, like any building, Race Rock had cracks and places where water could find its way in. With the amount of waves and water that had washed over the porch outside, Caleb was glad the first floor wasn't flooded.

The eye was a brief respite. A few minutes when it would be safe to go outside. He grabbed his foul-weather gear from the peg by the door.

"I'll be back in a minute," he said. He opened the door and went onto the porch that circled Race Rock. It was dusk. Caleb walked around the top of the caisson, aiming his flashlight down at the cement dock and the heavy rocks that surrounded it. They were half-submerged in the boiling surf. Eliot's boat was gone. Jennifer's boat was gone. The lighthouse's skiff, which hung from a davit perched at the edge of the caisson, was also gone, torn away by the wind and waves. Not that he would have tried to leave, but now there was no option. No way off the rock.

Caleb went back inside.

"Boats are all gone, Jennifer."

Jennifer sat on a chair, knees drawn up to her chin, mug balanced on them. She looked up at him.

"I'll miss my little boat. It was my friend," she said.

"Sorry."

Caleb stripped off his gear and poured himself a fresh cup of coffee. He sat and cupped the warm mug in his hands.

"Where's our guest?" he asked.

"I think he's in the basement."

"I think it's time we asked the reporter some questions," said Caleb.

As if on cue, Eliot emerged from the basement stairway. He looked agitated, nervous. There was some dirt on his pants knees, a grease mark on his cheek. He was scratching his arm. He looked around and seemed surprised.

"The storm's stopped," he said.

"Hardly," said Caleb. "It's just the eye passing over. It will be back. Soon. And it will be worse."

"Worse! I can't imagine it being any worse," said Eliot. He turned and stood before the mantle and seemed to study the watercolor above it.

A minute passed. Distant thunder reverberated across the water. The waves outside hissed. The wind, a mere twenty knots now, hummed.

Caleb needed some answers, and he needed them before all hell broke loose again. He knew how to deal with a storm, though this one might be beyond dealing with. He needed a better idea of what threat Eliot might pose.

"Okay, Eliot," Caleb said, his voice angry. "Just who the hell are you and what are you after out here?"

Eliot did not react. He sniffed. He looked at the watercolor, hands holding the edge of the mantle. After a moment of silence he spoke.

"Why do you ask?"

"I'm sure as a reporter, if that's what you are, you are used to digging deep for you story," said Caleb. "But I think looking at the backs of drawers and ripping up floorboards goes a little beyond being thorough. What are you really looking for? Why are you here?"

Eliot gave a quiet snort. Shook his head. Said nothing.

"Well?" asked Caleb.

Eliot turned slowly toward them. The windows rattled with the wind.

"Do you know who did this painting?" Eliot asked, gesturing to the watercolor he'd been staring at.

"No, Eliot, I don't. And I don't care. What difference does it make who painted it?"

"Oh, all the difference, Caleb. All the difference. It was painted by Madeleine Covington. See: 'MC'—she signed it down here." Eliot pointed to the two small initials painted on the rocks surrounding the stone caisson.

"Okay. It was painted by Madeleine Covington. I don't think you came all the way out here to look at a watercolor."

"No, Caleb, You're right. I didn't come here to look at a painting. I didn't even know it was here. It's not one of her best. But it was done a long time ago. She got better."

"You *know* her work?" asked Jennifer.

"Yes, quite well."

Caleb was losing patience. He was in no mood for riddles, for this game of revelation that Eliot seemed to be playing. The anger in his voice ratcheted up a notch.

"Listen, Eliot. The storm will be back with a vengeance. I don't have time to play games with you. So cut to the chase. Tell us why you're really here. What you're after."

Eliot blinked his eyes slowly. He was strangely calm, the inverse of Caleb. The angrier Caleb got, the calmer Eliot became.

"I realize that you didn't expect me here today. I understand that you're busy with the storm ... and with Jennifer. Believe me, I'm not so happy about being here myself. But I came a very long way, and it's important to me."

"Damn it, Eliot! I don't care how far you've come. What the hell is so important to you at this lighthouse?"

Eliot's placid smile turned to a frown.

"You really should be nicer to me, Caleb."

"Nicer to you! You drop in here unannounced. You poke around, ask a lot of questions. You pull apart desks. Rip up floors. This storm is about to come back and it will be worse— a lot worse. I have more to worry about than being nice to you."

"Still, you shouldn't be so angry with me."

"Why is that, Eliot?" asked Caleb, his breath quickening as his anger festered. Their brown eyes met and the two men stared at one another.

There was a long pause.

Then, with the slightest of smiles, Eliot spoke.

"Because, Caleb, I'm your brother."

There was a second or two of silence, as if the sound was moving slowly and hadn't reached Caleb.

"Brother!" Caleb was stunned and shouted the word. "What are you talking about? I don't have a brother. You're a madman!"

"I'm not mad, Caleb, though some who know me may think I am. I *am* your brother. Well, half-brother to be exact."

Eliot folded his arms. He seemed pleased with the stunned looks on their faces. There was silence in the room, a silence set against the growling of the waves outside. The few seconds that passed were heavy and charged.

"How are you Caleb's brother?" asked Jennifer.

Eliot looked at Jennifer. Blinked slowly again.

"We share a father. My mother, Madeleine Covington—or Maddy as she was called—spent one night out here with Caleb's father, Nathaniel Bowen. I am the product of that night. A memory of it. An echo of a brief encounter." He paused for a moment, sniffing, then added: "A bastard."

Caleb was bewildered. If what Eliot was saying was true, then indeed, they were half-brothers. A half-brother he never knew. From a father he barely knew. Caleb forgot about the storm a moment as he tried to understand this new bit of family history that had washed up like a piece of driftwood. If it was true, it didn't explain what Eliot was after out at Race Rock. Caleb was wary of the man. He was unpredictable. Maybe dangerous. He was after something, and the story might be a ploy of some sort. He might just be setting a trap.

Caleb knew that the storm would unleash its full fury soon, and when it did, there would be no time for conversation and riddles. He spoke with a barely controlled anger and growing urgency.

"Eliot, maybe you are my half-brother. I don't know. You're still a stranger, as far as I'm concerned. You still haven't told us why you came to Race Rock. After all this time, why now?"

"Yes, indeed, Caleb—brother. What *am* I doing out here? That is the question." Eliot had turned back to the mantel and was again staring at the watercolor.

Jennifer looked at Caleb. She saw the confusion and doubt on his face. She took his hand in hers and squeezed it. The wind had picked up a bit. The first tendrils of the storm were beginning to wrap themselves around Race Rock.

Eliot turned and faced them again.

"Would you believe me if I said I was out here looking for treasure?"

Caleb closed his eyes. Shook his head. "Treasure! You really are mad!"

"Goddamn it, Caleb!" Eliot hissed, erupting in anger. "Don't call me mad! You don't have a clue. You don't have a fucking clue! I know so much more than you do! You should listen to me!"

"Treasure!" said Caleb again in utter disbelief. "Treasure! What, do you think some pirates buried a treasure chest here at Race Rock?! Why should I listen to you, to your crazy story?"

Eliot gritted his teeth, the muscles in his jaw flexing. His eyes burned now, and he glared at Caleb. He was struggling to maintain his composure. Both men were.

"I wish you'd just leave, Caleb! Go ashore. Get out of my way!"

"Not today, Eliot. Not tomorrow. It's *my* lighthouse. I'm not going anywhere. Treasure!" Caleb spat the last word with scorn and anger.

The two men faced each other. Jennifer gripped Caleb's arm, partly in support, partly to restrain him from a more violent confrontation with Eliot. Eliot was breathing quickly. His eyes flared wide. Then he closed them. After a moment, he opened them and looked at Caleb.

"Let's not argue, brother. We need each other. We need to work *together* to find the treasure."

Jennifer jumped in, trying to diffuse some of the anger in the air.

"What treasure, Eliot? Why do you think there is a treasure here?"

Eliot looked at Caleb, but he seemed to be looking beyond him to a different time and place altogether. His tone shifted completely. He was measured, calm. It was unsettling.

"Like I said, my mother spent a night out here at Race Rock. Just one night. With my—your—our father. She asked him to tell her a secret that night. And he did. He told her he'd found a box washed up on the rocks. A box full of jewels. Not just some trinkets. No, these were huge gems. Diamonds. Emeralds. Rubies. Sapphires. Big jewels worth a fortune. An unimaginable fortune. Nathaniel told Maddy he'd hidden them on the lighthouse. When he was ready to retire, he'd take them, cash them in, and lead a life of luxury."

"But he didn't retire," said Caleb quietly.

"No, he didn't," said Eliot. "Things didn't go as he planned. He screwed up and let the light go out. A ship was wrecked and people died. He was taken off this rock immediately. He had no chance to take his treasure, and he never returned. Nobody knew there was a fortune hidden out here. Nobody except Maddy."

Eliot turned to the mantle, to the watercolor of the light-house keeper. It was his father. The only image of him he had ever seen. It was just a few quick brushstrokes, as vague as any other reference to the man he had ever uncovered. He knew his father through some newspaper articles and the entries he'd read in the logbooks, and they were about as revealing as a grocery list. For a moment, he envied Caleb. At least he had spent time with the man. Talked with him. Heard his voice. Looked into his eyes. As had his mother. The one day they had been together. The day she'd painted this watercolor. He turned away from the mantle.

"Did your mother ever try to contact Nathaniel?" asked Jennifer.

"I don't know. He died just months after she visited, so she probably didn't reach him even if she tried. I doubt he ever knew about me."

"Why didn't your mother tell you about the treasure sooner?" asked Jennifer.

"I'm not sure. Maybe she forgot about it. Until the end. I received a letter she'd written a few weeks before she died. Lung cancer. She always smoked a lot. I suppose that killed her. She was reaching out to me. We'd drifted apart. She was a good painter, but not so good a mother. She tried, but it just wasn't in her nature. Maddy was just too much a drifter and free-spirited person to be tied down by a family. She took up with a succession of men, hoping one of them might be a good father to me. They weren't. Some of them ... well ... it doesn't matter now."

Eliot's voice drifted off. A look of sadness played across his face. Jennifer felt sorry for him. Caleb was trying to keep up with the story and with the jumble of feelings swirling through him.

Eliot turned, reached up and put his fingers on the water-color, as if trying to touch his father through the glass. Or maybe it was his mother he was trying to reach.

"When did you know that Nathaniel was your father?" asked Jennifer.

"I don't remember exactly. I was quite young when she told me. She told me he'd died at sea, which is true. I left home in my late teens. Or what passed as home in Maddy's itinerant life. She was living in Denver with a construction worker. He was a creep. I'd had enough. Denver was a good jumping off point. Plenty of trains to take me away. So I went. I always had a wan-derlust. A desire to see other places. Do forbidden things.

"I won't bore you with my life story. I've been around. I've done things. I'm not proud of some of them. I tried to keep up with Maddy. We'd write letters and do our best to let each other know where our gypsy paths might take us next. My travels took me to New Mexico. That's where I was when I got the let-ter from her. Her last."

Eliot looked up, his expression haunted.

"I'm glad I didn't see her sick. Maddy is ... Maddy was quite a little dynamo. She was small but filled a room with her energy. She was incandescent. I wouldn't have wanted to see her dimin-ished. Dimmed. I was spared that. I'll always remember her as vital."

Caleb glanced at Jennifer. That's how he thought of her. He couldn't imagine her sick or frail.

Eliot continued: "Anyway, I guess she wished she had something to leave me. But she didn't. She was born to great wealth, turned her back on it, and died poor. Actually, her father didn't do so well, either. He lost a great deal of money investing in the White Star line. At first, he did fine. But then their biggest and most beautiful ship—the Titanic—was launched. We all know what happened next.

"Whether Maddy was happy in her life I can't say. I like to think she was. At the end, I think she remembered Nathaniel telling her about the treasure he'd found. Maybe she hoped against hope that it would still be here for me to find. It was a long shot. But she was a gambler and she was dying. It was her last and only hope of giving me something. A legacy."

"How do you know this is all true?" asked Jennifer. "She was sick, dying. Maybe it was just a fantasy."

"I wondered about that, too," said Eliot. "So I decided to check, to see if I could verify it. I figured Nathaniel's logbooks from Race Rock might have some clues. I went to the National Archives, got the journals and looked for myself."

"And?"

Eliot pulled out his little notebook and thumbed through the pages.

"And I found what I was after," Eliot said. "Here's the entry in the Journal of the Lighthouse Station that confirms he found something of value:

December 1, 1905. Snowy. 28 degrees. Winds from SSW at about 10 knots. Visibility 4-5 miles. Seas 1-2 feet. Oiled lamp bearing. Caulked window. Found wood box, a real treasure. Checked kerosene levels. Need 100 feet of rope."

Caleb and Jennifer were fascinated. It was the strangest of stories that this strange man was telling them. And it just might be true.

"Here's the entry for the following summer that shows Maddy was here:

July 8, 2006: Foggy day. Very calm. Hot. 85 degrees. Winds 1-2 MPH from the south. Daily routine. Visited by Painter MC."

Eliot closed the notebook.

"I think my mother's story is true. I think Nathaniel did find a little box of gems and hid it on Race Rock. And I think Maddy did visit him."

"Aren't you the proof of that?" asked Caleb.

"Well, yes and no. She told me about her night with Nathaniel and that he was my father. But she knew enough men in her time that I couldn't be certain. I took my last name—

McPherson—from one of them. Anyway, the entry in the journal verified it for me."

Caleb tried to imagine his father and a young mysterious woman sitting in this very room. He tried to picture his father opening a small box and finding a fortune inside. He thought about Eliot. His father, it seemed, might have left more legacies than Caleb had ever imagined.

Jennifer asked: "So you came out here pretending to be a newspaper reporter on a story and thought you'd open a drawer and it would be full of gems?"

Eliot laughed, a rueful short snort. "Something like that. I figured I'd have to dig around for it. I knew it would be hidden. I didn't know Nathaniel so I couldn't crawl into his mind and figure out where he might hide it. I didn't think this place would be so big. There are a lot of places to hide a small box out here."

"So you're not a reporter," said Caleb.

"Not exactly," said Eliot.

"And you didn't make any arrangements with St. Clair to come here today."

"No. I just rented a small boat and headed out."

"Nathaniel didn't tell your mother where he hid the treasure?" asked Jennifer.

"Certainly not. Nathaniel was no fool. He wouldn't tell a stranger where to find it, no matter how wonderful their lovemaking had been. It was his retirement. The ship he would sail to his dreams."

"Still, it seems like quite a long shot," said Caleb.

Eliot shrugged. "Sometimes, long shots pay off." He turned and looked at Maddy's watercolor again, unable to take his eyes off the simple picture that connected him to his parents.

"I am not, shall we say, particularly flush at the moment," said Eliot. "It's not so easy to find work these days. When I got her letter, it seemed like destiny calling, so I acted on impulse. Like Maddy tended to do. I hadn't thought it all out. I got on the train, did my research in D.C. and New London, and here I am."

"So now what, Eliot?"

"We make a deal, Caleb. We search for the treasure together and we split it. It's fair. You wouldn't have known about the treasure if it weren't for me. It's your lighthouse and I need you to help me look for it."

"What if I just throw you off my lighthouse, Eliot? What then? I live here. I have plenty of time to search. I'd find the box eventually."

There was a very long pause. Eliot looked from Caleb to Jennifer. His mood had shifted again, as quickly as the winds of the storm. She could see it in his eyes.

As Eliot stared at Jennifer, he said quietly, matter-of-factly, coldly: "You may do that, Caleb. You may even succeed. But it will cost you. If we don't share the wealth we find, I promise you I will take something from you far more valuable than any gems." The direction of his stare left no doubt what he meant.

"You son-of-a-bitch!" said Caleb angrily.

"A bastard, yes. Son-of-a-bitch, no. Maddy had class," said Eliot. "Accept my offer and we may both prosper nicely. Otherwise, you may end up very rich, but very sad."

Thunder rumbled. The rain began again, rattling against the window. The storm was back.

"Think it over, Caleb. I'm not going anywhere. Not on a day like this."

"A day like this," Caleb said, shaking his head. "There has never been a day like this."

Caleb banged open the fire doors and stepped onto the spiral staircase, slamming the doors behind him. Eliot and Jennifer listened to his footsteps, loud on the metal stairs as he climbed to the lantern room. They remained in silence a moment.

"If you love him, Jennifer, you'll persuade him to help me find the treasure. It's the only way he'll ever get away from this cursed rock. The only way you two will have a future together."

She said nothing. She stood and left through the fire doors leaving Eliot alone with the ghosts that seemed to have come in on the winds of the storm.

20

Caleb came down from checking on the light. It was working fine. There was plenty of fuel in the reservoir, and four full cans in the lantern room. He and Jennifer met on the stairway just as she came out of the living room. The storm had returned quickly and with renewed intensity. The waves were smashing higher now, against the building and tower of Race Rock, some forty feet above sea level.

It was loud inside the tower. Jennifer hugged Caleb and spoke into his ear, trying to be heard above the roar of the cataclysm outside.

"I'm scared, Caleb. I'm scared of this storm and I'm scared of Eliot."

"I can't protect you from the storm, Jennifer. The lighthouse will have to do that. But I can protect you from Eliot. There's a gun in the study, in the desk or maybe on the shelf in the closet. Go get it and meet me down in the basement," he said into her ear. "I want to check something."

As Caleb turned to go down, she pulled him back and kissed him. It was a long, hard kiss, infused with an urgency of need and fear.

"I love you so much, Caleb."

They held each other for a moment, eyes locked. Then she turned and went up and Caleb started down. As Jennifer passed an arched window, a wave broke against it. Instinctively, she recoiled. It was hard to imagine a wave big enough to hit that high on the tower. She watched as the wave receded back into the night, lit by flashes of lightning. The waves were like rabid animals, lurching at the lighthouse, trying to consume it. It was hard not to think of the storm as purposely trying to get at the three humans inside the stone building. Caleb had said the lighthouse would protect them. She hoped he was right. She hoped it was strong enough to withstand the attack of the water and wind, of the entire ocean pounding against it.

She exited onto the second floor hall and went into the small study. She turned on the light switch. Nothing. The power was out! She felt her way over to the desk and found the flashlight she'd left there earlier. She flicked it on. She opened the top drawer and looked for the gun.

Eliot walked down the hallway, his footsteps lost in the howl of the wind. He saw shadows dancing wildly in the study. He stopped at the doorway and looked in. Jennifer was looking for something in the desk, her back to him. His dilated pupils were well suited to seeing in the gloom. He looked at her luxuriant chestnut hair flowing down her back. He followed the curve of that back down to her buttocks.

Eliot sniffed. His eyes narrowed. Where was Caleb? In the basement, he thought. He'd heard him going down. Even with this wind, it was easy to hear footsteps on the metal stairway. The tower was a natural echo chamber. Caleb was two floors down and at the other side of the lighthouse.

Eliot stepped into the room, crossing a line.

Jennifer was searching for the gun. It wasn't in the top drawer. She pulled out one of the side ones and rummaged there.

"Hello, Jennifer," said Eliot. "Looking for the treasure?"

His voice was eerily calm.

Jennifer turned. A flash of lightning lit Eliot's face. She did not know the man, yet she knew the look in his eyes. Adrenaline shot into her system.

Eliot saw it in the next flash of light. The slight dilation of her eyes and the slight part of her lips betrayed her arousal.

Arousal.

What was the difference between fear and sexual arousal? Were they entwined? Jennifer's subtle signs of anxiety and alertness were very provocative to Eliot. Her reaction was spurring him on. His latest dose of powder, a big one, had tweaked his awareness. He could see and hear and sense things much more acutely when the powder worked its magic. It also loosened the reins on his darker impulses.

He said nothing. He stared at her, and his stare pinned her to the spot. Her breath quickened. His eyes narrowed a bit more seeing that. He was taking control. Everything slowed to a silent shadow play of menace. The moment stretched on. Each was waiting for the other to move. Nothing had been said. No gesture had been made. But Eliot and Jennifer both knew that they were locked into a duel.

She broke the spell. She turned and opened another drawer, hoping Eliot wouldn't see her hands shaking, hoping she'd find the gun. The gun would even the equation. The drawer was full of papers. Nothing more. Then Jennifer realized that even if she found the gun, she could probably never bring herself to use it. He'd take it from her, and then he'd have a weapon. He could easily kill her and Caleb. The lighthouse and the treasure, if there was one, would be his.

She turned and took a step toward the doorway.

Eliot's arm shot out and landed with a thud against the doorjamb, blocking her way.

"Don't leave, Jennifer," he said. "Let's talk. Get to know one another better."

"I know all I need to know about you, Eliot."

"You know, Jennifer, there are a lot more exciting things to do in life than grow old at a lighthouse."

She glared up at him, her green eyes fiery.

"Get out of my way!" she hissed and started to duck under his arm.

Like a snake attacking, his arm spun around her. He tightened his grip around her back and hugged her close to his chest in one swift and brutal motion.

Jennifer was startled it happened so fast. She reared her head back and saw his face just inches from hers, lit by flashing lightning, one moment a bright mask, then a silhouette. She felt his breath. Another flash revealed his sneer.

For an instant, their eyes met. They had reached the crucial moment, a moment when either he would defeat her or she would defy him.

With a fury and strength that surprised Eliot, Jennifer peeled away his arm and spun herself free of his grasp. She walked backwards into the hallway. She was in the shadows, but her voice was strong.

"You know, Eliot, your plan may have one flaw."

"What is that, Jennifer?"

"You think you can just take me, have me, kill me if Caleb doesn't play along with you."

"Something like that, Jennifer."

A flash of lightning lit her like a spotlight. The look of hatred and determination on her face was startling. Eliot blinked. Jennifer leveled her gaze at him.

"But so help me God, Eliot, I might just kill you first."

Jennifer walked down the short hallway, threw open the fire doors, stepped onto the spiral stairs, and slammed the doors behind her with a loud and frightening bang that echoed through the lighthouse like a gunshot.

Eliot stared at the fire door. The wind howled around and through Race Rock. The storm was uncoiling itself. Unleashing its full and deadly fury. It would not go away. It had to be reckoned with.

So did Jennifer. Her defiance was exciting. A little storm in itself. But unlike the one roaring outside, he could tame this one.

Eliot walked into the study and sat on the edge of the desk. He took out his metal case and went through the ritual of carefully inhaling the powder. Like Caleb, he had plenty of fuel left for the night. He savored the sizzling buzz the powder brought. Images of Jennifer flashed across his mind. She was a beauty. Strong. Willful. Her defiance would only make his conquest that much more satisfying.

He needed a new plan. For her. For Caleb.

Eliot pondered his next move, a dark figure in the shadows, occasionally lit by a blinding flash of lightning.

21

Jennifer was shaking. She had left the flashlight in the study. She made her way down the stairway, following its spiral. She was breathing heavily, her adrenaline pumping from fear and anger.

Eliot was not just a man after a treasure. He was a predator. She knew that he wanted her, too. She wished she had found the gun. She no longer doubted she could use it.

She also knew there was something very odd in how quickly Eliot's moods changed. Maybe he was just a madman. Or maybe something else was at work.

She made it to the basement. The sound of the waves hitting the stone walls sounded like explosions.

"The power's out!" she shouted.

"I know. Do you have the gun?"

"No, Caleb. I don't. I ran into Eliot. We had a confrontation. I had to leave before I found it."

"Are you all right?"

"I'm fine."

"I won't let him hurt you," said Caleb.

While she appreciated his sentiment, Jennifer knew she'd have to look out for herself. Eliot was dangerous, unpredictable and probably ruthless. So far as she knew, Caleb had never been involved in violence. She suspected Eliot had. Eliot would be the aggressor. He'd strike first, and he would be deadly. She didn't like the thought of being trapped in the lighthouse with him, with nowhere to go, no place to hide. Not after their face-off in the study. They'd have to keep their guard up. Try to get a step ahead of him.

She decided to change the subject.

"Do you think it's true what he said, Caleb? That there's a treasure here?"

"Could be, Jennifer. Who knows? It's possible. My father did love to collect stuff from the rocks, and I know he never made it back here after the shipwreck. Like Eliot said, there are plenty of places on Race Rock to hide something. If nobody was looking for it, it could still be here."

"Why wouldn't your father have written to Carla or you, or told somebody about it?"

"I don't think he would have trusted anybody. And I don't think he knew where we were. It had been a few years. We'd moved around. I doubt he had any idea where to reach us. And don't forget, he didn't have much time. He left the morning after the storm. He had no warning, no time to make plans. They just took him off here and a few days later he ended his life."

"He could have left a clue," said Jennifer.

Caleb shrugged. He was poking around some of the wiring on a wall, a flashlight balanced on a box. He traced one of the wires with his fingers, groping in the shadows.

"Well, well, look at this," he said. Jennifer came around the tank and looked. Caleb was holding up a wire.

"The telephone line. Cut. No wonder we couldn't call out. Eliot's been busy."

"Yes, he has," said Jennifer. "Yes, he has."

"I think he's a madman," said Caleb.

"Well, he's certainly determined, mad or not. And I think he's taking some drug. His eyes seem glassy at times. His moods change. He's volatile."

"Do you know where he is now?"

"No. I left him in the study."

"Damn. He may have gone to the light." Caleb said. "We better get up there and see if it's still okay. We need to keep him from destroying anything else."

Grabbing Jennifer's hand, holding a flashlight to light the way, Caleb led her out of the basement. They made their way up the stairs. Up and around, up and around. They went slowly, cautiously, expecting Eliot to be around every turn. The roar of the storm, even through the thick masonry walls, was deafening. The metal stairway thrummed beneath their feet.

As they neared the top, Jennifer pulled on Caleb's arm. He stopped so she could talk in his ear.

"It's getting wet in here," she said.

"Probably just salt spray finding its way in through crevices or the windows."

"No. No. Something else. On the stairs. Look: it's flowing from above."

She was right. Liquid was flowing over the stairs, cascading over them like miniature waterfalls. He swiped at the liquid on the stair in front of him. Smelled it.

"It's kerosene! That crazy bastard is pouring the fuel down the stairs!"

"But why would…"

Her words were cut off by a loud whoosh in the stairway as a flame suddenly curled down the stairs toward them like a fiery snake.

"Go down! Get out of here!" Caleb yelled.

He pushed her down the stairway as he recoiled away from the approaching wave of fire.

Down and around they went, spinning around the sixty-eight stairs, the fire at their heels. Caleb pushed Jennifer ahead of him. The inside of the tower glowed with the burning fuel. It dripped off the stairs and dropped down the tower. The burning liquid spread out across the stairs and onto the walls. It was quickly becoming an inferno. Flaming drops rained down on the two figures frantically trying to escape. They reached the fire doors on the first floor. Caleb pulled at them. Locked! They were trapped in a stone chimney full of fire. He remembered the screw had been holding the cotter pin chain had been loose.

"Help me!" Caleb shouted, throwing his shoulder against the door. The flaming liquid was still pouring down. The floor at their feet was burning. Jennifer joined in. Together they slammed against the door in desperation. The screw came loose and the door swung open into the living room. As it did, Caleb saw flames on the side of Jennifer's leg. She saw them, too, and bolted through the open doors across the small living room, shedding fire as she went.

In an instant that fragmented into a collage of impressions, he saw the flame at the side of her leg, growing. He saw chairs and rugs catch on fire as she ran through the room, shedding flames in her wake. He saw her running toward the front door. He understood. She hoped to douse the flames in the waves washing over the porch. She grasped the huge bolt in her hand, slid it open, and turned the doorknob.

"No!" he yelled. Too late.

Jennifer pushed the door open. The tremendously power-ful wind yanked the door outward violently. She was still hold-ing the handle and went with it. Jennifer flew outside and lost her grip. She went airborne out into the darkness, into the teeth of the storm.

The wind howled through the open door. It sounded like a train slamming on its breaks. Chairs, books, tables, lamps—everything in the room—swirled around, crashing into the walls, bouncing off the ceiling. Caleb covered his head and ran across the room. He stood in the doorway, braced against the frame. Usually, he had to look down to see the water. Now it seemed as if Race Rock had sunken down into the sea. Waves crashed across the porch and into the room. The wind howled through the door in a blast that pushed him back. He couldn't see Jennifer anywhere. He'd have to go out there. He looked back over his shoulder. Already the room, or what was left of it, was awash with a few feet of water. At least the flames were out, doused by the sea.

Goddamn Eliot! He was trying to kill them. The man was crazy. Caleb's anger rose and added to the adrenaline already pumping through him. Later. He'd deal with Eliot later. He had to try to find Jennifer.

He knew he'd need a safety line. It was the only way he could hope to have any chance of getting out there, finding her and getting back. The waves were enormous and hitting Race Rock on the second and third floor levels. Water was pouring into the doorway. The beam from the lighthouse swung around and lit the scene. The swells were huge, the waves on top of them enormous. The rain was almost a solid wall of water.

He ran to a supply closet and found a coil of rope. Two hundred feet of it. He hoped it would be enough. Working quickly, knowing every second counted, he tied the rope to a heavy oak desk. He tied the other end of it around his waist, then threw the coil outside. It started to lash around in the wind. Another thing to watch out for.

Then he stepped outside.

He thought he was prepared for it, but the violence of the storm shocked him. He was immediately caught by the wind and slammed into the railing of the porch. He winced, the breath knocked out of him. The water rushed by in mountainous swells that broke around the lighthouse. On top of them, ragged waves collided and roared and shredded into the wind. The wind! It was a wind to shake the world. It seemed to occupy every octave, from a high screech to a low rumble that shook him, filled him, stunned him. It was a world of wind and water mixed into a violent, deadly froth. A new element. The soul of the storm. Caleb had stepped into an apocalyptic nightmare.

His back was pinned to the railing. His front was being bludgeoned by the storm. He dropped down to his knees. He tried to present as small a target as possible.

Something rolled by his feet. The lightning rod. It had finally broken off and tumbled down to the porch. It rolled about with each wave. His lighthouse was coming apart. The world was coming apart.

The wind had the occasional pocket where it slowed a bit. Sensing one, he rose up and looked out. Visibility was maybe fifty feet, a bit more when lightning flashed, and the lightning was flashing almost constantly. He couldn't tell where the sea stopped and the sky began. Maybe there was no division anymore. They had become as one. It was as if Race Rock was inside a bottle that a giant had taken and shaken.

He didn't expect to see Jennifer. She would have been carried far away by this wind. Or she would have been slammed down and broken on the rocks.

Caleb had a sudden feeling of such loss that it was like a deep, sharp wound. "Oh, Jennifer," he moaned. "No, no, no!" He couldn't lose her!

He scanned around frantically, but he saw nothing but a seething sea and black rocks. Waves swept over the porch, knocking him over. The water was ice cold. He crawled back up, grabbed the railing, searched the seas.

Then he spotted her, a small white figure out in the water. She had been thrown a hundred feet or so and had landed beyond the rocks. She wasn't moving. The foaming sea was tossing her closer to the rocks with each violent surge.

Overcoming his fear and a primal urge to flee, Caleb crawled forward to the ladder. Waves crashed below and the cold spray rained down from above. The noise was terrifying. The howl of the wind. The explosive hiss of the waves. The hollow throb of the water boiling through the giant boulders. There was a more ominous sound: the creak and grind of the boulders as they shifted from the force of the sea. He almost lost his nerve. To descend that ladder was to descend into hell.

He gripped the ladder railing. He had to go. He had to try to reach her or die trying. He stepped back and down and into the maelstrom. It was all he could do to hold on. In moving an arm or leg to get to the next rung, his body was pitched to the side. He was soaked. Clumsy. The rungs were slippery. His hands were scrapped raw. He wondered if the railing would hold him. If he was torn loose, he'd be smashed on the rocks.

The waves slammed into him. Some completely covered him when they hit. For about four seconds, he'd be underwater. Then the wave would retreat and he'd be free of it, gasping and clinging to the ladder.

Caleb moved on the desperate hope that he could reach Jennifer. The storm was so violent he couldn't think. It seemed to suck his very being from him. He wondered if he could be ripped apart by this wind, which was gusting to 150 miles per hour. All his concentration was on staying on the ladder. Down with his foot. Get a solid step on the rung. Let go with his hand. Quickly lower and grab the next rung down. Over and over. The ladder seemed endless. It was like a dream. No, a nightmare. A far more terrifying nightmare than he ever could have imagined. And all too real.

At last he was at the bottom of the ladder at the flat landing slab. The boulders rose up on either side. Caleb looked up. The beam of the light spiked through the rain and spray. The air was so laden with water that the light beam seemed a solid, tangible thing. At least Eliot hadn't cut off the light. Not yet.

Caleb's rope still had slack, and it whipped around crazily. If it hit him it might cut him, break bones. He heard thunder. He pictured a lightning bolt slicing down and hitting the metal ladder. Time to step off.

The boulders looked like wet beasts ready to pounce. They were black, slick and deadly. He stepped onto the concrete dock. At least down here, the wind was not as bad. The rocks and the whole lighthouse provided a bit of cover. But the waves were huge. He looked up at them as they surged in. They crashed with no pause against the island. He used the boulders as cover, using the crevices and cracks their jumble created to move toward where he'd last seen Jennifer. The sea funneled through those same cracks and pushed him back. He heard and felt one huge boulder shift above him. He thought of Shane Fitzgerald, the keeper who'd been trapped and drowned in the rocks of his own lighthouse. Now Caleb was clambering about the same kind of giant rocks in a storm capable of tossing them around like pebbles. It was madness to be out here.

The rocks were half submerged and strewn with pieces of wood, half a boat, all sorts of junk. Their jagged tops poked up above the hissing seas like the teeth of a great beast. Precious seconds ticked by. He made slow progress. The rocks were slippery. His clothes were soaked. He spent so much time underwater he was having trouble catching his breath. He was tiring. He pushed on. The waves crashed. Not rhythmically, as waves normally due, but in an angry cadence, like the mutterings of a madman.

At last he crawled between two huge boulders and saw her. She was still in the water. Was she alive? She was face-up, thank God. She was light enough that she rode the water. Maybe she hadn't been smashed against the rocks. When he saw her move her arm, he suddenly had hope. She was alive!

220

He was ten feet from her. Almost there. He took a step forward and stopped short.

He was, literally, at the end of his rope. He tugged at it and backtracked a bit and freed it from a rock. That gave him an extra few feet. Not much, but maybe enough.

The ocean rolled back and Jennifer was pulled away. Then she came nearer as the waters surged forward. He found a foothold and planted himself where he though she would be with the next wave. Two more crashed over him. She was still out of reach. Then a big wave came and she was suddenly there, pushed against him. He wrapped his arms around her as he fell backwards. When the wave receded, Jennifer lay on him, cradled in his arms. He looked at her face. Her lips were blue, her eyes were closed. He could not tell if she was breathing. He remembered the passion of her recent kiss, the glow in her eyes, the warmth of her as she hugged him. Just minutes ago. Now she seemed a corpse in his arms—cold, white, unresponsive. The cold water had sapped the life from her.

Caleb rolled over and lifted her limp, soaked body. He threw her over his shoulder. He had to have at least one hand free to climb back. He knew that bending her that way could be deadly if she was hurt. It could push a broken rib through her heart or snap a weakened back. He had no choice. She moaned in his ear. It was a sweet sound to him. She was still alive.

"Stay with me!" he shouted, though he doubted she could hear much over the wind and waves. "I'll get you inside. Hold on if you can." There was no response.

It was a rough journey across the rocks. The waves knocked them down. The boulders were slick. A few moved as he crawled across them. There seemed to be no break between the waves, just a constant hammering. He looked ahead to the ladder. Twenty feet. Ten feet. He paused in a crevice by a huge boulder to try to catch his breath. Jennifer was still on his shoulder. Her arm looked blue. The exposure was getting to her. She was getting colder. Hypothermic. He was shivering, too. They'd gone from the inferno of fire to the icy grip of water.

A huge wave hit. The giant rock above them groaned as it slowly turned, unbalanced by the force of the surf. It seemed to pivot in slow motion. Caleb dove down between two rocks as the boulder rolled over and onto their crevice.

The waves surged through the gap they were in. Caleb felt his adrenaline surge even higher in panic. They were trapped!

He forced himself to calm down. The rocks on either side supported the boulder that had rolled over. He didn't know how long they would do so. With each swell and surge, the boulder shook. It was a tight spot. Caleb gasped for air between waves and crawled forward, but the opening was too tight. He'd have to try to back out. Another wave crashed over the rocks submerging them. Again it receded and he gasped for air. He pushed back, scraping his knees, scraping Jennifer along the underside of the boulder, praying it would hold. Another wave. He pushed back against the sea. The other end of their crevice was wider. They could escape there. He pushed between waves and at last they were out from under the huge rock. Jennifer moaned.

Caleb crawled around the boulder and through the angular rocks toward the lighthouse. He felt his way, bumping along, scraping and bruising himself, still carrying Jennifer on his shoulder. The water was ice cold as it washed over them relentlessly. The lightning was frequent, lighting the scene with a strange flickering like a jerky old movie.

Finally, they were at the dock. He rode a wave onto it and made his way to the base of the ladder. Caleb looked up. It seemed impossible that he could make the vertical climb with Jennifer on his back. He didn't know if he had the strength. He was exhausted. The fight had been pummeled out of him. He had no adrenaline left. Nothing to push him on but his will. A vague notion of just letting the sea take them crossed his mind. Just let go and sink into the cold waters. Admit defeat. Embrace death. Be together forever in a better world.

Then he thought that his father had chosen that path, pushed by shame and remorse.

Caleb had neither, and would not give in. He shouted to himself: "This is it, Caleb. Now or never. Reach down. Find the strength. You can do this!"

He needed both hands to climb the ladder. He considered untying himself and retying the rope to Jennifer, climbing the ladder, then hauling her up. But that seemed like too much work, and he might lose her to the waves in the process. Or he might be sheared off in his climb with no safety line to save him.

He decided to wrap the rope around Jennifer and tie her against him so that she hung over his shoulders. At least it would give him two hands to climb with. His hands were cramped and bruised. He was shaking from the cold. Handling the flailing rope, handling Jennifer's limp body, all while trying not to be swept away, was very hard. His knots were clumsy, but Caleb managed to secure her as he'd planned. Jennifer was petite, thank god, but she was still dead weight on his back.

Caleb started to climb.

In the middle of the sea, in the middle of the worst storm to ever hit New England, Caleb Bowen made his way up the slippery ladder at the base of Race Rock lighthouse.

"Hold on! Hold on! Hold on!" he kept shouting, as much to himself as to Jennifer. He shouted in time to his climb, like a coxswain goading on his oarsmen. A few times, he slipped, and for a few terrifying seconds they'd hang over the waves below. Their white foamy mouths looked like sharks waiting to swallow them if they fell. Rung by rung, he climbed. The swells and waves smashed him so hard against the ladder the breath was knocked out of him. He couldn't bear to look up. He just took it one rung at a time. Reach up, grab the rung. Lift his foot, get it firmly planted. Reach up, another rung, a little higher.

They reached the top of the ladder.

With a final heave Caleb pulled himself up and over. He fell heavily on the stone porch. He was gasping for breath. A sharp pain in his side made him wonder if he'd cracked a rib. Jennifer was still tied to him in a tangle of rope and limbs. He didn't know if she was still alive. Water washed over them. Again, as he lay there, completely spent, he had to fight the urge to let the storm take them. It was far too powerful and he was far too weak. He lay on his side and looked up at the tower, at the glistening wet stone. He scanned down it to the carving above the door: *"1878."* His eye caught the glint of the plaque by the door. *"God bless all those who serve here."* He didn't feel blessed this day. Just damned.

Race Rock's light rotated overhead, its red beam shining out into the night. He wondered how many boats were out there using that beam to find safety. If there ever was a day when a lighthouse was a life saver, it was this day. September 21, 1938. This was a day that nobody would ever forget.

As he lay there, the end of the rope blew by. He couldn't imagine it coming undone from the desk. He'd tied it as he tied every knot. Hard. And as was his habit, he had double-checked the knot. He raised his head and looked toward the front door of Race Rock.

It was closed.

He crawled toward it, Jennifer still lashed to him. The rope whipped around on the porch. He rose to his knees and reached up and grabbed the doorknob. He gave it a twist and pulled.

Nothing. It didn't budge.

The door was locked.

The goddamned door was locked!

22

It had been a slow, rough passage through Long Island Sound aboard the *Catskill*. The tremendous wind, tidal surge and waves had battered the ship. Windows broke. Lifeboats were ripped from their davits. Seams flexed from the torque of the hull and began to leak. The *Catskill* was coming apart.

Captain Freedman regretted leaving Montauk. He would have to find Race Rock, round it and try to get to the more sheltered waters of the Thames River. He peered into the darkness looking for a single red light blinking. Though his ship was constantly smothered by the enormous waves, there were a few precious seconds between them when he could look for the lighthouse. His life and the life of everybody onboard depended on the light.

He could not shake the fear that the *Catskill* would ride down one of the waves and keep going down. There would be no recovering from that death dive. He also feared he'd lose steering and get turned broadside to the waves. They might last a little while, but eventually a wave would hit them full abeam and knock them over. They could also be overwhelmed by a following sea. There were so many ways to lose a ship in a storm this big.

The problem with being at sea and in danger is that there is seldom a "Plan B." The only way to get to safety is to sail to safety. No one can help you. No one but the light keeper laying down a beam of light for you to follow—a blessed thing in the darkness of a storm.

23

Caleb was furious.

He was locked out of his own lighthouse. Jennifer was near death, and they were at the mercy of a merciless storm and a murderous madman. It was an exquisitely diabolical nightmare they found themselves in. In a few hours, his calm life, like the day, had exploded into violence. Eliot had failed to burn them up in the stairwell. So he locked them out and left them for the sea to take. They'd either be washed away and drowned or die of exposure.

"Goddamn you, Eliot," he yelled, "Damn you to hell, you fucking bastard!' The anger made him feel better. It focused his energy.

Caleb huddled against the wall near the door. He rested just long enough to get his wind back, then untied Jennifer from his back. He retied the rope around her waist, left a few feet of slack, and propped her up against the stone wall. Then tied a loop to the heavy iron door handle.

He'd have to break into the lighthouse. That wouldn't be easy. The windows were thick, double paned, and crisscrossed with inner wire for strength. He remembered the iron lightning rod that had broken off and lay on the porch. It was heavy, pointed, about three feet long. It would make a perfect spear to use to smash through a window.

The rod was still rolling along the porch, bumping into the railing. It was angled so that it didn't fit through the railing supports. A bit of luck for Caleb. Untethered and grabbing the railing to keep from being washed away, he made his way to the rod. He hefted it in his hand. It was heavy. He saw the ragged edge at the bottom where it had sheared off the cupola.

Caleb hugged the stone of the light tower and made his way to the leeward side. In this storm, with the winds so high and confused, the leeward side was not much calmer than the windward side. He edged along the wall until he reached a window. He stepped back, planted his feet, held the rod in both hands, raised it above his head like a sledgehammer ... and paused.

Caleb had spent countless hours maintaining this window. Cleaning the salt off the glass. Sanding and painting the wood. Filing, priming and painting the lead between the panes. Now he was about to try to destroy it. Lightning flashed and he saw himself reflected in the window.

The keeper of the light, poised to attack it.

His nightmare continued.

24

Eliot stood in the lantern room at the top of Race Rock, panting. He had run back up the stairs after he'd untied the rope and locked the door. He flinched when a spray of water hit the glass just inches away. The howl of the wind seemed to cut into him. He couldn't think clearly.

He looked into the revolving lamp. Its center burned a bright, molten orange. It was the very soul of the light. Around it, the prisms of the Fresnel lens caught and focused the beams out into the night. He sat down on the metal floor that was strewn with empty kerosene cans. The light spun, alternating between the glowing glass and the blacked-out panels. Red. Black. Red. Black.

His plan was not going well at all. No, everything was a mess. This storm! He hadn't planned on a storm. The day had been so clear. So calm. Then this storm had come along. It terrified him. He had never been out in the ocean, and had no idea it could be so violent. What rotten luck to pick this day to be out here.

He hadn't counted on the woman, either. How could he? He had thought he'd just come out, talk to Caleb, look around, maybe be lucky and find the treasure. If not, maybe he could get his brother to help. Whatever. He'd have figured out something.

It had all gone wrong.

Now he was up here at the top of this damned place with all hell breaking loose. Could the waves knock this thing over? He had no idea. He had no idea that waves could even get this high! The tops of a few seemed to rear up almost to the light before their foaming white tops were blown by the wind. He had no idea that wind could get so strong! And seeing that house go by—that had really spooked him.

He looked at the light. That's all Caleb cared about. Lighting it and keeping it lit so he could be the hero of the storm. Not tonight, brother. The damned fool was locked out of his own lighthouse. He was busy trying to rescue his woman. Eliot hoped they'd just be swept away. Then he could have the light to himself and look around all he wanted once the storm was over. He'd tear the place apart if he had to. The treasure was here. His legacy was here. His mother was right. He knew it.

With Caleb gone, he wouldn't have to share any of it. Not that he really would have. No, as soon as they found the treasure he'd have taken care of Caleb. Accidents could happen easily at a lighthouse. Caleb had said so. He'd have taken care of Jennifer, too. The bitch had snooped around and caught him. Ruined his plan. He'd have enjoyed throwing her into the sea and watching her drown. Too bad he'd miss that bit of fun.

They'd actually made it easy for him. Caleb had provided a supply of kerosene. Eliot had used it as a weapon. Like an old medieval castle where they'd pour flaming oil from the parapets onto the invaders below. It had been an inspired move. He hadn't burned them up, but he'd chased them outside, and that was even better. Let the storm take them. He could explain that away. Caleb and Jennifer went out to fix something. He'd tried to tell them it was madness. They insisted. They were washed away.

He should make sure they were gone. He stood up and looked out over the rocks. The lightning was frequent. He couldn't see them anywhere. They must have been swept away by the waves by now.

He stood and looked into the light, so bright it was painful to his dilated pupils. As it flickered and danced, the flame seemed to take on form. At first, Eliot wasn't sure what it was. He looked closer, ignoring the pain in his eyes, a pain that had seeped deeper into his head. He stared at the flame and saw it was really several entwined figures, vaguely human, yet deformed. He watched them writhe and gyrate. They were demons! He could see that now. Horrific things that danced and seemed to beckon him to their world of fire. It was unsettling, but mesmerizing. He couldn't look away.

He fingered the case in his pocket as he watched.

He felt trapped in the small lantern room. Trapped with the damned demons that danced in the flame, whose shadows writhed on the cupola above. Maybe he could burn them up in the flame that had spawned them. He opened the door in the lens. He pumped the fuel and the light glowed brighter. Red. Black. Red. Black.

The waves. The wind. Lightning. Demons. Spiders.

He wished he could shut it all out. Just for a minute. Just a minute of quiet and calm, like before. He wanted to think. He needed to have a new plan of action. Wait, then search for the treasure? Search where? The attic? The basement? The closets? The walls? Maybe the desks? Had he searched the desks? He couldn't remember. His thoughts were getting more chaotic, like the storm itself, coming at him from every direction.

The light spun.

The demons danced.

His mind ricocheted from plan to plan.

He scratched his arm.

25

Caleb slammed the lightning rod down as hard as he could against the window. It cracked and crumbled from the blow. The mesh kept the shards together. He hit it again. And again. And again. With a renewed strength, with a fury fueled by desperation and anger, he struck the window. Finally, it gave in. It buckled and fell with a crash into the front room.

Caleb used the rod to scrape jagged glass off the bottom of the windowsill. He threw the rod inside, then pulled himself up and over. He pitched forward and into the living room. He landed in two feet of water laced with broken glass, books, cups. He wasted no time. He got to his feet and went to the front door. He pulled open the bolt and kicked the door out. Caught by the wind, the door slammed open and back against the wall. He had tied Jennifer just right. She was dragged to the open doorway. He again stepped into the maelstrom and untied her from the rope and pulled her inside the lighthouse. He left the front door opened. It was too much effort to try to close it against this wind. He wondered how Eliot had managed to do so. Perhaps madness, like anger, had given him extra strength.

Again the wind swept into the small living room. Things flew around and bumped into the walls. Caleb hunched over Jennifer trying to protect them both from the flying debris.

The waves came in too. They hit the walls and sprayed upwards. Caleb was knocked back. Maddy's watercolor spiraled into the surging surf that flowed across the porch and into Race Rock. He was losing. The wind and water were winning. His lighthouse was being destroyed by the storm.

He struggled to his feet, now waist-deep in the water.

"Hang on, Jennifer," he yelled. "We've got to get to higher ground!" He hoisted her over his shoulder, again hoping she didn't have a broken back or ribs.

He wondered about Eliot. Where was he? Was he lying in wait? Caleb stumbled back to the window he'd broken. He picked up the lightning rod. It was his only choice for a weapon.

Soaked, with Jennifer slung over his shoulder, he went to the fire doors. They were open. He willed himself into the stairwell, holding the lightning rod in front of him like a sword. He stepped into that cold spiral where he feared a madman lurked, waiting like a spider, patient and deadly.

26

Eliot stood by the lamp. He was still transfixed by the demons in the light, still overwhelmed by the storm outside the small glass room. The howl of the wind was an agonized scream, as if the ocean were in pain. Or maybe it was the voices of all the people who had ever perished at sea crying together, a chorus of dread and despair. Maybe it was their souls that danced in the flame.

He took the metal case from his pocket. The silver reflected the red of the spinning light. He opened it and took out the vial and tube. He dipped the tube into the powder and inhaled sharply. Once. Twice. The red light spun above him, alternately casting his face in shadow and blood-red light. He closed his eyes and felt the drug infuse his mind, his body, his senses.

He stood there and let the kaleidoscopic images play across his eyelids, the sounds morph and form and re-form.

Then his hearing, so acute now, so very acute, picked up something new. It was subtle. Maybe he was just imagining it? But, no, no, it was real. Yes, very, very real. The thunder seemed to fall into a rhythm. It sounded like huge distant drums booming a steady cadence. The wind was chanting: "Come in, Eliot. Come in. Come in!" How hadn't he heard it before? He opened his eyes. He stared at the light, at the demons. Theirs was a dance of death, in time to the thunder and the chanting, terrifying and hypnotic. The light was no longer a beacon to mariners but a portal to hell.

Red. Black. Red. Black.

"Come in, Eliot. Come in. Come in!"

His mind drifted to the powder. Had he taken it? He couldn't remember. He should take some. It always helped him see things clearly. Helped him act. He took out the vial and the tube and took a deep sniff. He put it away.

His arm itched. He scratched it. It only made it worse. Christ, that was where the spider had been on him! It must have bitten him. He gaped at his arm. He was horrified to see the skin rippling and writhing. There was something below the skin. The spider must have laid eggs! They'd hatched! He had spiders crawling inside him!

He scratched frantically, drawing blood, waving his arm like it was a flaming branch and he was trying to douse the fire. It *was* a fire, a burn of pain and agony. Eliot felt a surge of terror as he imagined spiders beneath his skin, crawling about inside him. The powder took him further into his fear. He was over-whelmed by the sound of the chanting voices. He ducked when he saw the writhing demons on the ceiling. They were getting ready to come after him. He was surrounded by these creatures; he was invaded by them. The light spun its cycle of black and red, black and red, a heartbeat of horror. He had to get out of here!

Eliot put his ear to the door. Carefully he opened it. Peered into the darkness of the stairway.

27

It was hard to carry Jennifer up the tight spiraling stairway. Though she was small, she was soaking wet and
deadweight. The lightning rod clanged as it bounced along the
stairs. He struggled up and around, up and around until he got
to the second floor. He pushed the fire doors. They opened a
crack but no more. Still locked.

"Damn you, Eliot," he spat, "Damn you!"

Caleb jammed the rod into the crack and slashed it up.
Hard. It took a few times but the small chain snapped, the cotter pin tumbled out, and the latch swung up. He kicked the
doors open.

He took a quick look in. He half hoped Eliot would be
there. Caleb was angry enough to bash him with the lightning
rod. Brother or not, he would kill the bastard.

Caleb stumbled down the hall and into a bedroom. He lay
Jennifer on the bed and quickly shut the door.

He was cold and wet and shivering. In the strobing illumination of the lightning, Jennifer was pale. Her lips blue. Her
breathing was shallow. He took her pulse. It was faint, slow. She
was hypothermic. In shock. She was shutting down. He knew
he had to get her out of her wet clothes and warm her up or she
would die.

He stood there and looked down at her. It was a strange
moment. Caleb and Jennifer had never slept together. Whenever his kisses and hugs had become insistent and passionate,
Jennifer had smiled and said, "Not 'til we're married." He had
accepted that. Not that he had given up fantasizing about making love to her. Hardly. Yet they never had, and he had never
seen her naked.

He sat her up on the bed and started to undress her. His urgency was fueled not by lust but by pure love, by a desire to save this woman who had captured his heart. Taking clothes off someone who is unconscious is not easy. Especially when the clothes are wet. As he undressed her, Jennifer shivered violently. She was getting worse quickly.

He got her shirt, pants and socks off and lay her back on the bed. She wore only a bra and panties.

Caleb stopped. Should he take off her underwear? The whole scene was a bizarre parody of a man undressing his lover. He decided they needed to go, that he needed to get her warm and dry. Completely. He pulled off her panties and unsnapped her bra. In the dim light, she glowed like a ghost. He gazed at her naked body for just a moment. He went to the closet and found a towel. He sat on the bed, sat Jennifer up, and started to dry her body with brisk rubs.

Caleb was so intent on drying her off that he hadn't realized that he, too, was shivering, almost uncontrollably. His teeth were chattering. He was also tipping into hypothermia. He dried Jennifer some more then lay her back down and pulled the sheets and wool blanket over her.

Again he went to the closet and found another towel. He stripped off his own clothes and started to dry himself. The towel felt good. He rubbed hard, trying to get his blood flowing.

Jennifer mumbled something unintelligible.

She was disoriented. Maybe hallucinating. More signs of hypothermia. At least she was still alive. Caleb dried himself for a few minutes. He had to get Jennifer warmer. She had been in the water longer than he, and was suffering more as a result.

Without thinking about it, Caleb walked over the bed, pulled up the covers and slid in beside her. He rolled Jennifer over on her side and curled himself along her back, spooning her. He wrapped his arms around her and hugged her tight to him, hoping to share his body heat. It was all he could think to do.

"Come on, Jennifer. Hang in there. You're going to make it. You're going to be all right. You have to be!"

He had dreamt of being naked with her many times, but now there was nothing erotic about it. Not at all. Her alabaster skin was cold, clammy. He breathing was very slow, very shallow. She still shivered. Occasionally, a violent shudder wracked her body.

Caleb hugged her tighter. She smelled salty. Jennifer mumbled and whispered, as if her mind was trying to latch onto something coherent that would bring her back.

"flomtng ... mnnn ... lutht ... seecol ... tethure... cofy ..."

Caleb grasped a word and tried to connect to it. To her.

"There's a fresh pot of coffee," he whispered in her ear. "Nice and hot, Jennifer. Can you smell it? Feel the heat?"

Caleb hugged Jennifer and prayed she would survive. He had never thought about losing her. They were relatively young and quite healthy. Such thoughts didn't cross their minds. Now it was possible, and it scared him. In the fear of losing her he realized just how much he loved Jennifer. How much a part of his life she had become.

He held her closer.

28

Eliot ran down the spiral staircase. The fire was out. The stairs were blackened. He spun down the steps. Down and around. Down and around. His eyes were so dilated, he could see in the unlit tower. The flashes of lightning hurt, and he flinched every time one knifed through the windows.

Near the bottom, he saw water flooding into the bottom of the tower, coming in from the living room. He stopped at the threshold to the living room and peered in. It looked like a bomb had gone off. It was a shambles. The wind and waves were still wreaking havoc. Furniture was being tossed and broken. The front door was open! He had locked it, hadn't he? Maybe not. He couldn't remember. Maybe it had blown open. Or maybe Caleb and Jennifer has survived and come back in? If so, where were they?

Damn!

He started back up. Up and around. Up and around. He was panting when he made it to the top. Through the open door to the lantern room he saw the red glow of the evil light. He recoiled, turned, and ran down the spiral stairs again. Halfway down, he stopped. No! He had to get back up there. If they got back in, he should be up there at the light. Caleb wanted that light lit. Needed the light lit. That was it! If he controlled the light, he could control Caleb!

He spiraled back up, gasping. His footsteps clanged in the stone tower. The waves and wind and thunder all roared outside. He got to the lantern room, went in, and slammed the door shut.

29

Caleb heard the door slam. Eliot was crazy, drugged, frightened and desperate, and now he was in the lantern room. The light was at his mercy. So was anyone out there who depended on it. Caleb was not going to let him destroy it. He wasn't going to let the light go out on a night when it meant survival to those caught in this storm of storms!

He would not let history repeat itself. *This* Bowen would not fail in his duty. He could not stay with Jennifer. He had to get to Eliot. He had to protect the light.

And he had to save Jennifer.

Caleb was torn. He had to choose. He had to choose between Jennifer and Race Rock. Between love and duty. Between the past and the future.

He got out from under the covers and sat on the side of the bed. Jennifer didn't look much better. Her lips still had a bluish cast. She was shivering, and when she mumbled it was more whispered nonsense. Her breathing was very shallow. His embrace might have warmed her a bit, but as soon as he was gone, her body seemed to slide back into hypothermia. She had gone over the edge, and he might not get her back.

For a minute, the storm vanished. Caleb was lost in memories and thoughts, in fleeting impressions of his father, of other nights at Race Rock, of Jennifer and days and nights to come. He had arrived at this moment, and this moment was a prologue to two possible futures. He had to choose one.

Caleb sat on the edge of the bed a bit longer.

Then he crawled back under the covers and curled himself around Jennifer.

30

Eliot emptied the final grains of white powder from the vial. Like the light, he had pumped himself up to a hot, bright intensity. Like the light, his mind spun. The demons. The voices. The unearthly moan of the wind, wrapping itself around the tower, snaking its fingers into him, tearing at his senses. His arm was on fire. He felt the spiders making their way through him. He lay on the floor of the lantern room, tormented and terrified.

He looked up and watched the light spin, sending its beam into the storm. A sliver of light in the darkness. He laughed. He wasn't fooled by the light. He knew it was just a trap, that the beam would draw the unwary in, in to the clutches of the demons, the devils, the horrors that lived within the flame, waiting.

No, he was not fooled it all!

He knew what he must do. He must kill the light before it killed him.

* * *

Caleb had been with Jennifer for perhaps another thirty minutes. He had hugged her close and massaged her hands, arms and shoulders. Her breathing had slowly grown stronger. Her skin was no longer icy to the touch. She was still unconscious, but the warmth of his body against hers had helped. He had pulled her back from the brink.

He got out of the bed and carefully opened the door. He waited for a lightning flash. The hall was empty. Naked, Caleb darted to his room. He went inside and got some clothes.

He dressed himself. The dry, warm clothes felt wonderful. He rooted around and found some clothes for Jennifer. They'd be big on her, but it little mattered.

He went back to her.

He laid the clothes on the bottom of the bed. He picked up the lighting rod and cautiously went back to the spiral stairway. No sign of Eliot. Caleb descended to the first floor. It was soaked by the sea and battered by the wind, which still howled through the open front door. The kitchen was a mess, too. Caleb searched a few cupboards before he found what he wanted: a bottle of whiskey, kept at the lighthouse in case someone who'd been rescued needed to be revived.

Caleb made his way back up to the second floor. He returned to Jennifer and sat beside her on the bed. He sat her up. He uncorked the bottle and tipped it to her lips.

"Here, Jennifer. Take a sip of this."

Her eyes opened halfway. Her pupils were dilated.

"Iththistha...?" she said.

"Take a sip." He parted her lips with the bottle and tipped it so that a little whiskey trickled into her mouth. She sputtered and coughed.

"Good," thought Caleb. "Anything that gets her body working is good."

When she stopped, he tipped the bottle again. A little whiskey trickled down her chin, but some made it in her mouth. She sputtered and coughed again. Swallowed.

"Caleb?" she moaned, suddenly seeming to snap into awareness. For the first time, he thought she might make it.

"Yes, Jennifer."

She dropped down on the pillow. Eyes closed. She was on the borderline of recovering or lapsing back into shock.

He still held the bottle and raised it to take a sip himself. But didn't. A night a generation earlier flashed across his mind and stopped him. He gently put the bottle on the bedside table. He sat on the bed and felt Jennifer's cheek. Warmer. He bent close to her face and felt her breath. Stronger. Every so often, a shudder would run through her body. She still had a long way to go to pull out of her hypothermia. Caleb lay down behind her again and hugged her through the covers.

He put his lips to her ear and spoke. "Jennifer, can you hear me?" There was no response for a few seconds. Then: "Caleb?"

"Yes."

She was struggling back, trying to stay conscious. She was still weak. Still confused. She closed her eyes.

"Stay with me, Jennifer. Come back."

A minute passed. Two. He hugged her tighter, hoping some of his warmth would flow to her. Another few minutes passed.

Her eyes flickered open. "Caleb?"

"Yes."

"What happened?" Her voice was still weak.

She had regained some coherency. Caleb let out a long sigh and without warning, a sob caught in his throat. Now he was the one who could not talk.

"What happened?" she asked again.

Caleb told her. He told her about the fire, about how she'd run down and out and been blown off Race Rock by the winds. He told her how he'd rescued her, how he had to break in, how he'd taken her up to this room and revived her. During the time it took him to tell her what had happened, she seemed to gain some strength.

"What happened to my clothes?" she asked, her tone one of simple bewilderment.

"I had to undress you to get you dry and warm. I'm sorry," said Caleb.

"No. It's okay. It's okay. You had to."

There was an awkward pause.

"Besides," she added, "You'd see me this way sooner or later, when we were married."

"Jennifer?"

"Yes?"

"Can we set a wedding date?"

Caleb said this impulsively. It just came out. Because he was behind her, he could not see the wide smile that spread across her face, or the sparkle return to her eyes. Now that he had her back, Caleb knew that he would never let her go.

He would not lose her. Not to a storm. Not to a madman. Not to his own blind dedication to the light.

"I'd like that," she said.

"How about November 17?" he asked.

"Why November 17?" she replied.

"You don't remember?" he asked, a little surprised. "We met on November 17, when your hat blew off."

"Ah, yes," she said, "you're right. It *was* November. That sounds good to me, Caleb. November 17 it is. Where?"

"We'll have to work on that. A church if you want a priest. Maybe someplace like the Lighthouse Inn if we have a Justice of the Peace."

They lay there a few minutes. Jennifer was not sure if they had really had the conversation or if she had imagined it.

"November 17?" she repeated. She had to hear it again to be sure.

"November 17," said Caleb.

Jennifer smiled. The seventeenth was just a few months away. She trusted that things would be back to normal by then. She could just see the diamond engagement ring on her finger in the gloom. She felt beat up, half dead, yet more alive than she could remember. She had come out to Race Rock this day to get Caleb to agree to a date. To ask him to leave Race Rock once they were married. Well, she'd accomplished at least one of her goals. Damned near died trying!

Caleb was happy, too. Setting a wedding date gave him a sense of resolution. A feeling that they had charted a course. What would happen after they were married he did not know. For now, just having a date was enough.

"Jennifer, I have to get to Eliot. He's locked himself in the lantern room, I think. No telling what he's going to do to the light. This storm .... this storm is the worst I've ever seen! Probably the biggest to ever hit this area. There are boats out there and they need this light lit. I don't think he's going to let me in. I've got to figure out something."

"He's a madman, isn't he, Caleb?"

"Yes. And more: he's taking something. Cocaine, maybe. You mentioned his changing moods. So he's a very dangerous madman. He's tried to kill us already."

"Son-of-a-bitch," said Jennifer.

"No, 'bastard'," said Caleb. They both chuckled.

"Do you think there really could be a treasure, Caleb?"

"Maybe. I don't know. He sure thinks so. But it all may just be a fantasy, the wild dreams of a madman."

"When this is all over, Caleb, we'll have to look."

"Yes. With Eliot looking over our shoulders, no doubt. We'll deal with that later. Right now, I have a light to keep lit and a brother to calm down." He shook his head. *"Brother."* It was an odd thought.

The lightning was frequent. The thunder loud. The wind screaming. The waves boomed like cannons as they continued their relentless attack on the lighthouse. The storm was at full intensity. Urgent as it was to get to the lantern room, Caleb didn't want to leave Jennifer. It was so good to hear her voice. To know she would not die. He stayed a few minutes longer, then sat up. She rolled over and looked up at him. She could just see his face in the gloom.

He looked at her with a smile, then spoke: "Okay. Time to deal with Eliot. I don't think you're hurt too bad. I was afraid something might be broken, but I don't think so. You're a tough little thing. You've got a lot of cuts and scrapes and bruises, and a nasty burn on your leg. Nothing that won't heal. You were stunned and you were hypothermic, but I think you're going to be okay. There's a first aid kit in the bathroom, and some clothes here for you, when you feel up to it. Big, but they're all I've got."

He kissed her on the cheek. She turned and before he could pull away, she kissed him on his lips.

"I love you," she said.

Now Caleb smiled. He stood to leave, but she grasped his hand and held him back.

"Caleb, I have an idea."

"An idea? For what?"

"For getting to Eliot," she said. "I think I know how."

31

Crouched in the lantern room as the light spun, Eliot shut his eyes as the red sector, the one with the demons in it, lit his face. He couldn't bear to look at them anymore. Couldn't bear to watch their grotesque, writhing dance of death. Their eerie, seductive cries merged with the wind. Both were calling to him. He knew the wind wanted him, too. All the sea and all the sky and all the damned creatures that lived in the light wanted him. His senses, so acute, so exceptional, took it all in. The world vibrated through his mind with a hot intensity. He had begun to take energy from the storm. The powder had shown him the way. Now he sailed through the mayhem.

"Eliot!"

What was that?

"Eliot!"

Something—someone—was calling his name. A new voice!

"Eliot!"

He could barely hear it above the wind and the waves and the thunder and his heart.

"Eliot!"

It was coming from below.

"Who are you?" he shrieked, "What do you want?"

"It's me, Eliot. Caleb. Let me in!"

"No! Go away!"

"Damn you, Eliot. Let me in!"

"No!"

"Listen, Eliot, I have the treasure!"

"I don't believe you. Go away! Leave me alone!"

"It's incredible, Eliot. If I show you a piece, will you let me in? I just need to adjust the light."

A pause. Eliot was scratching his arm, blood dripping. The light spun. The voices chanted. He was trying to cope with so much! Too much! But the treasure … that was what he'd been after. Just this morning, when everything was so calm and clear. Before this journey to hell. The treasure. Did Caleb really have it?

"Eliot, can you hear me? Open the door a crack and I'll slip in a ring. It's a diamond. The smallest of the whole lot. You were right. The treasure *is* here. Once you told me about it, I had a hunch where to look. I remembered someplace my father had shown me. And I found it, Eliot. Do you hear me? *We* have it! It's wonderful!"

Eliot sat back. The treasure, found? Where? Blood dripped down his arm. Red. The light spun. Red, black, red black. "Come in, Eliot. Come in!"

"Eliot?"

"You have the treasure?" He shouted through the door, above the din of the storm.

"Yes! Open the door, I'll show you. Just a crack so I can give it to you!"

Eliot shuffled back around the base of the light, bumping the empty fuel cans out of his way. He stood and leaned against the door with all his weight. He turned the metal latch, unlocking it.

"It's open!" he yelled. "I'll open it just a crack."

He leaned back just a bit and pulled open the door. As he said, just a crack. Two fingers snaked in and dropped a ring on the gray metal floor. They withdrew and Eliot slammed the door shut. He did not throw the lock. He was too distracted by the ring.

It *was* a diamond. He picked it up and held it to his eyes. The sparkling gem caught the red light.

"I know it's small," yelled Caleb. "But it matches one that must be ten times the size. Maybe it was a little girl's ring to match her mother's. I was afraid to take out anything bigger in case I dropped it. You wouldn't want that, Eliot. The treasure's half yours. That's only fair."

246

Eliot turned the ring in his hand. The demons and ban-shees faded back a bit as he stared, mesmerized, at the stone. It glowed like an ember when it caught the red of the spinning light.

At the top of the spiral stairs, outside the door, Caleb waited. He had the lightning rod with him—his weapon. He wished he had the gun. Jennifer hadn't found it in the desk and he wasn't sure where it was. He hadn't wanted to waste time looking. So he'd headed up to the lantern room with the light-ning rod.

Caleb had caught a bit of luck. Eliot hadn't locked the door. He had a chance. Caleb closed his eyes. He calmed himself. He'd try something Nathaniel had taught him. Something he called "selective listening." It was a way to shut out distractions and focus on one sound. It was useful for a mariner trying to home in on a bell buoy in the fog or the sound of waves break-ing on an unseen rock. It took concentration.

Caleb told his mind to shut out the sound of the waves, to focus on the noises from above him. The waves dimmed. They weren't gone, but he'd pushed them to the background of his perception. He told his mind to shut out the sound of the wind. The wind dimmed. One by one, he pushed away the sounds of the storm. The thunder, the rain, the echo of the swells hitting Race Rock. He focused his attention on the lantern room above. He could hear the faint sound of Eliot. Caleb waited until he heard him take a few steps away from the door.

It was his chance.

Caleb rammed through the door. Like a football player try-ing to muscle his way through defenders, he kept his legs mov-ing, his head down, his body tensed. He kept the lightning rod with him as he crashed through the doorway into the lantern room.

Eliot was only a foot or two away. Caleb slammed into him and knocked him onto his back. The ring flew out of Eliot's hand and bounced about. It rolled into the gap around the cen-ter column and clattered down into the shadows.

Caleb went down too. Eliot was quick. He flipped over to his hands and knees. He started to scramble about, swatting aside empty kerosene cans. It was hard to see in the lantern room. The spinning light blinded him when it swung around and beamed into his dilated pupils. Caleb rolled to his left against the wall. He stood. Eliot stood. The brothers were separated by the spinning light. As it turned, Eliot's face would glow red, then Caleb's. Rain hammered against the roof and the windows. The tops of the enormous waves sheared off and pelted the lantern room. The wind and the thunder were a constant roar. Lightning bolts zigzagged everywhere. They were in the middle of an apocalyptic nightmare.

The Fresnel lens turned, the flame pumped as high as it could go.

Red. Black.

Caleb. Eliot.

Caleb stood against the lantern room wall, the lightning rod clenched in his hand, his anger as hot now as the light that spun between them.

"You don't try to burn us up, Eliot!" he yelled. "You don't lock me out of my own lighthouse! You goddamned don't fuck with this light!"

Eliot pressed back against the wall. They were only about seven feet apart. Caleb took a step around toward him and Eliot inched away along the wall.

The light spun.

Water hit the window.

Lightning flashed.

Caleb took another step. Eliot did too.

Caleb peered through the glittering glowing lens at Eliot. He looked wild, a force of nature gone crazy. Like this day. Whether the man was really his brother he did not know. Did not care. He was a murderous stranger who had to be stopped, stopped before he killed them, before he damaged the light.

Eliot looked back at Caleb through the lens.

Then, slowly, very slowly, Eliot reached out and put both hands on the hot spinning lens, stopping it. Tiny tendrils of smoke wafted up from his fingertips.

"Jesus, Eliot, no!" Caleb yelled. He couldn't believe what he was seeing. Touching the lens must have been excruciating.

Wild-eyed, smiling, Eliot let the lens go. It spun again. It was so bright! Eliot had pumped the flame so high! Caleb was blinded for an instant. He blinked.

Eliot pounced like a cat. He lunged down and around the light and yanked the lightning rod from Caleb's hand. It happened so quickly that Caleb barely flinched. He could not believe someone could move so quickly! Along with madness, the drug had given Eliot speed.

The tables were turned. Eliot had the weapon now.

"I don't what?" he yelled, waving the rod above him.

"Eliot! Watch out!" Caleb yelled back. There wasn't room in the lantern room to wield that rod without hitting something.

"I'll do what I want, Caleb!"

"Kill me," yelled Caleb, "and you will never have the treasure!"

"But you already have it, brother. You already have it."

"No, Eliot. That was just Jennifer's engagement ring. The treasure is still hidden. I think I know where. You'll never find it!" It was a bluff. Caleb had no idea where the treasure—if there really was one—might be.

The brothers circled each other around the small lantern room, the light spinning between them, the storm raging outside. Eliot looked even wilder and angrier when he realized he'd been tricked.

"I knew I shouldn't have trusted you, Caleb!"

They continued to circle the light. Then Eliot smiled just a bit.

"No matter, Caleb. No matter. When you're gone, I'll take care of Jennifer. Then I will have Race Rock to myself. I'll find the treasure."

"Listen, Eliot..." He never finished.

Eliot jumped a few feet closer and swung the lightning rod at Caleb's head.

This time, Caleb reacted quickly. He dropped to the floor as the metal pole swung by. It missed him by inches.

It didn't miss the glass window.

The force of Eliot's enraged swing carried the lightning rod through the lantern room window. It shattered in a spray of glass.

The full fury of the storm rushed in, a blast of wind and water whistling into the room at ninety miles and hour. The cold water doused the spinning light. Eliot stood there, arms extended. The lens hissed as the salt spray turned to steam. The glass cracked.

Then it exploded in a blinding flash.

Caleb was already down from ducking the blow. He covered his head with his arms as bits of hot glass sprayed around the tiny lantern room.

Eliot had no time to protect himself. The hot shrapnel peppered him mercilessly. His face was torn by a hundred tiny cuts, one eye horribly shredded. Still holding the lightning rod, he howled in pain. After its bright explosive flash, the light went out, extinguished by the wind and water. It was dark in the lantern room of Race Rock, except when lightning illuminated the horrific tableaux.

In agony and fury, Eliot began swinging the rod down towards Caleb.

Caleb crawled away from him. The blows followed him, clanging off the sides of the lantern room, off the fuel cans, the center column. Eliot was blocking the door. Caleb was near the hatch leading to the catwalk. He opened the latch and pushed. It slammed open and back against the lantern room, pinned there by the hurricane's winds.

Eliot continued to swing wildly, screaming in pain and anger, his words inarticulate. They were part of the storm, now, another sound woven into the cacophony of wind and thunder and waves.

Caleb scrambled through the hatch onto the cold metal catwalk. The wind slammed into him and he rolled to the edge and over, catching himself at the last instant on one of the railing supports. He hung there, out over the boulders sixty feet below. He clung to the support pole as gusts of wind, some over 150 miles an hour, tried to tear him loose. The waves were so high that some of them hit his legs as they crashed into the tower of

Race Rock. Caleb looked down at the foaming sea below as he held on for his life. It looked like the mouth of a ravenous monster, waiting for him.

In a lightning flash, he saw Eliot crawl out of the hatch.

Caleb knew he had to get back onto the catwalk. If he didn't, Eliot would take a few swings at him with the lightning rod and either kill him outright or send him to his death in the sea and rocks below.

Mustering all his strength, helped by a gust that blew his body sideways, Caleb pulled himself up and swung his legs onto the catwalk.

Eliot was there. He stood, wobbling in the ferocious wind, his face bloody, his one good eye wide and burning with hatred. He held the lightning rod in both hands, raised it high above his head, and slammed it down at Caleb.

Caleb tried to react.

Too late.

The rod thudded into his right knee with a sickening crunch. Caleb's scream of agony was lost in the howl of the hurricane.

Eliot was yelling something but it, too, was torn away by the wind. Despite the searing pain of his shattered knee, Caleb pushed himself back and away from Eliot along the wet metal catwalk.

Eliot swung again but the rod clanged against the railing, just inches from Caleb's head.

The catwalk was cramped and slippery. Caleb pushed further back. He was slow, the pain of his knee so intense he was close to passing out. He realized it was just a matter of time before Eliot delivered a deathblow.

The spray, the rain, the wind were all so thick it was hard to see. The light was out. Only the lightning, growing in intensity and frequency, lit the scene.

Another bolt. Then another. Each showed Eliot, his bloody face wild, screaming, a madman intent on murder. Another blow glanced off Caleb's shoulder. He was losing. He would die defending his light against a storm embodied in a man.

In the next flash, Caleb saw a ghostly figure behind Eliot. He thought the pain had made him start to hallucinate. Another flash: he saw it was Jennifer. She was trying to stand against the wind, but kept getting knocked down to her knees. She was holding a gun.

Eliot raised the iron rod. There was a bright flash and explosion behind him. On her knees, Jennifer had pulled the trigger. The wind had made it almost impossible to keep the gun up and aimed. Her shot had gone wide.

Eliot heard it. He spun, saw her, and lashed out. He was too far away. The rod hit the catwalk two feet in front of her. Rocking in the wind, Jennifer stood and fired a second shot. Again she missed.

Caleb could not move. His crushed leg was useless. He was beginning to lose consciousness. If it weren't for Jennifer, Eliot would have finished him off by now. He could do nothing but watch as Eliot and Jennifer squared off.

Eliot took a few steps forward and raised his arms high, the lightning rod poised for another blow.

In the same instant, a lightning bolt burst from the sky. It zigzagged down to the sea, then changed direction toward Race Rock, as if God in his wrath had directed the full fury of the storm at them. As the arc of Eliot's swing reached its apex above his head, that lightning bolt, crackling with 100,000 volts of raw power, sought out the metal in his hands. To Caleb, it looked like a flaming comet about to crash into Race Rock.

It happened in a heartbeat:

There was another flash from the gun.

The lightning rod fulfilled its destiny.

The lightning bolt sizzled into it. Into Eliot.

The entire top of Race Rock was bathed in a blinding light.

Eliot's body absorbed the full force of the lightning. He glowed. Sparked. Then exploded in flames as all that hot white energy consumed him.

For Caleb, there was an instant of absolute silence, as if the film that was the moment, that was the storm, had stuck in a projector. The scene was frozen: the fiery shape of Eliot. Jennifer holding the gun. Raindrops. Spray. Clouds.

Then there was a deafening boom and concussion that blew Caleb back around the catwalk.

Then nothing.

The keeper of the light was engulfed by darkness.

PART III

Fall, 1938

1

The day began slowly, as if in a restful sleep it was reluctant to leave. The sun rose over Eastern Point and dawn came, but the mood of the seas and skies seemed sluggish, weary, as if they barely had the energy to greet the new day. Like a child after a tantrum, the morning of September 22 was one of exhausted calm.

As the sky brightened, the smoke that rose above New London was silhouetted against the blue sky. The fires started by the storm, by downed power lines and ruptured gas lines, still burned. The waterfront of New London was piled high with automobiles, telephone poles, pieces of buildings, and all manner of junk that had been washed ashore. Train cars lay on their sides, half submerged in water. Boats of all sizes littered the coast. Some were perched in fields and lawns far inland.

The docks along the Thames had been splintered and washed away. The pilings that remained stuck out of the water like the bones of some giant stranded fish. The small shed at Burr's Dock where Eliot had rented his boat had vanished. So had Paul Tremain.

Low-lying areas were flooded. Houses that had once looked out over broad, landscaped lawns and gardens now floated in small lakes. Some people stood on their front steps and looked around bewildered. Their houses had become like lighthouses, buildings surrounded by water. Others returned to where their homes had once stood and found only stairways or chimneys, poking into the sky like accusing fingers. Across the region, whole neighborhoods had been swept into the sea.

Shell-shocked people roamed about, traumatized by the violence of the previous day, stunned by the destruction they encountered. The large-scale devastation that greeted them the morning of September 22 was beyond their experience. Beyond anyone's experience. It was as if a gigantic bomb had exploded above New England.

Nobody was thinking of recovery yet. They were still trying to believe what they were seeing with their own eyes. Had a storm done this? Could wind and waves possibly move such large, heavy objects? In the years ahead, as war erupted and spread across the world, scenes of such devastation would become common. But in this fall of 1938, New Englanders had no reference point for the destruction left behind by the great hurricane. Even the birds seemed stunned. They sat on pilings or rocks or atop junk, watching, seemingly wary of the world about them. They, too, had been traumatized by the storm and found themselves in a world utterly transformed.

Photographers and reporters fanned out and tried to put into pictures and words what had happened. They photographed the fires and ravaged buildings, the lakes of floodwater, the hundreds of thousands of flattened trees. As the day unfolded, the news would only get worse.

Nearly eight hundred had died. Fifty-seven thousand had lost their homes or found them severely damaged. Millions would find their lives forever changed. It was not just the natural geography that had been assaulted by the storm. The geography of the human spirit had been attacked as well. Some would fear the sea the rest of their lives. Some would turn their backs and move far away, never to smell the salty air again. Most would stay, but would always look at the ocean warily, wondering when it might erupt in savage violence. On that morning when summer turned to fall, the gentle and genteel way of life along the coast had changed too. Forever.

As morning unfolded on September 22, the seas were calm, undulating in a gentle swell. Borne on those seas was all manner of debris: boats and fragments of boats, pieces of houses, trees, furniture, dead animals, dead people, automobiles, mailboxes, signs, papers, bits of clothing, and unidentifiable fragments of junk. It was as if a giant had picked up the land, turned it upside-down, and spilled its contents onto the waters. It was the detritus of destruction, and it flowed down the Thames River and throughout Long Island Sound.

A boat with four men made its way through the debris toward Race Rock. Their boat was too small for them to recover the bodies that floated by. They could only note a general location and hope that the larger boats that would soon be heading out could find them. They did hope to find some survivors, people who had managed to cling to something and ride out the storm. People had ridden roofs and chairs, mattresses and desks, barrels and automobiles. Some had survived. Others had been swept out to the Atlantic, never to be seen again. The men on the boat saw no signs of human life in the junk around them.

The small boat had been dispatched by the Coast Guard station to go out and see how the keeper of Race Rock was faring. All communications with the lighthouse had gone down early in the storm. Eventually, the light itself had blinked off after two brilliant flashes. The worst was feared. Early reports indicated the area's lighthouses had been severely hit by the storm. One, along with its keepers, had been lost altogether.

The four men on the boat surveyed the wreckage as they slowly made their way through it. They were silent. The day was clear, and they could see Race Rock as soon as they headed down the river. God knows what they might find when they got there. So calm and bright was the day that it was hard for them to believe that they were in the same world that had been so dark and violent just hours earlier. It was like waking from a nightmare.

On the ride out, Seaman Gilmore tried to imagine what it had been like on Race Rock. He could imagine the giant waves rearing up as their onward rush was challenged by the lighthouse. He could imagine the cyclonic winds wrapping themselves around the stone tower as they barreled by. Gilmore had been to Race Rock once and had wondered why it was built as it was. Why such huge stones around it? Why such a massive caisson base? Why such thick stone walls? Now he knew. He had seen the hurricane yesterday. Felt its elemental power. It would not have surprised him if Race Rock had been swept away. Yet it hadn't been. It was still there, out in the middle of the sea, battered, but there.

They slowly, carefully rounded Race Rock, inspecting it from a safe distance. Some of the huge riprap stones had been tossed about. A few balanced precariously, ready to tumble down. The station's rescue boat and exterior storage tanks were gone. Looking up at the lantern room, they could see one of its windows was blown out.

"Thompson, take us in," said the officer in charge, Captain Lopergolo.

The small boat swung around and threaded its way between the boulders to the end of the concrete pier. The helmsman cut the motor and let the boat drift to a stop. Gilmore hopped out and tied a line to one of the large iron cleats that lined the pier.

The men walked along the dock and climbed the iron ladder. The front door was open. A frayed rope hung from the handle. A window was smashed.

"My God," whispered one of the men. "What happened here?"

No one answered.

"Let's go in," Lopergolo ordered.

Inside, the small living room was a mess. It was soaked with water, and the men had to slosh through puddles as they walked about. Furniture was upended, water dripping from bookshelves and doorframes. Coffee mugs, books and pictures lay on the floor. Gilmore bent down and picked up a watercolor painting. It was soaked and the paints had run, but he could still make out the image of a lighthouse keeper in uniform looking through a spyglass. He righted a table and put the painting on it. From the condition of the room, it was clear that the door had been open during the height of the storm. The kitchen was a mess, too. Thompson and another seaman, Ketteringham, went to the basement. They emerged a few minutes later.

"Nothing," said Ketteringham.

"Let's check the second floor," said the Captain. The group filed through the fire doors and ascended the spiral staircase. On the second floor, they fanned out into the rooms.

"Nobody here!" yelled Gilmore.

"Room's empty," yelled Thompson.

It didn't take long to search the small rooms, and they again joined up for the trip to the lantern room.

"Odd," said Gilmore as they climbed the spiral stairway. "These steps look burned."

The men stopped and Lopergolo bent and took a close look at one of the metal treads. "I think you're right," he said. The men looked at each other.

"It must have been quite a night out here," said Gilmore.

"Apparently," said Lopergolo.

They continued up the stairs. At the top, the door was open. Squeezing in, they entered the lantern room.

The men surveyed the damaged room. The light was blown out. Shards of glass from the intricate lenses lay all over the metal floor. The light itself was a tangled mess, ruined by the intense explosion. Empty kerosene cans littered the floor. One pane of the surrounding lantern room glass was shattered. The lower walls were blackened. A light wind blew in from the south. Bright sunlight flooded in.

The door to the catwalk was open, swaying on its hinges in the breeze. They could see someone lying outside on the metal walk. One by one, they crawled through the door to the metal catwalk.

Caleb Bowen lay there. They couldn't tell if he was dead or alive. He was soaking wet. His left leg was bent at the knee at an odd angle. A metal pole—the lightning rod—lay at his feet. Lopergolo climbed over the man and crouched down at his head.

"Keeper Bowen?" he said. "Keeper Bowen?"

Caleb did not respond.

"He must have cranked the light way up and it blew. Hurt him when it did," said Gilmore. "Then he somehow crawled out here. Look: his leg is burned. Maybe he was trying to get away from a fire."

"The stairs were burned," said Thompson.

"And the lantern room, too," said Ketteringham.

"Hard to know," said Lopergolo. He felt for a pulse. "He's alive, but he's hurt badly. Look at his knee. We've got to get him to land where he can get some medical treatment."

Gilmore picked up the lightning rod and tossed it over the rail. It clattered on the rocks below. The men knelt and tried to figure out how to get Caleb back through the tiny hatch. Two went back in. Gilmore and Lopergolo gently lifted Caleb and turned him so his head was at the hatch. The other men grasped him under his arms and started to pull.

It was difficult, but they managed to drag Bowen into the lantern room. It was a cramped space, and he was dead weight. It took a lot of maneuvering to get him onto the stairs. His broken leg flopped about. There was no way they could protect it. Thankfully, he was unconscious. It would have been agony otherwise.

Finally they got him to the stairway. The men were winded and took a break.

"It must have been hell out here," said Thompson. "From the looks of it, this place took a direct hit from the storm."

"I imagine so," said Lopergolo. "Race Rock is the first thing the wind and waves hit after they come up the Sound or over Long Island."

"He's pretty beat up. I wonder what happened to him," said Thompson.

"Only Bowen can tell us," said Lopergolo. "And I don't think he'll be able to do that for a while. Okay, men. He's not getting any better with us standing here. Let's get him down the stairs. Gilmore, you take his shoulders. I'll take his legs. Thompson, Ketteringham, you try to support him in the middle as best you can. I just hope his back isn't broken."

The men took up their positions as ordered and slowly made their way down and around, down and around the spiral stairway, being as careful as they could with Caleb. He moaned a few times but never came to.

They carried him all the way out to the top of the caisson. They lay him down in the bright sunlight and caught their breath. Another arduous climb down the ladder faced them. Race Rock was not conducive to rescuing someone.

"Sir?" asked Gilmore.

"Yes?"

"Sir, maybe we can use the rope that's on the door to lower him down the ladder. It will be secure and easier than trying to manhandle him."

"Good idea."

They started to tie the rope around under Caleb's arms and tight around his chest.

"He must have used it as a safety line. Probably had to go out during the storm," said Ketteringham as he cinched a knot tight.

"I think you're right," said Lopergolo. "Though I can't imagine what would be so urgent that any man would venture out in a storm like that. This caisson was probably half under water."

"Not to mention hundred mile-an-hour winds!" said Thompson.

It took a few minutes to secure the rope around Caleb. Lopergolo and Gilmore scrambled down the ladder. Ketteringham, the biggest of the three, helped by Thompson, carefully lifted Caleb up, dangled him over the side of the caisson and lowered him down to the waiting men.

They caught him and laid him on the cement pier. Lopergolo untied him while Gilmore pulled the boat to the edge.

Ketteringham and Thompson scrambled down and they moved Caleb into the small boat.

"Thompson, you stay here," ordered Lopergolo. "Start cleaning this place up. I'll put in a request for a new light. If you can rig up a lantern or something up top, do it. I'll send out some supplies tomorrow. "

"Right, sir," said Thompson. "I'll do what I can."

"Good."

Ketteringham cast them off and Gilmore backed the small boat away from Race Rock.

Thompson was back up on the caisson. "Good luck," he yelled down. "Send me some help as soon as you can."

Lopergolo waved at him. Gilmore spun the boat around and eased the throttle higher. The small boat made its way back across Fishers Island Sound. They couldn't go full speed—there was too much debris floating about. Gilmore was a good helmsman and managed to weave around the larger things that blocked their way. Lopergolo tried the radio with no luck. The radio tower at the Coast Guard station was down. Transmissions weren't working. Very little was working this day after the storm. Electricity was out. Telephones were out. Roads were washed away or covered with sand and downed trees. People had to fend for themselves.

"When we get ashore," said Lopergolo, "we'll need a car to get Bowen to the hospital."

"The Lawrence and Memorial?" asked Ketteringham.

"Yes. He's too injured for the guys in our infirmary to deal with."

"My station wagon's at the boathouse," said Gilmore, never taking his eyes off the water. "We can use it."

"Then we just need a clear road to drive on," said Lopergolo. "Which might not be so easy to find."

The boat threaded its way through the wreckage of lives to New London. Flames still glowed along the waterfront, and smoke hung above the downtown district. It would take a very long time to recover from this storm.

Lopergolo looked at Caleb stretched out along a bench at the stern. He wondered what he'd endured during the hurricane. How he'd been injured. He did not know the man, but thought he embodied what a lighthouse keeper stood for: someone who tended his light in defiance of even the biggest of storms.

2

There was tapping.

Incessant, nonstop, tapping. And a bell every so often. He was not aware when he had first heard it or for how long it had been going on. His dreams had vaporized like a clearing fog as he drifted toward consciousness.

Caleb's climb from the darkness was slow. Finally, his eyes fluttered open. Everything was a bit blurry.

He saw an island.

He was looking down on it from a great height. He wondered if he had died and come back as a bird and was soaring high above the sea. He did not know where he was. He did not know what island he was looking at. It was vaguely round with articulated shores suggesting many inlets and coves.

He stared at the island a long time. It was his world. Otherwise, he felt disembodied. Then his eyes focused and he realized that he was looking at an island on a chart. He could see the grid lines. So he wasn't a bird in the sky. Where was he? What was that damned tapping?

Caleb faded out again. He was floating on the sea of his own consciousness, sometimes above the surface, sometimes below. He had not yet connected fully with his body.

Again he awoke. He looked down, or maybe it was up, at the island on the chart. But no, it was not a chart at all, he realized as his mind cleared a bit. It was a ceiling, a ceiling of acoustic tiles, spotted with water leaks. He was looking at a water spot directly above him. Not an island in the sea or on a chart. Just a dark stain on a ceiling tile.

He was in a bed. A hospital bed. There were rails on the sides, and when he gazed down his body, he saw his leg, in a cast, elevated in a sling. There was an antiseptic smell. So much for being a bird soaring with the wind.

He felt like shit. His mouth was dry, his head throbbed, his body was stiff and ached everywhere.

He heard voices, and the tapping, and the bell, and he realized it was a typewriter he'd been hearing. In the next room, or maybe out in the hallway. Someone typing up medical reports. He put his head back down and stared at the spot again. He was alive. Beat up, but alive. He was still disoriented. He knew where he was, but couldn't remember what had happened to put him in the hospital. He concentrated on the spot in the ceiling, and worked on pulling in memories, like a fisherman trolling a net. A few came back. A storm. A man's face. A spiral stairway. Fire. They were like pieces of a jigsaw puzzle. He was trying to connect them into a larger, coherent picture. He heard commotion down the hallway. A man swearing. Really cussing a blue streak. Then he quieted down, though the hospital continued to hum with activity.

It was perhaps a half hour later that a nurse came in.

"I see you've rejoined the living," she said with a smile. Her nametag read "Bettie Ferciot, RN."

Caleb tried to say something but his throat was so dry it came out as a croak.

"Here, take this," she said, pouring a drink into a cup and holding it to his lips. She helped him raise his head and he took a sip. It felt very good. He drank more.

"What happened?" he asked, his voice hoarse.

Just then, a doctor entered. He was a distinguished looking man wearing a dapper suit beneath his white gown. He had a thin, trim mustache and brown horn-rimmed glasses. His badge read "Edward Falk, M.D."

"He's awake at last," said the nurse. She took Caleb's wrist and checked his pulse. Dr. Falk looked at him and picked up his chart from the end of the bed where it was hooked.

"At last?" asked Caleb.

"Yes. You've been out for almost two days. A concussion, I think. Though it might have been lightning," said Falk.

"Lightning?" asked Caleb.

"Yes. You may have been hit by lighting. Or been close to a strike. I can't tell. You have some superficial burns. And they tell me they found a lightning rod near you. So it's possible. Maybe you can tell us?"

Caleb tried to recall. He had vague impressions, but nothing very specific. He shook his head.

"Do you remember the hurricane?"

"Bits and pieces. I remember I was out at Race Rock and the weather was very bad, but I'm having a hard time with the details."

"Well, that's okay," said Dr. Falk. "It will all probably come back to you in time. Memory loss is usually like that. Short-lived. Don't work at it too hard. Just let it happen."

"I feel like a train hit me," said Caleb.

"Well, you look like a train hit you, Keeper Bowen," said the doctor. "And in that storm, one might have," he added.

The nurse pulled open the curtains. Bright sunlight streamed in and cast hard shadows. Caleb squinted and then slowly opened his eyes, letting them adjust.

"Call me if you need me, doctor," said Nurse Ferciot, and left quietly.

Caleb mulled over the phrase "Keeper Bowen." Yes, he was a keeper of the light. Race Rock. A few more images surfaced: brilliant flashes of light. Huge rocks. Enormous waves. He just let them join the others.

"So what's broken?" asked Caleb after a minute.

Dr. Falk pulled up a chair and sat down next to the bed. He still had Caleb's chart and looked it over. He seemed reluctant to answer.

"Doc?" asked Caleb.

Dr. Falk sighed. Put down the chart. Looked at Caleb.

"Well, you have a lot of cuts and bruises. A nasty bruise on your shoulder, and a burn on your leg. They'll heal. Your memory will probably come back just fine. Like I said, just give it some time. Your worst injury is your knee. And I won't beat around the bush. It's quite smashed up. How, I don't know. Either you hit something or something hit you. Hard. Very hard."

He looked at Caleb, waiting for an explanation. If Caleb knew what happened, he didn't say. After a moment, Falk continued.

"It will mend, but I'm afraid it won't be functional."

"What does that mean?"

"It means you'll have a stiff leg." He paused and shook his head. "I'm sorry, Keeper Bowen."

Caleb lay his head back and looked at the ceiling. At his island. The implications of having a stiff leg did not take long to sink in. He could not work at Race Rock again. He couldn't work at any lighthouse again. It would be impossible to climb the ladders and stairways of a lighthouse. Impossible to do any meaningful physical work. His days as a keeper of the light were over.

There was an awkward silence.

"At least you ended your career a hero," said Dr. Falk.

"A hero?" asked Caleb, still confused over what exactly had happened.

"Yes. You kept the light lit. At the height of the storm, you pumped it up for two very bright flashes before the light blew. Those flashes saved a ship and all aboard."

"They did?"

"Yes. The captain made it to port and immediately started to sing your praises. It's been in the papers. I'll show you."

Dr. Falk got up and walked outside. Caleb was trying to absorb what the doctor had said and connect it to the memories that were starting to surface: the storm. Eliot. The fire in the stairwell. Climbing through the rocks. Houses floating by. Trying to revive Jennifer.

Dr. Falk returned a few minutes later with a day-old copy of the New London Day. On the front page, below the fold, was a short article: "Race Rock Keeper Saves Ship. Captain says Bowen a hero." It described how Captain Freedman of the ferryboat *Catskill* was all but lost at sea at the height of the storm when he spotted two very bright flashes from Race Rock. They let him regain his orientation and navigate his way into New London, or what was left of New London that night. Passengers, too, voiced their praise. The article concluded with a quote from the Captain: "He gave us a beacon to steer by, and because of him we made port safely."

Caleb read it, disbelieving and confused. Had it happened that way? He closed his eyes and let the memories play across his mind: Eliot. Jennifer. The struggle in the lantern room and out on the catwalk. The lightning bolt streaking down and incinerating Eliot in an instant that would last a lifetime.

Jennifer! What had happened to her? Suddenly, Caleb realized he did not know.

"Doctor?"

"Yes?"

"Did they rescue anyone else at Race Rock when they found me?" Caleb asked with desperate urgency.

Falk was confused.

"Anyone else? I don't think so," he said. "So far as I know, you were alone out there."

"You're sure?"

"Yes. The officers who brought you in briefed me. They found you at the top of the light. They didn't say anything about finding anyone else."

"Oh my God!" Caleb let out a long sigh and lay back on the pillow.

Jennifer.

Lost.

She must have been blown off the catwalk by the lightning bolt. Cast for a second time into the teeth of the storm. The wind had brought them together that day on Fishers Island, and the wind had torn them apart that night on Race Rock.

Sensing there was nothing he could say to help and that Caleb needed to be alone with his thoughts, Dr. Falk said, quietly, "You get your bearings, Keeper Bowen. I can't tell you much more. I'll check in on you later. I have a lot of patients to see. The hospital is full of injured folks from the storm."

Falk left.

Caleb's mind was in turmoil. He tried to sort out his memories. He contemplated the end of his career and the mystery of his heroism. He thought about Jennifer. He closed his eyes and tried to fix her face in his mind.

Out in the hallway, the tapping continued, but he no longer heard it.

3

Over the next few days, Caleb's memory improved. The events of September 21 came back to him. Gradually, as the pieces fell into place, the fragmentary details connected and the full picture was revealed.

Along with the memories came a deep, intense sadness. He had lost Jennifer. This time, he could not rescue her. The pain of his injuries was nothing compared to the pain in his heart. The day he had come to realize just how much he loved her, just how much potential their love and life had, she was taken from him. Abruptly. Violently.

Forever.

The hours dragged. Sleep was a mercy, an escape from his thoughts. Nurses came and went, feeding him, dispensing pills, checking his vital signs. They were cheery and tried to engage him, but could not. There was an empty bed in his room. One day, an unconscious man was wheeled in and transferred to it. A curtain was drawn. That was fine with Caleb. He didn't want to talk with anyone. He withdrew into a shell of despair.

He had lost Jennifer. He had lost his job, his lighthouse. He was adrift, carried along by the tide of sad emotions. Over and over he played out that day of madness, a day when Race Rock was assaulted by two storms: one outside, one inside. He had been overwhelmed by them both. When he wasn't grieving over Jennifer, his thoughts turned to Eliot. Was he really his brother? Was his story true? Was there a treasure hidden somewhere on Race Rock? Eliot had come in out of the blue and vanished in a blinding flash. Caleb wondered if he was even real. But he need look no further than his knee to know. Eliot had been real, all right. Real enough to destroy his light and his knee. Real enough to change the course of Caleb's life.

Jennifer, too, had come to Race Rock that day unexpectedly. He had lost her once and gotten her back, only to lose her again. He never thought she would come to the lantern room. Yet she had. She had saved his life. If she hadn't distracted Eliot, he would have crushed more than Caleb's knee. His next blow was aimed higher, at his head, and Caleb knew it would have been fatal.

He didn't know if she had shot Eliot. It had all happened so quickly. He'd seen the flash from the gun just before the lightning bolt hit. To his dying day, Caleb would never forget the horrific instant when Eliot was consumed by the lightning. It was seared into his mind. The man—his brother—a figure in flames, like some demon from hell. He wished the image had remained lost to him, but it had come back along with all the other memories.

Caleb never saw what had happened next. He prayed that Jennifer had gone quickly, that she had not drowned. He could only hope she'd been knocked unconscious and had not suffered.

The storm had passed. The days were sunny. Yet in his hospital room, Caleb still battled dark clouds of regret and bitterness and despair.

He was a hero who was not a hero. A man in love who had lost his love. A keeper of the light who had no light to guide him.

4

The man who was in the other bed in Caleb's room was sleeping. He was almost always sleeping. Whenever he woke up, he'd eat, stumble to the bathroom, do what the nurses said, then start to swear and raise hell. The nurses would give him a shot and he'd quiet down and fall asleep again.

When he was awake and not swearing, he'd rant at Caleb about all sorts if injustices in his life. Caleb learned that he was a Coast Guard seaman named Michael Shivers who had been manning a weather station on Eastern Point. His injuries seemed mostly psychological. He had become a bit unhinged by the storm. They'd found him wandering around up the coast on Shore Avenue, cursing at seagulls. They were trying to figure out someplace else to send him. They needed every bed for the physically injured. But with communications and transportation still a mess, for the moment, the Lawrence and Memorial Hospital was stuck with Shivers. So they knocked him out whenever he became hard to manage. He snored away, occasionally muttering gibberish or swearing.

Early in the evening, four days after the storm, there was a gentle knock on Caleb's door. He turned to see an old man standing there.

"Yes?" asked Caleb.

"May I come in?" asked the man.

Something about the man, the look in his eyes, a tentativeness, made Caleb say: "Yes."

"My name is Robert Martin. How are you feeling?"

"I've felt better. My leg is the main problem."

"I see. I hope it heals."

He paused.

"May I sit?"

Caleb motioned him to the chair by the bed. The man sat down. Martin was a kind-looking man and looked at Caleb with admiration.

"We are all grateful for what you did that night," he said at last.

"Mr. Martin, I assure you I was no hero the night of the storm." Even as he said it Caleb realized it came out all wrong. It sounded like he was being modest. Martin's look of admiration became deeper, almost reverent.

Caleb let out a gentle sigh. He'd been hearing this praise for several days. The accolades seemed hollow and misplaced, as if meant for another man, as if he was assuming a false identity and reaping unmerited rewards. It had been too hard to explain about the phantom brother who'd come to Race Rock. They might just think him mad, like Shivers. He hadn't told them about Jennifer, either. In fact, he'd said little about the day of the storm. What could he say? He was still trying to make sense of it himself.

But this talk of heroism: it pained him. The truth was, and it was quite ironic, that in destroying the light and trying to kill them, Eliot had caused the bright flashes that saved the ship. It was accidental heroism. Evil that had ultimately become good. Caleb had accepted the label of hero. Hadn't that been what he'd really wanted for years? For a lighthouse keeper named Bowen to be appreciated, thanked, praised? If he could not exonerate his father, he could at least replace his infamy with heroism. In a strange twist of fate, he had gotten his wish. But there proved to be little satisfaction in it.

"I brought you something," Martin said. He reached into his coat and pulled out a small beat-up cardboard box. He handed it to Caleb.

Caleb was curious. He took the box, laid it on his chest, and opened it. Inside was a watch. A beautiful, elegant silver pocket watch. Inscribed on the face of the watch was "United States Lighthouse Board."

"It was your father's watch, Caleb," said the old man. "I was the one who found the boat that he ... that he used for his last voyage. The watch was on the bench. I kept it. All these years. I forgot all about it. Then when your name came up in the papers, it jogged my memory. You should have it."

Caleb held the old pocket watch in his hand. It was tarnished, dented. He realized that it was the last thing Nathaniel had held before he'd taken his plunge to oblivion. Caleb's eyes misted and he turned away from the old man, fighting for composure.

"Thank you," he managed to whisper.

The old man had the good grace to sense Caleb's emotions and take his leave.

"Good luck to you, Caleb Bowen. Thank you for your years of service. For what you did during the storm. God bless you." Then he was out the door and gone.

Caleb held the watch and looked at it. It was the only thing of Nathaniel's he owned. He remembered the times his father had let him hold the watch. Caleb would push the little button that popped open the lid. He would bounce the sunshine off the shiny silver of the lid, creating a little spotlight that he'd shine about. "Be careful with it," Nathaniel would say. It was perhaps the most valuable thing his father owned.

Caleb turned the watch over and pondered the engraving on the back: "JLS 12~1~05." He did not know the significance of the date or the initials. Who was "JLS?" What was so important about the date that Nathaniel would engrave it on his watch?

Caleb thought about that cold night in 1907. About the shipwreck his father had caused. The deaths. The guilt. The shame. He tried to imagine his father's final day and night, his final moments when he gave himself to the cold dark waters.

It was too much for him. All of it.

Caleb clutched the old silver watch tightly in his hand and wept. He wept for his father and for Jennifer and for himself. He wept for all the sadness that had washed into his life. As overwhelming as a storm surge and as impossible to turn back.

5

Over the course of the next few days, more visitors came to see Caleb.

The Captain of the *Catskill* stopped in to thank him personally for saving his ship. It was a strange conversation. Freedman praised Caleb for creating the two bright, bright flashes: "The most beautiful damned things I ever saw!" Caleb tried to minimize things, wishing he weren't living a lie, but knowing it was too late to do anything about it. The best he could do was to say: "I'm glad you saw the light at Race Rock," which was true. He never acknowledged he was responsible for that light. He tried to temper his heroism with ambiguity. It didn't make him feel much better.

Hastings came by to hear what it had been like at Race Rock during what was being called "The Storm of the Century."

St. Clair came, too. He apologized for not coming sooner, but with the harbor and port in shambles, every able-bodied man, on active duty or retired, was called to serve to get things running again. Martial law had been declared. Troops were everywhere. The President of the United States was sending in workers to help clean up and rebuild New England. He'd been working long hours, managing a million details that had piled up like the debris on the waterfront.

St. Clair sat down by the bed and rubbed his eyes. He looked weary, but his voice had its old sparkle when he started talking.

"You know, Caleb, you did well out there at Race Rock. I'm sorry you busted up your knee. I guess it happened at the top of the light? I don't think you'd have been able to climb any stairs with a bad knee."

"Too long a story, Commander. Far too long a story."

St. Clair looked at him a moment. It was clear Caleb didn't want to talk about it. Why, St. Clair had no idea. He sensed more had happened the day of the storm than Caleb would let on. He didn't press.

"Okay. Don't worry. We'll always have a job for you in the Service. We need some heroes. I'll find you something. I promise. It may be at a desk, but I'll find something for you."

"Thank you, Commander. I'll need work, and I'd like to stay involved with the Service in some way. It's been my life."

St. Clair seemed to be mulling something over. He looked at Caleb thoughtfully, then spoke quietly.

"Caleb, I never told you this, but I had some doubts about your being the keeper at Race Rock."

"Doubts?"

"Yes. I wasn't as fixed in my thinking as Armstrong, but I worried about you. Your motives for wanting to be at Race Rock. I figured you had something to prove. Figured you wanted to clear the Bowen name. So I was a little wary. But I thought I'd give you a chance. I thought maybe you'd be more motivated than most of the guys to be an excellent keeper."

"And?" asked Caleb.

"And you proved me right. Whatever your motives might have been, you were a very good light keeper. One of our best. And that's all that matters."

"Thank you for giving me a chance."

"Like I said, Caleb, you did well in that storm. You're a hero. Still, I don't know if what you did will ever make people forget about your father.

"Maybe not, Commander. But I hope I've created some better memories."

"Maybe, Caleb. Maybe." St. Clair sat back and looked around the small hospital room. In the next bed, Shivers snored away. St. Clair seemed lost in thought. He looked at Caleb.

"Caleb, memory can be funny. It can be hard to change. Show you what I mean: one time, my wife and I wanted to paint our living room a new color. We got a small can of paint at the hardware store, took it home, and brushed some on the wall. We weren't sure we liked it. So we went back and got another color, and painted it on, near the first try. We still weren't sure. We went back again. And again. I don't remember exactly, but I bet we ended up with eight or ten test spots on that wall. It looked like an explosion. Blobs of color all over. It was hard to decide on a color. But finally we did. We painted the whole room. And of course, we painted over all those trial spots. Funny thing is, whenever I look at that wall, I remember all those trial colors that were on it. They're still there. They're hidden, but they're there, underneath, and always will be. I know it. The wife knows it. Nothing can change our memories."

Caleb thought about what St. Clair had said a moment.

"I suppose you're right, Commander. Maybe I can't change any memories. Maybe the best I can do is cover an old history with a new one."

St. Clair smiled. "I think you did that."

He stood up.

"Well, Caleb, I'd love to stay here all day and shoot the breeze with you. But I have a small army to keep track of," he said. "No rest for the weary. This storm made a mess of everything. It's going to take us a long time to recover from it. I get discouraged when I see what's happened. What we need to do. Nothing will ever be the same. We've lost much of what made New London special. A lot of our heritage."

"I wish I could help, Commander. I hear the devastation is pretty bad."

"Beyond belief, Caleb. It's enough to make you want to get away from the sea. Far away. It's got everybody spooked. I think we'll always be looking over our shoulders, now. Always wondering what may be looming over the horizon."

St. Clair patted Caleb's cast.

"Take it easy, Caleb. Get your bearings. I'll get you a room over at the Griswold Hotel. Let me get New London back on its feet, then call me in a while. We'll talk about that job."

With a smile and a handshake, Commander St. Clair said goodbye to Caleb and left.

6

In the afternoon of his fifth day at the hospital, there was a knock on the door, sharp and decisive.

A gruff voice asked, "Can I come in?"

Caleb looked over to see the last person he expected to see: Commander Bullard. Caleb hadn't seen him in years. He was older, a little thinner, grayer. He didn't look so intimidating anymore. Retirement had taken his command, and age had shrunk his power.

Without waiting for an answer, Bullard stepped into the room. He was obviously ill at ease. He looked around. At everything but Caleb.

"What brings *you* here?" asked Caleb warily. He had never forgiven Bullard for the problems he had caused. For the delays. The anguish. Why had he suddenly decided to contact Caleb after all these years?

Bullard answered the question.

"I read about you. They told me you was here. I thought I should stop in." He busied himself looking at the calendar, studied the water pitcher, the sleeping man in the next bed, then drifted over to the window. He stood there, his broad back to the bed, looking out over the parking lot as if it held something of great fascination. He looked out the window for a good thirty seconds before he spoke.

"Caleb, for a guy like me, duty is pretty simple. It's black and white. You either do your job or you don't. I'm not a lawyer or one of these doctors here where everything is gray. A matter of opinion. In our work, there is no gray. You do your duty or you don't. You either keep the light lit or you don't. Your father

279

didn't, and I'll never forgive him for that. Never. A ship was wrecked. People died. Black and white."

Bullard did not look at Caleb. He paused, his hands clasped behind his back, fingers working nervously. They reminded Caleb of a cat's twitching tail. Bullard turned to him.

"A few days ago, we had the worst storm ever. You kept the light lit. Bright. You saved a ship."

Caleb wanted to point out that after the two bright flashes, the light had gone out. Nobody seemed to care about that.

Bullard paused again, looked at his hands. It was clearly hard for him to say what he was saying.

"I have to give credit where credit is due, Caleb. I was hard on you, and maybe I was wrong. Maybe I was just trying to punish your father. I know he took his life, but, well ... never mind. It don't matter now."

Bullard rubbed his big hands together. Reached back and ran a hand down the back of his thick neck.

"Anyway. I just wanted to come by and tell you that I ... we ... all of us appreciate what you did during the storm. It took guts. I don't know that I could have done as well out there."

Caleb was quite amazed that Bullard had made the effort to come see him and say what he'd said. Perhaps it was simply his sense of duty. His strict obedience to his code of honor. When he perceived something as "black," he was tough and unforgiving. When "white," he felt obligated to offer praise. His world was structured and so were his responses.

Bullard extended his arm, hand opened to shake Caleb's. It was a kind of peace offering. Caleb paused. How would Bullard interpret their handshake? Probably differently than Caleb. Though Bullard claimed the world was simple, just black and white, Caleb saw it as much more complex, like the surface of a stormy sea, pushed and pulled in different directions, confused and chaotic. No, it was not simple at all.

Their eyes met for an instant. Though a connection was made, it was also missed. Their perspectives were just too different to ever really align.

"What the hell," thought Caleb. "I'm too tired to fight Bullard. I'll just add a little paint to his wall and maybe cover

the ancient history that seems to haunt him—to haunt us both."
Caleb shook the big man's offered hand. Quickly. It was a handshake tempered with reluctance.

"You heal up," said Bullard. Then he turned and left without saying another word.

As other people came by to see him, Caleb tried to keep the
visits short, feigning exhaustion to help his visitors get the
point. He let them call him "hero." It was easier than trying to
change their opinions. Beyond that, he had come to realize that
the area desperately needed a few heroes. There was so much
death and destruction that anything positive was seized upon
and amplified. The taxi driver who dodged falling trees to get a
woman in labor to the hospital was featured on the front page
of a newspaper: "Heroic Driver Saves Mother and Child!" The
young boy who pulled his sister from the surf was all but can-
onized: "Tot Saves Sis!" Like them, Caleb was endowed with
the polishing of reality that only traumatized people can create.

Hero or not, nothing could fix his ruined knee. Nothing
could bring Jennifer back to him. She was always on his mind,
and little things hurt him terribly. Like when he overheard
Nurse Ferciot talking to another nurse in the hallway.

"Anything going on this weekend?" the nurse had asked
Ferciot. "You're finally getting a break after the long hours."

"Oh, no!" Nurse Ferciot had laughed. "Charlie and I will
be happy to share a nice dinner and curl up on the couch
together. You know Charlie: he doesn't like to go out on the
town."

"Good thing. There's not much town to go out on!"

The exchange had given Caleb such pangs of longing. How
nice to have someone to share the simple pleasures of life with.
A meal. A cuddle. He and Jennifer had never had much of that.
Now they never would.

When he thought about Jennifer, he felt guilt. Though he
had proposed to her, he should have told her more often how
he felt about her. How much he loved her. It is so easy, he
thought, to let daily life dull the edge of love. Without the
deadline of a wedding date, it had been so easy to drift along,

dreaming of some abstract future where they were together. The months had rolled by. He had meant to talk with her more about their future. To make plans. Somehow, he never had. These thoughts always stoked the pain in his heart. He felt so lonely. His life seemed to have no direction, no meaning.

Caleb lay in his hospital bed, injured beyond his broken knee. The late afternoon sunlight burned through the Venetian blinds in streaks. In them, dust motes drifted, glowing, like stars.

He idly watched them, some suspended almost motionless, others slowly drifting, bumping together, their paths and inter-actions random. He saw himself as a dust mote—drifting, head-ing somewhere unknown, pulled by unseen forces. He watched them drift in the late afternoon sunlight, passing through the light and disappearing into the shadows. Caleb felt his life was in the shadows now, too. Jennifer was his light, and she was gone. She left behind only darkness. Like all of New England, his heart and soul were devastated.

He was gripped by a quiet terror. He understood his father's desire to give up. Sometimes, life just piles up on you and you can't take its weight anymore. He had felt it out in the storm, rescuing Jennifer. He had been so battered by the hurricane that he had wanted to give in. Now, the burdens of life were crushing him. Starting over seemed like such work. He had been lucky to find Jennifer. Could he ever love again? He had been a lighthouse keeper for years. Could he possibly find hap-piness anchored to a desk? Caleb's life had always been orderly and predictable. Now it was without structure and direction. His future was in a different direction than any of his dreams. He had been blown off course and had no idea what heading to take.

There was a knock on the door. He slowly turned his atten-tion to it.

The door opened a crack.

"Permission to come aboard, sir?"

A head poked in.

It was Jennifer.

7

Caleb thought he was hallucinating. Perhaps grief had driven him to madness. He didn't say a word.

"May I take that silence as a yes?" she asked, stepping into he room.

It *was* Jennifer! Bandaged, battered, as beat up as he, but alive.

"Jennifer?" Caleb asked quietly, afraid that if he spoke too loud she would vanish, that he would wake himself from what surely must be a dream.

"Jennifer?"

She smiled and closed the door behind her.

"Yes, Caleb. It's me." She walked over to his bed and reached out, touching his cheek with her hand. "It's me."

He felt her touch. It was real. *She* was real.

Jennifer lost her composure and gave in to the emotions that she had suppressed for days. She began to weep in great wracking sobs. She sat on the edge of the bed and hugged Caleb, holding him so hard it almost hurt. She dripped her tears on him. She kissed him and rested her head on his shoulder. "Oh, Caleb. I love you so!" She said it over and over.

He had gotten her back. The relief that washed over Caleb was overwhelming. His happiness absolute. And the love, the love was unlike anything he had every experienced. All he could do was say her name repeatedly. Then he let his own tears flow, a sobbing release of joy.

Not many people get a second chance like Jennifer and Caleb. To lose a loved one and get them back for another chance at life is rare. It brings with it a kind of elation that is in a realm all its own.

Tears expressed what words could not. Hugs entwined them as were their souls. They held on to one another, afraid to let even the slightest distance come between them. Never again would they be apart. Never! Their reunion was like making love. It was a consummation. When it had peaked, it left them drained. They lay there and held each other for a while. Finally Caleb spoke: "Oh, Jennifer! I thought I'd lost you! I have been so sad. I love you so much. So very much!"

"I thought I'd lost you, Caleb."

"It's been so hard these past few days, Jennifer. When I thought you were gone, that I'd never see you again ...." He couldn't continue.

She sat up on the bed and dried her eyes.

"It was the same for me, Caleb. God, it's good to see you!"

He smiled. "You are a vision, Jennifer! If I could stand, I would dance. I would run around this damned hospital and shout!"

Seaman Shivers snorted and mumbled in his sleep. Perhaps their reunion had filtered into his dreams.

"What happened to you, Jennifer?" I don't remember anything after Eliot got hit by the lightning."

"I'm a little sketchy on some of the details, Caleb. I remember you two fighting out on the catwalk. I remember Eliot getting hit by lightning. God, what a sight! I've had nightmares about it. I've had nightmares about the whole damned day!"

"Why did you come up to the lantern room?"

"I heard you arguing. Heard the light blow. Even with all the wind, I heard it. I knew you might be in trouble. I ran down to the study and finally found the gun. It was in the closet. I got it and came up."

"Did you shoot Eliot?"

"I honestly don't know. I intended to when I saw he was about to kill you. But the wind was so strong I couldn't aim. My arms kept getting blown away. I went down. Eliot came for me. I fired in his direction. Whether I hit him or not I'll never know. An instant later, the lightning got him."

"You saved my life, Jennifer. Even if you didn't hit him, you distracted him. He would have killed me with his next blow."

"Well then we're even, Caleb," she said with a smile. "You saved me when I got blown off the porch."

"What happened to you after the lightning bolt hit?" asked Caleb.

"I guess I got blown off Race Rock by it. The next thing I remember, I was in the water. Clinging to a desk. A desk! I don't remember how I found the desk. There was so much stuff in the water, I'm lucky I didn't get hit by a bus!"

Caleb laughed and laughed hard. He laughed as he hadn't laughed in a long, long time.

"What's so funny?" Jennifer asked.

"Well, you hear about someone being so careful not to do anything dangerous and then they get hit by a bus. You just don't think of it happening at sea."

"No," Jennifer laughed, "I suppose you don't. But I did see a bus go by. It was like a dream out there. Or a nightmare. I was riding this desk. It was pitch black out. The waves were enormous. They must have been thirty or forty feet. Monsters! The wind was howling. It was so loud! I felt it with my whole body. There was rain and lightning. I had no idea where I was going. I was holding on for my life. My fingerprints are probably imbedded in that desk. I was sure I would get knocked off or it would flip over and I'd drown. But it was a good desk. A damned good desk. Very seaworthy. It stayed upright and I stayed on it.

I have no idea how long I rode that desk. Or how far. A few times, I caught sight of the flames over New London. Sometimes I seemed to be heading up the coast towards town. Then I'd be heading out to sea. I almost gave up a few times. I was so tired! I kept saying to myself: "November 17. November 17. Caleb and I are getting married November 17." I didn't know if you were even alive to marry. But thinking about us gave me hope.

All of a sudden, I heard surf. A wave tossed me and my desk onto a beach. I was back on Fishers Island! I got off the desk. It was perched on the beach, upright, like it belonged there. Like there had been a whole room that had vanished, just leaving the desk!

I took a few steps to get out of the surf and collapsed. Next thing I knew, I woke up in a hospital room like this."

Caleb shook his head, amazed at her story. She had been lucky. Not many people who'd been washed to sea in the storm had survived.

"Fate was kind to you, Jennifer. Or maybe God was looking out for you."

"You're right, Caleb. I don't know where that desk came from, but I owe my life to it. I was pretty roughed up. They say I've lost hearing in my left ear. Probably due to the lightning. I have a sprained ankle, three cracked ribs, and severe bruises just about everywhere. I have a burn on my leg. That really mystified the doctors. They couldn't figure out how someone gets burned in the water.

"I was sick with worry about you, Caleb. I couldn't find out what had happened to you. No ferries were coming out to the island. The phones were down. It was a mess. Then, this morning, I overheard someone talking about the hero of Race Rock. They were reading a newspaper from a few days ago. I asked to see it. The article mentioned you were recuperating here.

"I asked a nurse if someone could get me some clothes from home. She asked where I lived and I told her. She looked shocked. She told me that there were no homes there anymore! They were all gone. The neighborhood was completely wiped out! My home is gone, Caleb. Washed away. Probably halfway to England by now. Which is where I'd be if the desk hadn't bumped into Fishers Island."

Jennifer stopped. Sadness washed across her face.

"I'm sorry," said Caleb.

"Everything I owned was in that house. Everything. And not just things, Caleb. Memories. So many memories." She began to lose her composure. Caleb reached for her and she snuggled into his embrace. He stroked her hair. After a few moments, Jennifer calmed down, wiped away her tears, and continued her story.

"The nurse got me some clothes. They didn't want me to leave the hospital, but I did. The ferries still weren't running. It took me half the day to convince some guys on a fishing trawler to take me over here to New London. The harbor's so clogged with wreckage they had to drop me off up river a ways. Then it took me the rest of the day to get some rides that got me close to the hospital. It wasn't easy. The roads are still cluttered with downed trees. So many trees! The devastation is terrible." She sat up and smiled at him with pride. "I had to walk the last mile to get here. I was slow. I was limping. It was hard going. But I made it!"

Caleb looked at Jennifer. She was bruised and battered. Yet she was beautiful. The sparkle in her eyes, the determination in her voice, the love in her heart flowed over him like a soothing balm.

"Well, compared to you, my love, my story isn't very dramatic. They tell me some guys found me on the catwalk outside the lantern room. I was a mess. Half dead. I woke up here. No ride on a desk involved."

"How bad is your leg?" she asked.

"Bad. Eliot crushed my knee. I won't bend it again. No more climbing ladders and spiral stairs for me. My days at lighthouses are over."

"That son-of-a-bitch!" said Jennifer

"Bastard," Caleb corrected.

"Bastard!" they both said together, smiling. But Jennifer quickly grew serious.

"I'm sorry, Caleb."

He noticed how she turned her head when he spoke, so she could hear him with her good ear.

"What a pair. You're half deaf and I'll be walking with a stiff leg!"

"We'll make lousy dancers," she said.

"You have no home, and I can't get to mine," he said.

"I know where we can find a desk," she said.

Caleb laughed. "Well, St. Clair promised me a desk job, so I'm all set."

Then they got serious.

"I don't care, Caleb. You could have two stiff legs and I wouldn't care. We almost lost each other. We didn't. That's all that I care about. Half of New England has lost its homes.

Other people weren't so lucky. We'll make do. We'll start over—together."

She nuzzled in to him, holding him tight.

They were quiet. The enormity of what had happened to New England—what had happened to them—settled in to their thoughts. It was sobering to realize how close they had both come to dying. Coming back from the brink had changed them. Like New England, they would never be the same.

"So, you're a hero," Jennifer said after a few minutes.

"No, I'm not. They just think I am. If anyone was a hero that night it was you."

"You're too hard on yourself, Caleb. You were a hero because you were there, as you'd been for years. All those nights, lighting the light. You lit the light in the storm. It saved a ship."

"Not really. The two explosions saved the ship," said Caleb quietly. "First, when Eliot broke the window and the lens exploded, and then when he was hit by lightning. I was trying to save my hide both times. It was unintentional, but what saved that ship was his doing, not mine."

"You don't know that. You don't know that the captain wouldn't have seen Race Rock otherwise. It was *built* to be seen, so long as the light was lit. And it was."

Caleb said nothing.

Jennifer went on: "A few nights ago, the biggest storm ever hit New England. For whatever the reason, however it happened—right or wrong, the way you wanted it or not—you came out of the night a hero. The Bowen name has been redeemed. It may not be the redemption you want, but it's the one you got. You were lucky to get it at all. Life isn't always so kind. Accept it, Caleb. Live with it. It's over now, so leave it all behind: what your father did, the storms, Race Rock—all of it."

Jennifer paused. She looked Caleb deeply in the eyes and spoke from her heart with an intensity he had never heard in her: "We've been given a second chance, Caleb. I think we can have a wonderful future together. But only if you cast off the anchor of the past."

She'd said it. Not the way she had rehearsed it all those nights back at home on Fishers Island. But she'd said it at last. Simply and from the heart. Thinking back to how she'd set out the morning of September 21 for Race Rock, nervous, whispering her speech to herself, Jennifer smiled. Very little that day had played out as she'd planned. As anyone had planned.

Caleb listened to her and knew what she said was true. He'd always admired Jennifer's ability to see things clearly. She reminded him of an osprey, the magnificent seabird. When it spots the silvery glint of a fish beneath the jumbled confusion of waves, the osprey folds its wings and plunges to the sea like a comet. It swoops down, grazes the water and comes up with a fish in its talons. Jennifer was the same. She swooped down to grasp a truth, a truth usually hidden to him.

Caleb knew he had spent much of his life consumed by the past. It had given him direction and purpose. He thought about what both Jennifer and St. Clair had said. They were both right. He had redeemed the Bowen name, but he had not changed the past. He never could. At best he'd painted over it, and maybe that was enough.

"I think we have a wonderful future together, too, Jennifer. And you're right: it's time to let things go. Truth be told, I'm tired of it all. Only you and I will know what really happened that night on Race Rock."

"It will be our little secret, Caleb. I'll be your hero, and you'll be mine."

Their serious conversation slowed and stopped, too weighty to sustain any longer. They rested. After a few moments, Jennifer leaned up on one elbow and looked at him with a bit of mischief in her eyes.

"So, Caleb, I have a question for you."

"Yes?"

"Back on the light. After you'd rescued me. You took my clothes off to dry me and warm me."

"Yes."

"Did you like what you saw?"

"God, Jennifer, my only thought was to try to save you!"

"I know. I know. But, still, I was naked."

"It was dark."

"There was lightning."

Caleb smiled. "Well, I suppose I did catch a glimpse of you."

"And?"

"I liked what I saw."

"Good. It's good to know even heroes are human."

"Jennifer, are we still on for November 17?"

"I certainly hope so," she said.

"Good," said Caleb. "Then it will be your turn."

"My turn?"

"To see *me* naked."

She giggled. "I thought about that too on the desk," she said, cuddling in to Caleb. "Our wedding day—and night."

For the first time in days, Caleb and Jennifer shared hope. For them, the storm had finally passed.

A moment later, a squall blew in.

Seaman Shivers woke up from his stupor and sat up on the bed. His hair was standing up from his head in a stiff curl, like a wave in a Japanese painting.

"Jesus! What happened?" he said, scratching his belly and burping.

"You were half drowned," said Caleb across the room. "They found you and took you here to the hospital. They revived you. You started cursing a blue streak. You were ornery. So they knocked you out."

"Jesus! They woke me up to knock me out?"

"Repeatedly."

"Well sonofabitch! Fuckin' doctors!"

He jumped off the bed and started to tip over, still woozy. His hospital gown flapped about him.

"Jesus Christ! Shit!" Then he spotted Jennifer. "Oh! Sorry, ma'am. Beg your pardon." He pulled his gown closed over his rump, blushing.

He staggered towards the door.

"God damn! I gotta get out of here!"

Then he was gone.

"Who, or what, was that?" asked Jennifer.

"Weather station guy from Eastern Point. He was roughed up a bit by the storm."

"Weren't we all," said Jennifer. "Weren't we all."

8

Jennifer stayed with Caleb, sleeping in the bed vacated by Shivers. She was so beaten up, the doctors didn't mind. They just took her on as another patient. She and Caleb talked about their wedding and their future. True to his word, Caleb seemed to want to move on from his family history and the night of the hurricane. He did not talk about them, and even smiled a bit when one of the nurses asked: "How's our hero doing today?"

After a week of healing, they were discharged from the hospital.

They had nowhere to go. Both had lost their homes. True to his word, St. Clair had arranged for Caleb to stay awhile at the Griswold Hotel in Groton. Caleb managed to wrangle another room for Jennifer. Their lifesaving naked cuddle the night of the hurricane hadn't changed her feelings about waiting until they were married to become truly intimate.

Though the Griswold had sustained some damage from the storm—mostly broken windows and some basement flooding—the grand old hotel had become a refuge for the homeless. Unable to find any stores open to buy clothes, they had to make due. Jennifer still wore what the nurse had found for her, and Caleb had to borrow an outfit from the Coast Guard.

They managed to get across the river to Groton. For Caleb, it was awkward to walk with his leg in a cast. He'd have to get used to his leg being stiff and straight: when the cast came off in a few weeks, that would not change.

For a few days, they just stayed at the hotel and watched the activity around them. They heard extraordinary stories of death and destruction as well as survival. Jennifer regaled one dinner table group with the tale of her extraordinary voyage on the desk. As the papers reported the extent of the damage, people continually adjusted their perceptions of the magnitude of the storm. It was beyond big. It was apocalyptic. It was as if, for a day, the world had come apart. Chaos had reigned, and all that was human was swept aside by an implacable force unlike any before experienced or even dreamt of.

Yet slowly, the area was recovering from the storm. The sound of saws filled the air as people tried to clear roads and debris. Crews worked on telephone poles. Trucks carried rubble and junk. Reserve troops helped police stop any looters and directed people to shelters and soup kitchens. People were generous in helping strangers with food, clothing, shelter and transportation.

One morning, Caleb led Jennifer to a small room in the basement of the hotel. It was a storeroom off the main corridor by the loading doors. He opened the door and led her into the dark room.

"I have a surprise for you," he whispered.

He switched on the light.

There, in the middle of the room, was a desk. Jennifer's desk. The one she had ridden in the storm to Fishers Island.

"Caleb! How on earth?" she exclaimed.

"I heard some guys talking in the lobby about hauling stuff from Fishers to Groton. I asked if they could look for a desk on the beach and bring it here. I suppose they thought I was crazy. I offered to pay once I got some money in hand. When they learned who I was, they were more than happy to help. This being a hero has its benefits." He smiled.

Jennifer walked around the desk touching it almost reverently. It had, after all, been her salvation.

"We need to find a home, Jennifer. When we do, we'll have to furnish it. I figured this desk was a good start."

Jennifer just shook her head. "Amazing, Caleb. It looks so small. But like I said, it was a very seaworthy desk."

"The S.S. Jennifer," said Caleb.

"It's still a little wet."

"Yeah. The drawers will probably stick for a while until they dry out."

"We don't have anything to put in them anyway," said Jennifer.

"Good point."

"Thanks, Caleb. It will be a reminder of a day we'll never forget."

Caleb hugged Jennifer's shoulders and switched off the light. It was a little thing, but the desk was the first step in building their life together.

On October 3, a sunny day a few weeks after the storm, Jennifer and Caleb took the short walk down Shore Avenue to the Tyler House. It was a grand old Victorian home, perched at the windy curve of Eastern Point. The floodwaters had receded, but the house was still damaged. Windows had been boarded up. The Coast Guard's weather shack, where Shivers had been, was gone. Only a few boards remained. The beach was littered with trash and debris. Seagulls feasted on God knows what.

Caleb walked on crutches. They made their way to a stone wall at the southern side of the house. The owners didn't seem to mind that folks climbed around the big rocks that surrounded the large house. Indeed, there used to be a few benches, but they were gone.

They sat on the wall and looked out towards Long Island Sound. They were at the mouth of the Thames River. To their right, on the shore of New London, was the harbor light, tall and white. Out where the river widened into the sound was Southwest Ledge Light. Directly in front of them, a few hundred yards from their perch, was Black Rock. Behind it, in the distance, Race Rock floated like an anchored ship. To its left was the scraggily shoreline of Fishers Island. Way beyond it, a long smudge on the horizon, was Long Island.

They were familiar landmarks but also changed ones. The events of September 21 had added new chapters to their stories, chapters layered upon already rich histories. From where they sat, the stage of the dramas that had occurred here spread out before them. Those dramas were over. The stage was empty. The actors gone. It was up to memory to preserve their stories.

Jennifer watched as a flock of geese flew by, honking as they passed over. The ferries were running again to Fishers Island, Montauk Point and Orient Point. Lobster boats chugged along the shore. Life was returning to its normal rhythms.

"Jennifer," said Caleb. "I've had a lot of time to think this week."

"You've had a lot to think about," she said.

"I have. I don't know that I will ever make sense of all of it. Maybe it doesn't matter." He looked at her. "I do know that, come what may, I want to be with you. I don't know what the future holds in store. Where we'll live. What we'll do." He paused and looked out at Race Rock for a moment, then turned back to Jennifer. "Things have settled down a little. You've had time to think, too. I hope you still want me, even if I am a bit damaged. Even with so much uncertainty facing us."

"Caleb, I told you at the hospital your leg doesn't matter to me. And as for the future, well, the hurricane blew us off one course and onto another. So be it. If we could weather that day, I think we can weather anything."

Caleb smiled and took her hand in his. They were quiet for a while.

"I keep wondering about Eliot, Jennifer. Whether what he said was true. Did Maddy Covington really visit Race Rock? Was there even a Maddy Covington, or did he just make her up when he saw the painting?"

"You think it was all a lie?"

"It could have been. He was after the treasure. He would have killed for it. He *tried* to kill for it! He was crazy, he was drugged, and he was scared. All I have is questions: Did my father find a box of gems? Did he hide it on Race Rock? Did Eliot really find proof in the archives? I don't know, and I don't think we'll ever find out. If there is a treasure and I knew exactly where it was, we might be able to go out and get it on a quick visit. But I don't know where it is. We'd have to do what Eliot started to do: tear the lighthouse apart. And we're not in any position to do that."

"I've wondered about him too, Caleb. Sometimes, I wonder if he was even real."

"Oh, he was real. My knee proves that. It didn't break itself."

"No, of course not. His story, like you say, could have been just lunatic ravings. Wishful thinking. Madness."

"I don't think we'll ever know, Jennifer. If there really is a treasure on Race Rock, I'm afraid it will remain there forever, unclaimed."

"Not exactly," said Jennifer. She squeezed his hand and turned his face to hers with her other hand. She leaned in and gave him a long, loving kiss. "I found a treasure on Race Rock," she said.

He looked into her eyes. They sparkled in the late morning sunlight.

Maybe they had lost a treasure, but what they'd found was even better. It was priceless.

9

Caleb and Jennifer left Eastern Point and walked back to the Griswold Hotel. Though not far, it was a slow amble, as Caleb was not very fast on crutches. Their life would be at a slow pace. They were in no rush. They existed in their own world, a world of togetherness that had deepened immensely over the past week. Their love nourished them as it never had before.

Taxis waited at the Griswold Hotel, their drivers reading newspapers or leaning against their cars, chatting. Caleb leaned in and spoke to the driver of the first in line.

"Get in, Jennifer, there's someplace we need to go."

"Where?" she asked.

"The Colonel Ledyard Cemetery," he said, and Jennifer knew that Caleb was not quite finished with the past after all.

The Colonel Ledyard Cemetery was not far away—just two miles inland. It was an old New England cemetery nestled between nondescript houses. Except for the big stone archway that marked its entrance, it looked like a quiet park in a quiet neighborhood.

The taxi drove down the long road to the Avery Chapel. Trees used to line the road, but the storm had flattened them. Only their stumps remained, like stubble after a quick shave. Caleb paid the driver and spoke to him for a moment. The taxi left.

"He'll be back for us in an hour." They walked around the old stone chapel, still closed and boarded up from the storm.

"Let's go to his grave," said Caleb.

Jennifer knew that Nathaniel Bowen was buried here, but she had never been to his grave. They locked arms and strolled down a path towards the back of the cemetery. Caleb was quiet, trying to be casual, but Jennifer knew it was difficult for him. Death can be abstract and distant in many ways. But when you see the cold carved letters on a tombstone it becomes very real. There is no denying it. She knew. Whenever she visited her parents' graves it was a shock. She had never gotten used to the intense feelings of love and loss that washed over her when she stood there reading their names and the dates of their lives. Though it hurt, it also brought comfort, for she knew they were safely tucked in, their troubles over, their worries gone. At rest. At peace.

The leaves on the few trees that remained in the cemetery had been stripped off by the hurricane's winds. Fall had come early. The ground was covered with bright red, orange and yellow leaves, a beautiful patchwork beneath their feet. The early afternoon sun was bright. Crows made their loud calls in the trees, and just a wisp of wind rattled through the empty branches. A few remaining leaves fell from the trees like a dying flock of birds.

It took Caleb a few minutes to orient himself and find the grave. He had only been here once, years ago when he first arrived back in the area. He didn't like cemeteries. They were such irrefutable reminders of life's brief span. There were graves for fathers and sons and grandsons. Whole families had come and gone. Many of the inscriptions were almost impossible to read, worn by time and the endless assault of wind and rain. Who were they? What had their lives been like? Whatever triumphs or tragedies these people had seen were part of a distant past. Caleb found the cemetery a sad place, a place that made life seem futile. Here, all the dreams, all the struggles, all the moments that made up a life were over. Gone. All but forgotten. He thought of vigorous, imposing people reduced to brittle bones beneath his feet. He took no comfort from the place.

Nathaniel Bowen's grave was toward the back boundary of the cemetery near the crossing of two paths. The headstone was a simple granite slab. Jennifer had never seen it. She read the epitaph as they stood there.

Nathaniel Bowen
1864 ~ 1907
My legacy is in my dedication to the light.

"He arranged for this the day he died," said Caleb. "It was a final, defiant statement to the world. Though in the end he failed, he didn't want anyone to forget how much of his life he had given to serving as a lighthouse keeper. He was dedicated to his work. One night could not change that."

Then Caleb reached into his pocket and pulled out his father's watch. It gleamed in the sunlight.

"I thought I should return this to him," he said.

"I'll give you some time," said Jennifer. She kissed him and walked back to the chapel, leaving Caleb alone with his father.

The first time Caleb had visited the grave, he had read the epitaph, but the letters had also spelled out something else. They told of the irrefutable finality of death. Caleb had always thought he'd see his father again. They'd talk, laugh, share stories, do things together. That had never happened. He had returned to Groton only to find his father long gone, remembered as a failure, his life summed up in a few words chiseled into stone. At the grave, he felt close to his father and, at the same time, terribly far from him.

Though a lump came to his throat, there were no tears left in Caleb. He had shed them all the past few weeks. He looked at the old watch. He turned it over and read again its cryptic inscription. "JLS 12~1~05." He still had no clue who "JLS" was or why his father had inscribed the initials on the watch.

"This must mean something, Dad, but I don't know what. Why didn't you keep some sort of diary or journal?"

Caleb planned to dig a little hole on the grave and bury the watch in it. He stood there, staring at the watch, gripping it tightly. It connected him to his father, and he didn't want to let it go. He stared at it, and the thoughts in his mind began clicking towards something, working their way together. Just beyond his grasp, his unconscious seemed to be homing in on an idea.

The word "journal" floated into his thinking. He didn't know why. Thoughts were sometimes like this. They were like little bubbles, trapped under a log at the bottom of the sea. Then a fish swims by or the current swirls and disturbs one of the bubbles. It breaks free and floats up to the surface. So, too, could a hidden, obscure thought be freed from the grip of the unconscious to float its way into the consciousness.

Caleb frowned. He looked at the watch again. "JLS." Those three initials —why did they somehow seem familiar? They meant something to him! He struggled to place them. It was like trying to make out a ship in the fog. He could sense it, almost see it, but it was frustratingly vague. Just out of reach. "JLS," he repeated to himself. "JLS. JLS. JLS." He was fishing for an association, for something that would catalyze his thoughts and lead to an answer.

He thought back to September 21. To Eliot. He closed his eyes. Tried to remember every word, every detail. He heard Eliot talking. He listened. Caleb looked at the tombstone again. He read it over and over.

Then, like a flash of lightning that illuminates a scene with sudden, vivid clarity, the answer came to him. It all fell into place with startling suddenness.

Caleb understood.

He spoke to his father for the first time in over thirty years.

"I don't know if you can hear me, Dad, but thank you. You've finally reached me after all these years. I love you, and always will."

Caleb wanted to run up to the chapel to tell Jennifer. He could see her sitting on a low stone wall, backlit by the sun, her hair glowing. He could not. He had to hobble there slowly. He realized his life would always be slower, now. He would never run anywhere.

Jennifer watched as Caleb turned from his father's grave and made his way back to her. He swung himself on his crutches. His affliction had only made her feel more love for him. She felt responsible and protective. Whatever diminished him also made him more human.

"Jennifer! Jennifer!"

"What is it Caleb?" she was startled by his sudden animation. He was smiling, excited. She couldn't imagine why.

"Jennifer, we have to get out to Race Rock!"

"Oh, God, Caleb! No! I almost died out there twice a few weeks ago. I'm not giving it another chance at me. I've had enough of that damned place! I'm never going out there again!"

"No, you don't understand. We *have* to go. Just for an hour!"

Jennifer was afraid that the visit to his father's grave had pulled him back to the past, that the ghost of his father had wrapped its arms around him and would steal him from her.

"Why, Caleb? Why?" she wailed.

"Because I know where the treasure is, Jennifer! I know *exactly* where it is!"

10

It wasn't hard for Caleb to arrange to go to Race Rock. It only took a call to St. Clair. Caleb explained he wanted to go out for one last visit to the place that had been his life. Who could deny a hero that? Caleb explained that his father had left abruptly and so had he, with no chance to say goodbye or retrieve personal effects. Caleb also requested that he and Jennifer be allowed to be out there alone. Just for an hour. The temporary keeper could go ashore and do some errands or pick up some supplies. St. Clair agreed and said he'd arrange for a boat to take them the next day.

The rest of that day and night, Caleb was like a little boy. Excited and anxious. Jennifer pleaded with him to tell her what he had discovered at the grave that made him so sure there was a treasure and that he knew where it was. But, like a little boy, he had a secret, and he wasn't quite ready to share it. "I'll tell you when we get there," was all he would say.

Jennifer cajoled him and pouted, threatened and crossed her arms in mock anger, but Caleb would not budge. She was, indeed, very reluctant to go to Race Rock again. She did not want to tempt fate. She had escaped from it with her life, though just barely. Yet seeing Caleb so animated, so happy was heartening. Though he had spoken with optimism about their future, she knew he was troubled by the uncertainty of what lay ahead. Once vigorous and agile, he faced a life walking stiffly and slowly. He was leaving his beloved lighthouse and all the daily routines and rhythms that had defined his world for years. He would be a married man, sharing his life in ways he never had. Change is never easy, and Caleb was embracing a lot of changes all at once.

She had to admit that the idea of finding a treasure was exciting. He seemed so certain. She hoped he was right. A little money wouldn't hurt as they started to build their future.

Finally Jennifer had conceded. "Okay, Caleb, I'll go out to that damned rock with you one last time. But if there isn't a treasure out there, I may just throw you off it. You can paddle home with your crutches!"

Caleb laughed. "There are desks out there, you know."

* * *

The next day dawned calm. The air was heavy. The forecast called for fog. At ten, Caleb and Jennifer made their way to the long pier that jutted into the river in front of the Griswold Hotel. As promised, a small Coast Guard boat was waiting.

It took some doing for Caleb to get into the small craft. His stiff leg made it hard to negotiate the bobbing boat. With help from the young helmsman and Jennifer, he made it in and sat down on the long bench across the stern, his leg stretched out in front of him. Everything he did reminded him of how things had changed. He knew that, with time, he would adjust to his stiff leg. But now it was something new. It was awkward and frustrating. Jennifer was patient and sometimes called him "Gimpy." It was her way of making light of his infirmity and getting him used to it. Feeling sorry for himself wouldn't help anything.

The seaman who was their helmsman cast off the line and started up the motor. He arced the boat out of the shallow cove at the Griswold and headed out towards Race Rock.

Jennifer and Caleb were quiet as they passed the familiar landmarks. They glided by Black Rock, where cormorants stood, drying their wings. They passed Southwest Ledge Lighthouse. They crossed Fishers Island Sound to Race Rock. Caleb and Jennifer were lost in their own thoughts, and they were also becoming more and more anxious as they neared the lighthouse. In part it was excitement: were they really about to find a fabulous treasure? In part it was the trauma of returning to the place where so much had happened to them. For Caleb and

Jennifer, Race Rock was far more than a lighthouse. It was a place of triumph and failure, love and fear, danger and death. It was hard not to be anxious about setting foot upon it again.

Jennifer wondered about the treasure. Would it be fantastic or a disappointment? She squeezed Caleb's hand and he looked at her. She could tell he was thinking the same things. There was no need for words. Their tense silence spoke volumes.

The boat drew close to Race Rock. As always, it was surprisingly imposing as they crossed into its shadow and it loomed over them. It had taken a beating in the storm. The window Caleb had broken was boarded up. A temporary window had been jury-rigged in the lantern room.

Once again, the huge boulders loomed up on either side of them. Jennifer felt a sudden chill seeing them. Even though the day was calm, she didn't trust this place. It had become sinister in her mind.

The temporary keeper, Doug Allen, was there to take the rope and tie up their boat. She helped Caleb stand and together with the helmsman and Allen, got him out of the boat onto the pier.

"Welcome back to Race Rock," said Allen with a smile and a handshake for Caleb.

"Thank you," said Caleb.

"St. Clair tells me you need an hour alone out here?"

"Yes, about. No more. I just need to say goodbye to this old rock."

"I understand," said Allen. And he did. The bond between a keeper and his lighthouse is a strong one. Few keepers had more personal history with a light than Caleb Bowen. Allen could hardly begrudge the man a chance to say farewell to the lighthouse that had been his home and his life.

Allen hopped into the boat, untied it, and the helmsman backed them out and turned toward Fishers Island. Allen waved.

Caleb and Jennifer watched them a few minutes. Caleb hobbled over and sat on one of the boulders. Jennifer joined him, and they looked up at Race Rock.

On so calm a day, with the waves gently lapping against the boulders, with barely a trace of a breeze, it was almost impossible to imagine the nightmare that had engulfed Race Rock a few weeks ago. It was a different place, now, and the nightmare was over. Perhaps, as dreams do, the terror of it would fade with time.

Jennifer spoke first: "Okay, Caleb. Now we're here. You promised to tell me how you know where the treasure is." Her eyes flashed. Caleb thought she had never looked lovelier.

"Okay," said Caleb. "I guess you've waited long enough."

He fished in his pocket and withdrew his father's pocket watch.

"Here's what I think, Jennifer. You know I got my father's watch back."

"Yes, of course. His Lighthouse Service watch."

"Right. And it has 'JLS 12~1~05' engraved on it."

"Yes."

"Well, I couldn't figure out who 'JLS' was. Of course, I didn't know much about my father's life. 'JLS' could have been almost anyone. Maybe another, more enduring love than Maddy. I kept thinking it must be a woman. Or maybe a relative. I got nowhere.

"Then I remembered that I'd read that on the day he died, my father did a few errands. One of them was to a jewelry store in downtown New London. He had this watch engraved. Why? It didn't make sense. It had to be important. Given that he was about to take his own life, it couldn't be for him. It wasn't a keepsake or something to make him remember someone. No. He had it engraved for someone else."

"Who?" asked Jennifer.

"Me," said Caleb quietly.

"You? He hadn't seen you in a couple of years, Caleb. Why do you think it was for you?"

"Bear with me, Jennifer, you'll see."

"Okay. He engraved the watch for you. What does 'JLS 12~1~05' signify?"

"When I was at his grave yesterday, I told him I wished he'd kept a diary or a journal. Something that would have given us a clue to who 'JLS' was. And why 12~1~05 was important. It turns out he did."

"He did?" asked Jennifer.

"He did. He kept a journal of his daily life on Race Rock. I kept one, too. It was so simple once I realized 'JLS' wasn't a person, it was a thing."

"I don't understand, Caleb," said Jennifer. "You're speaking in riddles."

"Sorry. The problem was, I was thinking in one direction, and that was blinding me to the obvious. It was like looking at an optical illusion where you see one thing and then, with the tiniest shift of focus, it becomes something else entirely. I just didn't make the connection until the word 'journal' started rattling around in my head. Then, it came to me. 'JLS' isn't someone's name. It's a simple abbreviation for "Journal of Light Station."

"You mean the logbook for Race Rock?"

"Exactly, Jennifer. It's printed on the cover of every logbook. They are the Journals of Light Stations. 'JLS'"

"And the date?" asked Jennifer.

"Once I realized what 'JLS' meant, I realized '12~1~05' was simply the date of an entry in the Journal."

"To know what that entry is, Caleb, we'd have to dig out the old journal from some archive."

"No, no we don't. Eliot already did that for us. You remember: he said he'd been to the National Archives and requested the journals from 1904 to 1907 to see if he could verify that our father had found a treasure and that his mother, Maddy, had visited."

"That's right! He found both entries, didn't he?"

"Yes, he did. And I remembered them. According to the journal, it was on December 1, 1905, that Nathaniel found a box on the rocks on a snowy day."

"12~1~05," said Jennifer.

"I still don't understand why he'd engrave it on the watch," said Jennifer, warming to the unraveling of the mystery.

"I couldn't figure that out either at first. Then I thought about what I'd heard and read about his final day and it made sense. My father left Race Rock abruptly. He would never be allowed back. In his guilt and shame, he decided to take his own life."

Caleb stopped. Jennifer could sense the emotions swirling in him. Sadness played across his face. After a deep breath, Caleb continued.

"He realized that the treasure was as good as lost out here. He wanted to leave a clue. He didn't have many options. Who could he trust? How could he leave a clue? He was desperate. It was a long shot, but he took it. He took it, I think, because he knew I'd be back. I'd promised him that the day my mother took me away from here. I saw him looking at us through his telescope, and I said that to him: 'I'll be back.'

"So he engraved the entry date in the journal on the watch and carefully left it behind in the little rowboat. Engraving on a watch is a lot more durable than a piece of paper. It was a good idea. His gamble paid off. It took thirty years, and an honest man, but the watch *did* finally make its way to me. My father never knew I would become a lighthouse keeper myself, of course. But I think he remembered that I used to hover over him when he wrote his daily entries. And that I'd often pick up the journal and look through it. He had faith that if the watch ever got to me, I would make the connection. It did and I did. As for the date—Eliot just saved us a trip to Washington."

"Thank Eliot for putting the idea of a treasure in your mind, Caleb. I remember him telling us about that entry. Nathaniel wrote that he found a box that was 'a real treasure.'"

"Right."

"Caleb, the watch only confirms that there is a treasure here. It doesn't tell us where."

"True enough, Jennifer. True enough. But Nathaniel left a second clue."

Jennifer tipped her head as if to say: "go on." Maybe it was so she could listen with her good ear.

"My father was trying to tell me two things. That there was a treasure hidden on Race Rock and where it was. That's the second clue he left, Jennifer, and he left it in plain sight. Etched in stone for eternity."

Jennifer's eyes went wide. "His grave?"

"His grave. 'My legacy is in my dedication to my light.' I always thought it was a statement of defiance. Maybe it was. But when I realized the engraving on the watch was a clue, I read those words differently. In a flash I understood. He was telling me exactly where the treasure—his legacy—was hidden. It's not even a riddle."

"Caleb, I don't ..." Jennifer stopped. She was trying to put the clues together as Caleb had. She frowned for a moment, moved her hands like she was trying to organize her thoughts. Then she looked at Caleb and smiled.

"His dedication! Not his hard work and loyalty but, literally, his dedication. That little plaque next to the door. Didn't you once tell me he had put it there?"

"Yes. The first one was cheap and quickly rusted out. He had a nicer one made. He was very proud of it. He took great care to keep it polished and shiny. Hence the wording '*my* dedication to the light.' It had a double meaning, of course. He was nothing if not dedicated to Race Rock."

"The treasure is hidden behind the dedication plaque next to the door," said Jennifer, shaking her head in a mix of wonder and happiness.

Caleb smiled. "Yes, I'm certain of it."

"Isn't that a dangerous place to hide something valuable?"

"No, that plaque is screwed in to the stones hard and deep. I know. I've polished it dozens of times. And since the plaque is outside the building, Nathaniel could get to it any time. Even if he wasn't the keeper, he could row out, dock, climb the ladder to the porch, unscrew the plaque, and retrieve whatever's hidden there."

Jennifer was stunned. It all made so much sense. She herself had read the plaque many times. It was incredible to think it hid a treasure.

"Could it really be there?" she asked in a whisper.

Caleb reached into his pocket and took out a small screwdriver.

"Let's find out."

They stood up and walked over to the ladder. Caleb looked up it. He shook his head and turned to Jennifer.

"I don't think I can make it up, Jennifer. You'll have to go."

Jennifer looked at Caleb. It had to be a very tough moment for him. Looking up the ladder brought home to him how much his life had changed.   With his stiff leg, it was as insurmountable as a sheer cliff. Something he had climbed with ease was impossible for him now. She saw the pained look in his eyes when he realized it.

Jennifer hugged Caleb, kissed him and whispered in his ear: "You've got me now, Caleb. Together, we can do anything."

She took the screwdriver and clambered up the ladder.

Caleb watched and recalled the arduous climb he had made with her over his shoulder during the storm. He hobbled back to the boulder and sat down. As he sat waiting for Jennifer to retrieve the treasure, Caleb again recalled how very different it had been out here a few weeks back. The seas had been so high and violent. Eliot had come in with those seas, taking some of their violence with him into the lighthouse.

Eliot. His brother.

The man was crazy, drug-addled, and pushed over the brink by the storm. Eliot had destroyed his knee. In doing so, he had taken away Caleb's life as a keeper. Yet with his story of treasure, Eliot had also given Caleb the path to his future. A son his father didn't know had given the son he loved the legacy that would have been denied. How strange were the workings of fate!

There was a squeal from above. Jennifer was at the top of the ladder, jumping with excitement. She was waving a wooden box around wildly.

"I have it, Caleb, I have it! You were right, it was behind the plaque!"

"Well I'll be damned!" said Caleb.

11

Jennifer had no place to put the box as she climbed down the ladder.

"Jennifer," yelled Caleb when he'd made his way to the bottom of the ladder. "Drop it to me."

Her eyes widened. She was afraid they'd lose it.

"I don't know, Caleb...."

"Don't throw it, just drop it. I'll catch it."

Jennifer dropped the box.

The second it was in the air was an eternity.

Caleb caught it.

It had taken thirty years for his father's legacy to reach him. Time is a ship that never anchors, a ship that no storm can stop, no man can command. The treasure had ridden the current of time and finally washed up in Caleb's life as it had washed onto the rocks of the lighthouse so many years ago. Jennifer climbed down the ladder.

"Okay, let's take a look, Jennifer." They returned to the boulders at the edge of the concrete pier. Caleb turned the box over in his hands. It was a beautiful thing, with alternating squares of wood and metal—probably brass. He was so excited his hands shook.

"How do you open it, Caleb? I don't see any hasp or hinges."

"No, it's not your typical box. It must be some kind of puzzle."

"God, the anticipation is killing me, Caleb! It feels heavy. Something shifts around inside—you can feel it! I hope what's in there is worth all this."

"Let's hope," said Caleb, barely able to contain his own excitement. He turned the box over and over, looking for some way to open it. The box itself had been elusive. Now opening it seemed to be, too. As he fiddled with it, something beneath one of his fingers clicked in. He looked and saw that one of the small brass squares was depressed into the surface a bit, like a button.

"Look," said Jennifer, "that must be the release."

"Not quite. I think there's more." Caleb kept the button pushed in and now Jennifer began pushing the other brass squares. After trying ten or so, she pushed one and it, too, clicked in. Both stayed in, and the smallest gap appeared at the bottom row of squares near one edge.

"We've got it!" she said. "See: that looks like a lid."

While Caleb kept both buttons depressed, Jennifer grasped the lid and started to slide it open.

"Slowly, Jennifer. Take it slowly. Pull it straight off. We don't want to jam it."

Jennifer wiggled the lid and with agonizing slowness it parted from the rest of the box. Then it was off. The box was open, and they could see a leather pouch inside. They looked at each other and smiled.

"Well," he said, "the moment of truth. Shall we take a look at my father's legacy?"

Caleb put the box on the rock and removed the pouch. He untied its drawstring and parted the top of the bag. Though the sun had disappeared in the gathering fog, what was inside glittered and gleamed. Jennifer held her breath.

Caleb reached in and pulled out a very large, very beautiful green jewel—an enormous emerald.

"Jesus," said Jennifer.

Caleb could say nothing. As his father had been, he was overwhelmed by the stone. The size of the gem and its magnificent cut were stunning. He turned the stone in his hand and they admired it from every angle. It was as big as a grape, and the deepest green he had ever seen. He felt he could drown in it, like the sea.

"Do you know anything about carats?" she asked. "About gem sizes and weights and all that?"

"No, but I would describe this as 'very large.'" He put the emerald in Jennifer's palm and reached into the bag again. He pulled out a diamond ring. It, too, was huge.

"Oh my God!" gasped Jennifer.

Caleb held the ring in his hand. He had never seen anything like it. It had many facets, and just the slightest motion made the light shimmer and dance in them. He looked at Jennifer and smiled.

"Give me your left hand," he said quietly. She extended her hand towards him and slowly he put the ring on her finger. It fit well.

"Marry me?" he asked.

"Caleb, we're already engaged."

"True. But you lost your ring as bait to Eliot. It was a small ring. You deserve better. This is yours."

She wiggled her fingers and brought her hand up to her face admiring the diamond.

"Well?" asked Caleb.

Jennifer was mesmerized by the ring. She shook her head as if trying to snap out of a trance.

"Yes. Yes, yes, yes!" she said. They kissed and hugged, but the treasure beckoned. Caleb reached into the bag and withdrew a blood-red ruby. Like the emerald and the diamond ring, it was very large and very beautiful.

"Caleb, who do you think these belonged to?"

"God only knows, Jennifer. Judging from the size of them, I'd say a king or a sultan or ... I don't know. They're crown jewels."

He handed the ruby to Jennifer. She held it to her eye. It was like looking through a glass of wine.

He withdrew a stunning opal, yellow, with a cross-shaped pattern in it. It seemed to glow from within, as if on fire. He exhaled a long slow breath. He took out more gems and rings: another sapphire, another diamond, two more emeralds, a gold ring with a carved head of Medusa. They looked at each one for a few minutes. Jennifer carefully lined them up on a little depression in the rock they sat on. They were bright colors against the drab gray of the boulder. They were, indeed, a treasure.

"My God, Caleb. These must be worth...."

"A lot, Jennifer. A lot. I don't know much about jewelry or gems, but these must be worth a fortune. They're all bigger than anything I've ever seen, except in a book."

"We could bring them Mallove's Jewelers in New London. They could appraise them."

"Maybe. But I think this stuff may be out of their league. They'll probably refer us to someplace in New York like Tiffany or Cartier."

The bag yielded up more gems and rings. Twenty in all. A spectrum of colors and shapes. All of them were flawless, perfectly cut, huge, beautiful.

To see any one of them would have been breathtaking. To see so many –and to know they were yours—was mind-boggling.

"Pinch me, Caleb. I must be dreaming."

Not entirely sure that it wasn't all a dream, Caleb actually did give Jennifer a light pinch on her wrist. They both looked down at the gems lines up on the rock.

"Still here," said Jennifer, "no dream."

Caleb and Jennifer shared a wonderful few minutes together revealing their treasure. In a season of turning points in their lives, it was yet another. No matter what life held in store for them, they would always have this dreamlike, foggy morning alone on the lighthouse. They would never forget those colored jewels as they emerged from the darkness of the mysterious box into the light of their day. The treasure was not just in the gems themselves but in the moment they shared revealing them.

And they knew it.

The final thing in the pouch was a ring. Caleb knew instantly what it was. It was a not a precious stone. He knew it by its tobacco color and the flecks imbedded in it: amber. He held it close to his eye and peered into its golden depth. There was a tiny spider entombed inside. Not a fossil, but the actual spider, preserved for millions of years. While the gems were stunning, they were cold. The amber seemed to hold life and warmth, as if some of the light and heat of the jungle was captured inside along with the spider.

The amber ring struck a responsive chord in Caleb. As he looked at the tiny spider he saw himself. In the past few weeks, Caleb had realized that he was stuck in time, anchored by his fierce desire to reconnect with his father and clear his name. He had imprisoned himself on Race Rock. Like the spider, he had been trapped. He had become a living fossil, a man doomed to gaze out at the present from a prison of the past.

As Caleb studied the spider, he knew there was a difference. The spider could not escape his prison. Caleb could. He did not have to remain forever in the amber of regret.

Caleb slipped the ring onto the ring finger of his right hand. It fit him well. Now they both had rings. They would be constant reminders of life's promises and perils.

The fog that had been coming and going all morning had settled in. In the distance, they could see the Coast Guard boat slowly chugging its way toward Race Rock. They gathered the precious jewels and put them back in the pouch and the pouch back into the puzzle box.

"We'll sell these," said Caleb. "We'll realize a fortune from them."

"We'll have to decide what to do with all our money."

Caleb looked at Jennifer. Her hair blew in the gentle breeze. Her eyes glittered.

"We can help your 'Mariner's Widows' charity," he said. That brought a very big smile to her already happy face.

"We can travel like you've always wanted," she said.

"Yes. There are a lot of places I'd like to see, Jennifer. Maybe Tahiti."

"You and your islands. Let's go to the mountains!"

Suddenly Jennifer pointed to the boulders across the pier from them.

"Look!" She exclaimed, pointing.

He didn't see it.

"No, Caleb. To the right. Near that big rock with the curved top."

He followed the point of her finger and saw it: the lightning rod, wedged into a crevice. Before he could say anything, Jennifer had scurried into the boulders.

"Careful!" he yelled. The memory of the boulder rolling onto them in the storm sent a stab of fear into him. Luckily, she did not have to go far to retrieve the rod. She returned, holding it out to him.

"A memento, Caleb. Of Race Rock. Of the storm. Of Eliot."

"Eliot?" he asked, surprised.

"Eliot," she said. "Your brother. I know he was a stranger, and I know he tried to kill us. But if it weren't for him, you wouldn't have that treasure box in your pocket."

"Or a stiff leg." Caleb said. "I'll think of Eliot every step I take." He took the lightning rod from Jennifer anyway. For a simple piece of metal, it was charged with memories.

The Coast Guard boat was getting closer. They could hear its engine.

"Did you put the dedication plaque back?" Caleb asked.

"Just like I found it. Nobody will ever be the wiser."

"I still can't believe all the times I polished it and had no idea there was a fortune hidden behind it. My legacy. Just waiting for me."

"I wonder if we would have ever figured out the clues if Eliot hadn't come along," said Jennifer.

Caleb just shrugged. He didn't really know.

"You know it's sad, Caleb. Eliot came out here, lost himself, and died in the storm. Nobody knows. Nobody cares. No one will mourn him. Nothing. He'll vanish from memory."

Caleb balanced the lightning rod on his open palms.

"We'll see," he said.

Then he turned to face Race Rock. He looked up the ladder at the caisson. His gaze swept up the granite building, up the tower with "1878" carved into the stone. He tilted his head back and looked up at the lantern room, at the cupola capping it, missing the lightning rod.

Jennifer stood next to him, her hand around his waist, looking at the lighthouse, too. She could only imagine what he was thinking.

"It's time to leave," he said quietly.

12

The Coast Guard boat arrived at Race Rock. Keeper Allen hopped to the pier where Caleb and Jennifer waited.

"I see you found a memento," he said, noticing the lightning rod in Caleb's hand.

"Yes. We were attracted to it. A tangible memory of the place."

"And I'm the lucky bastard who has to put the new one up," said Keeper Allen. "Don't you want to take your personal stuff? Clothes? Books? Whatever?"

"No," said Caleb. "No. Use what you like. Or box it up and stick it in the attic. I'm starting over. I don't need any of it."

"Okay," said Allen. "Whatever you say."

Caleb was leaving Race Rock again. This time, he made no vow to return. He handed the rod to the helmsman and turned to Allen.

"Take care of the light, Mr. Allen. Always keep it lit. You never know who might be out there in the darkness."

"I will, Caleb. I will."

With Jennifer lending a steadying hand, Caleb stepped off Race Rock onto the boat. Jennifer smiled. "Permission to come aboard, sir?" He held out his hand and she stepped into the launch. The helmsman backed the small craft out of the notch in the rocks and turned toward New London.

Caleb and Jennifer sat on a bench and faced the stern, watching the lighthouse. Keeper Allen waved at them, climbed the ladder, and disappeared inside to get back to his daily routine.

Caleb checked his pocket again for the box. He wouldn't rest easy until he had put it in a safety deposit box at a bank. Jennifer snuggled against him. She looked out over the calm, silent sea. A cormorant slowly headed toward them, barely above the water, its reflection gliding along beneath it, two birds flying towards parallel destinies. She wondered whose spirit it might be. Nathaniel's? One of her parents'? Eliot's? She watched as the bird flew on and disappeared behind the light.

Race Rock began to fade away into the fog, its lines and details softening and fading, as if in a watercolor. With distance, the lighthouse seemed to dissolve into the fog until it was just a phantom silhouette. Caleb stared at it until it vanished completely, then looked a while longer, conjuring it up in memory.

He gazed out into the depthless gray emptiness of the fog. Caleb thought how fitting it was. He and Jennifer were heading into an unknown future. It was a blank journal in which they would write the story of their lives.

As if to bid a final farewell, Race Rock's foghorn came on. It warned ships of the perilous rocks nearby. It warned, too, of the fears and failings of the men who kept the light, whose secrets and faults lay just below the surface, ready to be exposed, as if by a receding tide.

Caleb knew the sound of Race Rock's horn would be with him always, a kind of heartbeat—a final legacy of the light.

Epilogue

The Hurricane of 1938 would live on in the memories of all New England. No one who had lived through that day would ever forget it. That monstrous storm changed the geography of New England. It forever altered how people looked at the sea. How they reacted when a stiff wind started to blow on a calm fall morning. The wounds of the day would heal, but the scars would mark the area for generations.

The Custom House in New London, where Nathaniel Bowen's hearing was held, is now a maritime museum. Like the National Archives, it is a repository of history. It houses a collection of logbooks and ship manifests, manuscripts and documents, artifacts and ephemera. In its basement, beneath vaulted arches of brick set upon heavy stone walls, are cabinets and piles of boxes. In the back of one drawer is a bundle—a piece of burlap wrapped around a bent lightning rod. A tag reads: "Lightning rod from Race Rock Lighthouse. 1938. Given by Caleb and Jennifer Bowen in memory of Eliot McPherson. It took life and saved lives. Acquisition Number G06-03195-2-6S" The lightning rod is slowly rusting away and crumbling to dust, all but forgotten. Yet who knows? The things stored in archives are bits of the past, but sometimes they are also prologue. Someday, someone may stumble upon it and wonder about its cryptic message. Someday, someone may try to tell its story.

Keepers continued to tend to Race Rock until 1978, when it was automated. Men had served there for a century, but their loneliness and dedication are no longer a part of the life of Race Rock. The lighthouse is deserted.

The glittering, beautiful fresnel lens is gone, replaced by a modern lamp of industrial design. Triggered by sensors, the electric light comes on at dusk and swivels around, its Cyclops eye a bright red. In fog, more sensors analyze atmospheric conditions and turn on the horn. As they always have, things drift up onto the rocks at the light's base, but there is no one there to collect them. The wood of the doors and windows is rotting. Railings and stairways are rusting. Paint peels off the walls and falls silently to the dingy floors. Race Rock is slowly decaying. It has become a ghostly place. Some even believe it is haunted.

But it is not entirely true that Race Rock is deserted. Lifeless. In the attic, back among the eves, in the shadows, a spider sits in his web. Who knows how he has gotten there or where he has come from. Perhaps he is just the latest descendant of a long line of spiders who've inhabited the lighthouse. Who knows what he expects to catch out there in the middle of nowhere.

The spider is Race Rock's final keeper, attending to his daily routine, waiting for something to come his way and give his solitary life meaning.

= • =

Todd Alan Gipstein has been a writer, photographer and media producer for 40 years, 20 of them for the National Geographic Society. He grew up in New London, Connecticut, where the story of "Legacy of the Light" takes place. He is a graduate of Harvard University, where he studied writing and filmmaking. Todd has traveled the world photographing for documentaries and lecturing. He has written hundreds of scripts for multimedia shows and films. His work has garnered many grand prizes in international competitions, and he is the recipient of several lifetime achievement honors. Todd and his wife, Marcia, live in Groton, Connecticut, within sight of the lighthouses and seascapes that inspired "Legacy of the Light." He is president of the New London Ledge Lighthouse Foundation, which is dedicated to restoring Ledge Lighthouse (formerly Southwest Ledge Light), a neighbor to Race Rock. He continues to travel the world, photograph, create media presentations, write, and lecture. This is his first novel.

Copies of this book may be ordered at his website, www.Gipstein.com, where you can also see some of his photographs, films and other projects.

CPSIA information can be obtained at www.ICGtesting.com
Printed in the USA
LVOW080152190412

278228LV00001B/3/P